FAVORITE

SONS

FAVORITE

SONS

A Novel by

JOHN RUSSELL

ALGONQUIN BOOKS OF CHAPEL HILL 1992

This is a work of fiction. While, as in all fiction, the literary perceptions and insights are based in part on experience, all names, characters, places, and incidents are either products of the author's imagination or, as in the case of some historical figures and events, are used fictitiously. No reference to the life of any real person, living or dead, is intended or should be inferred.

Published by
ALGONQUIN BOOKS OF CHAPEL HILL
Post Office Box 2225
Chapel Hill, North Carolina 27515-2225
a division of
WORKMAN PUBLISHING COMPANY, INC.
708 Broadway
New York, New York 10003

Southern Regions of the United States, by Howard W. Odum.
Chapel Hill: The University of North Carolina Press, 1936.
Used by permission.

LIBRARY OF CONGRESS CATALOGING-IN-PUBLICATION DATA
Russell, John, 1954–
Favorite sons : a novel / by John Russell.
p.   cm.
ISBN 0-945575-36-X
I. Title.
PS3568.U76675A78   1992
813'.54—dc20   92-45   CIP

2   4   6   8   10   9   7   5   3   1
FIRST EDITION

for Sallie

Grant that the old Adam in this child may be so buried,

that the new man may be raised up in him.

—Public Baptism of Infants
Book of Common Prayer

Contents

FAVORITE

SONS

I

—— ✖ ——

MAN'S ESTATE

1938–49

Chapter One

1938–39

ORTH Patterson not only had a distinguished name, but his family had kept its money and diversified it so thoroughly and subtly that no one could actually be sure where it was. "The Pattersons are in railroads," Roger heard it confidently said and just as confidently denied; "No—they are in tobacco" or "trucking" or "furniture." Roger thought it safest to assume they were in all of it. But Worth himself seemed to be beyond getting and spending, beyond striving of any sort. Roger got the impression that he had done all of his thinking in another, somewhat higher life and was now occupied with remembering what he already knew.

Roger met Worth at "Leaders," a special orientation held on a remote farm estate; the faculty singled out new men whom they flattered with tales of their families' importance around the campfire, trying to instill in them the proper regard for alma mater before they had the chance to matriculate. Roger had little idea why he was attending, a bow perhaps to the Albrights' better days and to his father's speeches. Everyone, however, knew the Pattersons of Fairington, the benefactors who had built the Piedmont city from a mill village. Some said they were carpetbaggers, others that they were crooks, but whatever they were, they were exactly that. Thus, Worth stood out from his ill-defined classmates, a seventeen-year-old man fully formed *sui generis* from the Carolina clay. Roger watched the curiosity's face as he sat, chin inclined and liquid eyes unblinking, during the recital of alma mater's sacraments and the speculation as to the ideals of the Carolina gentleman.

"I think I already know this stuff, don't you, Albright?" Worth said; he'd seen Roger dozing during the debate over whether the honor code

3

was fully an extension of the Ten Commandments. They hitchhiked to Chapel Hill and went to the movies.

Their rooms were on the same hall during freshman year, and they talked about everything, or rather Worth talked and Roger listened. Roger did not feel ready to talk just yet. Worth talked and Roger listened through the breezy pastel autumn and the misted winter, when the fog and chilly rain enveloped the tiny town like a London movie set, and on to cacophony in spring, as the blossoms of the dogwoods, the redbuds, the Judas trees, and cherries floated down on the heads of the lounging young men. Worth Patterson's talk cut through the distracting harmonies; it was direct talk, full of feeling and thought, not mimicked from an opinion heard at dinner last night or aped from Father. He talked so well about everything — girls, sports, courses, politics, cars — even the world outside Carolina, which he seemed to know, and which seemed to allow him to fight, far better than Roger, the madness that set in around the ides of March, when nature rampant and youth rampant took over and the professors gave up.

In April Worth joined the Deke house, which Roger knew he chose by instinct, and which in turn welcomed him with relief. Worth Patterson was more Deke than the Dekes, and they needed him if for no other reason than to continue to persuade themselves that they were who they were. None of the other mainline fraternities would do for Worth, Roger could see that. The KAs were too wet, the Chi Psis too professional, the St. As too northern, and the SAEs positively sybaritic. The Dekes possessed the manner and the necessary funds to retain the correct liberal style of old. They had conquered, too, the question that perplexed Roger: how does a gentleman spend all his time making money and still remain a gentleman? Apparently he just didn't talk about it.

Or he didn't talk about it around strangers. Left to themselves, the Dekes talked about it plenty. The next fall, when Roger rushed the house, one of the brothers had the poor taste to remark that Mrs. Albright was known to dispense but ice water from her silver service, and that to make ends meet, even after the family had sold its land, she had become a self-employed caterer. As laughter resounded through the vaulted main hall, Worth Patterson smashed his cocktail glass against the mountainous stone hearth and proclaimed in a voice hardly above a whisper, but which carried to the very marrow of everyone present, "I will remind you, gentlemen, that Mr. Albright's great-grandfather commanded North Carolina's brigades at Gettysburg." And that was that. Roger was in.

Years later, the Deke house burned after an especially lively party, and the fraternity suffered the further indignity of probation when even the most discreet onlookers could not fail to testify that half of the unclad undergraduates leaping from the inferno on the upper floors were coeds. All that remained standing of the old wooden frame was that same hearth. It was Roger Albright's donation that rebuilt the house, composed this time of solid, incombustible North Carolina bricks, manufactured by the company his wife had inherited from her father. At Roger's instructions the architect rebuilt around the hearth, which Roger intended to be the rallying point for the old boys during the libations that preceded and concluded home football games. At the gala opening of his proud new house, Roger Albright was the guest of honor, and a classmate from pledge days, in a misplaced tribute, shocked the assembly by flouting convention, not to mention strict fraternity law, in recounting the words Worth Patterson (who was fortunately in Washington) had spoken to stave off the blackballing of the fraternity's most generous benefactor. When the besotted brother had concluded the humiliation, Roger, flushed from forehead to clenched fingers, managed to remark, not without grace, that Gettysburg was the last battle the Albrights ever lost. He then excused himself from his own party and never set foot in the house again.

In truth, however, the Albrights had lost many battles and several wars after the most glorious defeat whose memory served Roger so well. The Albrights had in fact developed a taste for losing. Each twenty years or so, money, chance, or fate would present itself to a recently reared son, and the hopes of the family would rise; then the spirits — the past failures whose portraits stared down darkly from the walls of the timeworn country manse — fluttered around the unlucky young man until he too made his routine failure, doused himself in a soggy alcoholism, and retreated to recount his missed chances to all who would listen until he died and found his place on the wall with the rest. Arranging these farces, from the fantasy of the China bonds to the collateralization of the wife's inherited deed, never proved difficult, since the avariciously gracious Security National Bank in Raleigh always loaned the Albrights money; the bank always loaned because the Albrights always paid them back, losing each time more and more of the land they had mostly already lost. The young man attired himself in battle plumage, prepared for the final charge, and placed his wager on Florida real estate, or peanut manufactures, or, as one of the young Icaruses inventively destroyed himself, on a country club in Raleigh for the "workingman," by which he meant teachers and insurance agents and the like. This last venture actually turned a profit, to everyone's astonishment, including the Security National Bank, which was looking forward to devouring still more prime Albright bottom land, and this young man, Roger's father, Charles, had dared to hope that the spell had at last been broken.

As the newly prosperous flocked to the country club (which was really more an amusement park), the Albright fortunes rose, and Charles began to invest the capital in the nation's most prudent enterprises, the glorious institutions that now commanded the nation's honor, replacing the AEF and the Rough Riders, the Seventh Cavalry and the armies of the Potomac and of Northern Virginia: great armies of United States Steel, the Pennsylvania Railroad, National Cash Register, and the Radio Corporation of America — names that rolled off the tongue like the duchies of the House of Plantagenet. The dividends did indeed flow in, and the manse's double-set columns and fluted grillework, detached kitchen and creaky breezeway, matched chimneys and smokehouse were primed and painted rather than whitewashed, and the croppers and tenants drove Crane tractors rather than mules, and parcels arrived from Saks Fifth Avenue in New York, and Marshall Field in Chicago, and Miller and Rhoads in Richmond. Cousin Edith was married on the back lawn, given away on the arm of her uncle Charles, she in her crinkly lace and Charles in a new morning suit. The striped tent, and the orchestra from Raleigh, elicited comment even within the salons of Richmond, or so reported *The News and Observer* in the account Roger found. He saw himself, too, in the picture, a smiling, fat, white-jacketed ring bearer standing between the happy couple, convinced that he was the center of attention.

Having won a battlefield commission for fighting mustard gas and Germans at Château-Thierry, Charles fought without fear against the superstitions of the Albright past. What weight had superstition in 1929, except in the silly dreams of old women who refused to ride in the new motorcar and in the stubbornness of the maid who refused to use the new wringer washer? Dressed in summer whites, the young officer drove the motorcar to Raleigh every day and carefully tended to his country club–amusement park. Roger drove by the remains of it once—the modest golf club now a municipal course circumscribed by two shopping centers and a beltline cloverleaf, its clientele now a dissociated set of harried men who understood that riding after a little white ball in a little white cart constituted one of the main aspects of the American Dream. Roger circled the cloverleaf, driving past the millpond with its ornate paddle wheelers and funicula that passed to the island in the middle with the gazebo Charles rented out for private parties. The millpond sat shrinking, filling with silt, and the city used what remained of it for show, a scenic spot to place picnic tables and charcoal grills. The clubhouse with its fantastical spires and leaded windows and brass caricatures that Charles designed still stood. Peering through the chained front door, Roger saw the moldy interior, linoleum laid over the wooden floors, the halls lit by fluorescent strips.

Gradually Charles bought back the land that had been oozing from the family's estates for a half-century. A lot here, a farm there; always the countrymen and the bankers named a high price, always he paid it. He sat on the gallery of the old house and looked in four directions at land that was his again. The land did not earn in tobacco what it should have, and he did not have time to oversee the operations himself just then. One more year in trade and he could sell the country club and devote his time to the land. One more year and the "unfortunate period"—as the sisters so delicately referred to the last three generations of their family—would be over. But he never had that year. Charles awakened one October dawn, his pulse thundering, his arms and legs shaking from the nightmare. In the early light he dressed and drove to Raleigh and sat at his desk, waiting. At noon the call came from his broker in New York, and then he knew it had gotten him too. United States Steel, the Pennsylvania Railroad, National Cash Register, the Radio Corporation of America—the legions of that grand army lay decimated.

The workingman's country club died a slower death than the creditors expected. It struggled into 1932, losing revenue each year after the Crash, but rescuing itself during the several false hopes that led the businessmen and the bankers to pronounce the panic over. Finally, as the summer of 1932 in all its stillness and fecundity gave the *coup de grâce* to the tobacco price on which Raleigh's government workers depended for their prosperity, the clerks and insurance agents who had been left to bring their families to the lake and try a round of eighteen lost their jobs and retreated fully into the general desperation. The patient officers at the Security National Bank finally executed the long-drawn papers of foreclosure, and the Bright Leaf Golf and Family Club, and all assets and liabilities thereto, passed on to the special drawer in the main vault reserved for Albright dreams. The meticulous junior vice-president newly assigned to the foreclosure branch made a point to leave space in the drawer for the land deeds he knew were coming.

Within eighteen months after he had locked the gates to the club, the funicula, and the gazebo for the last time, Charles disposed of every landholding he had patiently acquired over the last eight years. The bank officers were amazed at the speed with which the Albright lands were divested, but as for the white and black tenants in the two counties where the Albrights held their land—the men who had learned to drive the lumbering new tractors but had been cautious enough to lend their mules to friends—they were not surprised. They knew the Albright luck, and each time Charles inspected their credit under the new electric lamp in his study, sitting beside the oak shelves that held the leather-bound volumes he read at his leisure, they wondered when it was going to end. Charles Albright had fought in the Great War; he could strip and assemble a Browning automatic rifle blindfolded. And he could repair his motorcar without a mechanic because he had taken instruction in Raleigh to learn how. He knew superstition had not beaten him, but he knew something had, and he was going to find out what it was. He subscribed to journals and read the new books. He listened to the radio and talked to his professors at Chapel Hill. He wrote and thought and then he made a list of what had beaten him: growing too much and selling it for too little, this he underlined; the Federal Reserve Bank and the policies of Andrew Mellon, which he regarded to be the same, writing them on the same line; margin position taken by Wall Street broker, and by him, of course, but this was not an exercise in self-examination; and LARGE HOLDERS OF LIQUID CAPITAL, this the summation of the others. Having made his list he put it in his lockbox under the worthless stock certificates until the day he could do something about it.

The house was the last to go, but it went too, its newly bought and deftly arranged furniture from Saks Fifth Avenue and Marshall Field and Miller and Rhoads, and the striped tent from the grand wedding—the bondsman hauled away everything except the books that Charles himself apportioned among the family for safekeeping. They also left the dining-room suite for the new house Charles was building on the last of the land he owned, which was in fact his wife's dowry. Barbara Brent Albright accepted all, for she had known what to expect from the Albright men, and like them she was temperamentally better equipped to cope with misfortune than with success. She moved into her hew house without petulance, but since she had no belief in her husband's ability to keep that property either, she bound her mother's diamonds and her own store of Victory Bonds in trust to provide for the two events that were the most necessary for the family's survival: her son's education at the university and her daughter's presentation at the North Carolina Debutante Ball in Raleigh.

•   •   •

For Roger, catastrophe meant only the excitement of a new house. He scarcely remembered life at the old one, though he had memories, which he freely embellished, of his ring bearer's role in the grand wedding. Years later he brought his fiancée, Lillian Siler, to meet his stately and by now formidably widowed mother, and he took the shortcut from the main highway past the old Greek Revival mansion, well tended by the bland people who bought it in foreclosure and still lived there. As they drove the gentle S curve up the slope to the vista the house had commanded since the 1830s, bumping over the wide dirt road that carriages and mounted cavalry and Model Ts and his own Buick Special had all shared and that no one had ever thought would be the better paved in asphalt, Lillian Siler caught her breath. "Golly," she said. "I mean golly." And Roger said, "Oh, that's just the old house we used to live in before the Depression." Roger stopped the car in the driveway and walked through the front grounds to the small cemetery beyond the grove.

"Roger — you're walking right across the yard," she said, trotting behind him, holding her hat.

"When you sell a piece of property and reserve a use to it, they give you an easement," he told her, looking straight ahead. "We've got an easement to get to the cemetery, where my father's buried."

Lillian took off her hat and gloves and tried to stand as still as she could so that she would not sweat in the sun or sway on her spectator pumps in the clumpy grass. She squinted at the dim inscription on the old Civil War general's obelisk that dominated the plot, but she couldn't make it out unless she put on her glasses, which she wouldn't do. Roger stood stiffly in the new suit he had bought after throwing his officer's uniform into the garbage. He removed from the coat pocket his European Theater ribbon, his combat infantryman's badge, his Silver Star with oak leaf cluster, his Purple Heart, and his major's palms. Beside his father's clean marble headstone he buried the medals.

Then he took Lillian by the arm. "Let's go see Mother. We're late."

At afternoon's end, after she knew she had passed muster and they were on the way to Raleigh to dinner, after she had considered what she had learned and measured it in the balance of her love for this burning man, Lillian asked, "Why did you bury your medals?"

"What the hell was I going to do with the damn things? Keep them in a jelly jar around the house?"

Later, as they were driving back to Fairington, she asked, "That house, Roger, is really so grand. Is there any way we could buy the place and fix it up? Daddy would help."

"No, sugar. It's impossible to cool in the summer or heat in the winter. The plumbing is terrible. If we lived there I would have to farm and there's no money in it. Besides, you wouldn't have anything to do out here in the country."

•   •   •

Charles applied himself to growing tobacco. The few acres he was able to keep for himself and away from the bank were good ones, and he called his new farm Bright Star, a name that told his enthusiasm for the project and his hope that this new start would be his last. He resettled only one of his tenant families; the rest, of much worse prospects than even the impoverished gentry, who after all still owned what little they owned, disappeared, both white and black, into the maw of the ruined times, surfacing perhaps, if they were inventive and lucky, in Harlem or Baltimore or Washington, D.C., and if they were unlucky, remaining paralyzed to squat on land they had worked the day before. The smell of their blasted lives hung over the dirt roads and the slat-board houses, bringing white handkerchiefs to the nostrils of the bank officers who drove from Raleigh to inspect their new assets. They were greeted by the gape-mouthed children of pellagra and hookworm and the silent men. The sight and odor moved even the meticulous junior vice-president, who had regarded the tenants and sharecroppers before as either ill-behaved or well-behaved children — and in any case just harmless niggers or sullen white trash — to put off calling the sheriff to remove them from the little they could not understand they no longer had.

The situation, Charles thought, will surely be easier now. Surely he had righted his account in heaven and obeyed the injunction against worldly success. Surely a modest living would be allowed him, as it was allowed Father and Grandfather and the others who had also come around to their true stations. But the tobacco crop of 1932 grew again in terrible abundance. When the buyers from Reynolds and British American and the Duke Trust came to the barns to bid at auction, meeting the hopeful farmers who drove their families and their bright leaf to Wilson and Kinston and Goldsboro, the company men paid very little for the overproduced crop. As often as not, the farmer took his family back from the auction without the shoes or the dress or the meal at the town restaurant he meant to buy. Charles thought, Is human folly the winner at every turn? God did not mean us to be bankrupts. There has to be a method. We are not helpless people.

When Franklin Roosevelt won, Charles removed from the lockbox the list of reasons he had written down for the Depression. He could not do anything about most of the evils, but one evil he could attack, and when the movie-star voice on the radio said not to be afraid because there was a method, Charles listened and knew this was his time. We must plant less and charge more, Charles said to his friends. The government offers to guarantee our price and to buy whatever falls below it. We must organize ourselves. To that task the quiet Charles Albright applied himself. Helpless in the simplest effort at self-advancement, given a goal for society, a holy task, he was magnificent. His elegant speeches punctured the rough air of the tobacco farmers' meetings and they listened, the gruff and proud men, for they knew who he was, and that his grandfather had led their grandfathers in something more dangerous than a spate of hard times. He convinced the skeptical farmers, convinced every one of them, for they would not move until all had agreed, that surrendering part of their acreage as the government requested was for the good of all. He traveled from hamlet to crossroads in his well-tailored suit, at no one's behest but his own, for it was his mission and the right thing to do, and he convinced the free-holders, some of whom had brooked no interference with their land since the Revolution, that they should sign the letters of agreement drawn up by the federal lawyers and accept the allotments. Charles Albright felt the swell of the people beside him as he drove in the soft, quiet darkness down the country roads through the bugs as thick as Christmas snowflakes. He felt good, like a man again.

Roger knew little about all of these things, though he saw his mother clip from *The News and Observer* the articles that mentioned his father and put them in her album. He liked exploring the new house, and he felt it was more his own than the other one. True, it did not have the long rooms with the high ceilings that echoed back your voice, or the curving stairway and the polished banister and the row of scary pictures with the faces that stared straight at you. But it had new paint that shone in the sun and it stood right by the road, with trees on every side and neighbors to play with, even girls to play with Missy so that she wouldn't be around all the time to mess things up. He left the private academy and entered the county school, to which his father promptly donated some of his more serviceable books. The school taught the basic courses, preparing farm boys to read newspapers and almanacs, to figure their bills at the end of the season, and to know enough history to pull the big lever for the Democracy. Each evening, after Roger and Missy had finished their lessons, Mr. Albright drilled them in the Latin he required them to learn on their own. After he had retired to his "study" — which was really a corner of the living room where he placed his desk and papers — to work on a political speech or digest the newspapers from Raleigh, Mrs. Albright took them into the kitchen and read from her large folio art books, with the crinkly, pasted plates from Rembrandt and Leonardo, and they memorized as in a trance the names and faces.

When Roger was fourteen he went into the fields to top and to crop the tobacco, he and his father working side by side with the tenant until the work was done. Roger wore the tall, stiff boots that came to his knees and cut into his skin. In the spring he topped the flower from the tobacco plants; in the summer he cropped the leaves, taking them from the bottom up, keeping one eye on the plant taller than he was and the other on the lookout for the hostile copperheads that regarded the ditched rows as their domain. Mrs. Albright's final vanity was her refusal to join the other farm wives in the fields for the frantic days of cropping and barning, when they hung the last leaves in the barns to cure. She and Missy would do women's work, she announced, and one day, to her husband's astonishment, she presented him with the realized plan of her own business. Everyone had so complimented her sweet relish over the years that in the spring she had planted her own crop of cucumbers and peppers and had just now finished putting up her recipe. All those years of reneging on her promises to provide the formula to her friends would pay off, for she was sure they would buy her Bright Star Relish in the store. She had arranged on her own for two grocers to stock her relish, and she was sure there would soon be others. So while the countrymen and their wives brought in the tobacco, Barbara and Missy, clad in identical hats and matching dresses, drove into town to make their deliveries.

Roger grew in his father's likeness — the blue eyes, the straight carriage that made him stand even taller than his six feet. He began to see himself in the oil portraits that Charles had retrieved from storage and hung in the new house, at less imposing stations than in the old. Charles began to take him to the cooperative meetings, since the boy had gained age and height enough to be given a man's education, and Roger listened to his father's speeches in favor of Roosevelt's New Deal, his lips pursed, his arms shaking, his voice on the rise when he made gentlemanly stabs at the bankers in Raleigh who opposed the President and the party's platform, explaining to the shrewd men why they had to stand together against the tobacco companies and get a fair price for their crop. Mr. Albright took Roger to other meetings, too, meetings this time with the denizens of the Shelby machine that ran the state Democratic party. The professionals had at first watched suspiciously the efforts of Charles Albright on behalf of the tobacco program. When he made a success of it, they agreeably proposed to take things from there and put him up for Congress. But he refused. He would not stand for Congress, he said. He was not a lawyer who would gain useful contacts in political office. He had been a businessman, he was now a farmer, and he was satisfied to be that.

When the time came for Roger to enter the university, his mother did not have to sell her jewelry, or what was left of it; her Bright Star Relish was a money-maker; in fact, she now had several local girls in after school to help with the growing operation. She turned over the proceeds every month to Charles, who accepted the money silently, and she never questioned what happened to it. To do so would have been unladylike, and a violation of the truce between them on the subject. Roger went to Chapel Hill in a new suit. Like his father he was something of a dandy, and even in the absence of money he tried to dress well.

Chapter Two

1940-41

THERE has to be a method, Roger thought as he traversed the walkways of the front campus that merged with the streets of the town, so that the habits of contemplation and consumption joined amicably over the rock walls that formed a gentle barricade around the school proper and that seemed to but formally and without enthusiasm separate study from life. There had to be a method to the visible world, he insisted to himself, resolved on this point after two years of study on it. Surely man's society had a pattern similar, if on a lower order, to God's creation, and human enterprise prospered by conforming to that pattern. Each night he had engaged his mates at the dormitory, and later at the fraternity house, with this idea, and each night they had indulged him in it, for they were fond of Roger. He had what it takes, anyone could see that. "I'm not going to read history anymore," he announced in the beginning of his third year. "It's bunk."

At the fraternity house he observed his brothers. He asked about their family businesses. He wanted to know precisely not only how things were made — that bored him after a while — but also how things were bought and sold. The inquiries would have been rude coming from anyone else, but Roger usually made the children of mill owners feel flattered that their affairs had been pried into, and they generally found their own lives more interesting after discussing themselves with Roger than before.

Beneath its doe-eyed sleep, the university's underworld of ideas stirred for Roger, and he saw revealed the energy that powered the old buildings, met the wan and hurried men who darted from the library, having just written an article or proofed a treatise. Roger could tell that these men were different, though he didn't know who they were. They had come, many of them, from far away, hired by President MacGiver, who himself had just arrived. The university had brought in President MacGiver to shake up things, his father said. Roger took these busy men's courses. He sampled economics, which he thought false, since what it taught him clearly did not work, and he studied psychology, which also missed the mark for him, all the talk of drives and the several egos and the business with rats. It seemed like history, another fairy tale. Finally, at the beginning of his junior year, he attended a class given by Professor Ogden of the new Institute for Progressive Studies and found the something he was looking for.

Professor Ogden sported the reputation of an eccentric. He was always stopping people on the street and asking them questions about the most ordinary things, thanking them for their answers while writing carefully on a note card. When Roger heard that he was to lecture on the problem of poverty in tenant farmers, he thought the subject would be a good test for the man. Roger knew something about tenant farmers, after all.

"What do we know, really, about the tenant farmer?" Professor Ogden asked, his trim bow tie perched high so that it plummeted with every disgorging of the Adam's apple on each languorous Georgia vowel. "We may know one tenant farmer on a personal basis, or several." He paused, studying the faces in the room with the high-banked rows of chairs. "We may even know the terms of a tenant's contract, but what do we know about the tenant as a class? Where does he come from, from what background, I mean. Where does he settle — I mean in what districts does he settle, and in relation to what crops? What percent is he in a given farm population, and to what degree is he upwardly mobile within it and outwardly mobile from it?"

The students shifted in their seats, intent, following the questions with strained excitement, many writing quickly. Professor Ogden pointed to the top of his list of names.

"Mr. — ah — Albright. Enlighten us please. Tell us what hypothesis you would propose. First fruits, if you will."

Roger rose and looked tentatively around him. Though this was the introductory class, no one seemed surprised that recitation had commenced. His classmates in fact had the manner of tigers ready to pounce. He cleared his throat. "I believe, sir, that the tenant is a vanishing breed. Opportunities for factory work will increase in the future and the tenant will travel back and forth to nearby cities where he will find employment."

"Not too farfetched, Mr. Albright, not too farfetched a hypothesis, though this course does not speak directly to that question. What is your data?"

Roger hesitated and his silence commanded still more attention. "Sir, I would base that view on logic, experience, and hope."

A book closed with a bang, and murmuring rose from the back of the hall. Roger noticed that the heads turning to look at him belonged to older students, students who did not seem like they belonged in college at all, among them large numbers of women, and not of the junior transfer variety. One of them, a striking slender woman with long, flowing black hair and dark eyes punctured him with such a stare that his knees weakened. Several embarrassed students chuckled.

But Professor Ogden did not. "Logic, experience, and hope." His eyes drifted from the classroom to the main quadrangle of the campus, where the still September air held the leaves to the trees; beyond the new Georgian buildings, which in all their incongruous antiquity reassured the ghosts of the place that no matter what newfangled ideas issued from their walls their purpose was one with the beginning; and still beyond to the old library, where the portrait of Saint George slaying the dragon reminded men at study of their duty, whatever it was. Just seventy-five years before, Sherman had quartered his horses in the library under the painting, flanked by Thucydides and Shakespeare, Newton and Saint Paul. By and by he had decided not to burn the university down, and afterward he claimed that his horses were the best read in the army.

"We need more than experience and hope, even logic, Mr. Albright," the professor said, his eyes fixed on the middle distance. "We need facts."

Roger had found the method.

Through that autumn Roger worked for Professor Ogden's course to exclusion of his others, undaunted that it turned out to be a graduate lecture. After the first day he did not speak in class but instead watched the older students to learn how the method worked. His argyles and tweeds and buck shoes contrasted markedly with the worn shiny suits, brushed cotton work shirts, and twill trousers the other men in the class wore. Some of them even kept a thin mustache (as did Professor Ogden, Roger noted). The women especially intrigued him; intense, argumentative women, many of them with the razor voices of the North or the blunted tones of the prairie, they challenged Professor Ogden and sought his approval, lingering after class, vying with the men to engage him in private conversation. Passing the graduate smoking room, Roger would often hear the loud strivings of their raised voices, the noise of politics, though not the politics of his father's symmetrical phrases but of table-pounding doctrine about workers, and the Negro problem, and the necessity of supporting the Party.

He noticed, too, that his classmates appeared to be intrigued with him. Several invited him to lunch one day, and they seemed surprised that he accepted, but over sandwiches and warm Cokes they all laughed about the eminence of Professor Ogden and the fear of their inadequacy. After that. they invited Roger to dinners at the cheap student restaurants on Franklin Street and sometimes asked him to raucous beer parties in the dark single rooms they kept in boardinghouses. One evening, to his surprise, he found himself with his classmates at a table in a colored café in the adjoining mill town of Carrboro, eating barbecued ribs, kale, and cornbread and drinking buttermilk. No one other than Roger and several of the unindoctrinated colored diners thought this strange, and Roger, having shared the same meal with Negro field hands many times under the Carolina sun, had to admit that prohibiting black people and white people from eating in buildings together when they broke bread regularly in the bright light of day made little sense.

The woman who had distracted him during the first class — Judith Stern was her name — leaned close to him, her long black hair brushing his shoulder. "Does eating with Negroes make you uncomfortable, Roger?" she asked, her eyes fixing him with that direct gaze. As he sopped up the last grease with his cornbread and downed the last drop of buttermilk, he said, "Well, no, now that you mention it; I ate plenty of dinners in the tobacco fields with colored field hands." The group stopped their conversation and listened respectfully as he told them about how he had worked from dawn to past twilight in the fields, how he had topped and cropped the tobacco, stitched the leaves to long stakes to hang in the curing barns, and sorted for market until the stems made a pulp of his hands. He finished. He met Judith's eyes. Finally, looking challengingly at her compatriots, she said, "There is something I want to tell you, Roger." She gripped the table tightly. "I am a member of the Communist party." And as Roger remembered another creed's adherents testifying on Sunday morning before baptismal dunking fonts in the country churches near Bright Star, the other students — Julian, the elegant senior, Big Joe from west Texas, taciturn Ellen from Philadelphia, and Al from "upstate," meaning New York — announced that they too were communists. "So?" Roger replied, turning his pockets inside out as the testimonials concluded. "I guess this means we split the check from each according to his means."

•   •   •

After that they invited Roger to their meetings at Elston's Book Shop on Franklin Street, a place known to most as a harmless business establishment and a rather good bookstore, but to the cognoscenti as the center for Party organizing in the region. Upstairs, the bearded El, a Spanish civil war veteran who was younger than he looked, ran a printing press that any bona fide leftist group could employ for a price. El kept his profits to a respectably low level. He maintained his questionable community credentials by rigidly enforcing the segregation codes in the downtown restaurant he also owned — and operated at a much higher profit — and by writing long letters to the *Chapel Hill Weekly* haranguing against Negrophiles, New Dealers, and the like. Though the Party took a dim view of his capitalist enterprises and cranky reverse propaganda, they made allowances for difficulties in the southern division and marked down his eccentricity to a somewhat skewed Trotskyite concern for local conditions. In the forties he would be purged as a Browderite.

Judith became Roger's friend, which was an odd but not unpleasant thing for a girl to be, he discovered. She insisted that's what they be, friends, but unlike other girls who said the same thing, she meant it. She argued with him for hours, saying the most challenging things to him in her peculiar direct way, criticizing everything in sight, from the skimpy thinking in the local newspapers, to the unhealthy interest in sports she detected in the undergraduates, to the timidity of the authorities before the state's financial powers and the laziness of the workers she wished to organize and who seemed disinclined to fight for their own good. Roger at first took umbrage at the assault on the surrounding institutions, and he ended up mounting a halfhearted defense, which simply fed her ire. After a while he learned to defend himself by attacking her, and so their arguments, which sometimes for hours shattered the quiet of McCorkle Place, before the sacred Old Well — whose water she also attacked for its metallic taste — became mutual broadsides, she sallying forth against the injustices he tolerated and he against the stupidities she proposed in their place.

"You AGREE with me, dammit!" she said, throwing up her hands at the climax of one donnybrook. "But you won't DO anything about it. You sit there and smile and nod and you don't want to DO anything!"

He shrugged. "Do what? Burn down the university because poor people live in Carrboro? Do you think Comrade El wants to burn down the university?"

Some of the brothers at the fraternity took a joking but nonetheless concerned attitude toward Roger's frequenting of Elston's and his association with the longhairs. Roger explained to Worth, who was his intermediary with the rah-rah element of the Dekes, that one of the New York girls was putting out for him and the brothers better shut up about him going to El's or else it might foul things up for them and their girls at St. Mary's and Patterson College. In other words, the wrong parties might pick up on some well-placed remarks about the tomcatting and late-dating he knew was going on. The brothers regarded him with new respect and asked if he could arrange some dates for them with the New York girls.

At El's he met the unusual and the famous. Once he casually mentioned to Worth that he had spent half an hour in conversation with Clifford Odets, and Worth protested that he had the best connections in the state, since everyone else had to spend half an hour standing in line just to get a ticket to hear him speak. To his surprise Roger learned that Elston's was a regular stop for the celebrated in the arts and literature and that this most innocuous-looking establishment was a better-known landmark to people from outside the state than even the new football stadium. A whole new world of totems and hierarchies opened to him, a world of preferments as arbitrary as the ones he knew already, and as jealously guarded.

A giant figure in this new world, Roger discovered, was the apparently famous Professor Ogden. Judith worshiped the man. "His work with the Institute is central," she told him over the terrible black and grainy coffee they all lapped up at El's, where, Roger had decided, to ask for cream and sugar would be condemned as bourgeois. "Things are so wide open here," she continued. "His findings are establishing the base for certainly a reformist and perhaps a revolutionary movement in the South. He is, of course, personally just another New Dealer, but the work itself — that's something else again." She confessed that she felt her training to be too theoretical and her analyses inadequate before Ogden's methods. "I'm trying like hell to find a dissertation topic he'll advise. He only takes three a year, you know, and Julian and Big Joe have already got theirs. I could go back to Wisconsin, I guess."

As the end of the term grew near and everyone, including Roger, was working hard on their final papers for Professor Ogden, Judith called a special meeting at El's to discuss the upcoming Southern Negro Youth Conference. Judith's strong voice grew tense when she announced amidst gasps and applause that a proposal was going to be introduced advocating the integration of student bodies at several state universities, including Chapel Hill. Julian, Frank, Big Joe, and the others left quickly after the statements ended, and the hard union men from the newly formed local at the R.J. Reynolds plant in Winston-Salem piled into their old jalopy and sped westward in the darkness. The intense Negro in the suit and thin tie left also, smoldering no doubt at the thought of riding in the back of the bus all the way to A&T College in Greensboro. El excused himself and trudged upstairs to set a pamphlet against the America-Firsters.

Judith sat beside Roger on the floor, her long, free-swinging hair lighting on his shoulder. "Roger, we have decided that you should represent our district at the convention."

"Hell, Judith, you know there are a dozen people who could go and do better than I could; besides, what about exams—and Ogden's paper?"

"We've discussed it. The group thinks that you going, given your class background especially, would make all the difference. There is no way that any of the local forces can say that you are an outside agitator."

She grabbed his arm with her strong brown fingers, worn and calloused and kept proudly that way by her part-time work at Carr Mill, in the weaving room, where the loudest and most dangerous work took place, and where many worked as punishment. Judith had asked for the weaving room and laughed at the supervisors who taunted her with the stretch-out until she stretched out all they could deliver and begged for more. She was hard and pretty, and Roger knew she would not turn sour like his mother from being hard and pretty, but she would thrive in it and live to a grand old age still being that way and right with it.

"Judith, I can't go to Richmond for that convention and vote for those proposals. You know how I feel about the Negro problem privately, but as a matter of law—I mean, I just can't vote to bring in colored men. Not here. Why, you don't know where it could lead. Upset the balance and we could go back to corruption and vote-buying and the very worst elements in control."

She looked steadily into his eyes. "I suppose by the very worst elements you mean me and my friends."

Before he could deny it she had run out the door into the December night. Roger ran after her and cursed himself for losing her on Franklin Street. She shouldn't have had to walk home alone at that hour.

• • •

After his words with Judith, Roger noticed that he was very definitely dropped from the circle at El's. Old El himself, however, treated him much better, retrieving for him odd volumes of poetry and texts for various classes at bargain prices and always offering a wink and a boisterous "How's tricks?" Roger decided this was the most definite sign of his rejection: if El could treat him so well so openly, he must really be on the outs.

Roger absorbed everything in Ogden's class. He buried himself in the study of statistics and in the writings of Franklin Giddings, Thorstein Veblen, Frederick Jackson Turner, and William Dunning. For his first field study he picked the topic Professor Ogden had called upon him to recite— tenant farmers. One weekend he caught the bus back to Bright Star and befuddled his mother and father by riding around in the car all over the county and taking notes about the oddest things—the number of children in tenant families, whether the houses had plumbing or not, or electricity, whether the parents lived together, what food they grew in their small private patches of ground, what the terms of their contracts were with the landowners, what percentage of the tobacco or cotton was theirs, what they contributed in the way of supplies, and how they reported their crops.

"But, Son," his mother said as she bent over her own account books. Charles had given them over to her several years before when he realized that her business, which now required two outbuildings and a staff of seven, and which had expanded from sweet relish to chutney and watermelon pickles of the choicest variety, outstripped in net earnings the return from the farm itself. "At college you should study some uplifting subject. Who wants to know about those wretched people anyway?"

Charles looked up from his copy of *Progressive Farmer.* "I was under the impression you were reading history. Well, this fellow Ogden is well thought of, from what I've been able to gather."

They decided to let well enough alone.

Roger presented his paper, entitled "Conditions Among Some Tenant Families on Tobacco Farms in Nash County, North Carolina," to Dr. Ogden on the final day of the term. He had worked for weeks compiling his research, arranging it, composing careful conclusions. He had neglected all his other work, for he did not care about his grades in the other courses — he wanted an A from Dr. Ogden. On the last day before Christmas break he ventured to Dr. Ogden's office to speak to him about the paper. It was the first time he had talked to him in class or out of it since the first day. The professor, hunched over what appeared to be a limitless supply of note cards, which he stacked in carefully labeled note-card boxes under a filmy goosenecked lamp, motioned to Roger with his pipe that he should dump the yellowing paper and dust-bound academic journals from the seat of the wooden chair opposite the desk and sit down. Wordlessly the professor picked Roger's tome from one of several bulging mounds of student papers and tossed it to him.

Roger turned through the pages, his hands shaking as he passed notes in the professor's slanted script underlining and taking issue with some point. At the end he read: "Sound work. Good research. B-plus." Any of the more expert graduate students would have been grateful for such a grade from the great man, but Roger was not, and his eyes must have shown disappointment, because the professor said, "Your paper was one of the three best in the class, Mr. Albright. Quite sound work for an undergraduate and a newcomer to the field, I must say."

"In that case, Sir, why wasn't the paper an A?"

The professor tamped down his pipe. "Mr. Albright, it takes a certain amount of time to develop a feel for data, especially as to the significance of the sample one examines. This comes with experience. Your findings are sound as far as they go, but you seem to have reflected little on the importance of what you have found out. What does your sample represent, if anything?" He walked to the grimy window and looked down on the neatly landscaped grounds below.

"It's easy enough to see that the sidewalks indeed form a rectangle with diagonals," the professor continued, gesturing with his pipe. "But what of it? What does that mean to the universe of sidewalks? Or to the world at large of which that universe of sidewalks is a subset?"

Roger did not know what to make of this. He stood to leave.

"Mr. Albright," the professor said, "is this farm on which you base the bulk of your research your own family farm?"

Roger nodded.

"Ah yes." He pulled a card from the box at his elbow. "Bright Star Farm, seventy-five acres tobacco, one hundred corn, fifty timber, Nash County. I have admired your father's work, if I may say so, Mr. Albright, with the tobacco cooperatives. I am giving a course that may interest you in the spring term, if you have a free hour at noon on Tuesdays and Thursdays."

The professor bent back over his note cards and Roger assumed he was dismissed. A curious interview, Roger thought, running back to the Deke house through the sleet across the vacant campus. To have one's farm in someone's note-card box was unnerving enough, but he had never heard anyone call what his father did his "work" before, and never had he heard anyone praise it. And he was sure the great Professor Ogden had invited him to take his spring course.

•   •   •

In January nearly the same class convened in Professor Ogden's lecture hall. Roger had to do some last-minute juggling to change his class schedule to free the hour, as well as convince his skeptical adviser that two graduate level courses in sociology fit into his college program. Judith had decided she would talk to him in a clipped, severe way Roger was sure she imagined to be "correct," but that reminded him of the way a town librarian might regard a patron who perpetually lost his library card. "Always remember," his mother had told him, "that being a lady or a gentleman is often mistaken for never giving insult. Very untrue. A gentleman or a lady simply never gives insult unintentionally." He wondered what she would think of Judith. In the papers, he had read about the meeting of the Southern Negro Youth Conference and about the call the conference had made for the integration of colleges. *The News and Observer* noted approvingly that while there were delegates from the university at Chapel Hill, there were no "native sons among them." I failed my friends, Roger thought, and they must hate me for it.

But isolation from Professor Ogden's most talented core of students did not lessen the value of the work for Roger; it seemed to enhance it. He felt Ogden's eyes singling him out in class when making a point, and at times he felt the professor spoke only to him. He went giddy with the power of Ogden's mind as he explained the movement of capital, the patterns of investment and industrial expansion as they related to labor supply and price, the internal structure of the large corporations, and the methods of their operation on a regional and national scale. This course was not the research primer of the first term but the very heart and soul of Ogden. Each class he placed before them like the pieces of an abstruse puzzle his grand theory of the economic organization of North America, his construct of how the material conditions of ordinary life were determined by a particular ebb and flow of ideas and wealth, the United States an engine of financial empire with cities and towns and states and subnations within the pattern continually integrating in a grand scheme. What seemed perfectly random to Roger as he drove down a highway and saw a farm, a truck, a house, a factory now took the possibility of coherence. Sometimes the professor's lecture would spiral so rapidly to a distant point that all Roger could do would be to copy the words verbatim and read them slowly later:

... chief cause of uneven technology is ... contracted access to capital ... differential in rates of interest ... industrial borrowing 6 percent in N.Y. 8 percent in S.C., capital consuming project in S.C. must earn one-third more ... elaborate technologies avoid high capital charges because of need for expensive plant ... same applies to lesser degree in farm or home ...

South has status of agricultural country in trade with industrial countries ... imports manufactures and equipment, pays in raw produced and unfinished manufactures ... debt results from inequalities in income ... proceeds from exports should service current debt plus manufactures ... luxuries for the upper classes in fact added ... mechanism of exchange fouled up ... interest rates go higher leading to rationing of capital ... standard of living reduced below industrialized area ... MUST ENLARGE CAPITAL ..."

Roger underlined the last three words. He became drunk with the numbers, with the grand design arrayed magisterially in the dozens of continental maps and graphs and tables. The numbers spoke the symmetry of the epic he lived, the epic he planned for himself.

"I see that you're already well along on your paper for this term, Roger," the professor said as he examined the prospectus for the work Roger proposed.

"Yes, sir, I want to study the large textile corporations, what makes them tick. I've gotten started at the library already. I was waiting to ask you for more guidance with the materials."

The professor clicked a rubber band over the pile of note cards sitting in front of him. "Roger, before you proceed with—this plan, I feel I must ask you to consider certain issues. The précis as it stands is not appropriate for the course."

What does he want from me? Roger thought.

"What needs to be done here," the professor continued, fingering the five pages Roger had composed and condensed from the original twenty, "is for you to address the projected consequences of your subject, its relation to the present social and economic structure."

"I'm afraid I don't know what you mean, sir. I simply wish to understand and compare the workings of several textile corporations, trace their means of gaining capital, their techniques for securing a pool of labor, and their patterns of management. It's straight from your lectures—"

"I know that." He waved impatiently and fumbled in his pocket for his pipe. "But there are extensive assumptions in such a study. What are the effects of these corporations on the towns where they locate and on the people who change their lives to work for them?"

"Sir?" Roger shook his head. "I simply don't see how that fits into my paper."

"And I don't see that your paper fits into my course."

The young man and the older man sat silently and stubbornly staring at each other. Finally, the professor handed Roger a list of references in his own hand so he could begin work on the topic, scribbled names for the interviews and fieldwork and also the names of articles in obscure journals, some written by himself, all of which he apparently had by heart. Then he looked down at the note cards before him and began to place them, one by one, in a new position, the logic of the arrangement known but to him. Roger took this, as he had learned, to be the sign for him to leave.

When he and Judith reconciled the following summer, meeting again at the colored café in Carrboro, she put her hand to her mouth in horror when Roger told her this story. "You said that to him? And he allowed you to go on with the paper?"

Roger could not be fully truthful and say yes, for the week after their meeting, after Roger had spent most of five days in the stacks of the library worrying the student assistants and the old reference curmudgeons to a frazzle, provoking one young man to walk out following Roger's request for yet another copy of *Southern Manufacturer* with the remark that the Thirteenth Amendment had to his knowledge outlawed slavery forever and including librarians too, he received by messenger a handwritten summons from Ogden to appear at his office the next afternoon. When he arrived, everything was in its usual state of disarray, except that Professor Ogden had fixed them both tea in an ancient kettle over a hot plate that Roger feared would combust at any moment.

"Roger, I asked you here for a favor," the professor said, pouring a cup of tea so strong Roger thought it was cough potion.

"Confound it!" the professor exclaimed. "I can never make this blasted tea right. No matter. You may know I am the university's representative to the legislature on the matter of public school appropriations, and I need someone to prepare for me a county-by-county report on expenditures and how they relate to attendance, performance, and graduation statistics. This report could stand as your term work. In addition"—he paused, reaching under his note cards for a pipe cleaner—"provided the work is of high enough quality, I would sponsor it for publication in the *Journal of Social Forces*."

The proposition startled Roger, not least because a dozen or so graduate students would have killed to do the work and might yet kill him if they found out he was doing it. "Sir," Roger said, "I feel I should ask why you are offering me this chance and not asking a graduate student."

"Very well, Roger, I will tell you. I don't like graduate students very much. They are obsequious. I will have to work with this person rather closely and I would prefer someone I like. I like you. I also think you are one of the most gifted students I've ever had. This work should appeal to your—your pragmatic bent. It may also please you to be doing something beneficial for the state."

Chapter Three

1941

ROGER labored well past midnight for five weeks straight to complete the assignment before Professor Ogden's hearing. The professor gave him a faculty key to the library so that he could work late in the stacks, examining the recondite public books long after student hours concluded. He sometimes encountered sleeping graduate students, who, he surmised, never went home from the library, but evaded night after night the otherworldly acolyte who closed the musty halls each evening with the thin clear tones of an ancient hand bell. Like mice lured by the pipes of Hamelin the other students followed, all but Roger, who joined the surreptitious scholarly hosts in the deep carrels of the stacks below the earth. The midnight fellowship saw him as one of their own and took him in without question, their code the honor of thieves, grave robbers looting antiquity.

Roger wrestled with the faded, handwritten tables, sometimes despairing over the huge task, but he completed the work on time and presented the report, carefully ruled and annotated. Professor Ogden accepted the paper with but a brief glance from his note cards. "Thank you, Roger. It all seems in order." He tossed the paper on the chair with the others. "Perhaps you would help at the hearing next week?"

Professor Ogden drove his decrepit Packard to the front gate at the Deke house. Roger climbed into the backseat and became slightly overcome by the smell of mildewed upholstery. For some seconds the professor sat silent, eyes straight ahead, as the car idled. Roger, puzzled, started to ask, sensibly he thought, why they did not proceed to their appointment. But he didn't. Instead he reflected again on the mysterious internal schedule of this odd and silent man. Just as he moved himself to comment, Worth

Patterson bolted from the door and made a quick run to the curb. "Sorry to keep you waiting, Tal," he apologized as he opened the door.

"We have ample time," the professor said, flipping the cover to his silver-filigree pocket watch.

"Well, I say, Roger!" Worth bantered good-naturedly as he settled in the front seat, sinking low in springless velour. "I haven't seen you since dinner."

"You gentlemen know each other, I take it," Professor Ogden said.

Roger rolled his eyes at Worth. "We live in the same fraternity, sir."

"Of course, yes," Ogden said as he turned the lumbering car down Raleigh Road for the hour's drive to the state capital.

On the way Professor Ogden explained to Roger that he and Worth often appeared together for the University before the legislature. The representatives liked nothing better than to see the fresh-faced young men whom they funded asking for the money themselves. And apparently no one was more effective before the legislators than Worth. Roger did not even know that Worth and Professor Ogden were acquainted — Worth had never mentioned the professor and maintained a practiced silence whenever Roger had. But clearly the two were old comrades in arms, as evidenced by Worth's startling familiarity — calling Professor Ogden by his first name! Roger had never even heard it uttered before — the diminutive Tal for the ridiculously florid Taliaferro — no doubt a romance of his grim south Georgia origins. So far as Roger knew, Worth had no interest in Ogden's scholarship; he had never even taken his class. Yet they spoke easily, as equals, on the grand strategies of school funding.

The manner of both changed as they talked curtly of the issues at hand and the personalities among the legislators. The professor, who seemed not to care the least about personalities most of the time, was precise, cagey even in his assessments of the politicians, each of whom he knew by name and district. He also knew their business interests, their religious preferences, and their votes on every matter important to education in the last decade. And Worth became himself in combat. His shoulders bulged under his full wool suit and he pounded the dashboard as he sat forward to make a point about how to handle the irascible old Reverend Bellemeade, editor of the *Biblical Messenger* and sage to the powerful Baptist Convention, a body hostile to state expenditures for the university; or the fireworks of Senator Bobby Earl Foushee, whose rural constituents howled with glee whenever the high and mighty professors were shown up by country wit; or Chairman Foswell, one of the corporate lawyers who did the bidding of the industrialists and regarded service "down at Raleigh" as useful in establishing the correct lines into the offices of the important. In each instance the professor pronounced his succinct and strict judgment, gesturing blindly to Roger in the backseat with such violence that the car several times left the narrow highway (which the legislature saw remained unimproved as a lesson in power to the university officials). He told the young men to profess piety before the Baptists; succumb to the charm of Senator Foushee's country philosophy; and to mention often to the corporate lawyers the importance of a trained and docile work force.

They parked before the old statehouse, which stood proud but somewhat in disrepair, owing to the exigencies of the Depression and the scarcity of funds generally. Guarding the portico was a granite memorial to the three presidents born in North Carolina, their seniority a litany of descending greatness — Andrew Jackson, James K. Polk, and Andrew Johnson. Significantly, as was often mentioned to the impassive solons by various speakers making their pleas for money, each of the three left the state of their birth to pursue greater opportunity, and it was incumbent upon the legislature to spend more to insure that nothing of the sort ever happened again.

The professor preceded Worth and Roger into the committee hearing room, the two younger men forming a phalanx for the invasion of the state's coffers. Lined by undistinguished portraits of dead men who looked down from the shadows as though they suffered from eternal indigestion, and possessed of a ceiling whose baroque moldings vied with the watercracked and leaking plaster for attention, the chamber seemed an especially cheerless place to conduct the people's business. Roger noticed that the senators themselves took on the mood of their surroundings as they surveyed the latest petitioners before them. Perhaps because they knew they actually had to give some money to public schools they were more attentive than they were when presented with representatives of just about everything else.

Professor Ogden cleared his throat. "Good morning, gentlemen. As you know, President MacGiver is unable to attend today. He sends his regrets. He also sends his urgent recommendation that you approve the increase in the state's appropriation for public school education this year. You have before you a paper we have prepared . . ." And so the professor began his recital of Roger's report. The logic of the numbers and their elegant progression from thesis to conclusion conveyed in Ogden's echoing voice carried Roger onward to his own demonstration that more money leads to better schools, a fact construed absolutely, relatively, logically, and empirically. As the professor predicted, the paper had no effect on the committee whatsoever.

"We have in this state the finest educational system known to man in all his time on the earth!" exclaimed Senator Foushee. "Since God made Adam, with apologies to Reverend Bellemeade," he said, nodding to the white-maned disputant on his left, "there has been no people who have enjoyed and profited from the benefits of education more than the children of this great state, the greatest state in the greatest country on earth. I support education, I support it with my dying breath. My granddaddy made me get my lessons every day, and I have praised God and thanked my granddaddy for that. As my granddaddy said once, the only way to get around your elbow to Salwazer's barn and back is with education. I thank the gentleman from the university for his figuring."

Thereupon Senator Foushee sat down, and the Reverend Bellemeade, who had been listening with one ear cocked toward his colleague, begged of him to yield.

"I share with my esteemed and honorable colleague Senator Foushee the highest regard for education, for as Moses corrected the vices of the children of Israel—who would worship the golden calf—with Jehovah's Ten Commandments, brought from fire and tribulation down the summit of Mount Sinai, so we also must make it the public's business to save our children from the vice and the golden calf set before them even in our very own and beloved state. It is my concern, as I listen to the very—I should say very, indeed—cogent remarks of this fine servant of education and see before me the very cream of young manhood that adorns our institutions, I say it is my concern that our servants of education commit the public's money in the Lord's name and that they do the Lord's work. Now we should ask ourselves—are we doing the Lord's work? I ask that question of myself every day. And I would ask the distinguished Professor Ogden if he is doing the Lord's work in the classroom there at Chapel Hill. Are all his fellow teachers doing the Lord's work, uplifting the fine young minds and bodies to be instruments of the Lord? I would ask him that, Mr. Chairman, indeed I would."

Chairman Foswell stared ahead, absorbed in his own thoughts, perhaps trying to decide which particular strategy to use to obtain the lucrative highway contract for his client, the Biscoe Asphalt Company, as *The News and Observer* had reported that morning. Senators Foushee and Bellemeade appeared to have concluded that the official response to the professor's presentation was over. Unless Roger had missed something encoded in the senators' remarks, he was sure that no actual response had been given to their petition.

"Professor Ogden? Is this — it?" Roger asked in a whisper he felt sure carried to the corners of the cavernous room.

"I don't know, Roger. You can never tell with these windbags. I'm trying to decide if it would be an effrontery not to assure that horse's ass Bellemeade that I work in the service of Jesus Christ."

"Sir," Worth said, leaning over the length of the table, "if I might — I know Wilton Foswell — perhaps I could try something here."

The professor nodded.

"Mr. Chairman, if I could have the attention of the committee for a few more minutes on the matter of this report," Worth began. Foswell nodded, banging his gavel out of habit — certainly not necessity — as there was nothing resembling a disturbance in the room, unless one counted the plop, plop, plop of water leaking from the ceiling into buckets on the marble floor. "I would like to direct the attention of Senators Foushee and Bellemeade to the statistics for expenditures in their home districts . . ."

Roger watched as Worth used the statistics he had compiled to demonstrate that the senators represented districts where low expenditures coincided with high illiteracy and where school buildings were older than the average and teacher salaries lower. This deplorable situation, he suggested, could be righted by the courageous action of the senators, and he was sure their constituents would be anxious to know their views on the subject, as this afternoon he would be supplying the report to all the state's newspapers, including the several in their districts. Both Foushee and Bellemeade then rose to deplore the deplorable situation and angrily call for the legislature to right the inequity done their constituents by voting an increase in the educational appropriation.

Senator Foushee concluded his remarks, conveniently in time for the lunch hour, by asking Worth one of the pet questions for which Professor Ogden had prepped him: "Now, I know you are a young fellow, Mr. Patterson, and you aren't tainted by the ideas of the education lobby" — this with a deliberate glance at Professor Ogden. "How is it that we should pay a professor three thousand dollars a year when he's only working nine months. Young man, I have never understood the reasons behind that. Maybe you could e-lu-ci-date me."

Worth leaned jauntily forward in his chair, and his voice changed, approximating Senator Foushee's own as the professor had coached. "Now, Senator, I'm not a man of great experience in government affairs, as you are, sir, but it occurs to me that paying a professor for nine months' work is kind of like keeping up a prize bull. You're not feeding him for the time he spends in the bull pen, but for services rendered."

Roger winced with the corniness of it. Surely that tired question and the clichéd response insulted them, he thought. He waited for reprisals, but none came. Instead, guffaws and general laughter arose from the old hands. Worth's metaphor caught even Chairman Foswell's attention, and as he gaveled the hearing to a close he winked at the clever young grandson of Oswald Patterson who had managed, unlike anyone in memory, to have the last word with Senator Bobby Earl Foushee.

•　　•　　•

On the way back from Raleigh, Worth and Professor Ogden chatted in the front seat and Roger pretended to doze in the back. As they had done on the way up, the front-seat compatriots discussed the foibles and promise of rising legislators. Afterward, Roger was scandalized to overhear, Professor Ogden permitted Worth his gossipy insights on faculty members. Their intimacy — not only with each other, but with him — surprised Roger. After all, what did they know about Roger Albright? He could have been a spy for Wilton Foswell, a plant of the Biscoe Asphalt Company, or even an agent of one of Professor Ogden's formidable enemies. And yet talk on they did, as though he were either suddenly part of it all or altogether insignificant. I should not be so distrustful, Roger thought. Professor Ogden made a point of including me, and so did Worth. Perhaps this is just their way of teaching me. But what am I learning? Politics? What they mean by politics seems really a form of drama, rather like a high school play. They rehearse to each other the lines they'll say, the effect they wish to create, and when the moment comes, they perform. Ergo, Worth's joke on Bobby Earl Foushee. But if what we're doing is a vaudeville show, why research those damn figures?

However irrational the magic, it certainly had strong powers, Roger discovered. In the triumph of the hearing, Ogden bloomed. His gait was broader, his handshake firmer, and his demeanor not that of a scientist but a businessman, or a lawyer, or one of the legislators themselves. Even his speech thickened in imitation. Roger marveled at the ease of transformation. But then he thought perhaps there really was no transformation; perhaps the popular image of Ogden as the perfect scholar was false. Perhaps the same skills that brought him success among the legislators brought him success among his peers and his students. His legend at the university seemed to progress without any effort from him, and his activity, which was constant, and the note cards, which were everywhere, did not necessarily evidence new work.

What required transformation in Ogden, Worth took to naturally, Roger observed, as the rhythms of the old car slowed for the approach to Chapel Hill. It was as though Worth had been born knowing the centers of meaning around him, moving directly from apprehension to the heart of the matter and to the hearts of others. This must be what nobility is, Roger thought; nobility in the service of high civilization.

"But the Pattersons rose from the mud, too," he reminded himself, muffling his monologue with a cough, remembering his readings in the slim velvet volume, privately published, entitled *The Southern Railroad and the Growth of Fairington, North Carolina.* The author, mysteriously enough, was Dr. T. Ogden. The volume was not cited in the professor's curriculum vita. Although his writing attempted to sugarcoat the truth, Ogden had been honest enough not to hide what the note cards revealed — that Oswald Patterson, Worth's grandfather, had been a robber baron of singular rapacity; as the first President Roosevelt might have put it, a "malefactor of great wealth." Sure, Roger thought, he had obscured his origins with a well-publicized pedigree — rumors of Princeton, the J. P. Morgan connection, a devotion to philanthropy that could only be described as grandiose. But from the vantage of a changed world, his achievements — principally building the city of Fairington — appeared narcissistic. Even from the vantage of the last century, the single thing that saved him from earning the name "carpetbagger" was the accident of his rude (or, as Ogden delicately put it, "undocumented") southern birth. The only explanation for Ogden's authorship of Oswald Patterson's vanity monograph was that he was hired to do it for a lot of money and the resulting explanation for his reticence in listing the work was that he was duly embarrassed. Later editions did not even name him as author, being identified instead as "a paper of the Institute for Progressive Studies."

Roger laughed to himself, delighted to recall his discovery. Knowledge is sublime, he thought; the most sublime thing of all. The investigation of Worth, the investigations of and for Ogden, all tended toward the same end, which was the measure of Albright, the most sublime existential task. "Remember who you are." Had Father said that? Roger wondered. It didn't matter, he concluded. You can't remember yourself. You have to discover yourself.

Such a program for self-knowledge was not present in the apparently realized Worth Patterson. Smart rather than intellectual, and a bit touchy about it, he was sometimes arrogant in the way sensitive people could be, Roger thought. He gave great speeches, though. Because they were so good it was hard even for Roger to tell, until Worth revealed himself, that analysis, intellect itself, was foreign to him. The fact was that Worth could not tolerate more than one idea at a time, much less one contesting another. Each idea for him had its own virtue and place and could be selected for use in the way one might select the proper golf club. Such surefootedness made possible an attractive generosity in which the views of each of God's creatures had value, and one's opinion, while not necessarily right or wrong, had truth in that it contained a particular genius. And Truth? What of it? Big Truth bore little relation to the little truths one produced from daily logic, for one gathered Big Truth from the air, as it was self-evident in nature and in society. What after all was the truth that one deduced about the merits of a certain breakfast food compared to the Truth of the Golden Rule? Big Truth was simplicity itself, as an atom was simple, and therefore unfathomable.

But how did you get to all-knowing solon from all-calculating robber baron? How did the generous son spring from the greedy father? Worth's embrace of his own inevitability—for if not himself, then who?—gave him the previous authenticity that the father never in all his strivings could possess. In other words, Worth Patterson was a leader. The objects of the world to him had qualities of essence but not metamorphosis, and only mass and velocity when irritated. Thus, without really analyzing, but rather by apprehending Senator Foushee, he knew how to move that vast, inert ego in order to advance the cause at hand, content to leave the reality of the vast inert ego at rest. For he knew that in the cosmos there existed harmony; out there somewhere resided another vast, inert ego that coexisted in obscure *concordia discors* with old Bobby Earl.

• • •

Once Roger discovered Worth's method, he began to talk with him, really talk with him, for until that moment he had not felt ready to do anything but listen. He talked to Worth as he had talked to no one since Judith. He challenged and picked apart Worth's mind as Judith had challenged and picked apart his mind, insulting all icons, suffering his friend's pained silences until the movement of Worth's glacierlike intelligence scoured the hated idea clean. As the evenings in the spring grew longer they drove for hours in Worth's Ford V-8 coupe through the tidy village and the greening countryside, arguing and drinking, drinking and arguing. After especially tiring bouts they retired to the 220 Club in Raleigh, where they relaxed until morning with the girls, or Roger relaxed and Worth, still agitated, sat alone and drank more.

The Dekes noted Roger's camaraderie with Worth, and his stock rose accordingly, especially in the ever-present bull sessions that tensely took up the question of the war. The heaviness in this April's air told each of them that their youth was ending, and that they were to have the grand privilege of fighting for their country in history's greatest disaster. Not everyone was enthusiastic at the prospect, and only Roger and Worth spoke up for the virtue of fighting against the cynics whose voices ran stronger than the others, perhaps because they sought to convince themselves by their own doubts that they could remain undisturbed.

"We have to fight the fascists, Walter," Roger rejoined, pounding his fist on the table as the white-jacketed waiter served his dinner. "Even you have to think of some greater issue than whether or not to call Brandywine Symms or Rebecca Pogue for Saturday night."

Walter Degley flushed deeply. "I don't have to take that from you, Albright. I know what the Germans are, and I didn't have to learn about fascism from a bunch of Reds."

The silence grew deadly on this field of fire, and Worth rapped his pipe on the table many times to clear the bowl, and also the air, before extricating Roger from his latest faux pas.

•   •   •

Roger stayed the summer in Chapel Hill, vacationing only for three weeks with Worth at his family's mountain home in Roaring Gap. Actually, the family retreat seemed to house only Worth, the closest thing to a parental presence being the caretaker, a genial, if taciturn local man who appeared daily on the grounds and puttered about. When encountered he would speak briefly of the weather and then disappear, as though his conversation fulfilled a social obligation to the lonely young rich man who lived there. Roger's inquiries as to the master and lady of the house returned from Worth vague but chipper responses. Martha, as he called his mother, was away, and Phineas, as he called his father, was away too, though not with Martha. Perhaps, Roger thought, this is normal with rich people. His father, whom he would never call Charles, asked him to come home and supervise the tobacco cropping at Bright Star, but he successfully pled academic necessity and returned to the library.

Back in the stacks, he resolved to master the university's holdings on the history and techniques of textile manufacturing and to teach himself enough accounting to understand the financial reports the companies made. All of this effort he applied toward writing a précis for his senior thesis on the textile industry — to get back on the topic from which Ogden had sidetracked him during the spring — and to make the work so accomplished as to render it impossible for Professor Ogden to turn down his request to advise the project.

The summer school students, generally angry that some misfortune or misconduct had ruined their vacation with additional courses, walked the scorched campus with more surliness than the heat required. As usual, the graduate students worked in the library's depths, oblivious to the climate or to the disposition of lesser seekers after truth. Roger joined them again, losing himself in the tables and figures, drowning in the ocean of what he wanted to know, demanded to know, as though he were discovering for himself not profitable lines of fabric but the elixir of knowledge itself. Shaving became a lost art, and his clothes, constantly run through with sweat, began to resemble the garments of the holy supplicant Roger imagined himself to be.

It was in just such a feverish state of appearance and thought that he saw over his pile of marked books one morning the matter-of-fact face of Judith. "I've been watching you for three days," she said. "From my carrel over there." Hisses for silence came from the inhabited regions of the darkness. "Let's go," he whispered, taking her hand.

They began to eat lunch together every day, taking their sandwiches to the still grass under the ameliorating green of the oak trees near the library. The unspoken assumption between them was that eating lunch under scholarly conditions was no abdication of their estrangement. They talked no politics, restricting themselves to stories of personal comedy among the circle at El's or the brothers in residence at the Deke house.

"Oh, but you're wrong about Worth," Roger said, feeding crust to an aggressive squirrel. "He's very talented at leading opinion, he's got good instincts—"

"It infuriates me how you're taken in by these people. Worth Patterson has no passion, no intellect. He talks from a script, swaggering around here, greeting people: 'Good morning, sir,' 'Good evening, ma'am.' I don't know whether to laugh or give him my coat. Believe me, he's just a spoiled little capitalist," she said, spitting the word. "When you change the rules on him he won't play anymore. He'll just go count his—"

"Let's not argue."

"You're right. Let's not. Just tell me one more story about Walter Degley," she asked, puffing her face up like a frog.

Roger laughed. "No chance. You've got to come for dinner to see for yourself. You'd be a Hollywood smash."

"Oh, no!" She threw up her strong, lithe arms in horror. "Mah reputation, Ashley! Think of mah reputation!"

It almost happened after they had watched the town's small, stalwart Fourth of July parade, lounging in the dusk on the burned brown grass of McCorkle Place near the street as the volunteer fire fighters labored by. They shared a warm Pepsi-Cola to stave off the still warmer late afternoon, and as the first cool breeze lifted the husk of the day, the tenseness their bodies felt touching gave way, and she rested in the crook of his arm, her hard fingers making slow circles of pressure on his rising and falling chest. He walked her home.

The next morning she presented herself at his carrel as she had the first day. He busily compared the RPM capability of wooden spools of the Munford and Akron designs, holding his finger in the air to stay her as he checked the last row of figures.

She leaned close over the book, her long, dangling hair obscuring the open pages. "Have you ever made love to a woman?" she whispered.

He did not think that telling her about the 220 Club would do. They went to her room at the old lady's house on Cameron Street, and when he had taken off her clothes and felt her thin, muscled legs close around him, he was unsure that he could say yes, that before this time he had ever made love to a woman. They lay for hours, sleeping and coupling and sleeping and coupling, as though having desisted so long only complete abandon could satisfy. They woke up in the dark and dressed, exhausted by each other, and went to Carrboro for dinner; they sat in the rear of the colored restaurant, the acrid jukebox blues sounding in the summer night. The salty, smoky grease they licked from each other's fingers and from their lips cleansed them, replenished them for the plunder next time.

They met at her room every afternoon and made love. They agreed never to talk about politics, or about work, and it did not bother them, this rejecting of what they had before, because what they wanted was what they had now, the crush of their bodies. One day he didn't come, and she trudged to the Deke house and called for him at the window until the summer butler came to the door and told her Roger was sick. She pushed him aside and ran up the staircase to find Roger awash in fever; she bathed him down, refusing to command the butler but running up and down the stairs herself for water and towels, drenching him in the icy water until the fever broke. As his teeth clattered with the chill she lifted her skirt and coaxed his fever back to life, matching his delirium with her own until the shocked butler bolted the doors to the kitchen so that the girl maids could not hear.

Three weeks later she left him asleep in her room as an afternoon shower drilled the old tin roof above them and the unknowing landlady slept below. She kissed him on the forehead and took away her flat-board suitcase held together with string, not knowing that he saw. He knew where she was going because she wouldn't say, and there would be only one place she would go that day and not tell him. He took the next bus to Winston-Salem and ran the rest of the way to the cigarette factory that sprawled against the hill, below the imperial skyscraper of R.J. Reynolds. He spotted her immediately on the disciplined, tense line that covered the sidewalk, saw her lips move in the chanting of that ugly word that turned to a roar as the two floods of arms and legs and ax handles and picket signs converged, the hard, lined faces of the union men and women meeting the hard, lined faces of the scabs, and then he saw the hundred men from nowhere who waded into the morass with brickbats and the police line across the street that swept in for the arrests. He plunged into the falling bodies, heard Judith's scream as she went down before he could get to her, felt the sign in his hand as he pounded the goon bloody who stood over her, heard the far sirens that roared over the city's hills to take them all away. They separated him from the others, and in a room with a plainclothesman he refused to answer questions for the four hours it took Charles to drive from Bright Star and take him away, huddling with a stern-faced lieutenant of detectives as a plainclothesman removed Roger's handcuffs.

"Are you trying to ruin your prospects entirely?" Charles asked after they had driven for an hour to the east.

"No, Father."

"I forbid you to associate with these people. You are still a member of my household."

Roger sighed. "It's not these people, Father. It's a girl, a woman. I'm in love with her."

"I see."

The two drove Highway 70 alone, through the towns idle in the night, past the spreading fields alive with the season and full moon, ever eastward across the calm, flat land and the time that lay between them.

"They attacked the women. You would have done the same thing."

"I see."

At Hillsborough, where Lord Cornwallis had ordered cobblestones placed on the muddy road outside his headquarters so he would not dirty himself while subduing the colonial rabble, they turned south to Chapel Hill, riding the winding road until the university on the rise ahead straightened their way. "How do you propose to support her? Or is that of concern to young men these days."

"You misunderstand, Father. I said I loved her, not that I want to marry her."

Charles cleared his throat. "I see."

They stopped in front of the Deke house, and Roger felt every muscle and bone cry not to move. He rubbed the Plymouth's smooth dashboard that his father worked with linseed oil to keep in good care.

"Thank you, Father."

"Do you need any money?"

"Thank you, Father, no."

Charles pressed a ten-dollar bill into Roger's hand. "Write your mother. She's understandably upset."

Chapter Four

1941–42

WHEN senior year began Roger felt the guiding presence of Worth Patterson leading him to new responsibilities. At informal student leader sessions in the Deke house, Worth presented him as a man "with his eye on the ball, one of the go-getters in the class." To his surprise, Roger discovered that Professor Ogden had seen to his election to the Institute as an undergraduate, an honor previously only held by Worth. Each month the Institute men — politicians and professors, editors, lawyers and businessmen — met in the drafty banquet room of a local hotel and talked really about nothing at all, but in a way that let Roger know if he needed anything he could call on any one of them.

Thus armed, Roger felt ready at last for the arena. He had found the center of his universe and he liked it. Soon the men of the Institute were talking about the dark, intense young Albright with the rapid mind and the large ideas. "Brilliant scholar, Worth Patterson's friend. He wrote the education report, you know. They say Ogden is grooming him for the faculty . . ."

Worth delighted in Roger's success. "I confess that I thought you might find those fellows a little dull after the crowd at El's," he said as they waited for their dates to return to their table at the Carolina Coffee Shop.

"Not at all. There's really not many differences between the Institute men and the local Party membership."

"Oh? I bet I could list some."

"No, I'm serious. Both groups have a method. I'm sure the only groups on this campus who don't need an explanation why we're going to fight the Nazis are the Institute and the Party."

Worth finished his beer and picked up the check, a habit as regular with

41

him as opening an umbrella in the rain. "That's what I like about you, Roger. You're always thinking."

• • •

Professor Ogden reviewed Roger's summer progress on his honors thesis, "Patterns of Operation in Piedmont Textile Corporations," which Roger had begun without telling him. The professor agreed that Roger was off to an auspicious start as he returned the notes, prospectus, tables, and chapter outline. Knowing that he had lost this skirmish with his prize student, Ogden agreed to advise the project as Roger had advanced it.

"I have the same reservations about this topic I've always had, Roger," he said, pouring another cup of black tea.

What is the "reservation" crap? Roger thought. This is scholarship, right? No way he can say it isn't—the research is solid, and the results, as he himself put it, are interesting.

"But you do agree to sponsor the paper?"

The professor stared at his tea and then threw up his hands in what appeared to be scholarly surrender, but, Roger reflected later, might have been the beckoning to scholarly hell. "Of course, of course. But I warn you. The tutorial will be the most miserable two hours a week you will ever spend."

Each Monday Roger set out, traveling up and down the crescent of the Piedmont, from Greensboro to Winston to Fairington to Charlotte to Greenville and Spartanburg, observing the organization of the factories, the consolidation that was producing the conglomerates, the economics of the mill villages, the relations between the large companies, the banks, and the utility companies, and the patterns of ownership that enwrapped them all. At the fraternity house, every conversation Roger began turned eventually to a discussion of the textile business, and the men whose fathers owned mills, or who had sold out to the large companies already, found themselves collared by the relentless investigator who drew diagrams on napkins and extracted explanations they did not know they possessed on capital financing and interlocking directorates. Roger had facts and more facts. He mounted his note cards one on top of the other on his desk, shuffling them into proof after proof through the night. On Friday afternoons he marched into Ogden's office and submitted to interrogation, armed with his own note cards for support against whatever attack the professor mounted. It was a floating doctoral examination, Roger thought as he withstood Ogden's scorn for the errors he detected in Roger's weekly draft, which he compelled Roger to read aloud to open the sessions. Facing the executives who opened their doors to him in fear of or deference to the Institute presented little challenge after the professor's grilling. In fact, Roger had the growing feeling that few of them knew as much about their own businesses as he did.

Still, the reaction of the executives puzzled him. What happened if they got on Ogden's bad side? Did the Institute keep an enemies list? It was, after all, only a confederation of academics and public men united around the general idea of "progress" — material progress, that is. More good things for more people. In general that meant more factories, fewer farms; more cities, less countryside; more learning, less religion; and above all, electric lights, indoor plumbing, and protein-rich diets. Giving meaning to these desires was the intellectual's job — Dr. Ogden's job — thus the need for the Institute. Just how much of the Patterson Trust was dedicated to the Institute no one knew, but it was substantial. The last generous impulse of the creator of this wealth was to endow an organization whose aim was to increase the income of the people he kept poor so he could get rich. Why doesn't the Patterson Trust just give money away directly? Roger wondered. That would be progress. Maybe Ogden holds that threat over the heads of the recalcitrant few who don't fall all over themselves to help him.

The only things distracting Roger from his project were the activities surrounding the request of his adoring sister, Mary Ellen, that he be her chief marshall at the Debutante Ball in Raleigh. He was glad to squire Mary Ellen to the rounds of parties that preceded the event, which had the added attraction of placing him often in the company of her St. Mary's classmate and co-debutante, Lillian Siler. Worth had first brought Lillian, dubbed Lulu, to the Deke house in the fall, to the admiration of the brothers, and if Roger felt ashamed in wanting to date his friend's girl, it was a shame he could dissipate among the legions of Carolina men who shared it. Besides her looks, her spirit, her carriage, and her new money — all of which were evident to her admirers, the latter rather unfortunately so when her parents arrived in Raleigh — Roger detected something he felt sure she hid from the others: a sense of upward trajectory nearly acute as his own.

For whatever reason Roger chose to embark with Worth Patterson toward Raleigh and the St. Mary's debutante parties, his mother was ecstatic. Barbara had finally reconciled her image of her son with her observations, describing him to friends as "the scholar." He was to be a great professor, she had decided, and his earlier flirtation with Bolshevism, which he fortunately seemed to have outgrown, was a necessary phase in the development of a genius. Furthermore, she concluded happily, if he has set out to meet some nice girls in the debutante season, then the spell of that Jewish girl from the North must be broken.

He thought every hour about the day she left, imagining it as a coda to their frenzied summer. He could still feel her against him, could still remember whole conversations. Though he had never had or lost a woman like that before, he knew beyond doubt that what he felt for her and what she gave to him was so powerful it would never go away. He thought, eventually, that she left because of the power of it; that she, being always a step ahead, knew they could not go on, but she couldn't say so because they loved each other so much that saying it would be false. All she could do was walk out and throw herself in front of a billy club on a picket line and by doing so tell him who she was and who he was and why it had to stop.

But he didn't know how to go on. He kept a ticket in his wallet and walked past the station every other afternoon when the train north pulled in, but he knew she didn't want to see him. She was in New York convalescing, writing more and more distant letters, speaking of enrolling again at Madison for her thesis. He read the lines that were true to her speech over and over and wrote to her immediately upon finding in them a hint of the old desire and understanding, damning each page because he could not in his own words tell her how much he missed her and what he wanted for them since he didn't know. He never spoke of her, but looked for her in every girl he met.

The white dresses swirled in the Virginia Dare Ballroom at the Sir Walter Hotel, the girls swaying to the orchestra on the hands of their escorts, forming petals of an imagined rose that opened and closed and opened again; they curtsied again to their mothers, who sat in the front seats of honor and applauded the figure.

Was this the prize? he thought, with a bitterness that surprised himself, as he surveyed the belles and their marshalls, finally finding Lulu and Worth in the figure. He caught his breath as he had the first time he saw her, welcoming her overflowing figure and eager green eyes in the moment of perfection now celebrated, a perfection she wore uneasily because she knew it was of time and that she must get its use. She circled the room on Worth's arm, aglow in her handsomeness and her knowledge of it that together were not quite demure enough for the ritual and therefore all the more alluring, assured in Worth's animation that she pleased him. Standing aside at the music's end, she tugged absently at the strap of her gown and whispered behind her bouquet to the girl beside her, unconcerned, though certainly not unaware, of the eyes and the contest that sought her out.

They invited me in, Roger reminded himself as he studied her. They didn't have to, these sons of commerce. They thought I was one of them; they didn't know the first thing about it, about walking every day down a hallway of frightened men captured *in extremis* in oil portraits like flies in epoxy; about fearing discovery in a room of men without fear, wearing the same rented tux they all wore better than they did, but knowing it still didn't quite fit; about being the odd man out and despite all the protests and impostures, requiring the daily validation. Most of all they couldn't know how much it hurt when Judith left. A hundred times he had asked why they found each other when it was impossible, and a hundred times he had answered that it was for that reason they had, to know what another life was like before they each did what had to be done. Funny, he thought, the only woman who could understand gave me up because she did. And I let her because I understood, too.

It was not that the prize was mysterious or particularly elusive. Lulu, too, was one of the invited. He felt both rivalry and attraction when he saw her with Worth, as though they shared him for the same reasons. When they danced, he tested her, pulling her closer than form permitted, feeling beneath the layers of her dress the directness of muscle and bone against him. She stopped chatting, and he made her look into his eyes beneath the speckled lights of the spring German, before the soulful off-key horns could start again. In that interstice of movement she had until then avoided, she shook her head to free herself, and then she relaxed, knowing she was caught.

"You shouldn't, you know," she said, pulling back.

"Why?"

"Worth's over there, for one thing." She nodded toward the shadows.

"You know, Lulu, with Worth you get what you see. That's all that's there."

She stiffened and looked away.

"No. It's all right. I do it too. Imagine. He needs us to do that."

"You mustn't talk about him," she said. She turned and walked away, disappearing at the crowd's dark edge.

Since that time when he had stood with her, huddling against the tribal music of the mysterious chosen, he believed that by his particular talents he could win her, the prize, and that she would have him on acceptable terms. They had, after all, been seduced by the same idea, and that made them more intimate than they could be after years of courtship. They were certainly more intimate than either could be with the idea himself.

She was coming around; he could feel it in the ways she greeted him without seeming to. Perhaps she had already figured out what he tried to tell her—that the drive it took to reach the ideal disqualified her from ever enjoying it. She needed the thrill, the ride, and he, Roger, could give that to her.

How, though, would she choose? At the moment of decision the combatants would stand together—Roger and Worth—each in his evening clothes, each in his prime. How do women do it? he wondered. Are they born with a ready-made tally, a scorecard for looks, brains, prospects, style? Or is it overview, a distinct feminine sense that allows them to picture their life with one man, then another, until one or the other prevails? Across the dance floor he spied her again and resolved to go to work. Discovered, she waved discreetly, her gloved arm brushing her sash, living with him now the code of their trial by society.

"Thank you, Brother," Mary Ellen said, glowing full and red in the cheeks with the last of her baby fat, bursting out of the cocoon of her white dress. She tugged self-consciously at her long white gloves and, smiling, straightened his high collar. "Now you go dance with Lulu, I know you want to. I'll just have to make do again with old Worth after you elbow him out of the way."

Lulu stood comforting one of her band, who sobbed into the tissue Lulu provided. "Now, Garland," she said firmly, "you stop this crying. It's not like anything really happened. They just say you're a woman now, it doesn't mean anything."

Roger offered assistance, sacrificing his own pocket silk.

"Now, Roger." Lulu placed her fists on her hips and swung her crinkly taffeta gown to face him. "I will dance with you a reasonable number of times, but I will not late-date you on the night of my debut or stand by while your sister makes off with my marshall, as has happened several times this month already."

"Anything you say, Lulu." He took her in his arms, noticing that Mary Ellen had accomplished her mission of waylaying Worth, who was laden with punch glasses, to begin a halfhearted waltz with the oldsters. As the last chorus sounded, Roger turned to see Worth striding toward them, trying to keep his balance between couples, nearly tumbling one father and daughter to the floor. Poised to cut in, he raised his hand to Roger's shoulder as the music stopped. Awkwardly the three of them applauded.

"Lulu, dear," Worth slurred as she cast her eyes to the floor, "would you excuse Roger and me for a second?"

"Of course, sweetheart. I'll just check on Garland."

Worth took Roger by the elbow. "To the bathroom, Albright."

"What the hell is your problem, Worth? If you don't want me dancing with Lulu, why don't you just lock her up in a cage?"

"In the bathroom."

They pushed their way into the men's room, ignoring the startled towel attendant and the retching swain kneeling in the first open stall. As Roger turned he felt the sudden force of a right cross that drew blood from his nose and staggered him back against the row of sinks.

"Now y'all gentlemens can't fight in here," the attendant said.

"Keep out of it, boy," Worth said. He pressed a dollar bill into the attendant's hand without taking his eyes off Roger.

"What the hell are you doing?" Roger said, pressing a towel to his nose to stop the blood.

"You've been doing nothing all month but trying to steal my girl." Worth swayed back and forth, massaging his knuckles.

"You're drunk, Patterson."

"Damn right. And you're not drunk. You're dead sober and trying to steal my girl. If you were a gentleman, you'd be drunk."

"Look, Worth, maybe I deserve to get punched out. The truth is, I'm in love with Lulu."

"The truth is you just want a piece of ass."

"Now you're way out of line, Patterson."

"The truth is I love Lulu. You don't love Lulu. Now strip yourself."

"Hell no. This is — "

Worth grabbed the firm edges of Roger's starched shirt in his hands and threw him against the heavy ceramic sink, pressing Roger against it until Roger could feel Worth's breath rise and fall, hear Worth's heartbeat in the recesses of his aching head. He felt Worth's arms relax and then tense, felt Worth's fingers in the side of his chest. The heat rose in him; true heat that tightened his thighs and his buttocks and rose in his throat.

"I'll kill you, Worth," he cried sharply. "You're drunk. I'll kill you."

"Strip yourself, goddamn it."

Worth stepped back and they released their suspenders slowly, shoulder by shoulder. They dropped their studs and loosed their crackling white shirtfronts. For a moment they stood facing each other, Roger tasting the blood from his nose that now smeared Worth's bare chest. Like an Indian brave, Roger thought, the red blood-smeared war paint. For a moment Roger thought they would not fight at all, but instead paint each with the other's blood, to be brothers forever. Then the heat rose in him again and he buried his shoulder in Worth's stomach, sending them both to the floor; they rolled on the echoing tiles, their groans mocked by the hissing radiator.

"Get the hell up!" Worth cried, and he dragged Roger to his feet. They clutched and huddled before Worth doubled him over, his fist in Roger's stomach. The blood pounded red in Roger's eyes, and he punched Worth's open face, felt the flesh break against the bone. Again and again Roger pounded Worth down, but the alcohol brought him back up until finally he slid back to the wall, his head resting against the naked radiator. Roger slumped beside him, pulled Worth's head away from the sizzling metal, and wiped the blood away with a wet towel as best he could. He staggered to his feet and dragged Worth to a vacant stall, righting his head and ducking him gently up and down into the toilet, pushing back his matted hair until the red was gone.

"Can't fight you," Worth said. "I can't fight you. Goddamn it."

They greeted a curious crowd outside, their ties dangling, faces the color of circus clowns.

"Figures. A couple of Dekes," said a voice from the back.

"There's one of your KAs passed out in there," Roger said, feeling as though he were speaking through a catcher's mitt. "Maybe if all y'all try together you can sober him up."

When they found Lulu she was dancing with Walter Degley. A line of their fraternity brothers waited to break in. "You going to beat all them up too, Worth?" Roger asked.

"No I'm not," Worth said, working his tongue over loose front teeth. "Just you. Because you're serious."

They drove back to Chapel Hill the next morning after trying Worth's recipe for hangovers, aspirin ground up in tomato juice with a sidecar of beer. Roger cursed the hard couch of the hospitality suite rented by Herman Siler, Lulu's father, where both he and Worth had passed the night. The cold of the December morning infiltrated the Ford coupe's floorboards and attacked Roger's aching body, although it somewhat numbed his face and hands. He felt the bumps in the highway as a private torture. When Worth turned on the radio Roger winced, but he gave in to Worth's insistence that the afternoon concert would cure them. He listened, soothed by the suggestion, to the distant strings of the New York Philharmonic, and he was nearly asleep when the announcer declared that the Japanese had bombed Pearl Harbor.

●　　●　　●

The next day Worth Patterson led fifteen of his fraternity brothers to Durham to enlist. Roger did not join them. He had business to complete. The war he had wanted so badly could wait until June. He compiled his charts and tables and on the last day of April presented his bound thesis to Professor Ogden, who thumbed it through like a phone book and said it certainly felt interesting. A week later he said it was the best research he had ever seen from an undergraduate and that he had nominated it for the Burney Medal at commencement. During the month that followed students and faculty and large numbers of businessmen journeyed to the library to read Roger's paper. The astonished dean of the School of Commerce said that it was the most useful document to a man wishing to prosper in the textile industry he had ever seen.

Only half the seats in the roped-off corridors of Memorial Hall were filled at graduation, but the empty seats, each marked with a flag, echoed the names on the tablets placed in the walls throughout the somber blue room that recorded Carolina men killed in battle, class by class. The governor told the men of '42 that before they could have the chance to conquer life, they had the duty to conquer the Axis powers. Roger waited for the Burney Medal, which he knew had to be his. When he rose to receive it, and the applause of the student body, he searched for Professor Ogden, but he could not find his slate-blue Columbia robes on the rostrum.

At his room in the fraternity house, when he returned to dress for dinner with his parents and Lulu, he found the note under his door.

Dear Roger,

Congratulations on winning the Burney, for you deserved it. You may think it strange when you receive your grades to see that I have given your thesis a mark of B; I feel you also deserve that. Undertaking a scholarly contribution as important as yours could be, requires that one accept the responsibility of placing one's findings in the context of history and human aspiration so that the possibility and not simply the fact of what you have experienced is recorded for men to know and moves men to act. Surely as you enter the defense of our country in the very battle for all we love and cherish in the world you will learn this lesson far better than I could teach you. Good luck and Godspeed.

Tal. Ogden

Chapter Five

1944

ALMIGHTY *and most merciful Father, we humbly beseech Thee, of Thy great goodness, to restrain these immoderate rains with which we have had to contend. Grant us fair weather for battle. Graciously hearken to us as soldiers who call upon Thee that, armed with Thy power, we may advance from victory to victory, and crush the oppression and wickedness of our enemies, and establish Thy justice among men and nations. Amen.*

Well, he's got his goddamn wish, Roger thought. This Christmas Day is fine for killing Germans. He stood over the body of the SS Oberstmeister, sitting straight under a charred tree trunk with his rifle lying across his midriff and his winter coat buttoned smartly to his chin. Roger looked closely and saw that the man's right arm was missing — probably buried in the snow. Herr SS looked as though he had stopped to rest while wondering where his arm might be, wondering where he had misplaced it. Roger had seen many dead bodies, some of his own making, and waking up beside this dead German did not in itself arouse notice. He had, however, never before seen a black corpse, and this German's death mask was coal black. Roger bent over and unsheathed the man's bayonet, using it to pry, one by one, his fingers from the carbine. He attached the blade with a snap. He rammed the bayonet and rifle into the frozen ground and placed the German's helmet on the stock. The Oberstmeister lay stiff, his black hand open in rigor mortis. Roger crumpled the card on which General Patton had dictated his Christmas prayer for the glory of the Third Army and gave it to the German. In return he took the man's Luger and a belt of cartridges. He preferred the Luger to his own officer's .45.

"Let's move," he ordered, and the troops stirred around him. His impromptu command was once a company of the Seventh Battalion. Now it

51

was the remains of several companies that had been makeshift outfits even before the advancing panzer units had chewed them up. But no matter. They were his men now.

"Jesus H. Fucking Christ will you look at that," Sergeant Billy Roy Thumper exclaimed at the sight of the Oberstmeister. "A damn nigger SS officer. I wonder what a damn nigger had to do to get in the SS."

Roger regarded the blackened face of the dead man, his high Nordic cheekbones and thin lips set in the determined manner of the Nazi propaganda posters.

"I don't know what he had to do, Sergeant. But whatever it was, you can bet he thinks it wasn't worth it."

•   •   •

Roger and the II Corps had marched the length of France, from St. Malo to Fougères to Laval; from Angers to Tours and Orléans; from Troyes to Châlons. He had eaten a postponed Thanksgiving dinner two weeks ago within the dearly won walls of Metz, which, General Patton proudly informed them, no army had captured since 641 A.D. The quartermasters had turkey dinners for the battalion, but they unfortunately could not provide any atmosphere for the ditch in which they ate it. Nor could they furnish to the men new stomachs to tolerate the rich holiday fare after weeks of C rations.

The first time Sergeant Billy Roy Thumper saved Roger's life — though for all concerned except Roger the honor had been the other way around — was during the approach to Metz, where Roger learned for once and for all the criminal lesson that American .75s were no match for German .88s. He watched panzers destroy Sherman tanks with the same alarmed detachment that he had watched the Duke offensive line of the 1942 Rose Bowl team churn the Carolina defense to nothingness. If he had followed his impulse and retreated with his company from the plain, he would have been destroyed as well, but he stayed himself from this fatal choice when he saw a lone GI bouncing crablike through the carnage of the burning Sherman tanks. The GI mounted one of them, which was listing off its track, its gun in the air mimicking the snout of a dying bull elephant, and unhinged the machine gun, firing it wildly at anything German that moved, machine or man.

Perhaps the orderly Teutonic intelligence of the German panzer commanders dismissed as a mirage the sight of the single American shooting an auxiliary machine gun at them in the middle of what was now their own formation; perhaps they felt it was too amusing a spectacle to end. In any case, the sight of the man making his dying gesture to history moved Roger through the concussions pounding him and his men, through the smell of sulphur and blood, to conclude that retreat offered nothing but surer death. He ordered his troops to advance. In the citation that General Patton himself recited as he pinned on Roger's Silver Star ("My brave young Albright," he whispered in Roger's ear as he kissed him on both cheeks, "your great-grandsire lives in your deeds"), his charge against the enemy tanks, a charge joined up and down the American line, was an inspired act of field command in the highest tradition of American combat arms. But to Roger this heroism simply answered the logic of advancing before heavy guns methodically increasing their range of fire, logic given flesh by a crazy GI turning in a circle and firing from his turret at anything that moved. Roger himself dragged Billy Roy from the gun and into a shell crater as the P-51s made their timely appearance and routed the panzer attack.

"Sergeant, are you trying to beat the German army by yourself?"

"I'll be goddamned, pardon the language, Captain, sir, if I'm going to die sitting still."

After they secured Metz, General Patton in his jodhpurs and Eisenhower jacket, polished helmet with the three stars regnant, made Captain Albright a major in the company of the press.

"This man, Roger Pettigrew Albright, bears one of our country's greatest names in war, and he will continue to bear it to the Rhine, God help us."

Roger took command of the Seventh Battalion's Charlie Company. He requested that Sergeant Thumper be assigned to him.

•   •   •

The men themselves changed daily, it seemed, or maybe by the minute, killed by the enemy, or maimed, or driven to harm themselves to escape the terror. Roger felt the terror, too, not as sensation, but rather as the absence of sensation. Even the heft and measure of things — the barrel of a weapon, the distance between a stand of trees and a stream, a body dead or alive — could not penetrate Roger's senses beyond the present dread that although he lived now, he could die quickly. This nonsensation Roger fought more desperately than the enemy, using the things he could still clutch around him, the lists he made, the routines he followed, as weapons against numbness. He understood if others lost themselves. One evening during the withdrawal, Sergeant Thumper disgustedly hurled a buck private at the foot of Roger's bunk. The boy had hacked away his ear with a can opener, presumably after he had been unable to shoot himself in the leg. General Patton disallowed any injuries resulting from wounds in the foot, and anything lower than the thigh was suspect. Roger looked into the boy's eyes and held the boy's chin in his hand. The choice the would-be van Gogh had made was not different from the one he had made in charging the .88s, though one they called a coward's way and the other a hero's way. Sergeant Thumper looked aside and cursed as Roger wrote out the boy's transfer to the rear.

For two weeks the Seventh Battalion, along with the rest of the new Ninetieth Division, pushed toward the Saar. Roger marched beside the tanks and they advanced until there wasn't any more gasoline; then they foraged for German gasoline, and if they got it, they went on. They made thirty-five miles a day against rear guard detachments on booby-trapped roads, through villages where the Germans had set delayed-fuse bombs for their American pursuers. Outside Thionville, as the Argonne Forest stretched before him like a fantastical city, Roger sat down in the road.

"What's the matter, Major? You feeling punk?"

"No, Billy Roy."

"Well then, what is it? You got the trots bad?"

"No, Billy Roy. I think it's my birthday. I'm not sure, but I think I'm twenty-four years old. Yep. Have to be — I'm twenty-four years old."

Thumper signaled to another GI and they lifted Roger into an ambulance, where he rode the rest of the day.

Roger did not think he was cracking up, and he knew he was not a coward. But his solitary universe slipped more out of control as he placed one foot after another on the rutted highways. He felt he was already dead, and that he would decompose when the noise receded and darkness came. No, I'm not cracking up, definitely not that, he thought. It's the flyboys who crack up, sitting up there in those metal chicken coops. Flying is such a strange thing under normal circumstances, the metal skin keeping you aloft in waves of air, a membrane between you and the universe. The flyboys crack up, everyone knows it, so they get to go home after thirty missions. Your infantryman, especially your infantry officer, is solid as Gibraltar.

Won't even have a good luck charm, forbid it for the men, unless it's religious, of course.

He reached in his helmet liner for the letter from Judith. He had found out her War Information unit and searched New York for her on his one-day leave before shipping out a year and a half ago. It wasn't hard finding her; he had almost a sixth sense about it. There she sat, looking terrific in her olive drab and nylons, writing a war bond radio script with the same intensity she would devote to a labor *cri de coeur*. "Bonds build bombs," she alliterated, perky before the microphone, her back arched in a poetic S curve, overseas cap pinned to her bobbed hair at a jaunty angle, finally having found a good use for the capitalist's money and a reason to join up. She wasn't surprised, she said, when he found her, but she was silent, shy almost as they made their way to her apartment in Gramercy Park. This is the nicest place she'll ever live, he thought, knowing that because of the war she rationalized the luxury, but the roommates' disappearance and her practical entertainment in front of the gas stove, with even the right liquor handy, seemed disturbingly routine.

"You're going to hate being married to her," she said, feeling his sudden jealousy, and hers.

He looked up, quickly. "I was going to tell you."

"It doesn't matter. I mean it doesn't matter you didn't tell me."

It didn't matter not because of the failure of the voluntary act, which did matter, but because, he realized, she had known it would happen anyway. She knew, without him saying, that with Lulu he could get what he wanted, and he couldn't with her; she could see, without him showing her, the pictures on the wall at Bright Star and the dumb logic of time he had to reverse.

"It's really all right. For me, that is," she said. "I don't want you that way anymore."

He hoped she was lying, that she, somehow, would make him stay in the warm web she could create for both of them and bring him back from the design of his life. But she, knowing it to be hopeless, and wanting him to feel the price of his choice, ordered him to leave and stood by the open door until he did.

Now, reassigned to staff after his collapse, Roger sat at a desk in a bombed building away from the old château at Chaumont and compiled analyses of munitions requirements and the inexorable progress of victory as a function of available gasoline. The symmetry of the figures pleased him. Every day he passed by the erect and vacant figure of a suit of armor posed in the hallway, the figure ludicrously short, as though the knights of the Middle Ages had all been little boys. He wondered how the metal-man liked this new way of war. When he finished with his computations he joined the other staff men who were filling up the field maps with flags and pushpins, shuttling thousands of men like paper clips around the towns of Nancy, Soissons, Château-Thierry, names that engulfed Roger as the past recaptured. We are killing one another for the same ground, he thought. It was the old AEF campaign of 1918.

He had never asked his father where he had seen action in the Argonne offensive of that year, and Charles only discussed the Great War under duress. Roger now understood why it was unspeakable. Thoughts of Charles marching in terror through these fields and towns filled his mind, and now he shared the secret with his father, made old by fear and by failure and the renewed possibility of death. On impulse he took the afternoon to write Charles a letter recounting the campaign from Cherbourg to the Argonne, describing the old château town of Chaumont as it now stood and imagining it as not much different from when it was Pershing's head-quarters. He drew a rough map of the current front. The next day the sergeant in the telegraph room interrupted him with a wire between the usual mail drops, said he was sorry, and left. It was from his mother. She told him that Charles had been killed returning at night to Bright Star from his job in the Office of War Mobilization in Raleigh, running the old Plymouth off the road at the curve before the bridge at Lansing's Creek. "My dearest son," she wrote, "your father died a gentleman and a patriot, in the service of his country."

One more good man dead, Roger thought. So that's who it was after, back there on the road. Not me. It was after him.

Not by German guns, either, but by as fool a thing as a curve at night in the shadow of your own house. Roger put his head down on his desk and cried, and then he wrote out his orders to return to combat, initialing them himself as the officer of the day. Patton had already ordered him to the field, he learned from the hand-delivered pouch he received that after-noon in the Hôtel Chaumont, where he was drinking himself unconscious on *la spécialité de General Patton*, Armored Diesels. "What the hell is Pettigrew Albright doing riding a desk?" the general had roared when he saw the duty roster. He needed Pettigrew Albright to kill Germans.

•　　　•　　　•

After enlisting in June of 1942 and taking basic training at Fort Bragg, Roger had moved quickly to officers' school and was then shipped to Fort Hood in Texas, where he had learned how to command infantrymen in combat. He spent his last six weeks before embarking for North Africa and Patton's Western Task Force in Fairington, at the Atlantic Transit Billet. As opportunity had it, Lillian Siler was also there, enrolled at Patterson College.

The inevitability of his mission thus blessed by the War Department, Roger had attempted to close matters swiftly, while appraising his temporary quarters anew. He was acquainted with Fairington from visits to the Pattersons and from the research on his thesis that had taken him to the huge Galway mills there, but he scarcely recognized the calm streets he once knew; the little city had become a bigger city overwhelmed with wartime projects. With the other young officers awaiting their orders, he toured the clubs and movie houses of the place, took girls from Patterson College to dinner at the O. Henry Hotel, and tried to keep them there past hours. They were all marking the days before they boarded one of the trains at Southern Station for Europe and the fight. The other young officers also noticed Lillian, and many had asked her for a date; some had even gained entrance to the huge new house her father had built, having moved his family and his business from Salisbury to Fairington. But when Roger arrived he made sure the others stopped calling.

"Another letter from Worth?" he asked, closing the door to the living room, Herman Siler having retired to the basement to toy with the short-wave radio he had bought to monitor the war news, plotting the battles on relief maps of Europe and the Pacific. Lulu's melancholy on the days she received letters from Worth was by now well known to Roger.

"His PT boat was hit and three of his crewmen . . . it's too horrible." She disengaged herself from his grasp and pulled a sweater around her shoulders. "He asked me to visit his mother because she's frightened for him."

"So go. I don't mind. Worth's my best friend."

"Don't you understand? He's treating me like we're engaged."

"Okay, I'll go. I haven't seen Mrs. Patterson for a while."

"This is just a game to you, isn't it? The war, everything."

She sat on the sofa, waiting, as she had more or less for a month, as he moved their pirouette to the conclusion desired by both of them, making him conscious at every turn that he was her choice. How much crockery had been thrown, Roger thought, between mother and daughter over the decision to resist the entreaties of the town's, nay the state's, most prized suitor in favor of the enterprising best friend. All had been sweetness and light in his presence, of course, but closed doors, raised voices, and the made-over traces of tears had often greeted him as the end game ran its course.

That she loved him he did not doubt. Although his experience was limited, the evidences would have been apparent even to an emotional illiterate. But do I love her, he wondered, or just marvel at her? It was not like Judith, who still in memory had great power to stir him. Yet he desired Lulu, and he knew she wanted him, more, he felt sure, than she had wanted any other man — certainly more than she had ever permitted herself to want.

"Have you told him?" he asked.

She turned and stared him hard in the eyes. "What's there to tell?"

It's here, he thought, journey's end. He caught his breath, sat down beside her, and made as graceful a proposal as he could, surprised at how nervous he was even with the benefit of much rehearsal. Lulu, who seemed by her composure to have received proposals before, heard him out, nodding quickly at the end as though to assure him he had done an adequate job. The next day — for she had been sworn by her friends to make him wait at least overnight — she accepted him. In celebration, the gentlemen in residence at the Atlantic Transit Billet took over the O. Henry Hotel the next night and gave the party of the season. They sang a bawdy rendition of "Lillian, My Lillian" to the tune of "Maryland, My Maryland," and in the excitement of love requited and the romance of battle ahead managed to bed in that one night close to one-third of the entire female population of Patterson College.

17 Sept. 1944

Dear Roger,

I won't lie and say that I just found out that you proposed to Lulu and she accepted. She did write. I just couldn't speak about it until now. You see, I thought I would die and not have to disturb either of you. But now I know I'm not going to die and neither are you. Really, I guess I should have seen it coming. Anybody could see she loved you. But I hoped otherwise.

I don't want us to be driven apart by this but to be made closer. I think it is the work of God that we should be friends and that even this should happen. Fate is at work all around us—the war makes God's will more visible. We have so much to do when we get back home. Though the war makes it seem like we've lived forever, we've only just started. If I can say these things, I hope you can too.

The kamikazes hit us again last night [censored]. They don't have very many planes left. Some days go by [censored] and then it will be over. The Japs must know that and [censored]. If those chaps can carry on when it means the end for them, how can we not when it means the beginning for us? I know that after this I can go through anything and you can too. I've given up thinking about it. I just do what I have to do. It's my watch.

As ever,
Worth

Roger had reread and refolded the letter so often that it could hardly bear creasing again. He carefully opened again his equally fragile response:

10 Oct. 1944

Dear Worth,

I'm glad that you wrote me about the thing with Lulu. I didn't know how to talk to you about it either. It's remarkable how cowardly I could be about that and face the music every day here.

I don't know what God has to do with it, but I hope we can get back to where we were. That is, if we both get back home. Your odds have sure improved, moving from the PT boat to the *New Jersey*, although you have the kamikazes to make things interesting. All I get is tanks. At least they move in a straight line.

I hope we can work this out. I know it's crazy.

Yours,
Roger

Worth's reply hadn't come until the week before Thanksgiving. Well, he had a right to reflect on it, Roger thought.

17 Nov. 1944

Dear Roger,

You are my best friend, and it is not our fault that we both fell for Lulu. More and more the idea of fault or of cause, or of the idea that we have power over ourselves, grows remote. To be so close to death does that to me. Not that fault can be discarded—for there is still fault, don't you think, in the injury done others, or else how could society continue?

But I believe even with that, that we are on a string of one sort or another. You discount God (or do you?). Still, you have to account for circumstance, and for ethics, and for death, even your own, if what you must do ethically leads to your death in the circumstance given. Something must create that for a greater good; it is too hard otherwise. How else can we learn? How can there be faith?

As ever,

Worth

Roger replaced this latest in his belt pouch with Charles's medals that his mother had sent. He hadn't yet given his response as to the character of death and faith. The Christmas holidays had been hectic in the Ardennes.

Through his field glasses Roger studied the ridge, a steep rise transformed into a fortress by the panzer guns. Moisture rose from the snow in the dawn twilight. Down the line the troops dumbly awaited their orders to attack, wondering if this was the day their luck ran out. Roger surveyed the German gun emplacements, the panzer unit positions, the dug-in machine guns. What the frigging hell are we doing sitting here? he thought. This isn't war, it's murder.

"Billy Roy—bring me the map."

Thumper lay the case with the field maps before him in the snow and waited, smoking a cigarette. From the west came the rumble of howitzers as the American artillery tested the German lines in the caesura of the bulge around Bastogne.

La Côte de Notre Dame. That was the name of the hill; what a nondescript place the brass wanted to make famous, Roger thought. Apparently a church had once stood there in a grove of trees, the ruins of both partly obscured by the snow. Salvos from the American .75s and mortars sounded their familiar double thud. Satisfied with their high ground, the Germans did not answer the barrage.

Was this how it was going to end? Roger wondered. Is this crap what Worth would have us believe is fate, God's plan, doing what you have to do? He shivered, and not from the cold. Such a stupid battle. If he could hold the road and race the tanks to the river, then the hill could be flanked and this nonsense bypassed, he reasoned. Killing good soldiers in a frontal attack violated the code of logic; refusing to attack violated the code of war. Hills had to be taken, charges made; victory, he had concluded, depended mostly on how many more men and how much more money you could waste than the enemy.

The field radio crackled. Thumper threw away his cigarette and squinted at the German guns glinting in the first light. Incoming shells exploded two hundred yards in front of them, and then closer, as the Germans adjusted their range. The assault was beginning a half-mile to the east, and Roger heard the roar of men and the roar of fire mixed as one purposeless chant of death. He saw the American line advance to attempt the hill, and suddenly he was a boy again, dreaming of Cemetery Ridge, traveling the last steps with Great-Grandfather, his hat atop his sword and the battle flags falling like tenpins, riding the cresting wave of emotion and time, the dead and the soon-to-be-dead one against the steel of an army that fought with superior fire from the higher ground. Up and up again they charged into the powder and steel, twenty thousand men at full run for a mile and a half, for a cause so vast and a hill so modest; the high-water mark of the Confederacy, his weepy aunts called it. Roger knew his men, too, would charge the hill if he ordered it, bound by what many called honor but Roger thought to be little more than a failure of imagination. It was funny how honor, as men allowed it to destroy them, became ever more powerful the more it destroyed. In the end honor masked many faults, principally stupidity, but it couldn't mask death.

"Charlie Company, attack," the bird colonel's agitated voice crackled over the panzer blasts. "Charlie Company—over?"

The Sherman .75s stood silently akimbo at the bottom of the hill, many of them in flames; the stalled infantry hunched down, withered before the machine gun fire that held them at arm's length, as a bully would hold the head of a small boy.

"Repeat! Charlie Company, attack! Do you read — Charlie Company, attack! Albright — where the hell are you! Do you read, Albright? Over."

Thumper squatted in the snow beside Roger and looked expectantly at the radio. The bird colonel, Roger thought, was a mediocre Irishman who wouldn't have commanded a KP detail under Great-Grandfather. He knew, nonetheless, that he was bound to advance and that Billy Roy would follow him. Billy Roy would die at Roger's command because of the palm leaves Roger wore on his shoulders, as Billy Roy's great-grandfather had fixed bayonet and faced the cannon atop Cemetery Ridge on command, trusting his meager knowledge of the ways of honor to his betters.

"Charlie Company, do you read? Over. Charlie Company, come in. Repeat! Attack! Over."

Roger removed his Luger, looked at the unruffled panzers atop La Côte de Notre Dame and at the men who had made history for themselves in death on the gray and bloody snow. Too many Albrights had done stupid things for honor and died losers. This Albright would be smart and live to enjoy it, Roger resolved. The open road and the river lay ahead, and he could get there without more killing. He took aim at the radio in front of him and fired a round into the center of the dial.

"Damn thing doesn't seem to be working, Billy Roy. Guess we're on our own."

Chapter Six

1946-49

DURING the war, Herman Siler moved from Salisbury to Fairington in order to take advantage of the opportunity to make money building prefabricated barracks the military needed for the Atlantic Transit Billet located there. Acres of Quonset huts appeared, seemingly on a daily basis. Herman's crews could hardly throw one up before he would receive another contract for work to be completed yesterday. This largesse in the name of freedom made Herman a rich man from a merely affluent one, increasing his girth and his belief in a just God accordingly. During a rare business lull in the summer of 1942, he built in the substantial Patterson Forest section of the city a large home entirely from brick, using all of the inventory from Carolina's red earth that he held in stock before he became a baron of prefabrication for the country's defense. The simple Georgian lines of the house that his wife Iris had from her research decreed to be correct were altered with facades and false balconies and gewgaws of every description in order to use up all the surplus, until the house itself rambled outward and poked upward in an eclecticism that shocked the surrounding residents. Even after the last false chimney had been added and asphalt had been eschewed in favor of a brick circular drive, there was enough of the stuff left to construct an all-brick swimming pool on the remaining idle ground. The Silers' new neighbors on either side, not wanting to appear rude, but nonetheless wanting as little to do with the creation as possible, promptly relandscaped their grounds and placed some of the tallest stands of shrubbery ever seen in the Piedmont along the adjacent boundaries, closeting the mansion from street view as one might hide with a relative's distasteful curio on the mantel.

"Do I look presentable?" Roger asked, checking his tie in the front window before they approached the tall double front doors.

Lillian kissed him on the cheek. "Absolutely gorgeous."

Roger had bought a suit the day before as a condition of his new job as a salesman for Galway Industries. He had told no one that getting the job had been difficult. He hadn't expected it to be. Worth had arranged for Roger to meet with old Galway himself, a meeting that had occurred just several blocks away from the one he prepared for now. The jowly entrepreneur, who had built a mom-and-pop mill and a hunch about something called rayon into the country's fastest-growing textile concern, had looked Major Albright, war hero, up and down and, it seemed, judged him to be just another hungry GI looking for a job.

"Sales and marketing, eh, Roger? That's what you want, you say. That's what all the young men want these days. Nobody wants to get his hands dirty making the stuff anymore. You'll have to work in New York, you know, Roger. They don't like men without experience. Yes, of course I'll mention your name to Ray Overman; you should write to him directly. My regards to young Patterson."

Apparently Galway had not mentioned the name Roger Albright with any special force; for two weeks, Roger had paced the gallery at Bright Star waiting for an answer to his letter of inquiry. He knew the textile business. He had studied it scientifically. He knew that the action was at Galway and would stay there. Already the leader in synthetics before the war, Galway's position had grown immeasurably better with the jump in demand during it. Before it had occurred to competitors, Galway had established an independent marketing operation, to discharge its traditional relationships with factors and New York agents, so that the strategies for marketing diversified products were centrally controlled. With market share increasing in every area and the right leadership in the research and development dependent synthetics field, Galway was in a golden position to buy out and milk the older mills while investing in new lines. I know this damn company better than the old man himself, Roger thought. The mills he's just thinking about buying I could have bought months ago, if I had the power. Yet they won't hire me as the most junior salesman.

At last a letter came from Ray Overman's office. "We were happy to receive your résumé in application for a sales position," Roger read, "but we have difficulty in processing the request. The Department of the Army has yet to confirm that you received an honorable discharge."

He had missed the daily sleeper from Raleigh, so he carefully laid out his last remaining prewar suit coat in the luggage rack and rode all night on the bus, arriving in time to get a shave and shoeshine before the sales offices of Galway Industries at 2188 Broadway opened for business. At 8:30 A.M., precisely, Roger strode into the corner office of Ray Overman, and, warding off the secretary, presented his honorable discharge from the United States Army, signed by Henry L. Stimson.

"Sir, my name is Roger Albright, and you asked to see my discharge papers."

Overman stubbed out his Lucky Strike and took the document in his hand, still keeping his eyes on Roger. "Jesus, buddy, you didn't have to hand-deliver the thing."

"It's quicker than the post office. So now do I get the job?"

Overman looked him up and down for what seemed to Roger like a very long time. "Yeah, I guess you'll do. Start at the first of the month. And Albright, listen, before you show up for work, get some new duds, okay? If you're going to be in the rag trade you don't want to look like you just got off the boat, know what I mean . . . ?"

Iris Siler embraced him at the door with a proprietary hug, and Herman pumped his hand before Iris let go. Mrs. Siler, it seemed, had gotten over not seeing Worth at the door, and whatever battle between mother and daughter had once flared over the subject now appeared over. Roger felt sure that his second supplication before man's estate would be less difficult than the first. From previous experience he knew that Mrs. Siler had enough pot roast on the table to feed his old battalion. After Herman had eaten beyond all human imagination and Roger had been able to disengage himself from added helpings, he knew the two of them would retire to the brick den, leaving mother and daughter to gossip over their prize, and Herman would pour them both some very good bourbon from the bar he no longer kept hidden from Iris. He had recently grown so bold as to refuse to sign the pledge. Herman would wait, with the satisfied leisure of a man to whom fate, for whatever unknown and unsought reason, had been very good, to hear his future son-in-law mention a wedding date. Herman grudgingly liked the young man, though he thought him a bit too proud in the way of these Down East poorhouse aristocrats. Of course it would have made more business sense for the girl to marry Patterson, and the wife adored him, or his pedigree anyway. But life is good, Herman reminded himself. Let the girl pick who she wants. The Albright boy had proven himself in the service, and he had a solid job with that old windbag Galway. Herman thought Galway might finally remember his name the next time they met.

Roger lived out of a suitcase for six weeks, taking the training course that would make him into a Galway Man, a station he felt confident of reaching, having already successfully learned to be a Carolina Gentleman and an Officer of This Man's Army. On the weekends he searched for a house on which to apply the down payment supplied him by Herman and the mortgage guaranteed by Uncle Sam. Manhasset, Long Island, with street after winding street of starter castles, beckoned Roger like a surprise party for young veterans moving up their new chain of command. Roger put his father-in-law's two thousand dollars down on a six-room house in the banker's bungalow style. Shingled, with dull green shutters and trim, the house appealed to Roger especially because — apart from the working fireplace — it had not a trace of visible brick.

They were married three weeks later, only four months after he had debarked from Europe in January, after a short but tedious stint with the Occupation Army. Mrs. Siler would have liked more time to plan, but things moved fast these days, her friends assured her. The young people were so impatient. The First Lutheran Church stood packed with Silers and Sitzens and Setzers on one side and Albrights and Pettigrews and Brents on the other. Barbara, heroic in stature and comely with her widow's comportment, so charmed Herman that he discharged his courtly duties to the mother of the groom with enough enthusiasm to make a fool of himself. Not having yet been successful in his campaign to join the Fairington Country Club, Herman gave the reception in his backyard, under tents supplied by a funeral home. Iris had never had so large a party in her home, much less one as important as her only daughter's wedding. She exhausted her known supply of experienced girls for the affair, and perhaps for peace of mind she asked her Ophelia from Salisbury to serve as well as attend the wedding. So Ophelia, in her go-to-church gown, gloves, and hat, left before the vows so she'd be sure to have time to change into her white uniform before the guests arrived back at the house.

Worth drove from Chapel Hill, where he was finishing his last college semester, and his first law school semester, he being, like everyone else, in a great hurry to get on. "You picked a warm day," Worth said in the receiving line after the deed had been done and the flask passed to accompany the champagne that Mrs. Siler had allowed just this once to be brought onto the premises.

"Thanks for coming," Roger said, and he left it at that. He studied his friend's face for a trace of hurt and found none. Roger had attempted all week to clear the air. "I'm not really able to be very analytical about it," Worth had said finally when Roger got him to talk. "We're still friends and all that, aren't we? Things turn out for the best, you know."

Roger wanted to settle everything between them before the wedding day. A businesslike pact, he thought, would forestall any unpleasantness later. Yet Worth wasn't helping, and it was precisely in such circumstances that Roger felt the old inferiority again. Even here, on this battlefield, and even as a loser, Roger reflected, Worth seemed so sure of the right phrase and the right gesture, as though he had read a book somewhere covering the topic of how to maintain correct behavior when the girl you love marries your best friend.

In the end Roger relied on Worth's strength to enable him to stay clear of Lulu, to play by his own rules. Of what man could one be more sure than Worth Patterson? It is an enormous blessing in life to have honorable friends, Roger thought. In contrast he shuddered at his own continuing compulsion to call Judith. The very day he arrived in Fairington, he had dialed her number repeatedly from Lulu's own bedroom, each time hanging up before she answered, like a schoolboy.

He couldn't help thinking about her, and with an urgency he hadn't felt in years. He attributed his weakness to the finality of the day, a last wavering before commitment to the path she above all knew he would take. She had left long before anybody handed her some rice to throw, and he couldn't blame her.

Still, it was his own inability to rid his mind of Judith that made him unsure that even Worth Patterson, honor incarnate, could forget Lulu, for he knew his friend, and he knew that insofar as he was capable, Worth Patterson loved her. He feared that the same reason that would keep him from committing adultery with her would keep him from loving anyone else, and he feared eventually the combustion of those reasons. Honor squared, or honor destroying honor, would be the name of that farce.

So he stood, watching the solemn ballet proceed down the aisle beside Uncle Quincy, who had been impressed as best man, given Worth's incapacity. Roger cleared his throat to cut the tension that overcame him when the organ sounded through the boards beneath his feet and Lulu emerged at the head of the aisle, marching forward in her glory on cue as her mother and then the congregation stood. She searched for him at the end of the aisle and smiled tightly, nodding as though to confirm that they were doing the right thing. She swayed in her pumps, her march not quite virginal and her off-the-shoulder bodice bold indeed. Uncle Quincy caught his breath and Roger, thrilled by her feminine daring, stood transfixed by the coming finality as the organ's basso gave way to trumpet climax and they said their vows.

He felt that he could not press Worth further, but he convinced himself that his friend looked happy enough caught up in the wedding party. In August he would leave for Harvard Law School with his Chapel Hill credits and his determination, bound to finish the three-year program in two. He would return still in a hurry, Roger imagined, to an apprenticeship in the Young Democrats and the required veterans' organizations, concentrating, when he had to, on his law practice in Fairington, sifting through the cases, appearing in court to execute every lot assigned him, gathering from each experience granted him by God or Calvin lessons in his fellow men; then quietly, to no one's surprise, he would be about his greater business. A seat in the state legislature to begin with, perhaps, deliberating whether or not a road ought to pass over a bridge in just this way or that, whether the state should buy for itself a symphony, a new fleet of highway patrol cars, a new store of stationery for its representatives — or nothing at all, the favorite conclusion. Or maybe directly to Congress. Who could tell what Ogden and the Institute had in store for him. He had the talent and the money. He certainly had the backing. With luck he could even be on the ticket one day.

"You leave for New York tonight?" Worth asked as he said good-bye.

"We'll take a honeymoon someday, Counselor. Galway is a tough CO."

They settled into the little house in Manhasset, which Lulu immediately busied herself in improving with aggressive tracts of periwinkle and trellises around the small patio. When he would return from the city long after dark and see the yellow light of the kitchen where she waited for him with supper, he would wonder, on the bad days, if she ever imagined herself in the Patterson mansion with other hands to do her work and a husband, instead of the radio, to keep her company at the cocktail hour. Still, she seemed happy, at least for him. He bought her a cocker spaniel who followed at her heels as she made acquaintance with the other wives and led their little family through the easy suburban democracy of cocktail parties and picnics, small dinners for new friends, thank-you notes written under her proud new monogram. Gradually but firmly he felt himself bound to her demands on him as a wife, drawn into the complexity of the marriage she made for them. As she drew their separate lives together and worked for them to belong to this new place he discovered she was easy to love, and he did love her. Yet the one thing she asked for — a child — he couldn't seem to give her. "I've got to give that puppy some company," she would whisper in his ear after clearing the table on a night especially charted for fertility. And obligingly he would make love to her, a practice she took to quickly and well, he thought, pleased beyond his expectations even with that. Afterward she would lie still, with her knees closed and elevated for seven minutes, releasing her concentration only when the timer sounded. Still, months passed and nothing happened.

The more he settled into this quiet life with her, the more Roger worried about why she didn't get pregnant. She worried too, he could tell. But she plunged gamely on, planning and arranging and pleasing, as though by pursuing the project of their marriage even harder she could make the baby come. Seeing her try so hard made him feel worse, as though he were having the affair that he wasn't.

For Roger connected the strange infertility to some punishment for his inability to forget Judith. So this is what marriage is about, he thought: good food, steady sex, and guilt. He passed with the crush from the Long Island Railroad to the West Side IRT in Penn Station, hustling for a seat for the ride uptown and feeling guilty about that, too. Most days it began with the first lurch through the tunnel, the hurtling cadence of the passing cars below as the train drew nearer to her apartment. His heart raced as they drew into her station. Every day he expected her to get in the car at Fiftieth Street and to sit beside him; then the train would move and it would start up again. Despite himself he hoped for it, as the memories of their long-ago lovemaking, vivid as the night before, took him to the point he would cry out, the sound muffled by the subway clatter. Sometimes he dwelled for minutes on the feeling of her against him, the sound of the clock ticking beside her bed. Then the doors would open at Fifty-ninth Street and he would run out with the others.

For three weeks he sat in the Broadway offices without portfolio until someone took notice and assigned him a territory to sell on the far side of the Hudson in New Jersey. After that, unless he had paperwork to do, he got up at five-thirty and took the train to Penn Station, then took another train to New Jersey, where the company car sat parked, and sold fiber in the sooty offices of the apparel factories, which were often little more than urban shacks employing immigrants for less than minimum wage. Every month if not sooner his sales kit had to be updated, for without pell-mell revisions the salesmen could not keep track of the lines Galway acquired as the old man bought aggressively mill after mill of finished, unfinished, gray cloth, or wovens, rayon, nylon, Orlon — and whatever else made by whoever wanted to sell.

Exhausted after the return ride to the city, where he filed his triplicate order sheets, he often shared a seat on the late train to Manhasset with Charlie Walton, a veteran and a Galway engineer in product development whom Roger discovered to be nearly as ambitious as himself. Balding on top, shy, a chemist by training — he had been an Army Air Corps researcher — on the long rides in the crowded cars the two of them drank beer in the bar, standing elbow to elbow with other sweating young men, their suit coats over their arms, their voices loud in conversation about DiMaggio or the horses, or business.

"Dammit, Roger, you can't make any money without your own shop."

"That's what I've been saying ever since I joined this damn company."

Walton's voice dropped as low as the rumble of the wheels below. "I've hit on something, I think. I mean I'm developing a new formula. I need a sales guy to help me figure out what I got. You interested?"

Roger inched closer, sealing them from the din in the packed car. "What kind of formula?"

"It makes shirts wrinkle free. Cotton shirts. All cotton."

For two months Walton and Roger talked around the subject, testing each other, measuring the main chance before them. Every Tuesday Lulu made dinner for them and Charlie slept over, talking into the night, discussing the cost of setting up a small factory, establishing orders, where they could get the financing. Walton came to Fairington for Christmas, spending the holidays in the green and gold guest bedroom in the Siler house, taking it all in, the rawness, the growth, the air thick with it. He squinted over his glasses at the miles of turned orange mud and the earth movers mired in it, so many construction sites that the crews left the equipment in one at dark and a night shift took it to another. And everywhere, red Siler bricks. After the huge Christmas dinner, Lulu led her mother into the kitchen toward the mounds of dishes. Roger presented the plan.

"You're not serious, are you?" Siler roared, laughing, striking his knee with the curved-stem pipe he had picked from the rack. "You two want to steal a patent for some kind of cloth from Galway. And you want me to go in with you to set up a mill? I think this whole damn country is going crazy."

"We wouldn't be stealing a patent from Galway, sir," Roger said. "No patent exists, and Charlie's under no contract."

"I'm damn sure old Galway's lawyers won't see it that way. You boys could end up in the penitentiary. Still, by God, it would be a damn good game."

Mr. Siler declined to invest directly in the business, but he gave them free use of an old army barracks he owned that was fit for industrial assembly, and he put them in contact with a man who would lease them the machinery they needed without asking too many questions. No Carolina bank would touch the project (including Security National which had never before passed on a chance to loan — and foreclose — against Albright farmland), but when he asked for a line of credit with the First National City Bank of New York, finding, conveniently, among their junior loan officers a lieutenant he had known in France as anxious to make a name for himself as he was, they granted a modest amount against future orders for the New Man shirt. Giving two weeks' notice, Walton and Roger resigned from Galway Industries and returned to Fairington, where New Man commenced production.

Roger memorized the train routes, and he carried the folded schedule like an ancient manuscript in his army one-suiter as he traveled out from Fairington in great spinelike journeys — to Nashville, Memphis, Fort Smith, St. Louis; to Kingsport, Johnson City, Cincinnati, Cleveland, Buffalo; to Atlanta, Birmingham, New Orleans, Houston. His sales pitch was more than a sales pitch, it was a hymn to the future; for the dubious buyer he conjured the image of an army of New Man executives marching to work in their no-wrinkle shirts. Everywhere, from the department stores to the haberdashers, it seemed, he made a sale of some size.

Walton assembled a small force of workers who treated ready-made shirts he was able to buy in bulk, obtaining a small margin that could see them through with limited overhead. After the first flush of orders he hired a designer, and then a bank of seamstresses, and he bought bolts of broadcloth to make the shirts from scratch. The formula, which he constantly revised, for fear that a competitor would duplicate it, was kept in a lockbox in Walton's apartment. Early in the morning, before the first shift arrived, he would enter the small room to the side of the sewing floor that he had established as his laboratory and mix the chemical himself for the day's use.

Soon the partners discovered they needed another man on salary to manage the growing plant, and Roger, who had foreseen this, as so far he had foreseen most everything else, gradually sold Walton on Billy Roy. Sure, he had no direct experience, but they weren't exactly grizzled veterans. Besides, he had done a year toward the new degree in textiles studies at State College. He was a good man, a man to be trusted — and they wouldn't have to pay him very much. Roger sold Walton on Billy Roy like he sold Gimbels on New Man shirts, and Thumper, who had taken Roger's advice and used part of his GI money to learn about the textile business so he could join him in it, had a job.

The benevolent silence under which they worked and thrived for the better part of a year and a half — refinancing their notes, expanding their shop, getting order upon order — was shattered by the summons they received to appear in federal court and answer charges that they had stolen the idea for their business, the expertise to run it, indeed the entirety of their enterprise, from Galway Industries, whose corporate name was fixed menacingly to the thrice-folded complaint. At the club, Winston Galway had talked of little else for six months except the two young men who had stolen from him, two young men, he had told anyone who cared to listen, whom he had hired as deserving veterans and who had pirated away a formula for something or other that was his by corporate right! One of the young whippersnappers had even married the daughter of his neighbor.

The prospect of a lawsuit, which, Roger admitted, he should have factored into their costs, was daunting. The orders they had established were regular enough, but not in such quantity as they had hoped, and their inventory remained uncomfortably high. Unable to borrow money to pay Worth — provided he would take their case — Roger had to go to Siler. The old man had read about the lawsuit in the newspaper, which he examined at great length every evening after dinner, chuckling over each paragraph of duplicity and greed, daily confirmation of the weakness of the race. No, he said, I won't lend you the money to fight Galway on collateral of receivables the bank already owns, gesturing toward the brick wall of the den where he had hung the painting he liked of ducks falling in the autumn air. You boys made your bed, and now you'll have to sleep in it. Your personal note? What's your personal note worth? Are you going to pay me back with your mother's good sweet relish? Because you're married to my daughter you won't go hungry, but not a nickel for your company . . .

• • •

"It's me," Roger said.

"I've been waiting for your call."

"Will you take the case?"

"Of course."

Roger gathered all of the records and hurried to Worth's office. Without sleep and short of breath he felt he was living his life as a footrace, that even after all this, his flight from fate was vanity and discovery awaited him in the silent room of the successful to which he had been mistakenly admitted, and from which, because of the same faults that were his counterfeit virtues, he would shortly be routed.

"So Charlie remembers signing something after all."

"Yeah, but he doesn't know what it was. I could strangle him."

"Roger, people often don't remember what they sign when they start jobs. He was an engineer — I'm sure he signed an agreement not to compete with the company. Did he sign anything when he left?"

"He doesn't remember. We're through, then, aren't we — if he really signed it."

"Not necessarily. The contract could be overly restrictive as to time and territory. You make no-wrinkle shirts. Galway doesn't. Actually, the products don't compete. They could say Charlie misappropriated a corporate opportunity, but he wasn't an officer and probably establishing his ordinary duty would be difficult. At the same time, the fact that you don't have a contract doesn't get us off the hook for your actions — they have a legitimate right to their customer lists, for example, which you used. So that's a negative. I don't think they can get an injunction — you're too far along. They could try for damages. In which case they still have to show you actually hurt them."

"Dammit, Worth, you've got to get me out of this. This is my chance. This is it for me."

"Listen, Roger. We're going to beat this. We may lose the first couple of rounds. But we'll beat it."

"I know this is tough for you, Worth. Politically I mean. You don't want to piss off Galway."

"Forget it. I don't care about Galway. He's just another fat cat who came to Grandfather's Christmas parties. Listen, the guy made millions back here while we were getting our butts shot at. And now he wants to take the bread off your table. Besides that, I can't wait to get at his lawyers. They work for us, too. Snotty bunch."

"I haven't told Lulu. I can't. And now Herman won't loan me any more money."

"Then I'll tell her. She needs to know."

The first round went badly, as Worth predicted. The decision rendered against them, if upheld, would force payments large enough to wreck New Man. The creditors in New York refused to refinance the loans, and Worth had to persuade them more than once not to force bankruptcy. Customers canceled orders and suppliers accepted cash only. The nadir came in December when Billy Roy laid off the entire work force, save one faithful woman who alone was able to sew the shirts they needed for their small backlog. They couldn't pay their current bills any longer, and there were three long months until the appeal would come to trial.

Roger studied the accounts and saw in the relentless numbers the pattern of past failures. Gradually and then suddenly—that's how you go bankrupt, he thought. Some writer said that. The final slide was a peaceful cataclysm, like falling asleep with the gas on. He had thought he would have more time before joining the others in the portrait gallery at Bright Star, but he figured that fate had decided to deal with him early since he was more trouble than the rest. The standard sinecure awaited, and, Roger admitted, it was more attractive than the usual family alcoholism. Last week Ogden had offered him a post as a fellow of the Institute at a generous stipend, with the promise that upon proper publication, he would move rapidly into academia. At least I wouldn't have to work for Herman, he thought.

Late one night, Roger and Walton, unable to find a penny more on the ledger, agreed, as they locked the doors to their silent plant, to take the bankruptcy filing up with Worth in the morning.

Standing before their cars in the empty parking lot, the partners instinctively shook hands, the solemnity of the moment seeming to demand it. As they turned away the headlights of a fast-approaching car fixed them. It headed across the bare asphalt straight to the factory gate. Could the sheriff foreclose at midnight? Roger wondered. It was rather dramatic. They weren't exactly fleeing to Argentina with the company payroll.

He relaxed, suddenly, as he recognized Billy Roy's car. Roger had sent him home at eight, since he had worked thirty-six hours straight.

"You missed the end of the wake, Billy Roy," Walton said as Thumper alighted.

"Yeah, but it wasn't much," Roger said. "Hope we both remember how to crop tobacco."

Billy Roy smiled, his big white teeth flashing in the darkness. He gave Roger an envelope. "It's not a loan. It's stock, free and clear. See y'all in the morning."

Inside was a cashier's check drawn on Worth Patterson's account at the Security National Bank for thirty thousand dollars.

•   •   •

Roger never doubted the product. With each day he knew the New Man shirt was worth more than it was the day before. He knew it because no one had maids anymore to iron. He knew it because men still wanted the feel of a good cotton shirt. In Fairington, in Manhasset, everywhere he saw men like himself, hungry men; all you had to do was drive through the neighborhoods of tract houses, see the young beshirted executives kiss their wives and children good-bye. The market was there. He leveraged Worth's capital contribution against one bank loan and then another. He spent more and more on promotion. At the club the men asked him, "Are you still in business this month, Roger?" He knew what the gossip was. He was going under. He had stolen from august Galway Industries and now he was going to pay for it. Too smart for his own good. "At least the other screwups were private," he told Lulu, who had been as solid as a Siler brick through the ordeal. "Now they talk about the Albright curse at bridge parties." Hunched over his books in the office, he closed his eyes and willed himself to pray. Please, please give me one more month, he asked. Not for the past anymore — but for me, now. Just one more month.

Then it all changed. Roger sat in court in Richmond as Worth, alone, facing a squad of Galway lawyers, told the appeals panel precisely why they should throw out the judgment below. Three weeks later, to everyone's amazement except Worth's, they did, unanimously. The next day Macy's called, then Jordan Marsh and Belk and the rest of them. Roger sold shirts he hadn't made and bought cotton that didn't exist. He borrowed more money against his orders and convinced his father-in-law to build him another plant at cost. He and Walton and Billy Roy worked around the clock for six months, but at the end of it they were made. Roger paid Worth's bill and Worth offered Roger the chance to redeem his stock at cost. Absolutely not, said Roger. I want Albright Industries to be the best investment you ever made, he told Worth. At the club the guys began to ask Roger to round out foursomes, and their wives invited him and Lulu for cocktails. Lulu became chairman of the cookbook committee for the Junior League, the most important position short of being an officer, everyone knew.

II

——⚔——

SUMMUM BONUM,

HONEST INJUN

1950–52

Chapter Seven

1950

Thirty-five E *train called the Southern Crescent originates in New Orleans, travels the Delta lowlands east and north toward Birmingham, then curves east to Atlanta and rapidly straightens its arc through Greenville, Charlotte, Fairington, Greensboro, following the traditional north-south trade route from the Middle Atlantic states to the Gulf of Mexico and the Southwest.*

A few inches in track size on the line the Crescent traveled made a great difference in who would be rich in the Gilded Age and who would be ruined. Tracks in the states of the old Confederacy were generally of wider gauge than those elsewhere, and Pittsburgh steel manufacturers competed for the contracts let to conform the southern tracks to the national standard. Having hammered and forged away the physical difference in the railroad lines, those same manufacturers then invented a metaphysical difference to protect themselves from competition. By the rule of the differential freight rate, steel made in locales other than Pittsburgh and sold somewhere else carried the imputed freight charge of steel made in Pittsburgh and sold to the same place. This stratagem did not keep the independent and highly efficient Tennessee Coal and Iron of Birmingham from introducing the new open-hearth furnaces in 1907 and selling the Harriman railroad an order of 150,000 tons.[1] Surveying the potential disorder of the universe such a pattern would portend, J. P. Morgan, in the midst of the Wall Street Panic of the same year, convened the directors of United States Steel in his library and engineered, for a stock price of twenty-five million dollars — approximately one-twentieth the worth of the company's assets — the purchase of Tennessee Coal and Iron.[2]

Morgan had already bought control of the railroad systems themselves. Following the Panic of 1893, he acquired the assets of the Richmond and West Point

1. S. B. Perry, "Coals to Newcastle: Tennessee Coal, Iron and Railroad Company 1885–1907," Journal of Social Forces 5, no. 3 (August 1931), 1247.
2. The remainder of the acquisition was financed by debt. Perry, "Coals to Newcastle," 1247.

Terminal Company, which formed the base for his new creation, the Southern Railway, a vast corporation that eventually owned seventy-five hundred miles of track and issued $120 million worth of stock to the public against capital contributions by the Morgan group of nearly zero. Consolidation of the Southern gave Morgan control of transportation routes that served coal fields, tobacco barns, the textile mills, lumberyards and truck farms stretching from West Virginia and Kentucky to the Carolinas and Florida. Within ten years Morgan had also gained financial influence in or outright domination over the Louisville and Nashville, the Atlantic Coast Line, the Plant System, and the Seaboard Air Line. Soon, no freight traffic moved by rail between the coastal plain and the Mississippi River, from the Gulf of Mexico in the south to the Ohio River in the north, without Morgan's blessing.[3]

The provincial capital of these holdings was Atlanta, home of the Southern; as President of his queen line, Morgan installed Oswald Patterson, Indian fighter, graduate of Princeton, a man of such modern views toward the contemporary business organization that he had his secretaries make a card index of regional state legislators, rating them according to their friendliness toward the railroad and the House of Morgan. Moved by what he perceived to be his duties to public relations, and advancing on the problem as he might have attacked a Sioux hunting party, Patterson proclaimed in 1897 to the somewhat puzzled membership of the Atlanta Merchants Association that the "interests of the railroad and its patrons are identical."[4]

Aware of his lieutenant's tendency to make unhelpful public statements, Morgan dispatched to Atlanta one of his most trusted public relations men. Gradually Colonel Patterson was led to temper his speeches, and eventually he stopped writing them himself and simply read from the copy the public relations man prepared. Eventually, too, he began to see the wisdom of joining certain of Atlanta's civic organizations, though their activities bored him, and even of donating some of the railroad's profits to certain very conspicuous causes—a monument to Henry W. Grady, an orphanage, a hospital wing, a trust for the Confederate veterans' pension fund.

Morgan grew more satisfied with the performance of the Southern Division

---

3. Howard Hildegger, "J.P. Morgan's Other Empire: The Building of Southern Railway" (Ph.D. diss., Johns Hopkins University, 1934), 478.

4. Oswald Patterson, speech to Atlanta Merchants Association, December 4, 1897, Papers of Oswald Patterson, Southern Historical Collection, University of North Carolina, Chapel Hill, N.C.

upon reports he received from Atlanta that his railroad now enjoyed the civic comity necessary for the successful operation of a monopoly.[5] He was not even particularly concerned when the general counsel of the Interstate Commerce Commission announced that he was calling Patterson to testify on the matter of some large contributions the Southern had made to state legislators who had voted for the railroad land condemnation program. Morgan simply placed several additional public relations men in New York on the case, planting favorable stories with friendly columnists from the World, the News-American, and the Herald Tribune. The stories spoke of harassment of honest businessmen and "interference with the free give and take of electioneering."[6] Morgan spoke confidentially to several commissioners of the ICC. A week before the hearings he sent his top corporation counsel to Washington to prepare remarks for Patterson to make and responses to any questions he might have to answer.[7]

But when the corporation counsel arrived, he found trouble in the temper of Oswald Patterson. "I will not read a script like a play-actor before those young lawyer puppies who don't know what it takes to run a business," Oswald declared.[8] So before the disbelieving eyes of Morgan's lawyer and Morgan's public relations man, he tore apart the script they had written for him and instead treated himself to a colloquy with the obliging counsel for the Interstate Commerce Commission:

> COUNSEL: Let me understand what you are saying, Mr. Patterson. You do not deny having paid tens of thousands of dollars of the Southern Railway's money to the legislators I have just named in exchange for their votes on matters affecting the railroad?
>
> PATTERSON: I do not deny it. In fact, I am proud of it. We try to get on good terms with the state authorities as a matter of policy. It is an exceedingly difficult matter to protect the property of a large corporation in thirteen different states from confiscation by the people.
>
> COUNSEL: What people are you referring to, Mr. Patterson?
>
> PATTERSON: Why, the people of the country, of course. The people have a democratic government with a majority rule, and they create commissions and other forms of government with power to prohibit the proper uses of

5. Oswald Patterson, letter to J. P. Morgan, April 14, 1898, Papers of Oswald Patterson, Southern Historical Collection, University of North Carolina, Chapel Hill, N.C.
6. "ICC Targets Top Morgan Man," New York Herald Tribune, May 17, 1898.
7. Hildegger, "J. P. Morgan's Other Empire," 872.
8. Lucian Wadsworth, letter to J. P. Morgan, July 2, 1898, Papers of Lucian Wadsworth, J. P. Morgan Library, New York, N.Y.

private property. All such bodies are a menace and we have to protect our-selves against them.

COUNSEL: *So, as I understand you, Mr. Patterson, you consider gov-ernment by the people as dangerous, and you conceive it to be your patriotic duty to undermine it?*

PATTERSON: *I would not go that far, Sir. We do not want chaos, we do not want anarchy. We have no substitute for the government.*

COUNSEL: *The anarchist, Mr. Patterson, says all legislative bodies are a menace; in action they are a calamity.*

PATTERSON: *That is my opinion.*

COUNSEL: *You say all legislative bodies are a menace, and in action they are a calamity. Will you explain the difference between your opinion and the opinion of the anarchist?*

PATTERSON: *I am not acquainted with any anarchists. I cannot explain the difference between their opinions and mine.*[9]

When his lieutenants notified J. P. Morgan, then traveling in England, of the fiasco, he decided not to hurry home as though there were a crisis. He arrived on schedule, closing the house in Scotland in August as planned. He then occupied himself among his artifacts in the library on Murray Hill, sifting through the arcana his various alter egos had discreetly purchased—an Empire settee, draw-ings of pre-Columbian beast worship, an illuminated Virgil—waiting for Pat-terson to arrive. He decided to be generous to the Colonel. Morgan retired Patterson at half his salary for the rest of his life, plus fifty thousand bonus shares of Southern Preferred, and he included Patterson on the Morgan Insider's list, where he joined, among others, two former U.S. Presidents and three Supreme Court Justices, as recipients of privileged information on stock deals. Morgan also, as a matter of courtesy, insisted that Patterson retain his private railroad car.[10]

Patterson found himself a wealthier man after Morgan fired him than before. He brooded on his humiliation, but by and by he took to riding the railroad again, his steel blue coach becoming a fixture unnoticed by the switchmen who routed him through Richmond to Weldon and Lynchburg, Columbia and Atlanta. From his railroad car, always moving, he saw the changing land, the construction from nothing of towns and enterprises. The idea grew on him to build a city—that was

9. *Interstate Commerce Commission*, Proceedings before the Committee on Election-eering and Graft, *vol. 14, no. 357, xix.*
10. Hildegger, *"J. P. Morgan's Other Empire," 1048.*

indeed the way to recoup, to make one's mark. Between Greensboro and Charlotte, the small village of Fairington had expanded handsomely in the twelve years since its citizens had invested in a cotton weaving mill. From his railroad car Patterson could see the clean rows of the mill village, where farm families had moved to take up the factory work. He saw new stores on the paved main street and several new automobiles. For all the signs of prosperity, however, Patterson knew that the town would never progress far in competition with its neighbors if the railroad did not establish a freight and passenger station there. For ten years the citizens had requested it, and for ten years they had been turned down. On his return to Atlanta, Patterson saw to it that Fairington made the new station list. As the depot rose beside the tracks, Patterson secured the promise of his friend, Penrose Galway, that Fairington would be the town where he and his son Winston would establish their southern textile base. The citizens of Fairington could not believe their good luck.[11]

Galway began construction on the mill as soon as the railroad hookup began service, and Patterson, deciding to make himself more widely known to the curious and influential of the place, parked his railroad car on the siding and installed himself at the Hotel Fairington, which had recently been expanded from a boardinghouse. A delegation from the town, having finally researched their benefactor, called on Patterson and offered him what they had to give: land. He accepted the gift and saw to planning his home, and a compound around it, to house however many of his children he could browbeat to join him in his new demesne. The mayor even suggested that the name of the town be changed to Patterson, but Oswald felt that was too great a vanity.

The regional newspapers eventually reported on Patterson's new venture in Fairington, and bit by bit his reputation was restored in the public's mind. Instead of a Morgan henchman he became known as a genial benefactor: "New South Booster: Patterson Befriends a City," the Atlanta Constitution *reported.[12] Without commenting, he continued with his task; his house, which he supervised in construction, stood ready at last. He brought his wife from Atlanta, and she settled in the brick mansion on the condition that it be their "summer home." All but one of his children, who finally knew they had to take seriously the request of their father to move to this place, decided to decline, though they risked his displeasure. Phineas Patterson, the youngest, who had nearly run through his trust, or what*

11. Raoul Millsaps, "The Founding of Fairington, North Carolina, 1902–11" (Masters thesis, University of North Carolina, 1930), 84.

12. "New South Booster: Patterson Befriends a City," Atlanta Constitution, October 21, 1910.

he could get of it at twenty-five, heeded the summons out of necessity. An architect by training, he took a floor in the manse, spending the days in Oswald's employ, overseeing the construction of Patterson Forest, a residential neighborhood modeled after the designs of certain newly rich eastern suburbs. The first street, Founders Row, had at its center the Patterson house, soon to be flanked by other substantial residences on the lots Oswald parceled out to his lieutenants and the local notables. He set Phineas next to planning a golf course on the open land facing the new mansions, a proper links and clubhouse, Oswald informed the startled city fathers, being the next necessary addition to Fairington's cosmopolitanism.

Five years later, Fairington's harvest abounded. From the countryside more and more families moved in to work in the mills, which now stood atop three of the six hills that enclosed the growing metropolis. Merchants, impressed with the city's central location and the railroad station, installed themselves profitably; builders built fine structures on Patterson Street's newly laid blacktop in the center of town. Founders Row had no more lots for sale, and the Fairington Country Club thrived. The Chambers of Commerce of rival neighbors Winston-Salem, Greensboro, and Charlotte held secret meetings to plot the means to counter the new threat among them . . . .

Roger placed the monograph on the coffee table beside the other curios — the worn and crumpled *Harper's* articles by the ubiquitous Sidley recounting Oswald Patterson's Indian days, and then his time at Princeton, and the bundle, held by black string, of sheer blue overseas letters from Phineas Patterson to Worth — delivered from Paris twice each year, unfailingly postmarked July 4 and December 31. Roger remembered past references to Phineas, Worth's father. Whenever the subject came up, Worth said his father spent most of the year abroad, in Paris, where he had an architecture firm. Roger had never met him, and he didn't know any one who had except perhaps Ogden, who might have mentioned his name in passing. But he couldn't be sure.

"So you see why I thought I should give this to you to figure out," Lulu said, her legs curled beneath her skirt as she sat on the sofa.

"That's all well and good, dear. But what I want to know is why he gave these papers to you."

She sighed. "Because he tells me things."

"What things?"

"Roger, I'm sure you know—whether he should, I don't know, get on with this plan or . . ."

"Or what?"

"Or not."

"I see."

"You mean he never talks about these things with you?"

Roger had the feeling that Lulu was playing. She had enjoyed playing like this for a couple of months now. He didn't much like it. "Worth and I don't talk about that kind of thing."

"What do you talk about then?"

"Oh, I can't say offhand. The business, his practice. Sports. Things we need to get done."

Lulu stretched to her full length on the couch and reached for her cigarettes. "So that's why he needs me to confide in. You see?"

"I don't think I like the idea—"

"Now don't you start *that*, Roger Albright. You're gone four nights a week, on the weekend tired and mumbling to yourself, writing numbers down on the tablecloth—why, if I depended on you for company I'd be in Dix Hill by now. I do spend time with Worth. You told me to. You said if I got lonely to go see Worth."

He didn't know whether he had said that or not. He didn't think he had, or would. But she was always throwing things back in his face that he was supposed to have said to her. It was clear in any event that she hid things from him about Worth, and he couldn't figure out whether it bothered him more that she hid things or that she flaunted it.

"Now, honey, whatever I said I didn't mean—"

"Yes, you did too. You certainly did, Roger Albright."

So this is what it's about, Roger thought. She's angry because I'm gone all the time. He didn't mean to neglect her. The business required it, he had explained a dozen times, and it wasn't as though he was with other women. He was, in fact, as alone as he could be. Still, he couldn't fight the basic accusation or the guilt he felt at enjoying life on the road, away from the domestic stalemate.

Besides, he had pointed out, she suffered in common with the other Institute wives. Now all the young men were gone, again. Ogden had called all of them out to fight another campaign, this time the great cause was

Dr. MacGiver, whom the professor had gotten appointed to the Senate during the war and who now stood for election. Worth of course took a leading role. Nothing like re-creating in fact the high priest he was in legend to revivify Worth's image, Roger thought. That is, with Lulu, who was the one who counted.

When Ogden called, Roger knew he had to go too, if for no other reason than to keep on looking good in a uniform. Ogden was firm and businesslike, reverting to the prior relationship of tutor to tutored. "You understand I believe you to be a talented researcher. We still use your thesis," he said, his vowel-laden voice raspy over the telephone but still at once soothing and commanding, continuing the conversation as though eight years, a world war, and a business built from scratch were semester break. My thesis — good God, Roger thought. "We need you to try your hand at some research on one of the key opposition people — a fellow about your age named Joe Crain."

Without any summons other than that, and despite being in the midst of building a new house one block over from his in-laws and trying to drive his business at the usual clip, the next day he appeared at MacGiver headquarters in Raleigh to pick up his assignment. He ended up spending half the day there, as Worth and Ogden, the new man Ackerman, and MacGiver himself briefed him on the importance of the Crain project. The guy has them scared stiff, Roger thought, and he doesn't even have an official job with the other side. More like a Svengali. Initial research proved frustrating; there was only so much information you could get out of cold calls on eastern North Carolina types when asking about the childhood of a small-town youth religious leader. Especially when all they did when you brought up the subject was push on their rockers and talk about the weather.

Maybe for that reason the easier, almost whimsical task Lulu assigned seemed refreshing. "Just a fool for love," he muttered, flipping through the old manuscript she set before him. An old manuscript that shouted Ogden from every page. He retrieved the magnifying glass from the dictionary lectern and peered at the onionskin paper.

"What are you doing?" Lulu said.

"It's Ogden's typewriter. See how the *t* skips?"

"You mean Professor Ogden wrote that?"

"Yes, honey."

"Why? Why would he write something about Oswald Patterson?"

Roger paced before the windows, the light curtains billowing softly in the afternoon rain that misted his view of the golf course before him and the Patterson mansion across the fairway. He had wanted to build on a contemporary design, but she had prevailed with a Cape Cod. No brick, of course; that would have been a deal killer. It was a good lot, everyone had said, one of the last with a view of the course. They were lucky to get it.

"Probably because he was paid to do it by Patterson."

"Paid?"

"Sure. A house biography to clean up the old man's background. You see Oswald wanted the Pattersons to be nice people. He probably volunteered Ogden for the job — and Ogden did it. You know once people like old man Patterson give you money they act like they own you. And pretty soon you start acting that way, too."

Lulu waved as if to clear her head, or the air itself, of the implications.

"Fine. So Professor Ogden wrote it. All I know is that Worth is confused."

"Confused?"

"Yes. He said, 'Read this.' I said, 'Why?' He just mumbled something and left."

"What do you want me to do?"

"You're the only person who can make heads or tails of it. He's so blue, Roger. He'd never let on."

"But don't you think there are reasons he showed this to you and not to me?"

"It doesn't matter. I mean — we've got to help him."

What the hell, Roger thought. Why not indulge her. It was hard for Roger to decide who was more insincere — Worth trying to seduce Lulu by depressing himself, or she trying to get back at him by helping Worth. It would be so much easier if she would just say she was in love with Worth again, Roger thought, rather than display it degree by degree with this parlor game. Still, it was fun imitating Ogden, and the story he had concocted in the vanity monograph looked very interesting. That is, the missing link, Phineas Patterson — surely Ogden's real inquiry, but one he dared not pursue too far — looked very interesting.

Roger picked up the slender manuscript. What does one make of this Phineas, the mysterious father? he thought. Smaller than life beside the blustering Oswald, unlike his siblings he could not resist his summons to Fairington, having spent his trust fund in secret defiance. But he was not a wastrel, as Oswald probably thought. He was, at least in Ogden's not-to-be-underestimated historical sense, the key — to the son, the reluctant progenitor; to the father, Oedipus unleashed on a bank account.

Roger turned again to the modest entrance: ". . . he took a floor in the manse, spending the days in Oswald's employ, overseeing the construction of Patterson Forest, a residential neighborhood modeled after the designs of certain newly rich eastern suburbs." Roger smiled, locating himself again in Ogden's mind, seeing anew the hostility of the passage. Another joke on the patron, he thought.

Now engaged by the task, Roger paced the living room, dark with the afternoon and silent except for the clicking of the rain on the slate roof and the muffled rhythms of the standing clock in the foyer. He looked out the bay window and down the hill, across the tidy street to the golf course, now luxuriating in its May growth, and imagined Phineas in his favorite safari hat, nursing the imperialist's gin while commanding his dark army of shovelers, reveling in the placement of a bunker here, the employ of an overhanging willow tree there, the entrapment of an impossible kidney-shaped green that gave only the illusion of rest. He was, it had been made already clear, in Oswald's thrall; if the old man wanted to rule nature, too, then Phineas would be the agent of its subjugation. And so the links must have grown, hole by hole; more a maze than a course, it seduced the eager man, luring him into false safe harbors, broadening its way before his cocky onslaught, appearing to crown his momentum with triumph, until the monstrous hidden bogs and the vicious Scottish saw grass narrowed and narrowed his prospects and then with one slip the main chance was lost. All that came after was an endless game of compromise from the deepest trouble, a broken mind and spirit, and the last subdued march up the wasted fairway, relief that at last it was over.

What extraordinary and hated fealty, Roger thought. "All right," he said. "You want to know what it's about? I'll tell you."

"What do you mean?"

"I can make it up as well as Ogden. Just listen."

"It had to be at Oswald's command that Phineas marry, and then also at his command that he produce a son, and then also at his command that he give the

son to Oswald. Although Phineas had some stake in the cleansing action. He knew himself to be too insightful, and therefore too weak a vessel, to exact tribute; he did not honor the necessity of, nor possess the present ability for, resurrecting in the public mind the good name of Patterson. Phineas could only record, with some relish, its demise.

"For it was the opposite of the truth to suppose that Oswald Patterson cared little for the opinion of history. The debacle before the ICC was one of those odd times when one says exactly the opposite of what one believes, is motivated by the opposite desire. It was indeed the Patterson name for which Oswald wished success. The money, the sweaty influence, was just a means. What else, after all, had attracted Morgan's eye for talent? Not a mere urge for money. No, the young Oswald Patterson, fresh from the Carolina pinelands that ten years after the war were still a mound of debris, human and otherwise, and he at fifteen too young to have gotten his name in the conflict, turned up at Fort Kearney in Nebraska and enlisted to fight the Indians, finding refuge and instruction in the legions of blue and gray veterans who had done just that, so they would have more humans on whom to employ their deadly learning. Across the Platte and up the Missouri he rode, and then from Fort Lincoln west with General Custer and the Seventh Cavalry into Montana, following the fires and night cries to the Sioux encampment.

"Sometime before the end, on the red plains, fate called him away. He had some scheme, certainly; perhaps the force of that scheme prompted the young man to hear over the shrouded hills the ghost dance, to imagine the incomprehensible surging death of Little Bighorn, not knowing the horror he was dreaming, but knowing it was real and not his. He escaped Little Bighorn, he would say later, with a dismissive show of modesty, only because a courier had been required to ferry a message back to Fort Lincoln; though he delivered it without reading what it said—knowing Custer, Oswald would opine, the gist of it was to have some girls (he liked them plural) ready when he got back.

"No one ever inquired whether this story was true. No other white man owned up to surviving Little Bighorn. Oswald did arrive at Fort Lincoln with a message. He of course had to be told of the massacre. Whatever the real reason for Oswald's presence at Fort Lincoln—and facing it frankly meant either Custer's order or Oswald's desertion—he did, according to the account in Harper's Weekly, *suffer manly sobs and require restraint to keep him from going back after Crazy Horse personally. The correspondent, George Sidley, wished to take him east on the Chautauqua tour, sensing an audience for them both. 'The Only Survivor of Little*

Bighorn' was box office. East they headed, touring on the good name of Harper's *the genteel circuits of Albany, Troy, Buffalo, Allentown, Camden, Rye, Danbury, and back again until, by the end of the summer, Oswald believed his own story.*

"But he had to hurry on. That September, army discharge and Sidley's articles in hand, riding his quarter horse and wearing his dust-beaten chaps, he appeared in Princeton, New Jersey, and asked to be directed to the college there, whereupon he requested admission into the class of 1882, producing before the startled bursar the term's full tuition, in gold, which he authenticated by biting each coin as it was delivered from his saddlebags. In support of his application he also delivered a letter from Mr. Sidley, class of 1868, in which the particulars of his legend, as well as some glancing and not too specific remarks about his family background, were set out. He listed Fort Kearney as his hometown, the Seventh Cavalry as his preparatory education. The entrance examination he passed on gamesmanship and boyhood Latin, and the next day he matriculated, prompting another article by Mr. Sidley.

"At the table in Fairington, Phineas enjoyed puncturing, under his breath, the particulars of the tale. 'And how long, Father, did it take you to ride your horse from the Black Hills to Princeton?' he would ask, sotto voce, or, 'It's remarkable how one simply never loses those declensions.' Sometimes it was not so sotto, so that they together, father and son, with the bewildered little Worth as auditor, would engage in dissonant counterpoint, neither paying the slightest attention to the other. Later, Phineas suggested that Worth ask his grandfather how he got the honorary colonel before his name, studying his young son, searching for the sensitivity that would pick out the joke when he heard the answer: that Oswald was certainly not a colonel, was never more than a corporal, but that his friends in college had called him that and the nickname had stuck. Of course the joke, and Worth would get it when he himself went away to school, was that the appellation stuck as a clubby form of ridicule, but Oswald was too vain to notice. As for the money, Worth concluded, under the influence of Phineas's insinuations, Sidley gave it to him, and as for the test, he never took it, but rather, Sidley took care of it.

"Thus he progressed through Princeton, nodding to his fellows, lounging before Old Nassau, not thinking that his odyssey there was unusual or noticing that his classmates generally found him a laughingstock as he recounted in his Chautauqua-stump manner bouts of derring-do with the Red Indians, interspersed with hints of a lost plantation past that those who had reason to know found absurd, all told shifting from foot to foot in suits that while not badly tailored (Sidley saw to that too) were draped as foreign objects over his ill-practiced frame. The colonel

plodded on, however, sure in some mental recess of his errand. He met Sidley at the appointed intervals, taking the morning train to New York, reporting on his progress—on the men he knew, the clubs he attended. Periodically, to keep his name in front of the public, the magazine mentioned him in a society sighting— 'Oswald Patterson, Indian fighter cum Princeton class of '82, dined at the residence of the Hon. Judge Walcott, joined by Messrs. Joshua White, Theo. deBarry & cetera all taking the holiday at New York. The courtly Carolinian, known as Colonel Patterson to his college mates . . .' and so on. Season by season the place worked itself even on this raw product, so that eventually the scoffers graduated and the rest of the college viewed the colonel as less a buffoon and more a character, and one who had interesting connections in New York. By the time Sidley paid his last term's tuition, Oswald had succeeded to president of the Racquets Club.

"At some point in this elaborate peregrination Oswald and Sidley must have discussed the ultimate end. Or maybe not; maybe Oswald was so directed to the next step, and the step following, that Sidley seemed a likely muse and provider. His long days on the plains that stretched forever, his escape from death and the fame luck brought him, the appearance of Sidley himself, and the subsequent nurturing of a legend and a new self were the normal appointments of man's estate. Oswald, too, was confident that what Sidley saw in him was true: that he was restless, given to work hard for reward, that he knew the western territories from the back of a horse better than any white man his age, that he was tough beyond his years, smart enough, and determined to make a name where one did not before exist. Thus when the day came that Sidley said he was ready, Oswald nodded and took the train to make the meeting, never having once questioned because he never once felt unsure.

"The house itself disappointed him. Oswald had trudged up Murray Hill expecting to see a castle and instead found himself on the doorstep of an oversized brown cottage. Sidley led him in and then retreated to the darkness of the still study. Oswald stood before the leather-covered desk. Finally, Morgan set aside his pen.

"'You are Patterson,' he said. Oswald felt the deep eyes pore over him from the jellied encasement of his full, pink face.

"Yes sir.'

"'Patterson, I will come to the point. You are a busy man and I am a busy man. I have checked your record. I need a man to superintend our line from Chicago to San Francisco. The northern route, through the Dakotas. Indian territory. We are, frankly, having problems. Indian attacks. Inadequate army protection. Right-of-way disputes. Bad Chinese labor. Et cetera. Not to mention the local pooh-

bahs you have to amuse. Millions have been put out, Patterson. Investors here and in England rely on my assurances. I have no concerns regarding the limits of your authority other than that the job get done. You will have no residence but will travel within the western territories wherever you are needed. Because of your position, your life will be in danger from numerous sources. It is only fair to tell you that several men have already been killed. You won't have time for a wife. Your compensation, for a man your age, I daresay will be exceptional. Do you wish to consider the situation?'

"'Yes sir. I have considered it. I want the job.'

"Morgan nodded and rose from his high-backed leather chair. 'Good. Sidley, you will do the usual?' He offered his hand, and Oswald took it. 'Welcome, Colonel Patterson, to the House of Morgan.'

"And so it began, success following upon success, Morgan's first mess cleaned up with a minimum of deaths and out-of-pocket expense. Then labor riots on the Terminal system, again well handled, and then smaller railroads to captain before the big prize, the Southern. Along the way, when he was professionally able, he picked up a wife, Miss Adeline Stafford, of an ambitious New York merchant family, who, because of the Morgan connection, itself advantageous, assumed incorrectly that she was acquiring an a priori railroad prince rather than one in the making. The shock of that prenuptial miscalculation and the necessity of moving hither and yon at the whim of Morgan and the command of her husband provoked Adeline to a thousand rebellions, the chief being the subversion of her youngest child, Phineas, so that by the time he reached his majority and Oswald reached his zenith he knew more about his father's true origins than Oswald had forgotten. It was unfair to Oswald, certainly, because he did eventually provide what he had advertised—the manse, gentility, unlimited funds, the fawning of lesser beings—but it was the getting of it all that ruined him for his station.

"That deficit became the tragedy of Oswald's stewardship of the Southern. The performance before the ICC, the inexplicable lack of restraint—wasn't that the product precisely of the qualities that made his rise possible? To navigate the waters of opinion safely, must not the traits that enable one to defy opinion be bred out? Like Joshua before the Promised Land he must have seen himself in a new and cruel light—the preparer of the way, rather than the conqueror. So Morgan, after the fall, senses these things too, and invites Oswald to the shrine, the new palazzo of his grand library, which he placed beside his Murray Hill cottage with posterity in mind, and amidst the vaulted cases spreads out the drawings of quattrocento Siena and Florence and tells him what he must do: 'Oswald, to recapture your

good name, you must found a city. I made you bold; now you must make your children prudent.'

"That would explain the gift, don't you see, honey?" Roger said, jumping up to find the leather-bound illuminated Virgil that always, until Oswald's death, had stayed open on the credenza in the Patterson library.

"The gift?"

"Yes—that's why he included it with the rest of the things. See the inscription—'To my Colonel,' it reads, 'Then I gave way, and lifting up my father, made for the mountains.'"

"I know; it's a beautiful book."

"It's from Morgan. J. P. Morgan."

"I know that. I'm really not as stupid as you think."

"Honey, I wish you'd stop saying that. You know I don't think you're stupid."

"Yes you do. Go on with your story. You're more interested in that anyway."

"But of all of the children (and some grandchildren), why did Phineas alone make the journey to novo ordo Fairington? He the subverted and Adeline the subverter, skulking around with their cynicism while Fairington played the boosters' game. Still, Phineas did oversee the construction of Founders Row and the Fairington Country Club; Adeline still minded the duties of royal hostess and charity leader. A testament to Oswald's admittedly immense powers of persuasion? Even Phineas succumbed to Oswald's idea of a bride, one assumes, since he had no interest in marriage while finding ample opportunity in more seductive quarters than Fairington. Still, he married Martha Wentway, the daughter of the president of First Fairington Bank. She was young, precisely seventeen to his twenty-five. Oswald installed her, too, in the manse.

"Poor Martha. Immediately after the marriage she began, as people said, to become nervous. None of the various treatments worked, and neither did elaborate travel to restful places. Her duty weighed on her. After Worth was born, she got worse; the depression deepened, she became incoherent, and then began the private hospitals."

"'Well, honey, it's beginning to make sense," Roger said. He carefully lit a cigarette to keep his hands from shaking with excitement, or foreboding. He picked up the last blue-veined air-mail letter from Phineas to Worth, as always cheery, as always impersonal, greetings from a distant friend. Many fathers and sons, Roger thought, have a relationship that is more cordial than intimate. But in this case, distance did seem to have meaning. It was always Grandfather who saw to Worth's rising in the morning, his meals, his rides to school, his friends; it was Grandfather who comforted, instructed. In the background Phineas observed, an ironical older brother, or maybe not even that. Perhaps it hurt too much to be even that. After he gave Worth up, perhaps he could not bear to watch too closely.

Oswald formed Worth to redeem himself, Roger thought, but only because Phineas was irredeemable. Why? Not that Worth questioned Oswald's unwavering attention, at the expense of his own father. How could he even have thought it? The affairs between a father and son are so murky under the best of circumstances — how could he have fathomed the troubled coexistence of his father as the son to his grandfather? Also, he loved Oswald so much that to question his own primacy may have endangered it. Call his passion by a name — jealousy — which gave rise to contempt for Phineas's weaknesses and the opportunities he wasted to make Grandfather proud. And then when he learned the truth it was too late to make amends . . .

"Roger — Roger! You're going to burn that upholstery." Lulu, ashtray in hand, darted to the wing chair and retrieved Roger's cigarette, which had burned to the end in his hand.

"I'm sorry, honey."

"If you're going to sit there in a trance and mumble — "

"No. Really, I was just figuring something out."

"Well, are we ever going to get to Worth? All you want to talk about is his old dead grandfather and that worthless old playboy father he never sees."

"We're getting to Worth right now."

"Young Worth Patterson thrived on the education Oswald provided. He attended the public school to learn the town and learn tolerance for the common way; he studied with the tutor to learn the more refined lessons. He traveled with Grandfather, in his private car, to the important cities of the East. At fourteen, he went to Europe, and then enrolled at Andover. And always there was the con-

versation — Grandfather's unyielding survey of the world twice daily, at breakfast and supper.

"Oswald was training Worth, but for what? Often he said, 'For public service, my boy,' with those erect shoulders and solid stride his self-conscious physical model. Then the cliché — 'I am in trade so that my son may be a lawyer and my grandson an artist.' The inscrutable progression, spoken first by Socrates or Jefferson, Oswald was unsure which, convulsed Phineas, though he laughed without elaboration, remarking later that no Patterson had ever been any of these. On Worth's vacations from Andover, Oswald talked grandly of his new interest in the university at Chapel Hill, and he expressed his interest in the usual fashion — with a building and some chairs for professors to teach in it. Alert now to signs of destiny, Worth knew what his next stop would be and what it meant. The Patterson name would be hoisted not on Wall Street or in Washington, at least not immediately, but at home, in the place Oswald had once so urgently tried to escape.

"For all of his irrelevance, Phineas would not leave until the old man died. Perhaps he could not do anything to stop the process, but he could stand guard. He was the one who called with the news — who else would, after all? The flat and properly somber tone over the scratchy long-distance line in the headmaster's office that April day conveyed not only the crushing fact but the hint of a choice that had not before presented itself — namely, the choice to stop becoming what Grandfather had ordained. It was not the message but the tone that lingered; the sense of sadness and of freedom mixed, as though the both of them, the one standing in the bereaved house in Fairington, the other in the motley Massachusetts den, felt to their bones as brothers the death of the master. They wept, and not simply because of Oswald, but because what brought them momentarily together would not last, for they were not fellow travelers to be launched together by this grief, but a father who had made his son unwillingly and given him up unknowingly, and a son who knew too little of these things."

Roger paused and noticed Lulu sitting alert at the edge of the sofa. She stroked her hair, attempting to mask nervousness, but Roger had seen what he feared. The story meant too much.

"That's what you wanted to know, isn't it?"

"What?"

"Whether there is some secret, something Worth can't get past. Something he can't even talk about."

"That's ridiculous."

Roger shrugged. "Maybe. But why did he ask you to do this? Why is it all so damn mysterious? All of the great Oswald Patterson's children hated him. None of them wanted anything to do with him, much less to live in his house in Fairington, a place not even big enough to be a hick town. None of them was the least bit interested in saving the family name if that meant carrying on in old Oswald's footsteps. So what was Oswald to do? He started to build Camelot, but no one would sit at the Round Table. Obvious answer — start with the next generation.

"But even with that, the next generation, you see, there was a problem. None of the other kids would allow this guy to get near his own grand-children. Still, there was Phineas. Phineas, the youngest, the only son, the hope of the race — and he disappeared, after all. Why did he stay in the first place? He may have 'run through his trust fund,' as Ogden says, or he may not have. That wouldn't have been fatal, anyway. He could have turned to his sisters, or his mother, if money was all of it. They would have protected him from Oswald. But what they couldn't protect him from was Oswald's will to make his name good, even if it meant harming what was closest to him, part of himself, really. Oswald had something on Phineas — and he used it. That has to be the answer.

"That was Oswald's strength, you see. He could force the worst things on his own son — blackmail even — because he was not afraid to shame him-self. He would suffer even that, risk it, in order to get what he wanted: our own Worth."

"That's crazy. This is all wrong. How could he even do it?"

"Because he wouldn't quit. He was going to leave a legacy no matter how much he destroyed."

"How horrible."

"Horrible enough. Less so for some. Martha, for instance. At least she could go crazy. But for Phineas — he fathers the boy, and then, according to the bargain, he has to give him over to Oswald and then stay and watch Oswald make him into the redeemer, step by step."

"You've really outdone yourself."

"You mean about Phineas staying? But he would. He felt responsible. Martha cracked up after giving him a son, who he loved. You see, he didn't count on that, either. So he had to stay, as long as Oswald did, and until Worth understood. Then he could leave."

"It was after the funeral and before Worth graduated that Phineas left for Paris and freedom. He left alone. This must have been the hardest part; he could have taken Worth with him and broken the spell. He could have banished Oswald then and forever. Was it another act of abandonment, or an act of love? Or of pure necessity? It doesn't matter. Phineas left because there was no other way, because to vindicate himself for Worth at the expense of Oswald would have equaled the old man's egomania and therefore marked his surrender to him.

"No, there was no other way. Phineas took his own freedom because that was all that was his to take, as the price had been all his to pay. Oswald could not raise his banner on Phineas, for he knew he was irredeemable. But the price of that knowledge, and the price of forbearance Oswald charged the aberrant son, was that the son—for that one crucial moment of essentiality—renounce what he would not renounce and get him a proper son. Oswald would find the vessel, inexperience being a prerequisite. Who could be blamed if Martha's nerves could not take the shock—first of being unwanted, then of being taken but still unwanted. Finally, her self-contempt drove her to a breakdown bed rest couldn't cure. Even then, Phineas's penance was not complete. He had to act the good son, even though he was the bad, and watch as his own son was taken from him to be made into something he despised. Day after day he built the houses and made the golf course, at night hearing the lessons that savaged his heart. True to the bargain, he never interfered in the grand plan. In fact, he recognized himself as so much a part of it, and Worth as eventually so right for it, that, when given the chance when the old man died and he claimed his safely probated inheritance, he still did not interfere.

"So there was Phineas, close to his dream of Paris and life with the valet of family fiction, his long nightmare over, his inheritance no longer held hostage to the demand for a real heir, or that his energy be employed in creating a Potemkin village to glorify his tormentor, or even that he separate himself from the son whom he grudgingly created but loved nonetheless. There he was, alone. At least he shared his aloneness with the only one who understood, who though opposing him was bound to the hidden truth. Now the hated, the other, the father was dead; instead of jubilation, he felt the cold shadow of the last door closing between himself and the truth of the sacrifice of his best years. When Oswald died, Phineas was forty-two years old.

"But rather than celebrate the emancipation, he mourned the captor, officiating in every detail at Oswald's funeral, demanding that Worth's aunts and uncles, disaffected as they were, return and sit in the family pews, summoning Martha *from her repose. They sat in the front row of the stifling church — Phineas, Adeline, Martha, and Worth, Martha humming to herself and looking at the stained-glass panes, unsure as to even where she was, and Phineas gripping Worth's arm, and Grandmother Adeline dry-eyed and tapping her foot impatiently next to him. On and on soared the funeral oration, from the inflated beginnings to the Indian combat, scholar-gentility at Princeton, glory on the railroads and in the House of Morgan, to the founding of Fairington's sweet world — a remarkable story, whether true or not, but the puzzle was in its telling, as Phineas had control of all events and must have ordained it. Periodically he leaned back in the pew and surveyed his three sisters and their husbands and their various children; never had they all been in Fairington together and never separately for more than a day, each having been able, unlike Phineas, to have made their escapes cleanly. Was it for them that the story ran on? Did he enjoy watching them hear it, their otherwise blank and slightly resentful faces arched in wonder as their crude father, who had terrorized them all, became a saint in front of their eyes. That was why he did it, to show them what myth had wrought. '. . . and he gave many of the youth of Fairington the same sound advice that he followed to become a Christian success — "Join a big company," he told them; "Join a big company — big men join big companies . . ."'*

"Maybe it could have been different had Worth been prepared, had he known Phineas would leave. He could have said something, asked him to stay. But even though they were, are, father and son, they were really more connected to Oswald than to each other. Even as the conditions of life with him kept them apart, the conditions of his death — meaning freedom to flee him for Phineas and the duty to become his better for Worth — still kept them apart. So Phineas said, after it was over, 'Worth, I am going abroad,' and in that moment between them he waited for an instant, leaving Worth the chance to say, Stop, don't go, or, Take me with you, or even to ask when he was coming back. But Worth said nothing. 'Before I go' — and the way he said it seemed immediate, and so it was — 'I want to introduce you to Professor Ogden.' And then from the corner of the dining room stepped Tal Ogden, idly holding a glass of punch, wearing a shy but firm smile. It was clear among the three of them standing awkwardly together that Phineas was not simply introducing Worth to Ogden, but rather handing Worth over to him. 'Worth,' Phineas said, 'Professor Ogden is with the university.' Ah, so there it was. Worth's next stop.

"'Mr. Patterson,' Ogden said, taking his hand. 'Your grandfather was a very great man.'

" 'Thank you,' Worth said, turning too late. He looked for his father, but Phineas was gone."

"So — that's your tall tale?" Lulu said lightly, opening the high windows to let the coolness of the rain's end clear the room.

"You know the rest."

"I don't think so." Her finger traced the title page of the old manuscript.

Roger knew she was still angry with him for everything, and for nothing. He promised things would change, but they didn't. Now she had seemed to lose interest even in getting a baby. Making babies had never been among the Albright problems. It was mainly the waste later, in all its forms, that plagued them.

"I can't tell you what you want to know," he said.

"What are you talking about?"

"You really want to know if you should have married Worth, don't you? And you want me to know you're thinking about it. That's why you wanted to hear me go on."

"Damn it, Roger. Just stop. He asked me to read it. I thought you'd help rather than go off like that."

"Great. Next time you two want to go over old albums together just leave me out of it."

"That's not hard since you're never here."

"He didn't even touch you, did he, back in college when he had the chance? And you can't get over it."

Chapter Eight

1950

I T would have had to have been Ogden who sought out Oswald Patterson, Roger thought, as he sat studying surreptitiously the crack in
the hotel room door, trying to read the faces of his worried professor
and the reluctant politician inside. Jeez, it's been forty-five minutes, he
thought; none of these other guys has a business to run. Roger stood
abruptly and began to pace, rebelling against the straight-backed chairs the
Robert E. Lee Hotel had provided for the anteroom to Dr. MacGiver's
suite, the inelegant accoutrements perhaps a reminder that even the august
senator had to pay his campaign's hotel bills. It was May 1938 when Ogden
had taken Worth from Phineas, twelve years, less the war. Always Ogden
seemed to know the next step. He also knew his place before largess. Oswald funded the Institute — or rather, he gave the money to Dr. Ogden,
who funded the Institute and then credited Oswald with having done it, a
gesture that at first seemed modest but now seemed a rather extreme ag-
grandizement, since Oswald would be horrified if he knew what the Institute actually did.

What did anyone really know about Ogden? Roger had known him for
years, yet he could scarcely summon any personal knowledge other than
the vita — born, Milledgeville, Georgia; educated, Hopkins, Columbia,
Heidelberg; professor of sociology, Columbia, U. of North Carolina; executive director, Institute for Progressive Studies. He had a wife, Jill, who
kept out of sight. She was also a scholar, although without portfolio. They
had no children.

Diffident about himself, Ogden was absolutely tenacious about knowing
the Institute men. They were captured in his note cards, each of the ones
he had picked, and they all believed that he had their posts and offices
charted out for years to come. Would Oswald care that the Institute, which

each year turned his birthday into its own grand fete, spent money to organize local "friendship groups" to discuss the relationship between "free enterprise and war making"? I wonder how those little talks turn out, Roger had thought between rounds of champagne at the last birthday bash. He suspected that kind of harmless guilt-stricken knowledge administered by the priests of academe was exactly what Oswald thought would dress up the great name of Patterson. Once, in college, Worth asked Professor Ogden point-blank, "Sir, are you really a radical, I mean really?" Ogden paused, putting on the dutiful face he used with his most important charge. "I believe in service to man," he said. "I believe in leading events." Worth earnestly pressed on: "But, sir, doesn't a leader have to have—I don't know how to put it—a philosophy?" Roger thought Worth had him—a "philosophy," of all things. Ogden even stopped shuffling note cards. "Consider history," he said, turning deliberately to face Worth, which he never did unless he was put out over something.

"'There is a tide in the affairs of men,'" he said. "Shakespeare wrote that. You've got to find the tide."

Worth shrugged. "That's not a philosophy."

Ogden paused, stumped by an unlikely source. "I guess it isn't. Well, let's think. The truly great men—as a rule—led the poor against the rich. Jesus of Nazareth, Julius Caesar, Henry V, Napoleon, Abraham Lincoln, Atatürk. There's a philosophy for you."

One minute Ogden said these things, and the next he was fund-raising among the targets of the revolution. The summer before the class of '42 entered Chapel Hill, Worth spent a fortnight of research in the library attempting unsuccessfully a research report for the Institute. After reviewing a first draft, Ogden suggested that rather than complete "Southeastern Chicken Embryos 1930–37," Worth should join him and travel for a week. They drove to Charlotte and to Winston and to Greensboro and to Raleigh to see the late Oswald's friends, who were happy enough to see Worth; none of them would have otherwise received Ogden. All became habitual Institute contributors, and not a one of them ever complained about the fervent souls passing judgment on "free enterprise and war making," or indeed about any other Institute project. When Roger was a junior, Ogden asked him to finish "Southeastern Chicken Embryos" and sent him a check for the work.

Ogden had a plan for all the Institute men—except for Roger, who had the audacity to plan for himself. Even Dr. MacGiver had a plan. Ogden, no ingrate (gratitude being institutionalized in his business), knew that his power machine only ran with the approval of Dr. MacGiver. By the time the Senate job opened up, the Institute had placed enough people, who had in turn placed more people, all of whom at Ogden's direction had written and talked and puffed on pipes about Dr. MacGiver, so that the governor's appointment was inevitable, an inevitability arranged so discreetly the governor even thought it was his own idea. Roger made no points with Ogden by pointing these things out. Eventually the mention of Roger's name made the ends of Ogden's mustache quiver just so. When Roger delivered Albright Industries' first contribution, the size of it stopped Ogden in his tracks. "My, my, Roger," he said, "very generous. But how will it look?" Roger started, irritated with what he knew was coming. "Look, sir?" he replied. "Yes. When *The News and Observer* finds out that we have such large contributors. In the textile industry." The gaze was so fierce, so full of his special meaning, that it almost sent Roger packing. But Ogden knew just how far he could go. He folded the check and managed to inquire pleasantly about Lulu. Later, Worth asked — at Ogden's request, Roger knew — that Roger do the research on Crain. Ogden never gave up on one of his boys.

"I apparently do not have the luxury of making choices," Worth muttered to Roger outside the candidate's room. So why do you honor the tyranny of the note card? Roger wanted to say but didn't. He knew that the clairvoyant Ogden and his empire passed the results test. A study goes out, the Institute speaks, and roads are paved, cities built, tobacco farmers organize, textile workers strike; nothing surprises, all is measured, the future is in the cards. The other reason, the real reason was that Oswald, or Phineas, had made his choice already and Worth was bound to it. In the best Presbyterian manner, Worth assumed his duty freely.

It was the war, though, that threw Ogden off. He hadn't planned for it that soon, had never expected France to fall so quickly or for the Japanese carrier fleet to be ready in 1941; 1943—that had been his calculation. He had to adapt to his coterie going to fight, leaving others to become politicians. Enter Dr. MacGiver. Reflective, ascetic in dress, morally determined to a degree seemingly impossible for a man engaged in the compromising activity of running a university, he had hired Ogden out of the conviction, religious in origin, that intellect must be harnessed to lift the mass of men. Science, in the broad and ecstatic way he invoked the term, gave intellectuals the capacity to perform great good, and sound philosophy created the moral imperative for doing good. Grateful for the opportunity Dr. MacGiver gave him, and for the higher calling his conviction gave to practical projects, Ogden reciprocated early on by nurturing the president's image, crediting him with the group's successes, and generally making MacGiver the Institute's first public man, a knight who practiced holy science.

Because of the war, though, Ogden needed his beau ideal for more practical causes. Ogden saw to it that the relentless machinery of total mobilization found Dr. MacGiver and drafted his intellect and fervor. Soon he was arbitrating military land condemnations, running coastal blackouts, commanding the Office of War this or that, and doing it all so well and under Ogden's subtle promotion that no one — except Worth and Roger and other recently returned veterans — thought it odd that the governor had appointed him to the Senate. It was Ogden's, and the Institute's, finest hour.

Perhaps to Ogden's surprise, although he would never have admitted it, MacGiver quickly became a senator of national views, a strong leader beholden to nobody, eventually not even to the Institute. As he had done with every opportunity, MacGiver grew into the job, his moral stature filling the ever-expanding rooms of power into which Ogden had led him. Confidence born of conviction was the one thing about MacGiver that Ogden never understood, Roger thought, because Ogden himself never had it. Not that Ogden was not moral; his purposes led to moral ends, certainly. But for MacGiver, doing good was a personal moral imperative, born of a Scotsman's Christianity that was heavier on duty than salvation. That was why, Roger concluded, he had helped the Institute flourish when it would have been easier for him to assume a presidential distance. He had recognized it as an engine for good and thus he was personally compelled to support it, compelled by an imperative outside of ambition, and thus outside of Ogden's logic and control.

MacGiver's independence caused problems. There was, for example, the race question. An annoying part of his morality was the conviction — which he never hid as a university president — that Negroes had been done a disservice by segregation. This inconvenient opinion had caused him to support the civil rights plank at the 1948 convention up to the last moment of public commitment before Ogden had finally prevailed against it.

Even with scares like that from his headstrong former boss and current protégé, Ogden was having the time of his life. He should have known the fun wouldn't last. There was the matter of an election, and it was 1950. There would be no free ride. Whatever his virtues as a public servant, Dr. MacGiver's faults as a candidate had not begun to be plumbed. He was an academic by trade and had by definition done some woolly headed things that looked better inside the university than out, not to mention his heretical views on the great taboo. The other side had finally sharpened its Red-baiting claws on the Institute, and things were getting nasty. They even started a rumor that Dr. MacGiver was a Yankee, which the Institute had to dispel by repeated radio broadcasts featuring the senator's drawl. It would be handled, Ogden thought. The right people would rally and protect Dr. MacGiver, and him.

But it was the war again. Who were the right people? The war made new people, and extreme people, people whom Professor Ogden didn't even have filed on note cards. Joe Crain for instance. Didn't even go to Chapel Hill. Nobody knew him. Yet there he was, from some Down East swampwater town, leading a slick, Red-baiting, Bible-beater crusade against Dr. MacGiver. Crain was everywhere — on the radio, giving newspaper interviews, mobilizing the large youth religious organization he apparently controlled — and he was all of twenty-five years old. As he continued his research, Roger was amazed that someone so anonymous and so young could rise so fast. He defeated the idea of meritocracy and regard for channels the Institute men prized. Perhaps for that reason especially he had the Institute on the run. "You've got to find out about this guy," Worth said to him at least once a day. Roger would, and he assured them that he would; yet, the more he learned, the more he concluded that capturing Joe Crain on a note card would have little effect.

Then there was Narly Ferguson, the ostensible opponent and Crain's boss, whom Ogden had once thought a sensible man. Somehow, something — the war again, maybe — had gotten into Narly, too. Why else would a corporate lawyer, a former president of the Pinehurst Country Club, let race-baiters — the very people who smeared Claude Pepper — run his campaign? Too many chiefs and not enough Indians, Worth said. Men can't wait their turn anymore, Ogden said. All agreed that it was ugly stuff and that Dr. MacGiver was vulnerable.

To make matters worse, new people had gotten to MacGiver and Ogden too, and the Institute men often got shuttled into straight chairs in hotel suites. That slick-talking Ackerman, the Institute men would say, encouraged all of Dr. MacGiver's worst instincts. Delbert Ackerman was a New Yorker, a liberal beyond even Dr. MacGiver, and a tough man. We can be thankful he was never a communist, the Institute men often repeated among themselves. Roger dimly remembered Ackerman in college, an ascetic freshman lurking about the fringe of Ogden's circle, and later, in the weight room, burning off pounds as a bantam member of the boxing team. He had greeted Roger as though they had known each other, and so Roger behaved as though they had. He did recall Ogden mentioning Delbert to him once, in exasperation really, when he had been offered Institute membership and turned it down, citing some vague principle about how the true faith was incompatible with breaking bread beside fat cats. This view, Roger was sure, left Ogden cold.

Ackerman's purity of mind had reached irritating heights in the campaign when he had vetoed any participation by Judith. She had written, offering to organize in the mill villages. Ackerman protested her participation because of her late Party membership, provoking MacGiver, who remembered fondly her civil rights agitations, to a rare show of anger. Still, Roger supposed, Ackerman was probably right in fearing her detection by Crain. Just because you're paranoid doesn't mean nobody's following you.

Now, Ackerman was in the room with Dr. MacGiver while Worth and Roger sweated outside and the press waited downstairs for a statement on what the senator would do about the Willie Simpson matter. "The Negroes," Professor Ogden had said wearily, as though no one listened to his lectures anymore, "The Negroes are next . . ."

"What the hell are they doing in there?" Worth whispered to Roger, who stared at the cracked hotel room door, which seemed to suddenly swell in the liquid ninety-five degrees and then swing open.

". . . I must consider my remarks carefully on the West Point matter, Mr. Ackerman," the senator said. "It is a troubling charge."

Roger could never understand how Dr. MacGiver's collar points, which appeared prominently in the doorjamb, remained at their perfectly acute angle in the midst of disasters natural and man-made, in which category this one most surely fell. The first problem was betrayed by the words "troubling charge." The candidate was not a college president anymore, he was a senator, a senator running for election against a vicious, carefully camouflaged opponent with a strategy that proceeded minute by minute, financed by money that came from nowhere and managed for the most part by people who were from nowhere but who had knowledge of some sort about what would make a certain kind of voter — rednecks, that is — turn out in force against Dr. MacGiver. Add to that a disturbing number of the respectable middle class suddenly devolved to race hysteria by the appeal, and you had a huge problem. Charges were not "troubling," especially when you were dealing with professional slime like Joe's boys; charges were made and answered, the worse they were, the quicker the answer. But instead, the senator sat day after day in his hotel room with a tepid Pepsi-Cola, writing speeches on world disarmament, ignoring three radio interviewers downstairs in the hotel lobby and the supposed brain trust whose members languished and bickered among themselves inside and outside his hotel room.

The door opened wider and Worth jumped slightly to it, bracing it with his knee so not to let it close, almost falling inside as Dr. MacGiver, head bent over his papers, pulled the door open and ventured out with Ogden and Ackerman behind.

"I've gotten the point down, I think. How about this: 'While it is true that I permitted the Negro youth, Mr. Simpson, to sit for the West Point examination, which I am sure all North Carolinians would believe his right in the, in the spirit of American fair play, I did not then, and I would not now actually appoint him to the military academy, as his score, while high, placed him still as an alternate.' No, no; scratch that last part — begs the question, don't you think?"

The brain trust paused. Is this what kept him locked up in his room for three hours? Roger wondered.

"Senator — Senator, again, say nothing, say something about it, but we can't be paralyzed on this," Ackerman advised, sensibly to Roger's mind. "We can only fight on so many fronts. They want to go after you because you thought about appointing a Negro to West Point. Go after Crain because he's a know-nothing bigot. Attack, attack, attack."

The senator's gaze took in the entirety of the hallway of the barren hotel, silencing Ackerman. "I have to address this point, Delbert. It is a matter of principle. It is important that the Simpson lad have a chance at West Point. It is also important that I did not appoint him."

"Well then, dammit — excuse me, sir — what's the point? I don't get it. After all we've fought for — farmers, workers, civil rights, the UN . . ."

"The people will understand the principle, Delbert. The people."

Ackerman strained to keep from speaking, and his large, mobile eyes grew wide as he attempted to contain his frustration while communicating to the others as much disbelief as he dared show, gesturing slightly to Worth and Roger for assistance.

Reluctantly, for Roger could see Worth was angry with Ackerman for once again insinuating himself into the sanctum sanctorum, Worth obliged. "Dr. MacGiver, if I may, we perhaps, as Delbert suggests, need to respond more directly to the attack, perhaps informed by more knowledge about Crain's new men. I mean if Crain is rounding them up, and they really are all from out of state, with centrally funded sources they share with operations in Florida and California — "

"It does seem quite coordinated, I'll grant you that, Mr. Patterson."

"Yes it does, sir, and — "

"Still and all, gentlemen, I feel the matter of Mr. Simpson must be put to rest. We have been slandered, all of us: Mr. Simpson because the opposition suggests that he did not have the basic right as an American to take the test, and us because it was suggested that I appointed him. We must put this to rest." Roger wanted to laugh at the self-imposed futility of his position. Senator MacGiver could evade the charges by claiming correctly not to have appointed Simpson, but wasn't it absurd to have permitted him to take the test if he had no intention of honoring a positive result? What would otherwise have seemed fair play simply seemed weak, and there was no way out of the old drama.

"This is very difficult, sir, a very difficult problem," Ogden said, fumbling in his pocket for a pipe cleaner. "I might suggest first of all that we defuse the situation by referring to Mr. Simpson by his first name — William, I believe it is — therefore, Willie for the press. I think that would go a long way toward reasserting your control."

MacGiver shook his head briskly. "I can't do that, old friend. I know how it pains you to make that suggestion. In fact, that is the worst of this sorry mess. To make Taliaferro Ogden suggest something so — so intellectually painful. No, Tal, I will not do it. The young man has the basic American right to be referred to by his last name. I believe that to be inseparable from his right to take the test. It may be that we forsake an advantage, but I will not call him Willie."

"I suppose, then, that you will not deny meeting with him either."

"Part and parcel, Tal. Part and parcel. I see now what happens when we deal with the Crain type. I have only myself to blame for not issuing more explicit instructions."

"Sir, you are a splendid senator," Ogden said, bowing slightly.

"Oh go on, Tal. By the way—would one of you have this last swallow of my Pepsi-Cola? It's a little warm."

Worth, Roger, and Ackerman stared as one at the ceiling fan that punctuated strategy talk there in the Robert E. Lee Hotel of Winston-Salem. There were so many of them, Robert E. Lee hotels, in the South. Why would Marse Robert inspire hotel owners? Why not movie house operators, or car wash men . . .

"We were supposed to be holding hearings on the India-Pakistan resolution today," Ackerman whispered to Roger. "He knows more about the India-Pakistan resolution than any human being. And here I am. Jesus Christ."

"I think we've got the solution, boys, as painful as it may be," MacGiver said. "It's the only thing we can do. The speech will say that Mr. Simpson has the God-given right to take the examination, as any male graduate of our public schools, but that it is a lie to say that I appointed him to West Point. And I won't call him Willie, and I won't deny I met with him and his mother. That won't be in the speech, though. I'll deal with that in question and answer. It's a tough row to hoe, but I think that's what we have to do. Now I just need to write the speech."

MacGiver opened the door again to let Professor Ogden proceed inside, and then he almost closed it on Ackerman. "I'm sorry, Delbert," he said, smiling. "I guess I did not make myself clear. I need to work on the speech myself. Just be alone for a few hours. I mean with Professor Ogden, of course. I never get time enough to think. Tell Emma I'm here, will you?"

Worth and Ackerman stared at the door, each waiting for the other to renew their sparring. "Delbert," Worth began, "it's not helping that you try to get around every order he gives to get in the room with him and Ogden—I mean it's not just this time. The staff is getting pissed off."

"Staff, hell, Patterson, it's you who's pissed off. That doesn't bother me. In fact, you need pissing off. But that's not really the point. The point is

I have to do everything I can to make sure he wins. It makes more of a difference to me, you see. If Dr. MacGiver loses, you'll go back to Fairington and your little law practice. You'll probably even play golf or something with Winston Galway and your pal Albright here and out of politeness not mention that Galway's a total scab shithead. I can't do that. You see this is war, and you don't have a clue what to do about it. You people kill me, you really do; turned inside out because some Negro kid so dirt poor it's amazing he even had shoes to walk downtown scored well enough to make West Point, and we're going to lose because of that. Going to goddamn lose because of that! Here's a man engineers deals between Walter Reuther and Henry Kaiser so we can build Liberty ships and you clowns are all bollixed up over whether to call the kid Willie or not. And him too, for Chrissakes. Goddamn it, they really know how to push your buttons, don't they? It's like Joe Crain has introduced you to your secret friend, the guy you always set the extra place for at dinner who never showed. Now he's showed, and he knows all your secrets. A hundred goddamn years! A hundred goddamn years! And you're all pissing your pants over whether or not to call the kid Willie. Well listen, I don't give a shit about you Institute guys. You show up here, you know all the fucking answers, to hell with you. I'm with Dr. MacGiver—in Washington, here, every single fucking day. This is my life. And what they're doing to him is killing me. Because, you see, they've got him, too. He's in there, completely paralyzed, turning over their fascist propaganda, talking tomato plants! It's like the frigging end is here! I don't know what to do! I feel like the only goddamn sane person in North Carolina. Listen, Patterson, I'm going in there, and if you or goddamn Albright want to stop me I'd love for you frigging both to try. It won't be one of your frat boy fights. I'll rip your frigging heads off."

Ackerman pushed himself between Worth and the door, and Roger, feeling the fast breath and boxer's muscles as he hustled past, remembered Ackerman in the gym piling more iron on the straining barbells, until the coaches themselves got nervous, and then sweating himself in the rubber suit, turning the hot water hotter, rubbing his skin raw with the crusty towels until the last pounds, last ounces could no longer resist the flagellant. Roger thought Delbert was exorcising the demons that drove him, but that was wrong. What Delbert really was doing was exercising them until they got big enough to use.

"I don't know why you don't trust me, Delbert," Worth said. "I like you. I don't want to challenge your role—"

"Personal likes and dislikes have nothing to do with it." Against Worth's bulk he closed the door and locked it behind.

"I guess that shows me," Worth said. "Ackerman was always a histrionic type. I used to think it was only for show. Now I think he talks that way all the time. Belongs on a faculty somewhere."

"Yeah, maybe so," Roger said. "Why isn't he?"

"Quotas, probably."

Roger shivered. This is certainly a day for nastiness, he thought. Delbert was right about the secret friend. He had come to dine, and royally.

"We still have another card to play," Worth said. "The Pepper business. I really am convinced the key to it is that this is the same bunch that got Claude Pepper—and nobody's focusing on it. That's why Ogden got you for the research. Crain's got to be tied into them. Don't tell Ackerman about it."

"Don't tell Ackerman? Come on, Worth, we're not doing that kind of crap, are we?"

Worth flushed. "I've spared you the internal politics. Better trust me. So did you get the Florida handbill?"

Roger opened the manila envelope with the Albright Industries seal and handed the contents to Worth. "Great," Worth said. "You're the best, you know."

Roger shrugged. "It was nothing. I needed a weekend in Palm Beach anyway."

"Well now we know how he got it," Worth said as he read the cover page of the handbill from the anti-Pepper campaign in Florida. It mimicked to the type size the most egregious Joe Crain broadside, although the doped-up silhouette of a Negro teenager in a plebe's uniform was missing. Below it sat the North Carolina version:

WHITE PEOPLE WAKE UP!

DO YOU WANT YOUR WIFE, MOTHER, DAUGHTER

RIDING ON BUSES WITH NEGROES?

DO YOU WANT DR. MACGIVER'S COLORED BOY

TO GO TO WEST POINT?

VOTE FOR NARLY FERGUSON

BEFORE IT'S TOO LATE!

"Very good," Worth said. "Down to the type. Ogden was right about that. So where does Crain come in?"

Roger confessed that the mystery was still deep. Despite his ability to find fact and detail, to read the newspaper archives, to talk to those few willing to talk, the meaning itself eluded him. Crain just didn't have a past that made sense for his present role. Of course, he could be just as he appeared. He could be a religious enthusiast with a youth following who somehow got himself into the graces of right-wing money men. That was plausible, somehow, except it would be the world then that made no sense, not Crain. That was Roger's fear — that Crain was obvious and the world made no sense.

What was clear was that Crain had some gift of persuasion that mixed politics and religion. He commanded the allegiance of thousands of pubescent believers and their parents, who, one would assume, voted, and who were good for an uncertain amount of campaign money. Charismatic in a sullen way, he had a gift for the key moment, as when he personally led a torchlight march to Ferguson's house to urge his tired candidate not to quit after the first primary.

But why him? How did a nobody run a campaign for Narly Ferguson? The whole thing seemed a charade, yet maybe that was the answer. Perhaps, Roger concluded, only a truly new man could carry it off. The outrageous nature of the Crain attack was completely out of character for the known leaders, and without precedent — unless one counted the anti-populist campaigns of the 1890s, and no one could draw on that example. It all seemed so out of date — rape, pushing ladies off sidewalks, "black outrages," and the like.

"Nobody around here has ever race-baited enough to know how to do it," Worth said for both of them. "It doesn't add up."

"Well, maybe it makes some sense," Roger said, remembering the hillside revival that doubled as a political rally he had slipped into outside Asheville. He had had to sing in the choir to pass muster. "The messianic character of the religious crusader. The total commitment that confounds ends and means. The country club candidate who denies the actions of the hired help. It could mean something. And Crain truly believes MacGiver to be evil, I mean really evil, like the Antichrist — the Christian who serves godless communism, no less. So he doesn't care what he does. It makes some sense."

"Well, let's see it then," Worth said, sitting down again in his hard chair.
"Here? It's long."
Worth shrugged and motioned to the candidate's closed door.
"Looks like we're going to be here for a while. Might as well read."

To: *The MacGiver File, c/o Prof. Ogden, W. Patterson*
From: *RA*
Re: *Joe Crain — Bio, Part I*

Records show Crain's father to be a town alderman of Pockston from 1933 until his death in 1943, winning three elections as a Democrat. Newspaper death announcement in The News and Observer *calls him "dedicated" and "above controversy." (8/17/43.) No records of any controversial aspect of Joe Crain's youth. Can speculate on psychological developments. Resentment of authority figures. Traumatic sexual confusion. Picture dinner table with Father in his shiny black suit and the strict model of his mother, who instills in her only child a Sunday school education to be used every day. Church records show her as mistress of Christian education in the Pockston Baptist Church contemporaneously with husband's city hall terms. At Pockston High School, Joe was moderately successful — B average — in his studies, though not ambitious in his course selection. He played bass drum in the band and debated on the junior varsity team.*

In May of 1940 the Marine Corps began an expansion program at its training base on the New River, soon called Camp Lejeune, fifty miles east of Pockston. (N&O, 5/4/40.) The army also enlarged its training base at Fort Bragg, fifty miles west of Pockston. The citizens of Pockston found themselves dead center between the two huge and growing garrisons. The business community generally responded to the town's geographic fortune by organizing entertainment for the troops to make their fifty-mile ride worthwhile. This breeds the crisis. The town council discovered that its three-man police force was insufficient to handle the young men who came into the quiet town looking for fun. Alderman Crain, who apparently took more personal responsibility for civic order than other council members (the mayor being in the Pacific), watched powerless as Miz Murphy's, Pockston's one house of prostitution, which the police tolerated as long as it catered only to gentlemen, expanded for the new clientele. Indeed, several more houses opened for business nearby, until the basic training command had to caution recruits against the town's "honky tonk district." (Pockston Register, 11/17/42.)

Ill equipped to enforce the law, unwilling to see Pockston turn into a whore-

house, Alderman Crain appealed to the joint military commands, which issued orders for periodic raids, but on the whole the generals seemed content to have a nice little burg to foul up, free from gamblers and organized mobsters and any dangers to the troops more hazardous than the social diseases for which the town's name seemed humorously well suited.

Mrs. Crain may have been worried about her husband's long hours and frequent ill humor, and Joe may have noticed that his father was working very hard, but after all, there was a war on, and everybody worked hard. People walked faster, talked faster, the air itself seemed brighter, colors more vivid. Pockston was part of the big world, and Joe was part of Pockston, and if the soldiers were loud and rude sometimes and if they crowded the streets and bought everything up and turned the heads of all the local girls so that the high school boys had to work hard for dates, well, all that seemed like a little thing compared to Hitler and the Japs. Joe would graduate from high school the following year, and he'd enlist and be a soldier, too. When his father had worked so hard that he had to come home and stay home for a month, not talking to anybody, it didn't even cause much of a sensation, though people were worried, of course. Just a case of bad nerves, they said. He was a soldier on the home front; soon he'd be back in the trenches. Probably he had suffered a mental breakdown. (Interview, Lionel Spalding, Pockston Register, *3/17/50.)*

Joe was not permitted to go downtown after dark. Neither were his friends. Of course none of them could stay away. Before the war, the tradesmen had closed the shops in the early evening hours, and except for the last eight o'clock show at the movie house, and the drugstore that stayed open until nine-thirty, the streets stood still. Now jeeps clipped up the main drag and soldiers walked shoulder to shoulder down the narrow sidewalks. The lights of several new movie houses and restaurants flashed intoxicatingly. Where only the familiar drawl had once been heard in conversation, Joe now heard alien patois. He was fascinated by the talk he had heard before only on the radio—fast talk, boisterous talk, nasty talk. The men themselves fascinated him—their legs and bellies and arms in all shapes, draped in the tan uniforms that grew moist with the nights and rank with their male odors. Often he met new soldier friends and they drove him to the special spots of deserted land where they told him their lonely dreams of Detroit and Wichita or Brooklyn. Most of all the Negro soldiers fascinated him, their glistening cocoa and ebony bodies gleaming in the dusky uniforms, their limbs swinging free and direct, their speech careful, like schoolteachers, not averting their eyes, but brazen in the way that excited him, so forbidden and profane.

On Wednesdays when his mother thought he was at the Methodist study hour and on Thursdays when she thought he was at the Baptist study hour, he was really downtown, taking in with his soldier friends all of the delicious exotic life of the world come home to Pockston. One night after he and a friend had driven to Romney's Point and humid July ran fast within him, Joe heard the sirens and the jeeps full of MPs career down Main toward Cypress Street. His friends bolted from his side, running suddenly alert to follow the mob to Miz Murphy's house. Like a bow pulled to the tension point and no farther, Pockston's armies had exploded. The mob's force pushed Joe onto the porch where the girls sat huddled together, crying, watching the marines fight the army, as the combat seemed at first. (N&O, 7/28/43.) But Joe looked closer and he saw that it wasn't the marines fighting the army at all, but all the Negroes fighting all the white men they could take on. The gruff male cries pulled him to the fight until Miz Murphy yanked him back and held him on the porch. Soon the MPs pounded into the fray, with billy clubs and pistols drawn, and hauled away combatants of both races, infuriating the rest all the more. The crowd gathered storm force, scouring the street in its fury; black on white, white on black, the grappling men feinted, thrust, and fell, their eruption overwhelming the fire truck that arrived in full siren and turned the hoses on the frothing mob. Joe saw his father and the three town policemen run from the city car and wade into the limbs and fists, shooting sawed-off shotguns again and again into the air until the whole mass turned in upon itself, turned all its madness to attack Crain and his men. Joe saw his father go down and come up, go down and come up, and go down again, like a drowning swimmer, until the memory of his disbelieving eyes forever settled in Joe's brain. He disappeared in the bloody crush. The girls gagged Joe's screams and dragged him upstairs to Miz Murphy's room, where she held him between her legs, rocking him in her bed, wiping his tears on her negligee until dawn cleared the streets.

Harold Crain's death was a touchy matter for the War Department. (N&O, 7/30/43; Stars and Stripes, 7/31/43.) Three Negro draftees were court-martialed and one sent to Leavenworth for manslaughter, and though evidence pointed to a white enlisted man, prosecuting him would only have fed the belief that the brawl was a race riot, and the carefully cultivated relations with local authorities would have cracked. Two generals and a full colonel came to the funeral, and the joint commanders declared Pockston off limits to all personnel for six months.

"Or so the theory runs," Roger said, curling and uncurling the onion-skin pages Worth handed back to him. "The Willie Simpson story. The Negro seducer at Romney Point. The Negro seducer at West Point! Willie Simpson climbing over the fallen body of his father. So his attack, and his fervor, is not some strategy, which would be merely despicable; it reflects his pure belief—a much more awful thing—that Willie Simpson must never go to West Point and Dr. MacGiver is evil for permitting the possibility. Hence the origin of Crain's dementia."

"Yes, Roger, very interesting, as always," Worth said. "But what the hell is this about? It isn't research, for Chrissakes. It's some kind of a story."

"That's right," Roger said, pacing. "MacGiver needs a story. You get all these facts and charts from Ogden about every damn thing on earth and you still don't know anything. Believe me—no data will teach you about Crain. He is the antithesis."

"I still don't see how—"

"Just listen up, okay? Crain is terribly guilty because he couldn't do anything to prevent his father's death. He doesn't have anybody to confide in, and to increase his guilt, he's also not in uniform—but that's beside the point. Anyway, he's convinced that he's the reason his father died. Punishing him for skipping Bible study on Wednesdays and Thursdays, not to mention—you know, the nights at Romney's Point. Well, there had to be a reason—a big reason. People didn't just die, not good people like his father. And yet the weight of it is unbearable. He—Joe—his beloved father's killer! Later he found out that his father had also screwed the girls at Miz Murphy's as part of his payoff when business got good. Getting it off with Miz Murphy's girls is what gave the old man his breakdown, probably. So Crain can save his sanity by figuring that it's not his fault his father died, but it was his father's own sins.

"And then, back to race. He figures that the colored and white soldiers fought because colored soldiers made it in the whorehouse, too, maybe made it with the old man's favorite girls. And maybe they liked it more than they liked it with him.

"And so Crain figures that his father not only died because God was punishing him for screwing whores, but that he also died to protect southern white womanhood, and therefore died for honor and the law."

Worth cleared his throat. "I'll have to trust you on this. I see that. You are the ace researcher, after all."

"There's more, you know," Roger said, handing Worth a second memorandum.

To: *The MacGiver File, c/o Prof. Ogden, W. Patterson*
From: *RA*
Re: *Joe Crain — Bio, Part II*

Mrs. Crain, stony-eyed, more alive in grief than she had ever been in happiness, accepted the ten thousand dollars that the army paid her and signed the paper that said she would never go to court to get more. There was one last thing, she said: "You can't take my son for your war. You will arrange it," she insisted. "You will arrange it."

The next day Joe Crain's status changed to 4-F. When he tried to enlist he couldn't. The big world had come to Pockston, and the war continued, but Joe Crain would never see it.

That was God's will, Joe figured, as he tried to understand why he, perfectly healthy and of sound mind, could not fight for his country and avenge his father. He wanted a simple thing — to go off to Europe or to the Pacific and fight against Hitler and the Japs, but God denied him this. Instead of going off to war, as he wanted, he enrolled at little Baptist Caleb College, as his mother wanted. She also wanted him to live at home and drive the ten miles every day to class, but since gasoline was rationed, he did get to live on the campus, in a little room in a little dormitory that was, like the rest of the college, nearly all inhabited by women, the men having gone off to do men's work. Joe took the required religion courses and then business courses. As in high school he excelled at public speaking, becoming the president and one-man broadcast crew of the college radio station and, for fun, doing the play-by-play for the girls' basketball team.

Joe Crain liked Caleb College, liked knowing everybody and having everybody know him. He even liked doing the examinations in the crinkly blue books with the ragged paper they used because of the war. He did not graduate, however; before the war ended he took a job with an insurance agency in Raleigh, and he did what everyone said was a creditable job selling policies door-to-door. But when the war ended and the veterans came home, there suddenly wasn't a job for Joe, no matter how well he had done, no matter that he had sold lots of the whole life and converted as many of the term policies as he could. Out of work, he returned to Pockston to live with his mother, who was becoming still more God-fearing. The ministries of the Baptist and Methodist churches asked him if he would be interested in heading up the local chapter of Youth for Jesus, which, they explained, was a new national organization to take the familiar weekly Bible study of his youth to all the teenagers in the country. Joe said he would try his best. ("Do Politics and Religion Mix in N.C. Battle?" The New York Times, *4/15/50.)*

Soon the Pockston chapter attracted young people from all over, more young people than the tent revivalists or the other preachers combined. In his Sunday suit, Joe Crain told them that they must submit to God's will, that God's enemies were everywhere—in Soviet Russia, in sex perversion, in race mixing—but that with faith and hope and with the help of Wednesday night fellowship they could overcome Satan's troops. There was nothing mysterious to having your life make sense, nothing about the world that submitting to God's will would not allow you to explain and conquer. Joe Crain offered no fire, no brimstone, just the cool facts.

Exactly when or how the big-time guys found Joe Crain no one knows for certain. They probably recruited him. They needed young men whom they could control to fight communism, even in North Carolina. The big-time guys had heard of Joe Crain, and they had lines into Youth for Jesus. Do you have radio experience? they asked him. They sent him to train on the first team, slandering Claude Pepper in Florida. He shone among the green radio competition, even cultivating a tremolo. Crain's first broadcast in North Carolina declared that a vote for Dr. MacGiver meant integration, that his wife socialized with African diplomats, and that when the senator had helped to set up that United Nations he had thrown in with a lot of those same fellows who just gave away China to the communists. Later, when the rough crowd came in strong from Florida, the campaign got really dirty, and they told him he had to follow the formula, he balked. He had nothing against this MacGiver fellow, really. But then it wasn't personal; MacGiver was there and not there. He was Satan's illusion. Satan was the real enemy. Then there was Willie Simpson.

Back and forth across the state they battled, Dr. MacGiver calm and scholarly, pointing out the superiority of his record of public service in the long speeches he insisted on drafting by hand in his hotel room, Narly Ferguson denouncing communism while Crain's handlers passed out the hate mail. For four months they fought, and when election day came, Dr. MacGiver won the primary, with a plurality. Ferguson could call for a runoff, of course, but he was dispirited, admitting defeat to his handlers. Maybe it just wasn't going to work out for him to be a senator.

Enter again the big boys. They had seen this before. Ferguson needed more persuading, the promise of more dirt. They rallied the Youth for Jesus. If the politicians could not make Ferguson see God's mission for him, to save the degen-

erate nation, the children would. Linking arms, Joe Crain and the Youth for Jesus marched on Raleigh, gathering hundreds in their wake, spending nights and taking meals at the mobilized country churches, descending on the would-be senator's lawn to make their draft.

"And the mouths of babes shall lead us," Narly said to the multitudes, or something like that, but Crain didn't laugh; even if the anointed couldn't get his scripture quite right, he walked the righteous path.

"Thanks again," Worth said, folding the Crain memorandum and placing it in his pocket.

"Not at all."

"It's not very scientific."

Roger laughed. "We need less science around here, don't you think?"

"Oh for Chrissakes, I don't know. Now on this other thing, if you've had time. What about the financing leads we discussed—the business groups around the Youth for Jesus, Winston Galway and the textile crowd. Anything on those?"

Roger got up and stretched in an attempt to ameliorate the effects of the straight chair. He hadn't counted on this conversation today. "Worth," he said, "we've got to have a talk about that. I've found that I can't be helpful."

"What?"

"It's much stickier than I thought, and to be honest, the way things have developed, supporting Dr. MacGiver openly is beginning to be an embarrassment. I'll do what I can, privately—"

"What things, Roger?"

"Oh come on, Worth. You saw it today. The way this West Point thing has been handled—the colored boy, you understand. Very sloppy. Who was giving Dr. MacGiver advice? You simply can't depend on Ogden. Image. Image. And permitting Emma to be photographed dancing with the Liberian ambassador. Again, where was his judgment? These things worry me. And Ackerman. The man is in a political race and he takes advice from—I mean, Ackerman? I've seen what happens with Ackerman around. How do you get a word in edgewise? Maybe MacGiver's in over his head."

"You don't give a damn about the Liberian Ambassador. It's Winston Galway who's worrying you."

The subplot is clear now, Roger thought: this is a loyalty check. "That's ridiculous."

"Really? Two years ago I saved your company, and your ass, I might add, from Galway, and now he's your bosom buddy, the son he never had, and all that crap. Don't think I don't see how he saunters around the club with you."

"Goddammit, Worth. You of all people. You know I have to make a living in Fairington. You saved my ass—for which you were well paid, I might add—but I've got to play ball. I need to make money."

"The bottom line."

"You're goddamn right. Something you never had to worry about."

"I don't want to argue," Worth said quietly, straining to smile. "Dr. MacGiver is different. It's like going to church. You do it because it's the right thing to do. So you can look at yourself in the morning."

"Friend, you may not like reality, but this *is* reality. Dr. MacGiver has done everything he could in the Senate to advance unions—"

"Oh for Chrissakes—"

"Yes, unions. Now you listen to me, goddammit. If he had his way I'd be organized right now. I couldn't even get a goddamn shirt packed without taking guff from some shop steward. I couldn't clear the handsome twelve percent we made this quarter. As a stockholder you ought to think about that. And it's not just unions either—taxes, the goddamn regulations from the war, and the trustbusters. Why, the Justice Department is investigating Galway right now."

"Aha—so it is Galway. He's been working on you. Probably bragging about your conversion at the nineteenth hole right now. I bet you're on his Christmas card list."

"This is reality, Worth. I help Dr. MacGiver for a lot of reasons, but business isn't one of them. MacGiver doesn't represent our interests. I include you as a stockholder."

"I didn't invest in your company—"

"Oh, let me finish it for you. You didn't invest in my company to make money, did you? You invested to do me a favor. Because it was the right thing to do. Like going to church. Because you wanted Lulu—"

"Don't bring her into this."

He's tense as a lion at dinnertime, Roger thought as Worth gripped the worn back of the Robert E. Lee Hotel's straight chair. He wants me to fight so he can evade the point, that is, his suspicion of my betrayal. He doesn't even think it odd that he should be instructing me how to talk about my wife . . .

"If you feel that way you can buy the stock back at cost," Worth said deliberately. "I don't want to be a stockholder if I can't see eye to eye with you on the business."

Despite himself, and despite his refusal of the same offer two years ago, Roger paused. "No chance," he said, finally. "You're in the company. You couldn't give the stock back to me. I'm going to make you money. And I'm going to torture you by telling you how I'm doing it every step of the way."

"Well thank you for that," Worth snorted. "If you feel this way, then why in hell did you do that memorandum or whatever you call it?"

Now he looks puzzled, Roger thought. He still hasn't caught on. "I did it because you asked me."

"Because I asked you?"

"Because you asked me. I didn't like doing it for MacGiver. I should be doing it for you. You're the right man to take on Crain and his crowd, but instead you're being the team player, backing up the good professor, doing just every little thing — "

"That's not fair."

"Fair? Jesus. Is Crain 'fair'? Look — don't come back here again asking for help for MacGiver. Ask for yourself. I'll do anything in my power to get you in Congress. But I won't do one damn thing more for MacGiver."

Roger noted, to his satisfaction, that Worth's confusion increased commensurately with the appeal to personal ambition. Surely the thought of his own advancement had not been absent from his calculations in working for the campaign? In any case, Roger knew he would get no answer to his suggestion, as the character of Worth's ambition was both immensely abstract and personal. The introduction of the idea that Worth had some ability to accelerate the progress of his own pilgrimage evidently had quieting power, however, for Worth reflected and then shook his head in mock answer to temptation.

And aren't I guilty of another apostasy? Roger wondered. To assess realistically Dr. MacGiver's lack of appeal to businessmen who cared not a fig for some philosophical program that lay apart from their interests, was also a kind of free thinking alien to the Institute. In fact, the interesting thing to Roger was that something still made him show up and go through the motions when at every opportunity he faulted the program. Maybe they're right in inviting me to leave, he thought, if all I have to give them is bad news.

"You might as well know the rest of it," Worth said suddenly.

"The rest of what?"

"There's something else we need to talk about."

Roger sat up. "What are you talking about?"

"It's, well, it's hard for me to say. Very awkward. Ackerman's convinced —"

"Ackerman?"

"Ackerman's convinced that somehow you're tied into Ferguson's money. I mean, through Galway and that crowd. He doesn't believe — and he has some support in the inner circle — that Crain could raise all this money they're throwing at us. Do you see what I'm getting at?"

Roger decided not to waste the energy it would take to get angry. So I'm a fat cat now, he thought. This is one panicked group of people. He'd never considered himself a fat cat, or a friend of fat cats, but he figured it was a kind of advancement in the world to be distrusted by the likes of Ackerman.

"I've done what I can," Worth continued. "It's ridiculous of course, but —"

"It's bullshit. Total bullshit," Roger snapped. "Give money to Ferguson? Jesus Christ. Tell Ackerman he should try out for McCarthy's committee. This whole campaign is going straight to Dix Hill, you know that?"

•   •   •

"Don't bring her into this," Worth had said, his tone too proprietary for Roger's taste. And then that melodrama about something else he had to tell me. He probably thinks I left because of Ackerman, Roger said to himself. He probably doesn't even know what he said.

Roger ran to his car and sped two hours directly home.

When he reached the door he found a note left for the laundryman, detailing the washing instructions for the sheets bundled at the door. Through the windows he saw more and different furniture than on his last stop home, two evenings ago. He felt strange calling in the day, like an intruder upon the alien stage of his wife the homemaker, a role he had never witnessed. Just seeing the bundled sheets and careful note pierced him in a way he did not think possible, and he wondered for a second if he could learn anew about this strange person he had loved in a fashion for nine years by touching the trussed green wrappings and the careful hand.

"Roger? Roger—what's wrong?" Lulu ran toward him from the driveway in slacks and one of his old shirts with the tails out, a lock of hair over one eye. "I really look a mess—I was just next door returning the floor waxer, you know ours is broken and you really don't use them enough to—I mean, are you really all right, you look . . . tired. Let me fix you a drink. It's after breakfast."

She led him into the house and poured them both a scotch.

"I need to ask you something about Worth."

"My, my. I'm glad I'm having a drink."

"What's that supposed to mean?"

"Oh, nothing."

Roger's heart sank with the failure of what he wanted to say and the intimacy he had too long ago discarded, and he despaired, as much as he could, at the correctness of their future lives and the absence of truth it would require. He knew, too, that he had lost without fighting properly because he never learned the rules. Even though Worth was weak, even though he had set the money and the empire at her feet, Roger knew he still did not measure up to the romance his rival conjured. She waited for him to fight and he wanted to, but the magic was strong and the hour late.

"It's just that if you drove eighty miles—I mean what is it?"

Roger shrugged and lied again. "Worth thinks I don't love MacGiver with all my heart."

"You mean this is about politics? Politics? That's all?"

"Do I really have to have a reason to come home in the middle of the day?"

"All right," she said, her tone suddenly efficient. "Doesn't he know that whatever politics is good for your business is what you'll follow? Don't worry, for heaven's sake. I'll explain it to him."

"Go ahead, if you can. He's lost perspective."

"Lost perspective. Is that so? Nice people don't support Joe Crain and Narly Ferguson, do they?"

"Honey, I don't know what nice people do. Always had trouble with that."

She looked at him with her head cocked flirtatiously, waiting for him to reveal more, but he couldn't say more, not just yet, for he couldn't give in to his true errand. How could he accuse her because of Worth's tone of voice? She leaned over to take his highball glass and he caught in the air the scent of her morning powder and the warmth of her skin, slightly dappled with the flush of their closeness, and then she turned quickly from him and he knew then, by the way she did it, that nonetheless he was right.

He surveyed the sumptuous yet barren house, without children, without books, without well-loved photographs or music or the color of culture of any kind amid its expense. Lulu made this place knowing what I wanted, Roger thought. At all costs avoid the impediments of legacy.

She leaned in the doorway, smiling as she shook her head. "You two. It always seems to be about me, but it's really about you." She held the door open and he left without telling her she had it backward.

Chapter Nine

1950

R UN OFF day dawned still and full with dew and the efforts of those who had risen before the sun to stand by the precincts with posters and handbills, although Roger thought it a particular waste this year, since one thing Ernest MacGiver and Narly Ferguson had in common was that neither had a problem with name recognition. Yet it was what one did, he figured — stand with the placards, pleasantly hailing the straggling voters as would an exceptionally polite panhandler. From his front porch Roger saw the well-turned-out citizens of his precinct walk to the cafeteria at Patterson Forest Elementary School, where their children practiced letters and numbers, called the names of countries on the multicolored globe, and learned proper democratic behavior. On this day they could be late for the first bell to watch their parents vote.

The Institute men still had hopes for MacGiver's election, partly because of the typical optimism that all doubts would be resolved in favor of the good, and partly because the possibility of defeat in the face of such raw evil would mark too great a defect in the peaceable kingdom. Roger had no such hopes. Yesterday had marked the senator's last campaign appearances; Roger attended out of a morbid sense of duty. Dr. MacGiver gave what by now had become a fair stump speech — invoking President Roosevelt, give-'em-hell Harry, the triumphs of the New Deal and the Marshall Plan, ending with his special story about the farmer who got electricity, light itself from the efforts of progressivism. As he concluded to brisk applause from what had started as a skeptical audience, the voice sounded, the same flat tone singed with hate and scorn, the same words deadly as bullets: "Where's your nigger soldier boy, Dr. MacGiver? Tell us the truth about your nigger boy." As had happened a half-dozen times before, in spite of the briefing and the planned ripostes, the senator for a long moment stood stricken before the attack, while laughter, at first hesitant, then rolling through the crowd as a leonine roar, drowned out the county chairman pounding the lectern with the flat of his hand for order. Finally, his voice rising, MacGiver denied the charge, but with an explanation too long and too indignant to have effect. Ackerman pushed through the dignitaries, pulled the candidate from the platform, and elbowed his way to the car.

The road west to Raleigh (the rally, contrary to Roger's amateur yet commonsense view that you always leave them cheering, had been held in the Crain stronghold of Rocky Mount), stood clogged with a reprise of Crain's original march—buses with the painted legends of renegade churches, groups of ten or twelve on foot, dragging banners that called for the election of Narly Ferguson and the redemption of Christian America, a flatbed truck caravan bearing more marchers, water, and sandwiches—that gave in total the illusion, the nightmare, of being caught in a desperate migration in which you yourself had been made a refugee. Nature also seemed to conspire against them. As Worth drove the wordless party westward, the equinox-enlarged sun blinded them all, causing the senator to snap down the brim of his fedora for some protection, and, more importantly to Roger's mind, for the anonymity that would protect them. Carefully they passed through the purposeful infantry, which marked them comically as allies, Worth mechanically acknowledging the waves from the road with two fingers raised from the steering wheel. At the last stoplight before the highway turned into the boulevard leading to the state capitol and campaign headquarters, they stopped in a mass of marchers, one of whom thrust his last handbill—featuring the now-famous picture of Mrs. MacGiver dancing with the robed and unnamed African diplomat—triumphantly into the car the mob finally recognized as carrying their hated quisling. One frenzied man forced his sunburned arm through the open front window, clutching the incriminating paper as though it were a papal bull: "See th-there, Dr. MacGiver! See th-there. We knowed it! We knowed it! Tell us the truth about your nigger boy!" Worth tried to gun the car and run the light, but the gathering crowd blocked his path. "Nigger boy! Nigger boy! Nigger boy!" the shout arose. Ackerman jammed the window against the intruder's arm until he screamed and yanked it free. Infuriated, he pounded on the hood. Still louder the cry grew—"Nigger boy! Nigger boy!"—the mob unaware or uncaring that they encircled the senator's car in the middle of a Negro neighborhood and that their shouts had brought forth a complementary crowd of residents not happy with what they were hearing and not particularly concerned from what context the shouts arose. Still the broadside-bearing marchers massed against the car, pressing the handbills against the windows and windshield as though by their very weight and force they could wound the senator with their question-accusation. Roger felt quick fear as the crowd's angry rhythm caused the car to rock as though in the hand of an otherworldly power; he believed the rocking must be what an earthquake feels like, when the ground moves against all of your expectations and learning. "Don't worry, Dr. Mac-Giver," Worth said, leaning over the car seat. "These are our people. We're quite safe."

Swiftly Ackerman slapped Worth in the face. "For Chrissakes, Patterson, snap out of it. Drive the frigging car. The morons aren't so stupid they won't move."

"You must be careful, Mr. Patterson," MacGiver said. "You must be so careful."

"Yes sir, I will," Worth said as he gunned the engine at full throttle in neutral, which cleared enough of a path to begin.

"I am looking forward to the cottage this year," MacGiver said. "It's so hot already. Emma wants all of you to come to Nags Head to visit this summer. She wants all the boys to come."

At headquarters the first returns had arrived and already the staff's optimism had turned brusque and unconvincing. By ten the radio crews had gone to Ferguson headquarters, leaving a skeleton staff behind. By eleven it was over. Senator MacGiver conceded, pledging his support for the Democratic ticket. At the end he nodded to the remaining reporters as though dismissing his noon class. "Too bad for poor Narly," Dr. MacGiver said, clasping Ogden around the shoulders as they left the platform together. "He let that crowd use him. He'll go down in history this way." "A crying shame," Ogden muttered sarcastically, tamping down his pipe. Ackerman wept, rocking on his heels beside an embarrassed Worth in the corner of the board room, where the precinct returns would be indifferently posted throughout the night. "Delbert," Worth said, holding out his hand, "Delbert." Ackerman shook his head and turned his face to the wall. "Delbert, I'm going back to Fairington now. I can't stay around here. I just wanted to say good-bye."

Ackerman turned quickly and caught Worth's shoulder in his strong right hand. "This is very hard, Worth. Very hard."

Worth nodded.

"You have been my brother through this, Worth."

"Yes—well, I wanted to tell you it was right that you slapped me in the car. It was necessary."

Ackerman looked at him strangely.

"Yes, well I just wanted to say good-bye. Who knows when we'll see each other."

Worth motioned to Roger to join him outside, and Roger knew, as he saw anger replace the awkwardness of dealing with Ackerman, that Worth too had seen the returns from Fairington. It had settled the bet between them, a wager for the corporate soul of the enterprise over which they quarreled. Fairington had voted against Dr. MacGiver, down to Patterson Forest itself, even more resoundingly than the other precincts. But the knowledge that he had been right did not comfort Roger as it usually did. It's like the war, he thought, trying to place the heavy purchase of knowledge he felt; the revulsion at wasted death came over him again, and, like Worth, he could no longer stay in the room where the ballots, like casualties, reproached him mute and irrefutable on the wall. When presented with the choice of a generation his neighbors had made a bad, shameful choice, something more than wrong and less than evil, producing a dull moral ache in the lovely streets. That he had known they would, and even known why, didn't make the wrong less wrong.

"You saw the numbers," Worth said, motioning to the wall and meaning, Roger knew, the returns from Fairington.

"Pretty bad."

Worth nodded. "You were right."

"Worth—it's not your fault."

Worth removed from his pocket a black-bordered picture of Willie Simpson at high school graduation, artfully designed as a wanted poster, a boyish open smile belying the threat his very face now made without even the incitement of a legend. "I ripped this off a telephone pole. In Fairington, by the waterworks. In Fairington, for Christ's sake. The son of a bitch."

"Worth," Roger repeated, "it's not your fault. You did all you could do."

"Of course it's my fault. But it's no use. Who am I to remind them of their duty?"

Roger thought he was precisely the person to remind them of their "duty," or if not that exactly, at least remind them from whence they came and how they had gotten where they were. But it wasn't the time to press the point.

"I've got to go, Worth. I've got to catch the sleeper to Baltimore."

Worth nodded, folding and refolding the noxious poster. "No point really in staying around here. Dr. MacGiver's gone home."

"You'll be going back to Fairington?"

"I'll be going back to Fairington."

Roger puzzled at Worth's detached manner, the lack of *gravitas* behind his irritation. But perhaps this was the true response to Crainism regnant; one part sorrow that the people betrayed him, but another part relief that now he could leave duty behind. The dirty release from virtue could be thrilling. After all, once the peaceable kingdom has been set to war, what good is it to keep up appearances? Thus did Crain also corrupt his opponents.

"How long will you be away?"

"Oh, three days at least."

Why not inform him of my itinerary? Roger thought. It was really a kind of pandering.

Business is to wealth as love is to sex. Both relations are sort of negotiable, a reaping of profits as it were. Worth wants to spend into our moral capital? Why not, Roger thought. Everyone's doing it; just read the returns from Fairington. So Roger saw it happen, remembering the dozen cheap movies Worth would use as his model. There he is dialing the number, saying to himself that he really can't do it, that he'll really go to borrow something — but that above all he just wants to hear her voice, that that's enough, as it always has been in the past. But then he hears the number ring, he sees the light of her bedroom across the fairway, imagines her awake, rushing to the phone. Roger's away and God knows what's happened, she thinks. Now, as she answers, he can't deny it, he has done the thing, set the action irretrievably, and he begins to move with her, her robe gathered, her hair tossed back, her hand on the telephone . . .

"Hello? Roger?"

"Lulu—"

"Worth. What's happened?"

"Nothing. I mean I just drove back from Raleigh. Dr. MacGiver lost."

He sees her move back and forth before the window, the telephone in hand; he sees a burst of brighter light, a match for her cigarette.

"I know. You must feel awful. Roger's not here, he's—"

"I know. I mean—the window, I can see your window—just move to the window so I can see you. Please."

He waits in her silence, and then she stands in the window, cigarette cocked on her hip. She waves.

"This is strange, Worth. But it's kind of fun. What do you want to do now—Simon Says?"

He wishes he could see her face, study the clues to see if he could or should go on—but what's the point, he has to do it, even if she's laughing at him, he feels at that very moment his life depends on telling her.

"I want you to listen to me, Lulu—"

"No fair. First I have to see you."

"Sure." He shakes as his hand moves to turn on the light. He hadn't even noticed he was sitting in the dark.

"I don't know how to say this except to just say it. I need you now more than I've ever needed anything or anybody. I can't live without you. I love you and I'm not sorry . . ."

Yes, that's how it must go, Roger thought as he replayed the scene for the hundredth time, seeing Worth racing across the eighth fairway, his tie flapping in the breeze, the Galway's Scotch terrier baying in the empty heaviness of the spring air, fading behind him into time past, she holding the double doors open for him in diaphanous silhouette, the goddess of the hearth turned whore with another man, or an idea of a man. After night came the morning sounds—the swish of the dew-laden leaves, the faint squeaking brakes of the distant milk truck—and the newspaper dropped on the rough driveway announcing to the citizens of Patterson Forest the victory of Narly Ferguson. It would not announce that Worth Patterson had slept with his best friend's wife, or that many lies would be told about it. The crowd leered and applauded, the free and shameful energy of it overpowering all. "Where's your nigger-boy, Dr. MacGiver?" "Where's your husband, Mrs. Albright?"

• • •

"Ouch. Damn — darn," Lulu said. She looked up quickly, hoping, Roger knew, that Mother Siler had not heard her. Funny how the fear of being caught in a forbidden childhood act terrified her. Perhaps it's a rule that the greater the primary transgression the greater the fear of the smaller, Roger thought. Surely there's research on that. She examined her wounded finger, pricked as she tried to knit the baby sweater of valentine hearts she was incongruously packing for Christmas. Mother Siler bustled on, as always overdecorating the tree.

"Mother, could you — "

"What, dear?" Mother Siler looked up brightly from arranging the Nativity. *For heaven's sake*, she had complained last year, in that intense way she reserved for the most trivial matters, *Mother's hand-carved animals cost a fortune and then you buy enough of them for the Washington Zoo.* She had tried to think of a nice way to get rid of some of the menagerie, but she simply could not summon the will to reassert control over her own Christmas decorating.

"Oh nothing, Mother."

"Are you tired, dear? Here, let me get you another pillow. You've got to learn to use your back, dear. It's not going to get any better until that little fellow makes up his mind to come on out."

Roger noticed that Mother Siler often asked Lulu how she was feeling but seldom waited long enough to hear her response before reminding her that resting the back was the key to carrying babies and then assuming that the baby was a boy. *It didn't much matter,* she had said; *I wouldn't tell her anyway that I feel miserable, that I'm far bigger at six and a half months than I should be, unless, dear God, there are twins, that I can't breathe because the child is up to my windpipe and kicking all the time, and my navel might as well be in Winston-Salem for all I can see of it, and, to top it off, I'm just going to feel like this and worse forever . . .*

"You know that boy is awful big, dear. I know it's a boy, you've been carrying him high."

"Mother, that's an old wives' tale. The doctor says there's nothing to it."

"Sake's alive, what does he know? Has he ever had a baby?"

"He went to school, Mother. For a long time."

"Well, I tell you there's another thing he's wrong about, too."

"What's that?"

"The due date. Two weeks too soon. Mark my words. That boy will be late."

Lulu looked as though she wanted to cry, so Roger quickly gave her a cigarette, which he knew would calm her nerves. She rested her knitting on top of the shelf of her stomach and puffed, continuing as a spectator to the Christmas decorating while Mother Siler tried to untangle the lights. *You'd think she was the world expert on babies, but she just had one,* Lulu had said. *I guess it's the one thing that doing it once does make you an expert. If she doesn't stop bothering me I'm going to ask her if she wants to have this one, too.*

"Are you smoking, dear?"

"What's it look like?"

"You know that the little sweetness—"

"Don't start, Mother. It's an old wives' tale. Smoking does not hurt the baby."

"I'm just trying to give you the benefit—"

"What will hurt the baby is if you put me in Dix Hill."

Mother Siler sighed and set the lights down in a heap. "You're just tired. You need some rest."

"Good idea," Lulu said, stubbing out her cigarette. "I'm going to bed." She held out her hand for Roger to help her up.

"That's fine, dear," Mother Siler said. "Roger and I will entertain Worth. He called, you know. He's bringing over some presents in a while. Just wanted to see if you were at home."

Lulu collapsed back onto the sofa and started to speak, but Roger's firm hand on her shoulder stilled the combat.

Where the hell else would we be but at home? Roger thought. He wondered if Mother Siler found it strange that Worth visited all the time, or if she still tuned out anything she didn't want to think about, citing either her "gift" or the "time of life," which had lasted approximately seven years this holiday season, Roger figured. Coping with Worth, though, was a problem. He was used to having the run of the place, since the master of the house usually didn't show up until Friday afternoon, exhausted, to mumble about the price of cartons and cellophane bags and sleep until Monday morning.

"Worth—well God love you," Mother Siler said. Worth stood in the doorway, taking off his coat.

"The door was open, so I let myself in. Hello Little Mother."

She made a face to show her disapproval at the appellation, but as usual, Roger thought, Worth just went right on. Better pay attention, my boy, or it's the hook for you.

"Little Mother, I brought these for the tree." He produced a bag full of presents from behind his back.

"Worth, please don't call me that," she said sweetly.

"Oh, I didn't know you didn't like it." He set out the wrapped presents, evenly distributed between the silver wrapping of Montaldo's and the candy stripe of Higgins Toys.

Now he's staring at her stomach, Roger thought, watching Lulu put a throw pillow in her lap. Doesn't he know he's doing that?

"Worth—what a surprise. Not spending much time in your law office, eh?"

Amazing, Roger thought, as he met Worth's best Mount Rushmore gaze. Imperious to the end. And Lulu taking it all in without a hint of shame, just exasperation at the inconvenience. *These men have some kind of radar for each other*, she's thinking. *It's plain prehistorical . . .*

"Roger, dear, this bell has been waiting for you!" Mother Siler said, hanging a gold Christmas bell by a red ribbon around his neck. "New fathers have to be belled at Christmas—an old mountain tradition. Nice, nice. Hold still now, bless his heart."

My God, Roger thought, is she in on it, too? I wouldn't put it past the crafty old bag. Probably likes the idea of replacing me with the Patterson bloodlines. I wouldn't be surprised if she schemes with her garden club before it's all over. How would that go? Just after the samovar runs dry and before Clemantha clears: You know, girls, Lulu might leave Roger . . .

"You're right—I haven't been in the office much. Can't bear to repossess anything at Christmas. Just wouldn't do," Worth said, standing up, his hands behind him to hide a package. "Here's yours, old man—open it."

Roger put the small box under the tree. "We don't open until Christmas morning."

"No, I insist. I won't be here, and we won't see each other until New Year's. Besides, you can use it. Go ahead."

"We really don't—"

"Oh, Roger," Lulu said, "go ahead. It can't hurt."

Roger shrugged, retrieved the package, and quickly tore away the wrapping. Inside the box lay a silver cigarette case. He turned the case over, read the inscription, and passed it absently to Lulu, who stood beside him. My goodness, he thought, what a play-pretty. "For the best times. WSP to RPA, Christmas 1950."

"Ohhh my," Mother Siler said. "Lordy. And you don't even smoke that much, Roger. You'll be able to keep that real nice looking. I hate it when they get all stained up and the little flakes get caught all down in the joints."

I wonder if it's enough for her, Roger thought, enough for her right now that she can see us angry at each other, ready to hurt each other over her, and knowing that it will be like this for a long time. *I didn't make you be gone so much, make you stop paying attention to anything but that old company; dammit, you've done what you can do with that old thing anyway. Daddy said he'd buy you out and let you run his company after a while. We'd have more money than we have now, Daddy said. And you wouldn't have to be gone so much. That just won't do? Now what kind of thing to say is that? That just won't do. It's what you say about the wallpaper in your dining room when you want to change it, not when your wife's daddy wants to give you a good job so you can stay home with your family and have all the money you want . . .*

Roger removed the red ribbon and bell from his neck and handed them to Mother Siler. He put the cigarette case in his coat pocket and faced Worth, standing nose to nose. Maybe I should hit him, he thought. That would fulfill Lulu's fantasy. Maybe, for a moment, I could be the hero of the piece. No—it's too humiliating. He caught Worth in a great bear hug, the force lifting both to their toes.

"God love it," Mother Siler said.

Chapter Ten

1951

EVEN by the forbidding standards of the rest of the hospital, there is something uniquely inhuman about this room, Roger thought, extinguishing another of the cigarettes that he barely smoked and didn't like, surveying the stern green paint, cracked in the corners, that rose to an even more threatening color under the fluorescent lights that had been on all night. "Ten oh six," he muttered to himself, checking his watch again. He felt suddenly alarmed that he was the only resident of the fathers' waiting room left after the full house that had gathered and dispersed during the night. He didn't know why he should feel alarmed, though, as speed was not of particular bearing to the result.

The metal doors swung open with the businesslike whoosh that had announced arrivals throughout the vigil. Roger leaped up, as he had during the night, to hear the news of the station nurse. "The only rooster left, eh, Mr. Arkwright?" she said in a dimly accusatory tone, working the chewing gum that was her constant companion to the aft position and tapping her foot to the remembered rhythm of the tent hymns she had hummed off-key for hours. It had been "Throw Out the Lifeline" since around three o'clock.

"It's Albright."

"What'd you say?"

"It's Albright, not Arkwright."

"Uh-hunh," she said, marking with a mechanical pencil some unknown category on her clipboard. "That's your business, I'm sure."

"Any word on Mrs. Albright? I mean, it's been a long time, hasn't it? I mean, I don't know, but it seems like a long time — and all the other guys are gone, you see."

She stared at him as she removed a yellow-wrapped piece of gum from her pocket and in one motion transferred the old Juicy Fruit into the foil and replaced it with fresh stock. She tilted her head far back to savor the first flavors. "Mr. Arkwright," she said, "the Lord has His time. We can only serve the flesh. It is the Lord that has His time."

"Albright."

"Sure. Mr. Albright."

"Are you saying something's wrong—with the baby?"

"No, nothing's wrong—with mother or child. It just takes time. The Lord's time. If you have something to say to the Lord, Mr. Arkwright, you might walk downstairs to the chapel. It's never too late—not even at this hour—to get right with Jesus. There's a minister there, too, of all religions. Baptist, Methodist, all of 'em."

Roger drew himself to his full height. "Madam, when I have something to communicate with Jesus Christ, I typically do it in the privacy of my own house." When he said it he knew it sounded ridiculous, but something about the woman—or the time—put him under siege. The marginality of him to the enterprise (which had been reinforced all night by the men's segregation and the bare tolerance the woman had afforded them when informing them of slight events such as the births of their children) imprisoned him. Ah, freedom. He wanted it—and recognition. He deserved it. The vigil has drawn me closer to the life of the child, a boy, I am sure now it will be, he thought. By God, that boy is mine and no sadistic religious bureaucrat will take him away.

She nodded over her clipboard and the odd white pirate's crown that the hospital had adopted for hats should have, by the laws of gravity, fallen off, but it didn't. Pins, Roger thought. By God, they're full of tricks. Her eyes retreated into hooded flesh, far back into her head, until she became a phantasm of authority wholly renegade, a factotum of the high seas capable indeed of holding them all hostage for the voyage's duration: Lulu, the boy, him, all in the cabin under her complete control until her vengeance was exacted. "If it's me you want, then take me," he muttered. "But leave Lulu and the boy alone."

"Beg pardon?"

"I said, thank you for your advice about the chapel."

"That's your business, I'm sure." She clasped the clipboard to her trussed-up bosom and pushed through the double metal doors.

Vinson, he thought. She reminds me of old Vinson, all of the old top kicks really, except Billy Roy. Never could find a sergeant who approved of me. They cursed the army, but they meant me; ninety-day wonder, that sort of thing. Maybe they could have done better without me. I don't think so. The army tried to kill us, but I kept control. That was the key then, control. Couldn't save them — God, what were their names? Spivey, Henson, Matlock — just a boy really, Matlock, his mother wrote back that he was sixteen. And I was all of twenty-four. Couldn't tell her that. But I kept control. I kept control even over this . . .

Roger checked his watch. Ten-thirty and still nothing from Worth. Worth had insisted on knowing when they went to the hospital, and Roger had tried to reach him at the club and the office before giving up.

At bottom, Roger believed, despite the hurt, that he benefited from Worth's betrayal. It was a necessary act of ordering, he convinced himself. Once again, Worth had come to the rescue, although unwittingly. By forcing matters with Mrs. Albright, he had made Mr. Albright campaign to get his wife back and produce a child, a campaign he was determined to win. For whether Worth knew it or not, it was clear all along that Lulu would stay put given half the chance. Roger knew she had long ago made the choice between them for reasons good and sufficient to her.

Though the end seemed satisfactory — a baby for Lulu, an heir for Roger, the old fandango for Worth, a marriage perversely back on track — that still did not in Roger's dark moments satisfy the question of why she permitted it. Was it reason enough that she and Worth had never settled things between them? That Roger had ignored her like an idiot? Or was there any reason at all? Roger believed there had to be a reason; you just didn't do these things on impulse. Whatever the reason, the fact was she had permitted it. He believed, though, that what she had permitted was not really the man, but the act. She had permitted Worth in particular because he was the only other one she could imagine doing it with. It might not be pretty to think about, but it was logical. And she said it ended there. He took her word for it. As for the child, he would have to take her word for that, too, as every man did in the end.

With a whoosh the double doors opened and through them walked Worth, erect but bedraggled, his suit jacket under his arm, a somewhat smashed hat perched cockeyed on his head, eyes wide from worry or fatigue or both.

"Is it, I mean is she, or they—"

"No, not yet."

"How is she?"

"Okay, I think. They don't tell you much around here."

Worth began pacing, or rather circling, in the small room, fumbling in his pockets, retrieving an empty cigarette wrapper. Roger gave him a cigarette and lit it for him.

"Thanks. I ran out around Richmond. Funny place to run out, don't you think? Had to drive from D.C. Got your message—thanks, by the way—at court. Damn hearing ran on. Then what a damn comedy of errors—planes socked in, no fast train, so I rented a car."

"I didn't know if you'd gotten the word."

"I know, I know, I should have called. But I was convinced that the very moment I took to call would be the moment—you know."

The doors whooshed open again and the nurse appeared, scrutinizing Worth. "We don't have any new hens in," she said with the usual air of command. By now a veteran, Roger knew exactly what she meant. She was accusing Worth of being there under false pretenses.

"Don't think he can handle it alone, do you?" she said, nodding in Worth's direction. "Well, you're going to have to leave. Only the father can stay."

Worth picked up his hat and coat. "I understand. Roger, you call when—"

"You insolent woman!" Roger shouted, causing the doors to vibrate slightly. "Do you know who this man is? This hospital is named after his mother. His trust pays your salary."

"Roger, for Chrissakes."

"Dammit, Worth, I'm tired of this crap. Now Nurse whoever you are, this man stays," Roger said, pointing at Worth. "I don't give a man, or a dammit, a damn, about—" He made a flourish in her direction to end the sentence.

The nurse stared at him after he spoke, her arms folded across her chest, chewing her gum languidly, working it. A smile attempted to break through, but she beat it back. She is enjoying this, Roger thought.

"That's your business, I'm sure," she said with a renewed bureaucratic tone. "Only Mr. Arkwright can come back now. Mr. Arkwright has got himself a son."

Roger bolted after her, leaving the doors swinging. He collided with the nurse as she stopped before the room in which Lulu and the boy lay resting;

he did not listen to the directions she gave, even when she tapped his shoulder with the clipboard for emphasis. With a final shake of her head she walked away.

As he moved to the bed, Lulu saw him and smiled, turning her head to the boy who lay moving rhythmically, up and down, on her chest, his bristly, matted hair black against the tiny head, his wrinkled face having no complete human expression but all of them, mixed, in the first hour in this strange place. Lulu lifted him to Roger, and the boy stirred under his tightly wrapped blanket, opening one eye, and then crying the softest cry, a cry that Roger knew must be the strongest and only voice the boy could make. "Boy Albright" his wrist tag read. Roger held the boy to his chest, his son's head resting above his beating heart; the crying stilled, and with it the room. I had no idea, Roger thought as he cradled the boy. He felt the child's tiny fist relax against his chest. Gently he smoothed the boy's hair. "He's hungry, I think," Roger said.

The nurse had disappeared. "It's against the rules," Lulu said dreamily. "Nobody's supposed to be here." She lay back and held out her arms. Roger placed Boy Albright on her chest and his mouth found her breast. I had no idea it would be like this, Roger thought. So many important things he already knows.

We've got to go ahead now, Roger decided, the plan he had absently considered taking immediate shape in the figure of Boy Albright. Yes, he resolved; we must go to New York. The business demanded it.

"I love you very much," he said, kissing Lulu. She pulled him to her with one arm and he sat down on the bed and cradled both of them.

•   •   •

Four days later Roger called Worth to ask for a meeting. He showed no sign, no anger. He had waited for the natural world to take its course, and now that it had, men could make their mess. He heard the doorknob, left unlocked, turn easily and Worth walk into the house that now seemed filled with the life that had been absent before. He knew Worth would sense it powerfully, the life, and with satisfaction he saw in Worth's face that it struck him as a fist. "Back here," Roger called. He heard each step, so deliberate as to be on tiptoe, past the fireplace, down the hallway's Oriental runner, over the threshold, and into the study. "Throw your jacket over there. I'm just going over these certificates."

"Certificates?" Worth repeated. The anxious tone pleased Roger more than he liked. He had tried to reject emotionalism, to rationalize the best case, to solve this problem as he had many others, but in truth he enjoyed revenge. He had circled Worth for months, aware of where he was, imagining when Lulu left the house alone she met him; listening when she answered the telephone for that tone that meant he was there, or going to be; analyzing every phrase, every look, for favor lost or gained. The openness of their lives was a public blessing—scandal would not follow the sighting of Mr. Patterson escorting Mrs. Albright—but it was a private curse. Unable to absent himself, or to banish Worth, Roger suffered in double measure.

So the counselor's query, in Roger's jealous state, indicated a common and uncomfortable knowledge of what form his retribution would take. The stock. How would one of Worth's rambling legal documents—God knows, Roger thought, I've seen enough of them—recite the matter . . . *WHEREAS, on February 28, 1949, Worth Patterson gave thirty thousand dollars—or, technically, bought thirty thousand dollars' worth of stock in Albright Industries, a company being strangled in its crib by its chief competitor, Winston Galway; and*

WHEREAS this sum now represents one-fourth of the capital of a twelve-million-dollar company, and therefore a lot of serendipitous money; and

WHEREAS the above-mentioned Worth Patterson has slept with the wife of the above-mentioned Roger Albright; and

WHEREAS Roger Albright demands satisfaction, in some way other than divorce, which he has rejected as being of no help to anyone.

NOW, THEREFORE, in order to make things right, the parties promise:

THAT Roger Albright will redeem the capital stock Worth Patterson owns in Albright Industries for three million dollars, it being forever agreed by both parties that such price represents the fair market value of such stock.

IN WITNESS WHEREOF, done this 15th day of March, 1951, by the parties setting their hands and seals hereto in the City of Fairington, County of Essex, State of North Carolina . . .

"Worth, to get to the point—and by the way, I'm glad you were able to be with us the other night. It meant a great deal to me, and to Lulu. But, as I said, to get to the point, what I wanted to discuss is my, let's say, reconsideration of your offer regarding your stock."

"What? You mean after the Galway thing?"

"With Brent now—that's the name Lulu and I picked, for my mother.

The middle name, is — I mean we were under a lot of pressure — Pettigrew; shit, how I wish I didn't have to hang that on him. Anyway, I'm calling your stock. I believe your offer last year — most generous, I might add — was your cost. Thirty thousand, I think. I plan to register the shares in Brent's name."

"Under your control."

"Of course."

Worth wouldn't argue with him over the money, Roger realized, disappointed. Maybe this is really too abstract a game, he thought. Maybe I should just threaten him with a gun, or maybe with an open razor as the Puerto Ricans do . . .

"But I can't buy it from you at your cost, Worth. You supported me when I needed you. Our darkest days. This is really founders' stock. So I've had it appraised for the market value. I hope my personal check will do."

Roger placed the check in Worth's hand and watched for the one expression he craved — incredulity that the amount typed in alternating black and red was really three million dollars — ten times, no, one hundred times the original investment!

Roger walked from behind his desk and put his hands upon the high back of the Queen Anne side chair, trying to find the right vantage point from which to savor the moment. "Worth, old buddy, I realize that you must be taken a bit aback by the amount. I know that your original investment was love money. I try to repay in kind."

Worth pushed the check back to the center of the leather-topped table. "I can't take this, Roger. I would rather sign over the stock to you, or make it a gift for — for Brent, than take any of this money."

Damn you, Roger thought, angry that he was angry and that Worth could see. This was the one interview he hadn't rehearsed. He had forgotten that Worth was one of the few men on earth who could refuse three million dollars.

"But Worth, you don't need to think of it as a personal deal. Give the stock back to the company, and I'll retire it. Treat the payment as a political contribution. You'll need money to run against Bailey."

"I'm not going to run against Bailey. You know that. It would be a presumption on my name. Bailey isn't even doing a bad job — "

"Oh, bullshit. Bailey is a has-been. Ogden's already planning it."

"I've told Tal at the very most I'll be running for a judgeship. Hell, I could run for president on this money. What did Dewey spend last time?"

Roger stood silently by the window maneuvering the venetian blinds, fracturing the late afternoon sun over the desk between them, still marveling at Worth's ability to shrug away the cash, content not to argue but to let the reality and the power of three million dollars work. The money served a most eloquent command. Forget normal acquisitiveness, Roger thought; how could he honorably resist? As a lawyer he should understand the equity: once love has passed away, it's money that's left to pierce the heart's bottom line.

"And I'll tell you another thing," Roger said, closing his leather case and placing it casually into the open drawer beside him. "We're moving to New York next week. Got to stick close to marketing now. I don't think we'll sell the house just yet."

Roger had saved this blow, and even as he was disappointed by the failure of his check to exact the reaction he hoped, he was satisfied now to see that Worth looked as though the earth had opened beneath him. This was indeed the *coup de grâce*. Taking them away was the worst thing, and Worth was already in grief.

The screen door creaked open, and then the front door; outside Lulu's laugh echoed into the foyer and through the house. Billy Roy chortled as he set down her suitcase, preparing the passage for mother and child.

"We've got the bantam to bivouac, Boss," Billy Roy called. "And he's hungry." The tiny cries of little Brent filled the house, and for a moment all was still.

"Should I bring him in to you, sweetheart?" Lulu called.

"No, no. I'll come out. You shouldn't move around so much," said Roger, jumping up quickly, looking past Worth and smoothing back his hair as though life's audition waited in the next room.

Chapter Eleven

1951–52

WHAT bothered Ogden more than anything else was that Ferguson's people had broken the rules. Even the rantings of Bilbo annoyed Ogden less than Crain's stratagems. Bilbo, after all had been said and done, was a rogue; he didn't believe in another purpose for the racism he employed except to elect himself to a nice job. Crain and his national advertising squad, on the other hand, employed race as a means to obtain a proxy for their causes — namely Ferguson, a man who had long since ceased to own anything he possessed.

That aspect of true belief disturbed Ogden a great deal. The Crain people, who had no birthright to racism (except for Crain himself, who apparently did), used it to further an agenda and by so doing destroyed an equilibrium established for the greater good. No matter how much one believed something, there was, before Crain, the feeling that there were things you just wouldn't do to be elected. Because Crain believed himself to be so right, there was nothing he wouldn't do.

All the more important to accelerate our program, Ogden resolved. In Ogden's view, a shadow malevolence had arisen, one that fed on ignorance as the Institute extolled learning; that appealed to irrationality as the Institute relied on facts. Most incredibly, as predatory as Crain was, he believed his ruthlessness to be justified by faith in Jesus Christ.

On the practical side, Ogden admitted that MacGiver had been a miscalculation. One thing dangerous to overestimate was how success in one field would lead to success in politics. It was the war, really; the war had made everyone lose perspective. If Worth had been around, then the lineup would have been different. Worth would not have been ready for the Senate, of course; still, his advice, and Albright's probably, would have been not to run MacGiver but some less pure soul more difficult to spook, the kind of safe and honorable mediocrity that had been doing the party's business for the fifty years since the last race bloodletting. Such a man possibly would have won. He wouldn't have been caught up in the horror of the Willie Simpson attack; he could have deadened himself against it. Perhaps the attack wouldn't even have been made, Ogden thought. Perhaps the ugliness of it would not have taken hold without MacGiver's vulnerability.

In any event, they had to press on. These problems couldn't be solved in the laboratory, that was clear. If some variables came forward that weren't theoretically obvious, the Institute would simply have to improvise. What method was without its crisis points? To deal with the malevolent and the unexpected required a superior leader — even if that attracted the most hideous opposition. The younger men were restless with MacGiver to begin with. Well, now they would have their chance, he resolved.

Ogden recognized the disarray of the moment as signaling an opportune time for change. He was not blind to the friction between Worth and Roger in the last days of the campaign, which he attributed to the natural strain and also Roger's assessment, accurate as it turned out, that Fairington would vote for Ferguson. What better way for Worth to redeem the situation than to stand for Congress from Fairington's district? The obstacle was Ford Bailey, an amiable sort who had served five terms and looked quite comfortable. He was not an Institute man, but he was a good politician of the courthouse type. He had already heard Worth Patterson cantering up behind him. Ogden thought Bailey might be amenable to an early retirement if placement in a lucrative Washington law firm — quite a plum for an old slip-and-fall man — could be guaranteed to enhance his capital style of life. There would be adequate reasons: he had served a good spell, his wife had tired of it, he could make enough money with the firm to retire more than comfortably. Ogden knew how to help a man keep his self-respect.

He did the deal quickly. Bailey even seemed relieved in some way. Although Ogden left the matter unspoken, Bailey assumed all along, and correctly, that the appointment was being engineered for Patterson. He admired the young man for having such a classy bagman as Tal Ogden. In fact, things were arranged so quickly that Ogden feared he had overreached himself with the governor. He had to scramble to obtain the necessary commitment before the story surfaced. He even had to make it up to the governor for his inconvenience in a way he seldom did — by promising money. After the MacGiver affair, he feared the Institute's informal fund-raising would be tapped more often; such were the wages of lost campaigns and credibility. Still he persevered. All of these difficulties made more obvious his earlier conclusion that the younger generation's time was now.

Worth, he suspected, would resist the idea of taking Bailey's seat if he thought there was cunning in it. Roger would not have the same scruples, or, as he would put it, self-doubt. That was part of the difficulty in all this, Ogden thought. The boys could usually be prevailed upon to influence each other; what the one didn't understand, the other would. But now for some reason they'd had a falling out. He didn't even get a call from Roger before he moved to New York. In fact, very few people knew. To move your family at the drop of a hat to New York? With a new baby? He thought it highly erratic. In public he passed it off as shock, a sorting out of things after the MacGiver campaign. Some people took to their beds, he would say; Roger is so energetic, he needs a new environment. His business, you know. He is an example to us all, and so on. Privately he believed it to be serious, and a mystery. Only Worth could know, and he wasn't saying. All of this would make it more difficult with the Prince, as certain wags on the faculty now called Worth — not referring to Machiavelli, but Hamlet.

He could hear the tiresome conversation now. "I'm not going to take Bailey's seat from him . . . a judgeship at the most . . . I will not presume upon my name . . ." If only, Ogden thought, if only I had a candidate who wanted to hold office for once, instead of preside over faculty meetings, or get rich, or debate over casting himself upon a sea of troubles.

So he was, to say the least, surprised at Worth's attitude. "I'll take it," he said, simply, before Ogden could get in the front door, much less make the proposal.

"Say what?"

"I've heard. You're not my only source in this business, Professor."

"What've you heard?"

"Oh, everything. Now don't just stand there, come in . . ."

So much to Ogden's delight and surprise, Worth took immediately to the idea of being a congressman. In public, Ogden attributed his vigor to the righteous outrage of Crain's victory generally, and the Fairington boxes specifically — in short, the desire to reclaim holy ground. The fact that the favorite son had popped his head over the foxhole bucked up the troops considerably. In private, however, Ogden was baffled. After MacGiver's loss, Worth's useful outrage had lasted around three days, and then he had sunk not exactly into depression, but into disengagement. He had announced a month later he was interested in boats, and when Ogden had come for his fortnightly dinner, the house was littered with yachting brochures. Nothing came of it. He spent much of his time, Ogden gathered, around the house, or at the Albrights' house, often not even bothering to put on a tie during the day. Some afternoons, it was reported, he appeared at the floating poker game in the Men's Grill at the club, clad only in a towel after his shower, with fistfuls of twenty-dollar bills, which he cheerfully lost.

Burying himself in work, like Roger, would have been the decent thing to do, Ogden thought. Even a depression would have been better. Taking to one's bed could be dealt with. But this aimless, giddy behavior — what could one make of it? Time had been Ogden's only hope. And time worked! Thank you, Ogden muttered, to no deity in particular. Finally, some good luck.

The date of the appointment had to be coordinated to fall past midyear so that there would be no special election before the 1952 campaign. The press generally received the news enthusiastically; the appointment merited more comment than usual in *The New York Times*, which noted that barely six months had passed since Narly Ferguson had taken his Senate seat before his defeated opponent's protégé moved to the House. Bailey gave every indication of becoming a happy lobbyist very quickly; he was barely remembered in the Cannon House Office Building after the porter removed his leather desk chair, which custom permitted him to keep.

Worth moved to a townhouse flat on Capitol Hill, leaving the Fairington house open for weekends, though he seldom made it back. He liked the townhouse so much that when presented the rental contract he bought it. Without any introduction beyond his acquaintance with fellow navy PT boat skipper and bachelor Representative John F. Kennedy of Massachusetts, he soon became a favored dinner partner for capital hostesses. With his easy wealth, self-effacing charm, and young but distinguished good looks, Representative Patterson found himself quickly in the gossip columns and was actively targeted by social spinsters in cave-dweller society. One of those, Miss Mandy Scoville, whose parentage in the government service extended to the Buchanan administration, was especially diligent, and her campaign of small soirees, string quartets in various rotunda, and afternoons à deux in diminutive sailing craft putting out from Annapolis surprised even the hopeful with quick success. Following first seatings together at Thanksgiving dinner parties, the congressman proposed, and she accepted, barely in time to get invitations out for a June wedding. Contrary to Mandy's fears, the National Cathedral was booked in time. Roger arrived from New York to be best man, but Lulu and Brent did not make the trip. In Roger's vague telling, one or the other had taken sick, and all agreed that both should stay away from the heat that week. In the summer of 1952, air-conditioning was employed in the District of Columbia only on rail cars transporting beef; for humans, Washington remained a feverish encampment.

•   •   •

Seeing Worth married should have relieved Roger, but instead it provoked resentment, not especially at the event itself, although he found Mandy Scoville as supercilious a woman as God could put on earth, but because their apparent happiness together—and they were at least apparently happy, Roger concluded after hard scrutiny—seemed undeserved. Just two years before, Worth had been carrying on with Lulu, and Mandy had been scouting different quarry. Some people are just more emotionally nimble than others, he decided.

It was not exactly true that Lulu and Brent had taken sick; they were away because Lulu had taken to being bored, or disaffected, and had lately started to do something about it. Part of her new game was to remove the boy and herself to Fairington for several weeks at a time. This evidenced her displeasure at living in New York without the necessity of having a conversation about it. Brent made Lulu more independent, not less, Roger saw; he was now her constant companion, and the two of them had little need for Roger, really. Lulu had taught herself to live alone while Roger deserted her; now she didn't have to live alone—she could live with the boy, and he could live alone. This was not why he had brought them all to New York. The reason he had brought them there, apart from the evasive purpose, was to create a family, which he suddenly wanted. Once there, however, he saw that he didn't know how and that Lulu wasn't in the mood to help. He didn't know what he had done to make her shun him, or how to make her stop, or if he wanted to. What he did want was the boy, and she took him away whenever he woke up. Roger felt overmatched at this game. He didn't even know what game it was, much less how to play; it seemed that Lulu, maybe all women, not only knew the game, but was good at it.

While the disaster of his domestic life dragged on, business couldn't have been better. In a perverse way, each tracked the other, passing on axes of ascent and decline. The New Man shirt had exploded on the market Roger had envisioned — the newly busy businessman who needed that mass-produced high-class look, with easy-care fabric for the wife. The facsimile was what he wanted, not the real thing in laundered shirts. Because if he just looked the way he was supposed to look, it wouldn't matter that the product was slightly bogus, especially with the classy advertising in full color now blanketing the better barbershop magazines. William Holden for New Man shirts in *Esquire* — that moved some units. Lulu stayed home for that party.

The ironical thing, Roger thought, was that now he had time for the things he had earlier neglected; now he did come home for dinner, didn't travel so much. That was a virtue about New York — people came to see you. He wanted to be a Family Man as much as he once wanted to be a Carolina Gentleman, an Officer in This Man's Army, and a Galway Traveler. Yet he was stymied at every turn by his mysterious wife. How could she be angry at him? he wondered. She had had the affair; he had forgiven that. She wanted a baby; she had that. She wanted him home more; he tried, and he was. It had meant moving to New York, but the objective was accomplished. What more could he do?

On those evenings, sitting alone, waiting for the missing element to come to him, then waiting for anything to come to him, finally succumbing to Mel Allen on the radio for the Yankees again, he often came to ponder the nature of cause and effect. Before it hadn't bothered him, because he thought it all of a piece, one thing leading to the next — learning from Ogden, befriending Worth, courting Lulu, the war, the business, the marriage, the money. But what if he hadn't taken that route? What if he had stopped at that first thing, learning from Ogden? And what if he had never given up Judith? Except for the war — and that was a different matter entirely — he remembered that summer with Judith as the most vivid time of his life. He fought that conclusion, fought it with as much will as he could summon, because not to fight it would be to admit that his marriage had failed and that his life otherwise, of which his marriage was a part, was a vast mistake.

The price seemed too high when he stopped to ring it up. Knowledge turned to money, love turned to advantage; all day long he talked to strangers he employed, and at night he sat alone in a Park Avenue apartment listening to the radio. His life, this constructed thing, seemed impenetrable. He didn't remember when he had chosen it; the beginnings seemed so near, like yesterday, even the war, even college. But it was a long time ago, years ago.

Roger began taking long walks in the city on the nights Lulu and the boy were gone. He often wandered north to the Upper West Side, and then farther still to Morningside Heights. He knew from Ogden that Judith was at Columbia, and he thought by walking up Broadway he might just bump into her without seeming to want to, and then she might bump into him the same way and it could be accomplished without either one seeking it out. Sometimes he stopped at the West End Bar, where the jazz he liked played every night, and he imagined her there, too, because she loved jazz and that's where she would stop after a conference about this or that finding, an afternoon in the stacks; she could eat supper at the students' buffet and relax.

At the bar he saw her a dozen times, he thought, before the night when he finally did see her. She appeared from the shadows of the place and stood at his side, brushing against him lightly as he drank and dreamed of her in an apparition of women at the back of the dark room.

"Roger?" she said.

He started, not knowing fully whether he was awake or asleep, done in by the beer or the heat. "Is that you, Judith?"

She laughed. "It's me. What are you doing here?"

"I like jazz."

"I mean in New York."

"We live here."

"Oh. Where's Lulu and —"

"Brent." He waved his hand in the general direction of Fairington. "Gone."

She stood by him, her hand on his shoulder, talking and sipping at his beer. They traded compliments on how well the other looked, expressed amazement at the passage of time and the current meeting. He wanted her to join him, but she couldn't, pointing to a table at the edge of the room, where others sat, students it appeared, and one older professorial gent who seemed to be holding court. "Later then?" he asked, and she shook her head, seeming to make her mind up about something. "Be at the Long Island Railroad ticket counter at ten past eight tomorrow," she said. "Bring your bathing suit. And a towel."

"A bathing suit and a towel?"

"Roger," she said, squinting through the smoky confines of the bar as the evening's quintet began the first set of the night, "tomorrow's Saturday. It's very hot. We need to go to the beach."

At the station the next morning stood a line of would-be beach travelers waiting for tickets, and he looked at his watch nervously, thinking he would miss the train and her. Dammit, he thought, I spend my life just making trains. In the shadows against one of the dusky columns, he saw her, standing coolly, flicking the tickets in the air and smiling. Of course she would have gotten the tickets, he thought; of course she would be here ahead of time. She wore shorts, stylishly flared, and a polka-dot shirt, tied at her waist, with absurdly sequined sunglasses propped in her thick hair, just slightly askew from where she had removed her huge Oriental hat. As she moved toward him he saw clearly what had evaded him last night. Her carriage, her presentation, everything about the way she was had changed, making what was before a suggestion into a *fait accompli*. She moved with slightly more gravity than he remembered, a hint of heaviness in the legs and the torso not there before; her looks, ever handsome, were the good looks of a woman who has entered the long plateau of her own time. She had passed over from youth and had thereby become somehow more herself and, to Roger's eye, even more attractive because of it.

He remembered, though he tried not to, that Lulu's looks now displeased him; seeing Judith, in this light, in this way, he knew why, because Lulu had not passed over from youth. She still fought the end of girlhood, fought harder than she would have anyway because of the baby, and the results were awkward. The hair wasn't right, the clothes weren't right, the expectations for the face unrealistic. It was clear she wasn't comfortable with herself, and thus neither was Roger. None of this could he ever say to her, nor would he even know quite how to say it if he could. But in one stride Judith showed him the difference.

It was odd, too, to think of Judith as a woman who would contemplate this very matter. Yet she plainly did. She was two years his senior, he re-membered, crucial years for the transition he witnessed, but not generally so long a time. She must have been thinking the same thing about me, he thought. More *gravitas*, indeed. The fact is that neither of us is the same, and we were in love long ago.

He took the picnic basket she carried and they cut through the mass of beckoning and shouting passengers to the end of the train at its berth in the lower level of the grandiose hall. From the city they emerged to the flat gray fields of Long Island, rudely taken acre by acre for the spreading highways, the old ruling estates backed uneasily against Levittowns. She talked about her work at Columbia and the final journey she seemed to be on to the center of the mystery of her ideas and the world, a journey that seemed no less circuitous and demanding than his journey to the recla-mation by wealth he had promised to himself and delivered early.

"You could have been the one," she said as they changed trains in little Freeport, the station besieged by the multitudes gone to bathe, lounging in wait for their connection, making in that unlikely place a babble of lan-guages and bodies.

"Which one?"

"Oh, come on. He liked you the best."

He knew she was talking about Ogden, and that she was right. He could have had that life; Ogden had done all but beg him to take it. But the other vision was so bright then, compelling him to take the steps, one by one, including, as he realized, and as she must have realized long ago, giving her up. When she spoke of the other life, what Ogden had offered and Roger refused, he knew now that she spoke of the future that could have been possible with her and that he had discarded, knowing only incom-pletely, if at all, what he was doing.

"Are you rich? Ogden says you're rich."

He calculated for a moment his tangible net worth, thinking it funny that he would have to do it to honestly answer the question. He was rich but didn't think himself so; he had never believed it necessary to imagine himself as rich, or to imagine himself much at all. In any event, he didn't think it should make such a difference. But there, on the foreign concrete of a suburban train platform turned Saturday way station, between the per-fumed Italian men and their tightly coiffed women, the much-iterated Irish families prepared to do group damage to their peachy complexions, and the violin student who had taken to entertaining them all, her case sprinkled with dimes, he felt in Judith's voice the fact of change. Am I rich? he wondered. Ogden would remark on it, in certainty proclaim it, with admiration at the accomplishment he could never manage for the striving. For the fact made all the difference: he was rich, not attempting it, or wanting to be it, or any other less attractive variation. He was rich, and there the doubting stopped, even and especially for Ogden, and in her suddenly shy way, as though she had asked the most intimate thing in the world, for Judith, too.

"Yes, I'm rich."

She sighed. "Of course. My positive Roger. Of course you're rich. I'm going to be rich, you say. So you make yourself rich."

"What do you mean?"

"I mean you have this gift, dammit. You focus. You want something to happen, and it happens."

The approaching train saved him from response, and they squeezed with their blanket and basket into a wicker bench for two, facing backward, which was a more interesting view, Judith believed, if you didn't get sick from it. They rode to the end of the line and with the others piled out to make lines between ropes at multiple bus stops. The "jitney" as Judith called it, but which Roger thought to be a perfectly adequate municipal bus, and not at all what the pejorative implied, took them the last distance, and they emerged at a sandstone obelisk in the midst of the circular drive marking the entrance to Jones Beach.

"I don't feel different. From being rich, that is. Sometimes I think I ought to feel different, you know, feel better in some way. I mean, I feel as though I've accomplished something, for my family and so forth."

"Of course you don't feel different. That's your charm."

He followed her through the elaborate gates to the public bathhouses by the outdoor pool, which was meticulously marked for depth and for lap lanes to regulate the hundreds of swimmers. He admired it: the scale, the care for detail, the elegance it bestowed upon the masses who overwhelmed it. They changed and walked across the piazza of the arcade to the sea, past the vendors, each with his appointed territory to push his cart, with his license prominently displayed. One, in the white blousy uniform especially prescribed, no doubt, for service at the shore, winked at Judith, but with a broad and worldly understanding that seemed to include them both.

She motioned ahead and they walked to the edge of the promenade. Below them, on the flat and manufactured beach, lay bodies as far to the water as could be seen, until the water and the bodies together appeared as a fundamental evolutionary statement, from the prostrate at the tide's edge to the upright umbrella dwellers against the dunes. He took Judith's hand and felt the thrill he had denied himself until that moment, for he had taken great care not to touch her even in the slightest way. He felt the pressure of her touch and the pressure of the great mass before him, and her and himself in it, the great carousing mass that parted just enough to invite them to the imagined bare spot of sand, which was not really bare, but which opened for them enough for Roger to throw down the army blanket, his only military keepsake, and for them to sit, she wrinkling her nose at the roughness of it.

"You cooked," he said as she withdrew chicken and egg salad and fruit in waxed paper.

"I do when I feel like it. You—here, why don't you get us some Cokes."

He knew she meant to say something like "you bring that out in me" and had thought better of it.

When he returned she produced a flask of bourbon. "It's my drink now," she said. "It reminds me of the South. I don't think it's too early, do you?"

The way she said it—"reminds me of the South"—stuck in his mind as the expression often did, for he didn't ever think of the South as one place, but as many; he saw that for her, though, it meant a single place in memory, and a good time. It struck him that there had been bad times, uncertain times for her, and that in their half-dozen talks of the last six years she had never mentioned fears or missteps. Wisconsin again after the war, some murky direct Party organizing, though Ogden, who kept him obliquely informed—grudgingly and only when asked—was discreet to the point of incomprehension. He took it that she had hit a block in her research and, through a redirected commitment—Roger translated that as guilt—had jumped back into Party recruiting in the teeth of the McCarthy onslaught; she had gone underground, he suspected. Now, resurrected, purged of whatever would possess her to prove again that she was not intimidated by whatever it was that would intimidate her, she had traded world revolution for a cheery, secretive bohemianism. He suspected that success at Columbia had required a renunciation, and that it had been painful.

He closed his eyes for a moment as the liquor made its way to join with the heat of the day in the far reaches of his brain. She laughed, watching him, and he imagined it hit her the same way. Timing, he thought, everything was timing. She stretched her arms to the scene before them without saying a word, and he knew why she had brought him there, to her world. It explained her, this world, which was so far from the green kingdom of Carolina. In Carolina there lived single-fated people lost in themselves, often alone, but never anonymous. Here you were never alone and often anonymous. Even on the beach you were caught in the mass, immersed in the history that brought so many to one place to struggle; here the world impressed itself upon consciousness every minute, making a kind of delirium from which you emerged a hard person, if you emerged.

She lay down, squinting even through her bejeweled sunglasses, and he lay down beside her. There was a naturalness about it, their closeness on that blanket amidst a hundred thousand people as intimate as the summer days together in her rooms eleven years ago. The thought overpowered him and he could remember it all, her weight on him, her smell. He permitted himself to study her body beside him, her legs crossed jauntily in the air, her long fingers tapping a graceful tattoo on the sand. He was thirty-one years old, and he had been truly intimate with only two women in his life, and one of them was lying beside him, essential to him still. The closeness he felt beside her was more powerful than making love to her, so powerful that he was startled by the ease of drifting into the life he had known with her and now imagined as vividly as though it were both then and now, as though he had it still. The power of connection with her, and with time past, liberated him for that moment from the dead hand of his current life; he laughed aloud. She rose up, quizzically, but he waved her away from explanations, for what he realized in that moment was that the very same feeling of release and connection was what Lulu had with Worth. It had nothing to do with willfulness or a plan of any sort; it was an escape from those things to the other life, the unchosen path revisited, youth regained for a few hours on the odd day.

"You were right," he said.

"About what?"

"I'm miserable being married to her."

She groaned and put her hat over her face. He thought for a second he had blundered terribly. She'd probably heard that from a dozen drunk professors in the past six months.

"I didn't—"

She touched his arm to still him and say she knew he didn't mean it that way. "I reacted to something totally different," she said. "Really."

"What?"

"Oh God. You go to the West End a lot, don't you?"

"Recently. Why?"

"I saw you there, from the back, twice before I came up to you last night. I couldn't believe you were there. I mean I knew it was you, but I couldn't believe it was you. But I knew you were looking for me—to tell me something."

He hadn't thought of having something to tell her, but as he reflected on it, maybe that was it. He was shocked that he had said that; he had told no one else, or even formed the words before. But who else would he tell? Worth would be the only other person, and he was the problem.

"Do you remember that man at the table last night, the one I was with?"

"Sure," Roger said, trying to conjure the vision again of the older fellow with the goatee.

"That's Dr. Donald Freebaum," she said slowly, as though he should recognize the name. "He wants me to marry him."

The news affected him more than he liked or expected. Somehow it made it different to be with her and impossible to think of her with him years ago in the same way. He was ashamed he wished she wouldn't marry so that she might remain pristine in his memory, but he did.

"You don't approve, do you?" she said.

"What's not for me to approve? He's sort of old, isn't he?"

"Fifty-five."

"Do you love him?"

She laughed. "What a question to come from Roger Albright."

"Ordinary enough, given the circumstances."

"Oh my God. You still have this effect on me. You know, when we were together, at least when we started out, I thought I would teach you these things. Here you were, this brilliant, untouched boy—you could jump to ideas I had to struggle for months to work through—and you were throwing yourself at these people, you know, Worth Patterson and the rest, trying to become them, without knowing how second-rate they were."

"I thought it was Ogden we were all throwing ourselves at."

She waved her hand to dismiss the diversion. "Well, that's Tal's weakness, too, a kind of sweet weakness, really. He wants to get his ideas in power — he thinks — but what he really wants is to be invited to the parties. And you — my God, how you buffaloed him. You were the Frankenstein he created. You actually did have the talent to get invited to the parties, and you did just what he said, took his thesis to the limit, and, well, there you are, or here you are beside me."

He didn't know quite what she was getting at, but she had evidently thought about it a great deal; beyond that, she now called Ogden Tal. He supposed she was, now, a kind of colleague of his. He had mentioned her from time to time in a professional tone, as well as when giving personal news, but Roger thought by the way she spoke of him, so warmly yet with a kind of resigned amusement, as one talked of one's father when one realized he wasn't a world-beater, that he had hidden their closeness from him, yet another manipulation.

"But that's a joke, really, because all the time you were teaching me," she said.

"I don't follow."

"You were teaching me how to get ahead, how to expect the best instead of the worst, how to do things because you have to, without being guilty, how to get on with it."

"I don't remember doing any of those things. I just remember tagging along behind you because you were the most beautiful, incredible woman."

"Sure. So you married Lulu."

She said it not bitterly, or as an accusation, but rather to summarize her argument.

He figured he had been dense not to get it until then, but now he saw. Her marriage to Freebaum would be a type of career move: the mentor, the deep abiding friendship, academic success, and enough money to see her through.

"I do love Donald," she said quietly, as though he might be listening to her thoughts. "Not in the way I loved you. But he is brilliant like you. He is also alone. He cares about me. And things will be easier when I am with him."

"I understand."

She sighed and rolled over onto her stomach. "I can't get my dissertation through without a sponsor; I can't get a job without a sponsor. It's the past. It still matters."

"I understand."

Rain overtook them as their train back passed over the steel railroad bridges for the high approach into the city, the very same cooling afternoon rain that fell at home. As the skyscrapers came into view it was hard for him to imagine the island without people, without concrete and steel, when the rain had nourished trees and a crop, and the land had stood at the magnificent juncture of sea and river with only the suggestion of importance. He took her arm when she headed for the subway station and led her to a taxi, an extravagance for her, he knew, from Pennsylvania Station to Morningside Heights. They had been so easy with each other. He had thought that seeking her out would mean his own confessional, his own admission of doubt, but it was she for whom the moment had arrived. The meaning of their earlier lives together was with them still, this time taking her measure. The poignancy of it, and the sweetness of the afternoon, made him feel a gentleness for her that he could not have anticipated. Little by little, as the day passed and they made their way through the weekend-deserted city, the full memory of their passion together enveloped him like the water of the clearest lake.

There was one thing left undone, and he knew it: she wasn't sure about the good professor, and he had made the pass where she found herself more precarious by saying what he had said about Lulu. The truth was that he could have lived forever with the way things were, and would probably still; the key was not the sadness that they didn't love each other, but the fact that she had slept with his best friend. He hadn't thought of telling Judith that, but because she took from him the meaning she did he thought that now he must.

"I didn't tell you something before," he said quietly. "I didn't really plan on telling you. But I think I should."

"What?" she said, her head resting lightly on his shoulder.

"The reason why — why I said I hated being married to her. It's not because of any reason you would think. It's this one thing. You see, she slept with Worth, and I can't get over it."

Judith sat up to look at him, her eyes wide with a mixture of sadness and vindication. "I'm sorry," she said.

He walked her to her door in the apartment building on Claremont Avenue, aware of her silence. He kissed her, as easily as he would have those eleven years ago, and with close to the same effect.

She leaned against the wall and closed her eyes. "That's dangerous, Roger. Very dangerous."

Chapter Twelve

1952

"SOUTHERN Station," read the sign overhead, above the presiding bust of Oswald Patterson, and below, the epigraph: "Southern Serves the South." Roger paused to take in the echoes of the domed passenger room, crowded at the end of the day with white-gloved matrons returning from family visits; salesmen with the grim professional journeymen's faces; and the porters, who attended the sooty crossroads where Fairington met the world as dark centurions, silent, watchful. He was home again.

For eighteen months he had kept them all in New York. Lulu refused to do battle, even after he had mentioned Judith. Roger admitted that her serenity had beaten him. 'We're going home," he said simply one night. And the next day they returned, wordless except to cajole Brent not to cry for the five hundred miles in the Pullman. How can she do it, Roger wondered, resenting her closeness to the boy anew as he saw Brent asleep against her breast, as she too fell asleep, rocking with the train's steady flow.

Worth and Ogden met the train—Worth, because Roger had called ahead to announce their return, and, by default, the end of the stalemate between them. But why Ogden? Roger thought, the snap-brim hat approaching singularly with the train's motion and then stopping, the sad, dark eyes searching, passing Lulu as Worth took her valise and her arm, and fixing on Roger, not bearing the rebuke Roger expected, but part salute for his return from a bad choice, part summons.

"Roger," Ogden said, "Roger." Ogden gripped his elbow, propelling him ahead through the lobby. "Worth is at sixes and sevens."

"Oh?"

"I think you know why."

Roger did know why. The professor viewed the problem as serious business, not the petty personal mess of recent concern. The design was imperiled. The only thing this could mean was that Worth had rebelled in some way, and drastically. Mandy, pregnant, was away in Washington, or so he gathered from Lulu's deadpan congratulations; Ogden had hired a campaign manager for the post–Labor Day push against a listless Republican who had no chance of being the first of his party to win the district since Reconstruction against Fairington's favorite son. These weren't issues. No, Worth had rebelled in some way, Roger concluded as he watched him busy with the porter's job, piling suitcases into the luggage cart, giving his back to Ogden. Roger saw in an instant that there had been words today between them. As in a marriage, it could have been over money—the overpriced campaign manager mounting a race fit for the presidency of a moderate-sized Latin republic—or it could have been more fundamental, emotional and therefore unfathomable to the professor. If that was the case, Worth would fight no pitched battles, but employ passive resistance, and Ogden, who could understand any opponent except the heart, would conclude the problem was a simple unwillingness to perform his duty.

Later, as Roger sat in Worth's office waiting to hear the story, he could not help but reflect on the man's haphazard fertility. He was indeed inevitable. And yet that seemed to be a smaller advantage as the years went on. Roger appreciated now his own freedom, even to fail, his own luxury of directness. Worth, although inevitable, had to achieve adulthood by misdirection.

Worth pressed the telephone receiver against his shoulder and shrugged tellingly. "Ralph, I'll wire it. Yes, I'm very pleased with the leaflets. You think another—how many? For Chrissakes. Ten thousand? For what? Whatever, Ralph. Of course I'll be ready. I know—I—yes, you'll pick me up. Good. Good-bye. Right. Good-bye."

So that was the problem, Roger thought. Worth had no control over his campaign. He obviously disliked his manager, whom Ogden had installed with a prepackaged plan that, among other things, offended Worth for its excess. He was, finally, the candidate, although he had never decided to be and had no control over his candidacy. Now he imagined he wanted out.

"This is all wrong," Worth said, striking the desk top hard, as though it housed the phantoms he combated. "The Bailey thing. That was wrong. I thought it was right at the time, but I was just fooling myself. And all the rest of this." He gestured past the confines of his third-floor law office to the street outside, the passersby below, the woman leaving the shoe shop across the street, package of shoes in hand; the man at the newsstand, buying the afternoon paper, folding it under his arm and proceeding against the late-summer breeze of the darkening day. "What's the old saw — *mens sana, corpore sano*, all that? Bodies and minds, the whole man. Phineas used to repeat that to me. Born to lead, born to serve. What a crock."

"I've got a solution," Roger said.

"How's that?"

Roger got up and moved thoughtfully to the partners' table that still held the last law files Worth had worked on, left in place for his return from Washington, now mottled at the edges by the daily sun, enticing to the reluctant prodigal for their very irrelevance. "Shoot Ogden."

"What?"

"Kill him. Then no one would bother you anymore about your political career and you would disqualify yourself forever from whatever office the governor would give you. If you played your cards right you could go to Dix Hill for the rest of your life and no one would ever bother you. Except me. I'd come to see you on Sunday afternoons."

The suggestion first brought Worth's self-serious and tight-lipped silence but, as Roger knew it would, the laughter finally began, as the lawyer imagined himself the subject of one of his own after-dinner stories, the renegade client, coatless, chest heaving . . . *Sometimes you get them off the street, you know, "I killed my wife," they say. "Here, take my gun and hide it." That was the old law school problem. If you are sitting at your desk and a man walks in from the street with a gun in his hand and says "I've killed my wife, hide the gun," what do you do? Always stumps the first-year men. Can't incriminate your client of course, but you have to maneuver the gun out of sight without disposing of evidence to a capital crime. By your second year you know enough to tell him to take the gun away and convince yourself that he made no comment connecting the gun with any crime. You see, he simply said, "I've killed my wife, hide my gun . . ."*

"That's beautiful," Worth said, shaking his head. "Shoot him. Yeah, that would take care of a lot of things. Easy for you to say. You got out from under it years ago. I thought you were nuts. Couldn't figure it out. Now you've got the best of it."

Roger wondered at the sentiment, and Worth's sincerity. It flattered him, and he thought it must be the first time Worth had ever admitted to envy.

"It was easy for me," he said. "I don't have the baggage."

Worth laughed. "Baggage. That's a good way to put it. Jack, Jack Kennedy, you know, says I ought to be a judge. Get a federal appointment. Can sit for life and nobody will ever bother you."

Except the wrong party is in power, Roger thought. Or maybe that doesn't bother Kennedys and Pattersons. "Right, Worth. Be a federal judge. Jack is such an authority on how to run your own life. Doesn't he check with his dad before he takes a crap? How would you like to trade in Ogden for Joseph P. Kennedy? The only thing Jack does without the old man is get laid."

Worth roared and slapped the table. "I'll have to tell Jack. He'll love it."

"Look, Worth. You've got a good job now. Bailey's water under the bridge. He's making a zillion dollars at Covington and Burling, he doesn't care. Mandy's not going anywhere, you're going to have a kid—what the hell's the real problem here?"

"Oh, for Chrissakes, I don't know. Ogden is driving me crazy, and Ralph, Jesus, he's all wrong."

"So what do you want to do about it?"

"I don't know. I want another manager."

"Fine. Fire Ralph."

"Roger, I can't just fire Ralph. What about Ogden?"

"Screw Ogden. Is he paying for any of this? Let me answer that question for you. No. You're paying for it. You want to fire Ralph? Fire Ralph."

"Who'd run the campaign?"

"I would."

"Come on. You really would?"

"Sure. Take about a half hour a day. I don't even know who you're running against. Nobody else does, either." Roger picked up the telephone receiver and handed it to Worth. "Fire Ralph," he said.

Worth dialed the number. "I'm glad you're back, old man. Things are going to be better."

"I'm glad, too."

• • •

Although Roger didn't commit himself to the last proposition, he did believe things were going to be better. He enjoyed Worth's stumbles away from Ogden and felt for him in his dilemma to a surprising degree. Worth's better instincts had been aroused, and Roger admitted that he had for a time ceased to believe they existed, between the mess with Lulu and Judith's practiced dislike of him. Yet Roger could see it as the beginning. "I have to be free — to get on with it," Worth had said to him simply as they left the office, having sacked the clueless Ralph; Roger had nodded, knowing that the remark and the sentiment were not empty but incomplete, that what he meant was he had to be free to get on with doing something good and that it was very hard to do something good — even after you figured out what it was — when you had to do everything you were told.

In an odd way it was he and Worth who had the means to move on with each other, more than he and Lulu. She probably understood that better than either of them and had steeled herself against it. He remembered the moment of greatest intensity between them in New York, when he had discovered the picture of Brent in his mother's antique silver frame missing from the mantel, and imagined she had sent it to Worth. She preened as he exploded, laughed when he accused her, played through the tempest, and then when he was spent showed him where she had removed it to a sofa table to take better advantage of the light. That night he took to her bed for the first time since Brent's birth, and the first real time in months of bad memories. As she lay curled like a cat against him, he thought he remembered an odd thing she had said before it all began — that whatever happened was really about him and Worth. And he saw the rough justice of it, at least understood what she meant and had just illustrated: that the range of ways for them to love each other again was narrow and narrowing, and his life with Worth was just beginning, if he would let it. Was that, he realized with a start, the reason, her reason for going to bed with the man? A kind of spitefulness, a huge resentful joke?

As to fate and the reluctant congressman, Worth had sought to bargain, rather late, for his own terms. Not that Roger blamed him for the tardiness — Oswald and Phineas were rather tough guys to shake, especially with Ogden as the enforcer. Still, he was bargaining, in league with Roger. It was a kind of second adolescence, and Roger, for one, needed it, reveled

in it as a cure for his own exhaustion. He knew he could handle the rebellion and hoped he could handle the other part, which was Worth's desire to do "something." Rather than growing weaker, it grew stronger.
MacGiver still affected him, Roger could see that. Worth had changed the
day he saw his neighbors desert him; though subsequent events had kept
him from attending to it, the change was upon him. Worth had been seized
by certain ends, and Roger did not mind, but rather liked, to educate him
about certain means. It was almost as though he were doing good too.

Together they walked to the O. Henry, where Ogden had insisted they
have dinner, even though Roger had not yet been home from the train.
Worth made the pretense of informing Ogden that he had fired Ralph,
although of course the professor already knew that and, for all Roger and
Worth could surmise, had reversed the decision. But he heard Worth out
and simply nodded. "Whatever you think best, Worth," he said, his eyes
straying to the outlines of the room, rich in its late evening hues. Roger
wondered how much of Worth's money he had promised to Ralph for his
trouble and his silence.

Ogden likewise greeted the news that Roger would become campaign
manager with equanimity. "Whatever you boys want to do," he said, smiling. Actually he couldn't be more pleased, Roger thought, studying the
mock reserve Ogden affected for the occasion of Worth's uprising. He's
probably already given himself credit for the idea.

Worth waved to the maître d', a tall, dark man named Ozymandias, or
Ozzie for short, who ran the room behind the unyielding face of an African
prince. "Setups all around," he said, tapping his menu against the table's
edge. "The usual."

Ozzie nodded at the code correctly employed and motioned to a waiter,
who appeared moments later with three martini goblets, perfectly chilled,
and the accoutrements for the drink, without liquor. Worth produced,
from beneath the table, a thermos encased in a brown bag, from which he
poured the gin and vermouth he had mixed in the office. Woe to the neo-
phyte in Ozzie's dining room who did not know the code of the brown
bag. Roger remembered taking lunch one day with Worth and a law school
friend visiting from Wall Street, the room bustling with ladies in from
shopping who set their boxes in the aisles and whispered at tables beside
businessmen of the town and travelers on expense accounts hawking their
wares to the amiably bored. "I'll have a whiskey sour," the friend said au-

thoritatively as Ozzie visited their table. Ozzie fixed him with the stare he saved for the thickest of white people. "We do not serve liquor here, sir," he said and turned on his heel.

The code, Roger thought, ah, the code. One had to know it. Sipping his good martini and toasting the campaign to come, he believed he did know the code. He was thirty-one years old and rich, and although he resented the rushing past of the days it had taken for him to get that way, and a youth lost to the war and striving, he didn't mind the result. He thought the price was almost worth it. His friend, too, for all of the doubts and the false starts, was thirty-one years old and a congressman, soon to be elected, and then elected again, and then—who knows? As Ogden sat before them, his hands folded in his lap, waiting for them to tell him what came next, Roger understood the true message and the acknowledgement. At some moment, he didn't know where or when, they had stopped chasing the world, and the world had come to them. They had inherited.

III

---⊗---

OZYMANDIAS,

KING OF KINGS

1978

Chapter Thirteen

1978

ROGER accepted a scotch straight up from the downstairs bartender and settled into what appeared by evidence of use to be the absent owner's favorite chair. He admired the end tables facing him, and the sofa they flanked, which unself-consciously bore the scratches and gouges of their many postings. The objects atop the inlaid coffee table — a snuffbox, a weighted Oriental bowl, a Punjabi scimitar encased in a jeweled scabbard — sat composed as a memory book for the foreign service officer who owned the house and rented it to Pammie Patterson and her friends. A dour colonial matron and her laughing husband peered from the eighteenth-century primitive over the fireplace, looking down on the only item of questionable taste in the ensemble — a grinning lawn jockey guarding the wrought-iron kindling box.

He wondered what the eminent Ambassador so-and-so — now reportedly showing the flag in a West African metropolis — must think of the children who apportioned the fruits of empire. That is, all of them who played at night in his house and by day sat in the squat gray buildings doling out the last of the government's debased loot before Crain's deluge did its work. Perhaps he left his Dutch merchant to watch over things, he of the civic probity and unlikely humor. *Summum bonum*, honest injun, he assured, with his fingers crossed. Roger picked from the bookcase a volume of the ambassador's Frank Meriwether first editions. "Gentlemen, you are about to play football for Yale. Never again will you do anything so important." Dick Stover indeed, he thought. Just what these youngsters need, forced bedtime readings of *Stover at Yale*. He considered reciting to the assembled young notables but decided against it. I'm here to observe, he reminded himself. He replaced the book with the other solemn volumes — Kennan, Acheson, dull, duller, Dulles.

Pammie especially liked giving parties in this house, Brent reported, insisting Roger drop by on his free night in Washington. Roger could see why she enjoyed entertaining there over the more modest quarters Worth provided for his daughter, as the house exceeded her demands for luxury and her father paid the rent. She and Brent could be living here together, Roger realized, fighting the familiar dread that came over him when he thought of it. Who could ever know, and who would ask.

"I say, Albright. ALBRIGHT! Dammit, this is serious."

Roger looked up, startled, thinking for a moment he was the object of the shouted admonition, but then he saw Brent in the hallway, toe to toe with a young fellow he thought he recognized from the Sunday-morning talk shows as Richard Hassell, the President's man for something or other.

"What now, Hassell?" Brent said.

"Just trying to keep to the deal."

"Oh shit."

"As I recall, we agreed the tobacco people would not go public." He handed Brent a rolled-up copy of the *Star*. "Check page A three."

Brent read the article, frowning in a way Roger had recognized as anger since his son was a boy. "Jesus, Dick," Brent said. "I'm sorry as hell about that. I'll manage the situation personally. Personally, you have my word on it."

"The Old Man would appreciate it." Hassell gestured meaningfully in the direction of 1600 Pennsylvania Avenue. "By the way, have you seen my date?"

The article was not good news for Brent, or for Worth, Roger surmised. Neither had control over the Tobacco Institute lobbyists, even though the industry chieftains would flatter both by murmuring that Worth was the ramrod for their Senate strategy; all either would get from that was a lot of trouble, however, because when the fellows said something nasty, somebody like Hassell invariably extracted from Brent a meaningless promise to shut them up, so as to trot out the senator's impotence for all to see. The real ball game for Senator Patterson was not industry lobbyists anyway, but thousands of farmers, allotment holders, and tenants, most of whom voted, and voted overwhelmingly for Democrats; their mobile homes or white frame houses on painted cinder blocks held one or two children too many, and their big-armed wives worked too hard too often outdoors to stay pretty. She — the wife — also voted for Democrats, and if the crops did not quite make ends meet, which happened often, she worked at a cut-and-sew shop part-time, maybe as a substitute teacher if she was educated, in either case for wages that were too low to buy what they needed when the FCX loan came due, or so Brent lectured Roger.

Roger listened patiently and said nothing when Brent recounted the figures, having taught Brent that story firsthand; he never thought Brent would make such practical use of it. Years before, they had ridden Sunday mornings on single-lane highways through the tobacco kingdom. Roger kept a notebook in his pocket and quickly jotted down numbers and figures when the car passed a busy crossroads with a store or a stand of buildings going up in the middle of the black-dirt coastal plain. He counted carefully the new mobile homes the wives fancied up with window boxes and the new ranch houses of glossy red brick the more prosperous farmers stuck incongruously in the open fields, sometimes running corn or soybeans or the golden leaf itself to the back door. He drove onto the smaller, winding secondary roads where the smell of insecticide and ditchwater on a hot, silent morning stilled everything but the two city spirits foolish enough to venture out. He scribbled the details scrupulously, and when he was finished a satisfied, low whistle would issue from his lips and he would say to the boy beside him, "Like some barbecue, Sport?" And the boy would pretend to decide, because who would ever think of turning down a trip to Wilbers or Kings or the anonymous places Roger had a knack for finding, so the boy would answer, "Yes, Daddy." At the barbecue shack in the town down the line, Roger would inquire of the waitress how the crops were making out this year, were there enough new farm families, what was that industrial property going up back yonder? Before noon Roger counted the cars at the packed country churches on the highway — the Mt. Holly Reformed Christian Church, the African Methodist Episcopal Zion Church, the True Grace Baptist Church. And another low whistle would issue from his lips and he would pat the notebook in his sweat-damp shirt pocket and gun the big Sedan de Ville back on the interstate toward Fairington, sometimes stopping at Bright Star to see Grandmother or at the big old farmhouse with the family graveyard. On Monday morning Billy Roy would find a memo ordering him to acquire property at this crossroads in such-and-such county, and with it a hand-drawn map in the boss's familiar scrawl telling him where it was.

Every Christmas Roger crowded his top executives and two or three of the young MBAs into a small caravan of dusty company Plymouths to go to the parties in the prefabricated plants that Billy Roy had built. The countrywomen wore their long dresses and brought their stiff-gaited husbands to shake hands with the boss and his men, and they all ate the baked hams and turkeys that the company bought and sang Christmas carols, and then Roger asked the men what their tobacco had sold for, and the other executives, who were wondering what the hell they were doing in this little cut-and-sew shop in Wallace or Bethel or Holly Springs, saw that the boss was asking about tobacco, and so they asked about tobacco, too, and then hunting and if the Mullet Festival was good this year, until the food platters disappeared and they piled in the cars and went home. And the MBAs punched themselves behind the boss's back and whispered, "Is this what got the guy on the cover of *Fortune* magazine?"

•　　•　　•

"Brey-unt, honey, have you seen, unh, lesse, unh, Roger?"

"What?"

"I said, have, unh, seen, unh, Roger?"

Pammie was clad in a silver top with skintight black slacks and a rhinestone evening bag hanging from her wrist. She was a pretty woman who often mocked the crafted style of her upbringing, tonight strikingly altered by the huge orange and green comb stuck in her hair.

"Pammie, Roger's my daddy."

She considered this. "No he's not," she insisted. "Roger's a fig-a-ment. A fig-a-ment of your imagination. But he's coming. I'm going to make him."

"Make him come where, Pammie?" Brent said patiently.

"Why to my party, you silly thing. Where else?"

The band swung into a lusty "I'll Be There," and at the first chord Pammie gathered her evening bag and flung her arms around Brent, forcing him to throw his drink into the bushes.

"Day-unce with me, Brey-unt," she commanded.

Brent looked around the dark patio deck. "Roger's not here, is he?" He shook her. "And where did you get that looney voice — old Talullah Bankhead movies?"

"Why you old thing, Brey-unt, playing with me. If you're nice you can be my es-cort."

As the last notes faded in the summer air, Brent sat Pammie at the edge of the pool and pushed up her pants legs so she could dip her feet into the water. So intent, however, was she on maintaining her forward momentum, and so entwined at this point were the two of them, that they soon careened in woozy slow motion toward the water — until a firm grip on Pammie's shoulders halted the pas de deux.

"Whoa there, Pammie," Hassell said with a grudging glance at Brent. "Are we going to the Jetstream or what? Everybody's ready."

"Oh damn," she said, sitting up suddenly. "Damn."

"That's the spirit. Now why don't you just stretch Brent out on the concrete and we'll go."

"Sorry to disappoint you, Hassell," Brent said. "But I'm going, too."

They helped Pammie to her feet, and it occurred to Brent that the present plan meant the party would continue unattended. "Pammie, we're leaving, right? And the party's still going on, right?"

She reinserted her hair comb and in the process swayed backward dangerously, prompting Hassell and Brent to catch her again at each side. "Leaving my own party," she said. "You don't think it's the right thing to do, either of you." She looked from Brent to Hassell and disengaged herself. "Well, to hell with you both."

Gathered at Pammie's Fiat stood six other revelers. "I suppose we'll have to take two cars," Brent said.

Hassell laughed. "As long as you're not driving one of them."

No one had thought to consider the implications of seating a table of ten without a reservation at such a prosperous café as the Jetstream, especially on a summer's eve when many wore name tags and rubberneckers stood six deep at the bar. Hassell bribed the hostess with a twenty and assured her that yes, everyone would eat dinner. No sooner did all ten squeeze around a table for four than Hassell wrapped himself around Pammie, leaving Brent no gentlemanly choice but to talk to Hassell's slowly stewing date.

"Can I get you a drink, Leslie?"

"What did you say?"

"I said, can I get you a drink?"

She waved her finger at him and nodded. "You're from the South, aren't you."

Brent supposed that meant she didn't want a drink. "North Carolina. So what do you do?"

"I'm with the Chase Bank. What do you do?"

"Lately I've been taking it up the ass for Worth Patterson."

"I think I'm going to the ladies' room."

Hassell shed his coat and began a speech about how evil it was that no one had yet waited on them. Pammie napped, her head on the table.

"Brent, go get us a round of drinks, won't you?" she said, rousing herself. "And Richard, you go help."

They ordered draft pitchers at the bar, which was crowded several deep with patrons. Brent really didn't want a beer, but at that hour he drank by reflex.

Brent gave Hassell a ten for half. "You know what I like about you, Hassell?"

"What?"

"Your name rhymes with 'asshole.' "

Hassell stepped back from the bar and looked at the ceiling, mouthing the two words and shaking his head. "That only works if you say it with a drawl."

"No, no. Look—I can also do it in your mother tongue, Locust Valley Lockjaw. 'Hess-ule, ess-ule.' See?"

Hassell stuck a pitcher of beer in Brent's chest. "You're obviously drunk, Albright. Look, I'm sorry about the tobacco thing. It doesn't mean we're not going to help. I'll be glad to help. No, goddammit, I mean it, I—we—will be glad to help. Now, if you can stand up, why don't you concentrate like a big fellow on this pitcher."

Brent stared at his reflection in the bar mirror and set the pitcher down, deliberately gathering himself like a shot-putter and wheeling to punch Dick Hassell in the jaw. Hassell staggered against the bar, throwing beer in several directions, and Brent, not having hit anyone in some months, figured he had hurt his right hand as much as Hassell's face. Hassell shook his head a couple of times and a gleeful look came into his eyes and then he whooped and threw some punches at Brent, and with that they were in a full-scale, if amateurish, fistfight. The bartender climbed over the rail and grabbed Brent, giving Hassell an easy shot; he missed, and the bartender went down with a loud crash. A diner lunged at Hassell with a broken bottle and Brent decked him. "You're all mine, Hassell," Brent cried as he threw punches and parried flying objects from several directions, losing his quarry in the anonymous fraternity of friend and foe. "Zero at three o'clock!" Brent screamed, but he could hear no reply as the singsong of the sirens roared near and the one punch you never see laid him flat-out cold on the parquet floor.

Roger surveyed the carnage from the other end of the bar. He finished his club soda quickly, paid his bill, and then asked for the check from the other Albright table, making sure that he had enough cash to bail Brent out of jail.

· · ·

Roger awoke to a landscape of pipes that sprouted like demonic agriculture from the Jersey marsh. Mallards lounged in an estuary beside a landfill; behind them, mafiosi exchanged positions in the cab of a chemical rig. The train rolled on, passing easily the Cerberus of the Palisades and then rumbling below the black river. The Metroliner delivered him to the plundered remains of Pennsylvania Station, and he was glad he had taken it, rather than entrusting his ulcer to four circles around La Guardia in the shuttle. His head throbbed as the surge of commuter bodies to the rear, aided and abetted by the sharp end of an umbrella, pushed him onto the platform and he inhaled the clean whiff of urinated cinder waste he expected. The smell took him back to young manhood in a more civilized time, when Pennsylvania Station would greet him with the cool, quiet purpose of a temple after the train from Fairington to New York had deposited his silent family, neither he, nor Brent, nor Lulu speaking, the dread of being together gripping them all.

He stretched violently to rid his head of the dream. "Damn it to hell," he muttered to himself, unfolding with a shaking hand the *Star* gossip page with the chatty poisons of Nose on Washington he had saved as though it were the results of a Fairington swim meet he would clip for Brent's scrapbook, rather than evidence of the greater ruin.

Nose was shocked to sniff out a brawl last night at the too-chic Jetstream Café between a pair of Washington's most (and I mean most, girls) eligible bachelors — Brent Albright, AA to Senator Worth Patterson, and Richard Hassell, White House Boy Friday. Many beautiful people and much crockery were smashed by the he-men, according to the District's finest, who took the boys downtown and gave them a good talking-to. Witnesses laid the fisticuffs to the rumored Federal Triangle among the duelling swains and the fetching Miss Pamela Patterson, daughter of Senator You-Know-Who. Other wags in the know think the boys were fighting over boring old business — such as White House support in Senator Patterson's upcoming campaign. Yawn. Nose is so romantic; Nose just knows all that scrumptious old-fashioned passion was for love . . .

It was fitting, Roger thought, that Nose would capture their earnest lives and offer them back as farce. He supposed he had himself to blame. As in a trance he had delivered Brent to Ogden, on schedule, in the boy's eighteenth year. Wordlessly they exchanged him after the professor visited. "You know it is the best thing, Roger. Purpose I mean." Brent already had a purpose, Roger had replied — to raise as much hell as possible. But the different purpose, the one the professor meant, and the one Roger wanted, too — namely to prepare to sanitize the Albright millions — that purpose Ogden would instill as a master, Roger knew, and so he was right and the choice inevitable. "I know you want him in the business, that is, eventually," Ogden had said, thinking himself shrewd by offering it up as bait, Roger thought. "But I think some time with Worth is what he needs right now." That said, the end game played by the master's hand came easy. So Roger handed his son over at the wrought-iron entrance to the bleached white gingerbread house that stood incongruously beside the university's main hall, where the Institute had offices, on a still August day very similar to the one when he himself began the journey, though unlike Brent, with an unmarked soul. "Son, you remember Professor Ogden," he said, stepping aside as the gate clanked shut.

That Brent would be seduced by the same old illusion was by no means a sure thing. Exuberant yet still sullen youth had their own language and many silences around the elders, Roger noted as he unloaded Brent's possessions at the old dormitory he had reserved for his son in a bow to nostalgia, the dormitory where he and Worth had lived. By coincidence, Brent's room was on his former hall, which that day vibrated with rock music and the smell of what he had come to recognize as marijuana. Nothing else bothered him anymore — not the hair, the wrecked cars, the silent separation from the day-to-day. But the marijuana, so secretive, so powerful an escape — that bothered him. He felt suddenly proprietary as he passed his old room and saw the young strangers in it, lounging amid their possessions, and their insolence, waiting for him to pass before continuing their insurrectionary lives. He wanted to feel that he continued through Brent and through them, believed he deserved to feel that, and yet there he stood, feeling instead that he had rented his life much as he had rented the old room where he was no longer wanted.

Still, Ogden remained, his arms outstretched, welcoming them all — Roger and Worth, and then Brent, and soon Pammie, welcoming them and their different challenges because he was Ogden and the Institute was the Institute. I delivered him up as in a trance, Roger remembered again; Ogden had stood there, puzzled, sensing the hesitation but not understanding it. The boy would serve Worth, yes, certainly, if it would create the purpose, or the desire for purpose that would in the end smooth the Albright successions, but to give up the boy to serve Worth and grant him, just deliver to him, the advantage he could never otherwise have, that was the difficult point.

Ogden had done well, Roger had to admit that. He had fired Brent again with the old dream, which Roger could not. The old dream, if anything, was even stronger than before, alive with the glittery eminence of Senator Patterson, constantly burnished by the Institute. The Institute, and with it the House of Patterson, had moved finally from the primary to the tertiary, from self-consumed wealth to disinterested power, all invested in the mystique of Worth, who, under Ogden's constant revision, became the perfect public servant: omniscient, self-confident, tolerant, historically of the long view. He paid his staff little because public service demanded sacrifice. He championed civil rights and other causes, which often put him at odds with his social peers, because it was the thing he had been sent to do and because he had absorbed, probably at an unconscious level, the professor's lecture that the great men of history championed the poor against the rich.

Ogden introduced Brent to the secrets gradually, with the right coursework, the right research, the right Institute fellowships. Somewhere along the way he must have discovered that Brent was not the scholar Roger was, but that too seemed only a temporary disappointment. The newest prodigal took to the Institute mystique in this removed setting, far from Fairington and its inhibitions, as a consumptive to dry air, breathing deeply to escape the tawdriness of the Albright mills. Ogden turned him to the life of action. His senior paper, "Joe Crain and the Rise of the National Christian Network, 1968–72," which Ogden carefully shepherded, prepared him, in conjunction with the correct interim placements on the Hill, for his post at graduation on the senator's staff, and, eventually, for being point man in the challenge all knew was coming: the candidacy of Joe Crain to unseat Worth Patterson in 1978. Ogden had done his job, Roger admitted as he stood uncomfortably with Lulu and Pammie at Brent's graduation. In four years he had turned an angry, mysterious young man into a liberal careerist.

Yet that was the bargain Roger had made. He imagined Worth and Brent together, Worth now with the advantage of collegiality never afforded the father of record, ill served by the boy's inexperience but charmed by his flattery. Together they tried to combat the rising negatives, wondering at the new power of the familiar enemy energized by money and television, sweating defiantly behind the little floor fan that Worth required in his offices instead of central air (another course in virtue), letters unsigned and documents unread curling in the warm revolving currents, outside the afternoon becoming another steam bath as late August wrung out Washington like a tattered old sponge. Even as they sat, reasoning against something reason could not master, Crain climbed: one point, another. Outside, on Connecticut Avenue, a jogger ran with a handkerchief over his nose as the gray cloud of car exhaust spread south and west across the Mall, meeting the sunset's orange haze over the Potomac, framing the Washington Monument and Lincoln's reverie. "Polls?" Worth said. "What would Henry Clay have done with polls?"

But even Ogden could not fix everything, Roger knew. Newspaper gossip broadcast generally what must have been apparent to even the slightly interested observer. Judith, who herself had admitted to a professional interest in Brent, remarked on it. "They are lovers, my dear," she said to Roger matter-of-factly after seeing Brent and Pammie together at that restaurant the Capitol Hill people frequented. She had met Nose there the time she saw them, sitting rigid on one of the small couches that flanked the blond tables, pinpoints of light from the slanting sawtooth glass above striking the plants that camouflaged the players, each growth hanging alternately from the ceiling or thrust up from the floor, stalactites and stalagmites of fashion. "The Library" was an arch name for the place, Roger thought. Books on shelves between the tables suggested a literary motif; their actual effect on the gossip exchange that doubled as an eatery was to stand as ancient data forms among the talk processors.

"They are lovers, my dear," she had said with finality after describing Pammie in the new suit-uniform young women of serious workday mien wore and that Miss Patterson lampooned: very dark gray with thin pinstripes, appointed with blunt-tipped buckled shoes, starched white collar-clipped shirt, and a floppy red bow tie. She also mentioned how Brent, characteristically, had addled the waiter, ordering an imported beer he knew the restaurant lacked and then berating the server. She recounted these details in order to verify, Roger thought, both the sighting and her conclusions. She had purposefully brought Nose there to see and stir it up, Roger now realized, wishing he could be mad at Judith for doing so. Of course Brent had recognized her, and she welcomed that, too, nodding at him from the shadows. "What do you know," he muttered, smile in place as he revved up the insider's jaunty allusiveness licensed by the Institute for conversational use. "Neoconservatism's La Pasionaria—a great American. What would she do for a column if liberalism really died?"

Pammie turned in a proper deliberate fashion to see. "My goodness. Judith Stern? She's checking you out, sweetheart. Should I be worried—I mean, are you into older ladies now?"

"Maybe. That would be too hip for Dad, though. She and Roger have a past."

"I've heard," Pammie said, studying quickly the tailored, deep burgundy Chanel dress, the upswept gray-streaked hair, and angular jewelry. "She doesn't seem to be Roger's type."

Brent shrugged. "Does Roger have a type? It's a good story anyway. Roger Albright and the *Commentary* crowd. Too much pipe smoke for him. Of course in college she would have been very left."

It was only then that Brent noticed the signature flowered hat and hawk-like proboscis of Judith's luncheon companion. They paid the check quickly and made do without coffee.

•   •   •

Roger told the taxi driver to let him off at Times Square. He could use the surreal walk uptown, he thought. He had made the appointment to see Brent a week ago, and even though they had just been in Washington together, Brent wanted to keep the date. He had been very particular about it. The boy enjoys running me to death, Roger thought, but he didn't always realize what was at the end of the chase. The wind at his back propelled him with a herald's portent up Sixth Avenue, past Black Rock and Exxon and McGraw-Hill, past the Time-Life and RCA citadels, until before him stood the high revolving doors of the Albright Tower, the forty-seven-story glass and steel box that Roger believed to be his best investment, housing the international and marketing divisions of the company, along with the other tenants who paid royally for the address. Up the avenue the fleet of skyscrapers stretched before him in full array to the far green horizon of Central Park, trim and smart dreadnoughts of capital. He dodged a half-dozen bored picketers wearing sandwich signs protesting Albright Industries' unfair labor practices, as well as the policeman who seemed ready to guard them, or guard others from them, and proceeded to his aerie.

"Have a real Cuban, Dad," Brent said, offering a cigar from the office's own store, his feet propped up on the leather inlay of Roger's desk.

Roger clipped the end of the thick, aged stogie that Billy Roy had bought from the storage humidors at Dunhill, where they sat beside the cigars of British nobility, gangsters, and movie stars. That was the point, and the not-so-hidden dig, Roger realized — that the office used to be Billy Roy's before Roger decided he liked it, and that the cigars still were. If Roger could simply appropriate the office at will, then Brent could appropriate the desk and the cigars. The rule of the jungle, or the playground, extended to all participants.

It was Brent's special relationship with Billy Roy that fed the friction, too. Billy Roy's manner gave Brent a model of rebellion against Roger's style: a celebration of rusticity and a belief that the crude act bespoke honesty. Roger had pointed out that what Brent called being honest was merely obvious, but honesty (or obviousness) Brent trumpeted as the highest virtue, and one, not coincidentally, Roger was least likely to possess.

"Remember Billy Roy and the Camels, Dad," Brent said, laughing, expecting Roger to do the same. Knowing this was expected, Roger did laugh, though he hated the memory of them together, Brent and Billy Roy in the bushes behind the pool house at the Fairington Country Club, the night of the twentieth anniversary of Albright Industries. Throughout preparation for the black-tie event, which Roger had to believe Brent knew was the validation — political, financial, social — of one of the grand coups of American business, the veritable ushering in of the House of Albright, the boy engaged himself in Billy Roy's struggle to quit smoking. Smoke Enders had long ago exhausted its possibilities, and each day there was a new story of Billy Roy's psychiatric session, as he resorted to hypnotism, at last, to break the habit, a therapy that as a final deterrent irrevocably associated inhaling cigarette smoke with nausea. Two days without a cigarette passed; then a week. Finally the night of the anniversary party arrived, with Billy Roy, smokeless, in attendance. Yet after dinner was cleared and the testimonials began, Roger noticed that Brent and Billy Roy had left. What good were the testimonials if Brent didn't hear them? Trying not to cause comment, Roger slipped away in the middle of Walt Wriston's paean, furious at them both. He searched the dark grounds, cool in the early May evening, the sound of crickets superseded by the muted laughter and applause inside. Then he heard them, the rough strangled sound and the laughter, now exhausted from the long pleasure of it. Behind the pool house, in the fifty-year-old boxwoods, knelt Billy Roy, his tuxedo jacket and cummerbund beside him, his drive for nicotine overwhelming even the magic of modern psychiatry, smoking an unfiltered Camel cigarette and retching with every puff. Brent sat cross-legged on his dinner jacket beside Billy Roy, rocking with laughter, holding his sides with it. Pammie, at least, had the modesty to disentangle herself from Brent as Roger approached, but not the modesty to place the spaghetti straps of the gown she was too young to wear back on her shoulders.

"I remember, Son," Roger said evenly, aware that Brent could search him for the slightest sign of displeasure, struggling, and succeeding as he usually did, in supplying none.

"Billy Roy is very loyal to you, Dad."

"Loyalty is the most valuable thing you can — well you know that, Son," Roger said, stopping when he realized the rebuke in the question, and the danger. Whose loyalty would he point to? He could suggest Billy Roy's, the dogged hitch-your-wagon-to-a-star variety, which was obedience really, obedience that stood a hundred humiliations, like giving up your office at a whim largely because the boss enjoyed making you do it. For bowing to this greedy will of the patron you receive the assurance that your material life will never have to return to the inferior condition from which you hoisted it. Or would he point to the loyalty you felt to friends and lovers, which was fidelity really, to yourself in the first instance, and to a common end outside yourself? And then the two together, mixed as they were between father and son, when the stakes for obedience and fidelity were of the highest order.

"By the way, thanks for bailing me out," Brent said, reflexively massaging bruised knuckles on his right hand, the only marks, Roger noted, that he visibly bore. Since Brent had been in numerous battles of that sort, Roger believed he must have developed a technique to avoid bruising.

"No trouble. As I told you, I just happened to be in that bar when it happened. I hope it wasn't too embarrassing for Worth," Roger said, placing his copy of the Washington paper with Nose's column faceup on the desk.

Brent grimaced and, with a deft sweep of his arm, propelled the paper into the trash. "He joked about the piece this morning. Said it was the most positive press we've had since the latest Crain ads."

"He's finally getting worried about the negative ads?"

Brent shrugged the topic away. "The answer is no, but we could talk all day about that. What I wanted to tell you, in person, Dad, is that the fair trade bill is going down. It'll be on the floor today, but we don't have the votes."

Roger knew that from other sources, but he nodded appreciatively, leaning forward to show interest. Brent was making a gesture, he knew that, trying to smooth over the differences between himself and Worth on the legislation, which was only their latest disagreement. The bill provided a delicate combination of tariffs and tax breaks for "threatened industries" such as steel, cars, shoes, textiles, and apparel, the last two being North Carolina's concern, and, one assumed, Roger's. In return for protected markets and subsidized capital expenditures, manufacturers would dedicate a percentage of profits to a sinking fund, called an "opportunity chest," for workers and communities in case of plant shutdowns, and they would pledge that a percentage of proceeds on sale or liquidation be transferred to fired workers for retraining and that worker or management buyout groups be given first option to purchase companies going out of business.

Worth had been unusually secretive about the full design, which attempted to join the needs of displaced workers with the protection desired by his textile friends, with whom he constantly needed to mend fences for his stands with the liberal leadership on other issues. Roger thought in retrospect that Worth meant to surprise him, as though the legislation were a testimonial token for thirty years of service without complaint. At the press conference announcing his initiative, Worth had named Roger to the industry advisory panel. But soon, deliberately leaked rumors of Roger's opposition made the press, and the senator, furious, demanded that he resign. A shouting match ensued in Worth's office, which Brent, in the anteroom with suddenly fascinated Sierra Club lobbyists, delicately made a show of ignoring. "I still don't know what you're on your high horse about," Worth had shouted. "You keep ranting about the market for corporate control as if you'd ever sell that goddamn company. I'm saving your life here." Roger had stalked out and a new rumor of their estrangement was born, timed, per the senator's bad luck this year, the same week as Crain's announcement.

"And I hope, Dad," Brent said, relighting his cigar, "that we can put the whole thing behind us. I mean, without messing in something not my business, after the bill goes down — and between you and me we didn't push for it after it came out of committee — I think it would be helpful if you could spend some time with the campaign, you know, patch things up. Besides, we need you."

"I think something can be arranged," Roger said, surprised by Brent as he often was these days, hearing in this plea a new cunning that artfully mixed request and probe. He feared for years that what he admired in Brent would be Ogden's or Worth's doing, but now he recognized proudly his own work.

"Good. By the way, there is something you can do immediately. We know that Crain has somewhere around seven million dollars. Seven million. That's partly from NCN, from other direct mail, PACs, you know, the usual suspects. But seven million. That's coming from some heavy sources. Big dollar guys. We don't know who they are. Maybe you could help."

Roger walked to the wall-length windows and looked toward the park and the high apartment buildings on either side of its elegant right angles. He didn't understand why Brent's question upset him, for it was obvious enough, and no more compromising than the request for fence-mending. Nonetheless, he stood there, at the apogee of Albright Industries, at the commanding prospect of Central Park that usually gave him pleasure, silent and angry that Brent would think he could list the parvenus who bankrolled Joe Crain.

"I don't know any of them," Roger said evenly. "They're new people, you see. In Florida, Texas, California, other places. Nobody knows them."

• • •

Posing in her new jumpsuit made it clear to Roger, as it was supposed to be made clear, that Lulu was in fine shape for a woman just this side of sixty — or, precisely, fifty-seven, he calculated, remembering her last-month's birthday. He still sent her a dozen roses on her birthday, as regularly as he had when they were married, the fact that they were not married making the gesture seem less mechanical than before. He wondered whether he only imagined that she looked better since the divorce. Her ever-tanned face seemed to have fewer lines; in fact her whole body had a newness about it, as though the surgical cocoon of her makeovers had given her an actual rebirth. More than the subtle tucks and gatherings elsewhere, it was the face-lift itself that raised and sharpened her features to an Oriental peak around the eyes and brought a physical attribute of wisdom never hers before. Even her hair, now turned artfully to ash, gave the look of a priestess, with distinguishing gray streaks in ensemble. She cocked her head like a girl, and her smile turned up flirtatiously, as he remembered it from the beginning. Could it be, after all this, that he wanted her again?

She had asked him for the divorce suddenly: "The marriage is over," she said. He thought that a strange thing to say — "the marriage is over" — as though it were a being itself, apart from them, with a beginning, a middle, and an end. He knew then, when he heard her say, "The marriage is over," what it meant for the marriage to have that existence apart and to end gradually. For him, until then, the marriage was not that being, but a condition, buffeted and scoured by much, a condition that one did not, or could not, pronounce as being over. In fact, he felt they had successfully faced down the greatest difficulties — infidelity, Brent, business demands — so that none was as crushing as when they were young. But the way she said it, and the action she took — moving into the New York apartment, beginning her self-improvement program, made him know that she, as keeper of the hearth, knower of their marriage for the thing it was, had attended to the corpse, said last rites, and buried it.

Surprisingly enough for Roger, Lulu's greatest defender and interpreter on this point was Judith. "Well, what did you expect?" she said, not adding what he should have indeed expected, talking instead about practical things, like children leaving and financial security, as though ending it for Lulu were a matter of balancing an emotional checkbook. In a way it was, Judith made him see; the end for Lulu, and perhaps the entire exercise, was ultimately practical.

"You're obsessed by this, Roger," Lulu said in the clipped way she now analyzed him.

"I am just alone in facing facts. And since you've encouraged it, you must put a stop to it."

"Oh, there you go again. You've held this over my head for twenty-eight years."

Roger sighed. "I haven't held anything over anybody's head. This is a problem. We have to solve it."

She threw her hands in the air. "Haven't held it over my head? Every day you held it over my head. And Brent's, too. That's the sad part—you did that to the child."

Dealing with her now over the slightest thing made him angry, much less dealing with her over the mystery of Brent. Years of conversational restraint only made her recent outbursts livelier. She skewered him with examples of his many failures—at marriage, principally at fatherhood, in fact at everything she now supposed mattered to her. Funny, he thought, his money ceased to matter to her once he got it.

"You just keep on obsessing, you never stop. I've told you a thousand times it's not true. But why listen to me? I don't know anything about it, do I?"

She bit off the last words with the anger that only the old wound could foster and lit another cigarette, turning her back to shield herself, Roger thought, from his imagined reproach on that subject, too. If he was obsessed it was a good obsession to have, he thought. She would be obsessed, too, if she had seen it. When the kids were in high school she hadn't been the one to go to Ocean Drive that night Pammie called. She hadn't been the one to retrieve Brent from the North Myrtle Beach police station and the mercies of his cellmate, who sat on the sink cutting his hair with a rusty knife, the officer with his round-brimmed campaign hat actually checking them out on a cash register, the human commerce on that May weekend being so active. And then the return, with Pammie, to the Spanish Galleon—a large, loud, acrid beer hall with the Stars and Bars and Jolly Roger flying side by side, and motorcycles parked beside the Volkswagens of the students, the teenagers on Beach Weekend ripe fruit for the ogling bikers. He asked her to show him the spot on the floor—he wanted to see it, to try to understand what he was unleashing before he got the lawyers to fix the matter—and so she did, the already faded chalk marks and the trampled yellow tape for the police line silently gesturing at the tragedy, the young man crushed by the cases of beer hurled one after the other down at him, Roger too frightened to ask whether Brent was hurling them or fighting the savages who were, and she not saying, the police accommodating them all, after Worth's firm did its work, to simply say he was "involved" but that no charges would be brought. Roger tried to force himself to be his son, to feel the drive to the elemental that provoked him to touch death itself, and suddenly; was this the greatest sincerity, the dedication to absolutely honor one's feeling and drive if it led to murder, to avoid compromise even if it meant that? And then it struck him. If Brent could do this out of a violent ignorance, what would he do if he believed the most basic truth of his life was a lie?

She led Roger from the spot, over the sawdust floors freshly swept each evening to rid the place of yesterday's stink; past the open wall to the beach where the children danced to what Roger identified as the old Negro music once played in National Guard armories for colored courtship, now so homogenized and connected to money that it was played for all; back down the beach road, lined with the bumper-to-bumper cars of the students in their Beach Weekend processional; to the house she did not need to tell him they all shared. "We were going to Dillon, I mean, if it hadn't happened," she said, fingering the aluminum beer can pop-top she wore on her finger and then idly pocketing it as he watched, he understanding what she meant: that their plan had been to be married by a justice of the peace. She revealed that, he knew, to place herself beyond the Beatrice she was playing, coyly tossing her waist-length hair as he witnessed the sights of hell; she placed herself beyond his torment and made herself one of the demons. How horrible he felt when she said it, and he could tell she saw the horror, and he thought too that she understood it as a horror apart from the trauma of a tight-lipped parent required to annul yet another South Carolina teenage marriage. He saw in her eyes, in the shadow of the seemingly innocent orgy, the knowledge of the true horror, and from that moment he knew that she too was his enemy, because she too loved Brent. Ordinarily it would be the highest good to join the houses of Patterson and Albright, and that made the impossibility all the more rending. A result so devoutly wished could only lead to idiocy and despair.

The buzzer sounded from below. "Send her up," Lulu called to the doorman. "It's Pammie," she said.

"What?"

"Pammie. Brent's coming along later. Have you forgotten? It's the night of the North Carolina Society Ball."

He looked at her, astounded. "You are encouraging them. I can't believe it."

"I encourage nothing," she said evenly. "I enjoy seeing my son and my goddaughter."

The elevator stopped with a rattle at the penthouse entrance, and Pammie opened the front door. "Pamela — God love you, child," Lulu said, taking her hand. "You look so pretty. Come in. Brent will be along."

"Hey, Lulu," Pammie said, kissing her on the proffered cheek. "I hope this dress isn't ruined. I held it in my lap on the plane."

"Oh, sugar, don't worry. It'll just hang out. I'll run some steam for it in the bathroom."

•   •   •

Things didn't seem to be working as they should, Brent thought as he sat between Pammie and Lulu in the backseat of a taxicab headed to the ball he attended under protest each year. The cab was not a Checker, which meant he had failed again, and Lulu, of course, was sulking, which meant Pammie was sulking, and there he was, again in the middle and at a loss. When they got there both Roger and the senator would appear, and then he would be in the middle again — between the relentless father and the serene hero, and without a decent place to hide. How much longer can I pull it off before they discover I can't keep it all together? The cab had to double-park outside the canopy at the Waldorf, and a Japanese family of four stared as they hurried to the curb unaided amidst a flock of limos. The Japanese studied them in their evening clothes as though they might be the movie stars the tourist guidebook failed to tell them no longer lived there. The man, dressed in the most sober of business suits, and with the mien of a mortician to match, produced a camera from his airline bag, but, thinking better of a photo opportunity, smiled quickly and simply bowed.

Not wishing to be unneighborly, Brent bowed back.

Pammie led him away. "Try not to be a jerk," she said. "Here, check our coats. Lulu and I are going to powder our noses."

He checked the coats and walked through the lobby, which presented itself as a posh United Nations — smug Scandinavian women, swaggering pastel Latins, vivid Tar Heels. The long corridors and high ceilings were a fantasy of opulence in blue and gold, lined with ivory couches and marble-topped tables, a baroque caricature of what luxury must look like to those who buy it by the night.

A portly, sideburned man, also in a tuxedo, shook his hand. "Bill Simpson, International Harvester. You must be John Deere."

"Well, no, actually. I'm Brent Albright."

"Brent Albright. Brent Albright. Is that the new Japanese outfit?"

"I'm sorry?"

"Wait a minute. Are you for North Carolina or equipment?"

"Do I have to choose?"

"Listen, son. You don't have to get smart-alecky. I'm trying to help you figure out what you're supposed to do. If you're for North Carolina you're supposed to be in the left ballroom, and if you're for equipment you're supposed to be in the right ballroom. This here's the right side of the hotel."

Pammie returned and led him to the left, to the table where they were supposed to buy tickets to get drinks. Brent did not have a good feeling about having to buy a ticket to get a drink at the Waldorf. "What's the cheapest thing you have?"

"Beer two dollars wine two-fifty drinks three dollars," said the keeper of the tickets, thumping his fingers on a metal lockbox.

"I've lost Lulu," Pammie said. "Can you spot her?"

Brent searched the crowd milling at the bars, filing into the ballroom. Finally, at the end of the formation he spotted Lulu, who towered over her portly escort, Walter Degley. The bon vivant Walter Degley was now well known to readers of the social columns as an upper-class escort for beautiful women, and as a lower-class mover in international trade. Brent had observed him at these occasions, but always from afar. He was a Deke, originally from Winston-Salem, Brent recalled from the detailed biographies Roger provided of those one ought to know. Roger attributed his livelihood to being the scion of fortunate R. J. Reynolds assembly line workers, who, sometime in the early years of that company, received their wages in common stock. Brent always figured that Roger made things up, especially about people he didn't much like.

"Brent, let me introduce you to Walter Degley, my very good friend," Lulu said, grabbing Brent by the arm. "Walter, my son, Brent."

"Oh yes, we've met," Degley said, offering his plump, manicured hand. "And what line are you in? Your father's splendid company?"

"I am not in the rag trade."

"Oh yes, I remember. You work for Worth. We were all fraternity brothers. I have a little import-export business, you know."

"I've heard that. Now what is it exactly that you sell — or buy?"

Degley's boredom seemed to paralyze him, as though to reply would exhaust him utterly. No mere question in any case was going to stop him from a methodical survey of the surrounding women.

"Do ladies in gowns interest you, Mr. Degley?"

"I'm sorry. Oh, I thought I saw somebody. Go to so many of these things. What was it you were saying?"

"Perhaps it is women that you export and import. There used to be a substantial trade in that, before the white slavery laws, I believe."

He paused from the rumps and bosoms. "My dear young Albright," he said, "as your father has no doubt told you, it does not matter what you buy and sell, so long as you do it often enough and at the right price."

"Walter, you're not boring my son with your old business, are you?" Lulu said, seizing them both by the arm. "We have to take our table now. The music has begun."

They made their way through the large and crowded room, past the orchestra, which had prospered in its forty years at the annual gala of the North Carolina Society of New York, playing the same swing music before the same happy dancers, replacing a saxophone player or a trumpeter as the fortunes of life or art moved on, even as the partyers replaced their own, each of them, the orchestra and the party, retaining the same face for the world. Because of Lulu's seniority they had a very prominent table, and Pammie and Brent, who in the common order of things would have joined the junior members in the back, sat front and center.

"Look," Pammie whispered, pointing beyond the dance floor to the double doors of the entrance hall where Brent could see the senator plotting his entrance. "He's here."

The senator moved through the room from table to table, greeting his old friends by name, speaking his private language of approval and disappointment with a touch on the shoulder, a joke, a slow laugh that sounded above the band's background. As he reached the center of the room, the chandelier's light sparkled upon his white dinner jacket and he found himself suddenly alone before the crowd, now his audience; the bandleader took the cue and played the Carolina fight song, and suddenly the entire party leaped to its feet, applauding and singing.

"They love our Worth, don't they?" Lulu said.

The senator looked in their direction and waved and Lulu blew him a kiss. "Love you!" she yelled. "Love you!" He bowed slightly, motioned the bandleader to keep the chorus going, and made his way to the table.

"Hello, Daddy," Pammie said, pulling at his lapels to kiss him on the cheek.

"Princess—are you going to keep Brent out of fistfights tonight?"

"She won't need to, sir."

"Good. You're in Fairington tomorrow?"

"Yes sir."

"Roger's coming, you know."

"Yes sir."

Lulu stood, waiting expectantly. "Don't I get a hug?"

"If Walter here will let me," he said, abbreviating her embrace with a businesslike peck. "You've been on Lulu's dance card since about 1940, haven't you, Walter?" he said, laughing.

Degley flushed. "Whatever you say, Worth."

As the last chorus died, the senator walked purposefully again through the applauding throng.

"How many of these people will vote for him?" Brent whispered to Pammie.

"Well, they're all his friends."

"Yeah, like Walter Degley. He's a Crain—"

Pammie grabbed his arm. "Look, I told you."

Silently Brent extended his marker to Pammie again; she had wagered him that Roger would show. It was her perverse fascination with Roger's gall, more than campaign responsibilities, that had driven Brent to this event, which he did not particularly like. And there Roger indeed shamelessly stood, alone among the crowd in his business suit, leaning against the double doors, swinging his scuffed briefcase, having stopped on the way to the airport. Like apparitions in silhouette, he and the senator locked arms in the shadows and for a second the crowd seemed to fall silent, waiters stopped in midmotion, and the orchestra played music for dancers in a faraway place, in a faraway time, in the Deke house, or the Sir Walter Hotel, or the Fairington Country Club on another summer night when the children had been put to bed and the cares of the week forgotten.

Chapter Fourteen

1978

"ROGER, for goodness sakes!" Mandy Patterson said as she opened the lacquered door. Upstairs rumbled a vacuum cleaner. The smell of furniture polish cut the air. "It's cleaning time, wouldn't you know it? Honestly, I can't believe I put up with it, but I won't have people thinking with this staff I can't keep a clean house. They're all in the back parlor. Abigail, now you come here this minute! Aren't you going to say hey to Mr. Albright?"

"Hey, Mr. Albright," Abigail, Pammie's younger sister, said, staring at the floor, clumping forward in her riding boots and jodhpurs. Her blond hair had turned the darker color of Pammie's, and her legs were too long for the rest of her. Roger remembered that as a public relations gambit Brent had once tried to arrange an afternoon for her with the president's daughter, who was nearly the same age, and had, he presumed, the same interests. As with many of Brent's early efforts, great enthusiasm had given way to inertia, and the event never came off.

"Hey, Abby. Looks like a good day to go riding."

She nodded. "MO-ther. If we're late I won't get to ride Sugar and I'll have to ride ICH-abod," she insisted, clenching her fists at her side.

"We just can't have *that*, can we, dear? If you'll excuse us, Roger, I'm just going to drive Abby to the stables."

Professor Ogden sat on the aged sofa that Worth had many times refused over Mandy's pleadings to remove from "his" parlor. Ogden had been driven a hundred miles from Chapel Hill and still managed to arrive first at the meeting, as though to defy any of them to believe that advancing age and declining sight would have any effect on his appointments. For forty years he had kept it all together, and he wasn't going to give it up for just another election. There had been harder things. When Ackerman

wanted the Institute to go ideological, to champion the Negroes and disarmament, he had given Delbert half of it and told him to follow his conscience, leaving Roger with the other half to plan economic development
schemes and raise money. The Institute survived. Meanwhile, he had kept
both factions in line with Worth, provoking Roger and the rest to move
the candidate when it was time to move: from the House; to Assistant At-
torney General for Civil Rights when Kennedy needed him (or his accent,
as the joke went); and then, when the seat opened, to the Senate in 1966.
He had even found time to train a younger generation to carry on.

"You're looking well, Brent," Ogden said, his voice firm.

"Thank you, sir," Roger said, clearing his throat. "But it's Roger."

Roger was relieved Brent hadn't heard their old professor confuse them.
Brent was always defensive when the comparison surfaced, believing the
legend — as indeed it stood uncontroverted — of Roger's stardom as an Ogden protégé, the paper, the plaudits, the business success related back,
probably inaccurately, to the academic achievement. Ogden encouraged
that myth, too — that the Institute could foster with its methods not only
do-gooders but hard-eyed industrialists like Roger Albright.

Ogden moved deliberately and wordlessly to the right, gesturing to
Roger to sit beside Brent at the end of the sofa closest to the senator. Always
the professional, Roger thought; the AA and the money man should take
the mates' chairs, even though it meant little, since if the professor was
invited the senator would turn to him first. Anyway, the others, Ogden's
charges, would conclude what he had coached them to conclude, so that
even as complex a contest as a resurgent Crain campaign would evoke in
the professor a type of omniscience.

"Brent was just showing around the schedule, Roger," the senator said,
handing him one of the photocopied sheets. "Next week is the NAACP,
the AFL-CIO, the Teachers' Federation speech — we need to hit that one
hard — the Uptown Rotary Club of Charlotte, a stock-car race in Rock-
ingham, and the fund-raiser tonight. How much will we get tonight, Brent?"

"We'll take in thirty to forty thousand, net."

"Where will that put us total?"

Brent peered over his glasses at a pocket diary. "Right at one million
five hundred thousand dollars."

"That would ordinarily be a good kitty," the senator said, leaning back
against the edge of the table. "A damn good kitty."

Brent clicked the diary shut and placed it in his briefcase. He took off his glasses and examined them in the light. "You get your name on the NCN list, you can buy Joe Crain for ten dollars a month until you get to seven million. Easy money for senators these days."

"You're in a cheerful mood this morning," the senator said.

"You want cheerful? Look at this," Brent said, reaching into the brief-case to produce a newspaper clipping. "This was in *The Wall Street Journal* yesterday. Jerry Brown got two hundred and fifty thousand from one after-noon's work by the Grateful Dead. That's a rock and roll group, Senator. I think the *Journal* wanted me to be angry about that. Instead, it just started me talking again about bands we could line up. What do you think?"

Professor Ogden began to laugh, rocking his head backward and for-ward until tears rolled down his face; he tried unsuccessfully to staunch them with a handkerchief. The senator stood, holding the newspaper clip-ping, while Brent and Roger sat, embarrassed.

"Mr. Ackerman is here, Senator," said Gudrun, the Pattersons' au pair, appearing at the door in a tennis dress. "And he said for you to help him with equipment."

Brent jumped up to help carry Ackerman's VCR into the parlor. "Let's get on with it if we can, guys," Ackerman said, jogging into the room and closing the door. "I've got to be on a plane for Miami in two hours."

"Delbert, we were just saying that we had raised a million five against Crain's seven million," the senator began. "They've already been com-mitting a lot of media money."

"They could spend seven million forever," Brent said.

Roger thought Brent had spoken too soon; he was nervous. Ackerman's presentation, Roger deduced, had been arranged by Brent as a ploy to pre-pare the campaign to go negative. Delbert had evolved from the politics of conscience to practical service at OEO in the Johnson years, then to political consulting in the lean times afterward. Fascinated by television, he gravitated to Madison Avenue and soon became the leading media man for aggressive Democratic campaigns. In political years he ran television for his liberal favorites. Other years he produced commercial advertise-ments, for which he won several awards, becoming especially associated with personal grooming products. He now was on a special mission to sell negative ad strategies to traditionalists like Worth. Roger had viewed sam-ple videos a month ago in New York, at Ackerman's West End Avenue apartment. Delbert's building looked prosperous, with small dogs clutching at tall ladies in the lobby and a crimson-uniformed doorman standing guard. His pitch was compelling. As Ackerman rewound his creations, however, Roger had trouble evaluating what he had seen; his attention was arrested by the sight of a pair of naked bums hitting each other with two-by-fours one block over on Broadway.

Naked bums bashing each other over the head with two-by-fours — is that the only way Worth could win now? Roger wondered. Or is that a sure way to lose? It's not something you can turn off and on. Once you're a naked bum, you're a naked bum. And Crain well understood Worth's temperament. If Worth's attack was begun halfheartedly, Crain would turn his opponent's inability to be truly mean into a liability. "He's got to have a new basket of issues, and he's got to repackage and resegment his market," Ackerman had said. "This Patterson Magic theme is bullshit against the NCN. I know those guys. They're not nice people. You wouldn't want to drink with them. Know what I mean?" He balled up a discarded high concept and tossed the paper into the wastebasket. "Sometimes I think I'm running a big emergency ward this year. Stanhope in Iowa, Dewey in Indiana, Finnegan in Idaho. They're all going down, hard, and they don't know what's happening to them."

"You're including Worth too, I take it."

Ackerman tossed another wad of paper against the far wall with particular violence. "I like Worth. Always have. I've even gotten to like you, you know. I mean we've all been through a lot together. But you're the one — not Brent and not me — who can snap Worth out of it."

"I don't know, Delbert. It's Brent's place now. Besides, Worth is Worth. He's got that stubborn streak. What he really wants — "

"Is to debate maybe? Blow the little jerk away with some elegant phrases? Sure, he wants to do the Lincoln-Douglas campaign. Who wouldn't with a nebbish like Crain? But that's high school bullshit today." Another wad of paper hit the wall. "Typical. What he doesn't realize is that the NCN guys are spending early on him. They want to take the lead now and ride it out. Incumbents don't come back, you know. Look, it's like I told Brent — we've got to take on their momentum now and give them a new look . . ." Delbert's voice trailed off, and Roger knew they were thinking the same thing, remembering with exasperation the subject and would-be project, five hundred miles south of their Manhattan strategy meeting. Even if Worth agreed in theory, he probably couldn't stomach actually doing it.

But Brent wouldn't know this, Roger thought, observing his son back in the Pattersons' study, tense with the battle for the direction of the campaign. Because of the malleability of youth, he couldn't appreciate how unchangeable his candidate was. "We could go out tomorrow for money except Crain bled us white in the primaries," Brent said. "There's always your personal credit, Senator."

"Scoundrels bled us white in the primaries," Ogden said, shaking his head violently.

"It seems, then," the senator said, trying to summarize, "that we just have to be conservative and save our media money until closer to the election. I see no reason to get into a spending battle."

Ackerman began to speak, but Brent beat him to it. "If I may, sir, I feel strongly that we should do just the contrary. We need to jump in now with big media buys. If we wait longer, we could be out of it. The polls show slippage across the board. If we slip much farther we won't be able to raise money anyway. I feel our best shot is to commit now for attack TV, to get Crain's negatives up and try for a bounce in the polls, and then go out on that basis for more money down the stretch."

"Worth, I agree with Brent on this," Ackerman said. "Last week in New York we developed a proposal for a strategy we could begin to employ immediately to combat the NCN. We need to retool and hit them hard now."

As if to underline the point, Ackerman set up his video recorder in front of the television set and played anti-Patterson advertisements done by the NCN. "This is what's driving up your negatives, Worth," he said. "I don't know if you've seen the full collection yet."

The thirty-second commercial spots showed angry motorists on gasoline lines, dark foreigners throwing rocks at United States embassies, crying matrons outside abortion clinics. American aircraft carriers fell off the screen and B-1 bombers exploded against a background of column after column of Soviet troops debarking at a port Brent swore was Morehead City, giving way to picketing black welfare mothers and gay couples holding hands, all marching from your television into your living room. At the end of each collage a map of America shrank against a map of the world and a voice said, "Do you want America to get smaller and smaller while our problems get bigger and bigger? VOTE AGAINST WORTH PATTERSON."

The last image faded into the room's darkness and Delbert rose to turn up the lights. "Very nice work," he volunteered, nodding appreciatively. "They use Bill Weissler."

Ackerman skipped his plane to Miami. The group worked through lunch. The senator was skeptical but not dismissive, and Brent had high hopes. Eventually, however, the senator and Ackerman argued.

"But dammit, Delbert, these Crain ads — they never say anything, not a damn thing. It has to backfire."

Ackerman turned off the VCR. "If what you mean, Worth, is that the commercials don't make an argument, then I agree with you. They have no argument, they're not speeches. It's ebb and flow."

"I don't follow."

"Ebb and flow. One image after another. Very antiauthority, you see. You're the authority, Worth, believe it or not. You tell people to be good, to help their fellow man, all that shit. But people don't want to be good. They want to be bad. See, Crain is telling them it's okay to be bad, to get angry, to kick ass — that's their nature, see. And then he'll save them and they go to heaven anyway, get it?"

"Metaphysics, Delbert. Metaphysics. What are the man's positions?"

Ackerman shook his head. "That's not the point, Worth. Oh, he has positions, all right. But it's not positions he's selling. It's an attitude thing. He says the country's on its knees and you're responsible because you want us to be good all the time. It's working. Your negatives are up fourteen points in three weeks."

The click of Ackerman's briefcase punctuated their exchange and the room fell silent, except for the chuckling of Professor Ogden, who tamped out his rancid pipe and with a shaking hand lit it up again. "The barbarians are at the gates, Worth," he said. "I'm afraid we're in for it. I think you should consider Delbert's advice. God knows Ernest MacGiver should've listened."

Brent looked grateful for the unexpected help. "Senator," he interrupted, seizing the moment, "this is what I meant when I said I didn't know what our position papers or the Truth Squad people were going to do. They can't respond to specific charges."

"They're out there doing something," Worth answered. "People listen."

"Maybe. But they can't respond to images or gut-level type stuff. Sir, I feel strongly that we have to take the initiative and mount a direct attack on Crain. I took the liberty of asking Delbert to bring along some samples . . ."

"Don't even bother," the senator said icily. "I don't want you, or anybody else, wasting any more time on this."

Ackerman, who, as evidenced by his smile and acquiescence had predicted the result, began to pack up his equipment. But Ogden halted him with a touch on the arm. "My question is, Delbert, or Brent," addressing the two of them as the good teacher would draw one or the other out, "what is there about Crain that could be exploited? The interesting thing about him, Brent, as your work has pointed out, is that he has no record. No private life, either."

Trust Ogden to get to the nub, Roger thought. Of course the job would be difficult for anyone, Roger thought, much less for people not much good at mudslinging. They all knew what there was to know, from the research Ogden orchestrated and Albright, elder and younger, had performed. The problem with Crain was precisely that he was a blank, a perfect television mirage. It was hard to focus bad news on him, because he possessed a negative capability that threw it right back. But Ackerman had discussed this in New York. Crain could still be vulnerable. All they would need would be the scintilla of a smear — and then the dynamic Crain had created would turn on him, too.

"I'm glad you asked that question," Brent said, flipping through his notes and stalling, seeming to calculate his answer. "As a matter of fact, Delbert can get us some terrific commercials on Crain's lack of a war record — you know, paint him as a draft dodger, especially good beside you, Senator. Or we could go after his television station — they were investigated once by the IRS. Or we could patch together some of his stupidest old editorials — some of the obviously racist ones from the sixties would be sensational."

"I'm just not comfortable," the senator said. "I'm not comfortable with this negative campaigning. I don't want to slander the man, I want to pin him down on the issues. I want to flush him out and make him defend himself."

Ogden shook his head and stood up shakily, holding out his hand first for balance and then to ward off Brent, who jumped up to help him. "No — dammit — leave me alone. Now Worth, you've got to listen, son. These people will break your heart. These people — they're not political people. You see, I trained you for politics, and these aren't political people. It's all an afterthought for them. What they really are about is a bump in the night — fear, that is. To debate them is no use. They just use you against yourself, because what you're doing — thinking, acting — is a threat because it's outside them, a thing of the world. Protect yourself, Worth. Listen, a little. I'm afraid Ernest didn't listen enough, or maybe I stopped him. They broke Ernest's heart that way. It wasn't the election. You can lose an election."

Professor Ogden slowly sat down and sipped on the glass of water Brent got for him. "You know, something Roger said once — I remember it, the first thing you ever said, Roger — 'logic, experience, and hope.' That makes you into a builder, see. That's what I liked about you right away. But Crain doesn't go for any of it. What he does on earth doesn't matter, you see. You know, why try to build something in Sodom and Gomorrah? Better to tear the whole thing down. Convenient, too, politically.

"But you boys can't do that. You've got to live by your lights. That's what he hates, you living by your lights. You're dealing with that awkward kid who couldn't stand the big man on campus. There's lots more of the awkward kids than the BMOCs, and don't you know they love to bring the BMOC down? But they have to do it for a reason, because all their lives they've been conditioned to follow. Now Crain tells them that the handsome people can be brought down, must be brought down, because they are hurting the country. Handsome people, Crain tells them, are traitors, which is what the awkward kids thought in their hearts all along.

"So, you see, he has to get you, just like he got Ernest. The race question we could have handled, politically, I mean, but it broke his heart. He'll try to break your heart, too, Worth, and you can't let that happen. You have to protect yourself. Bite the bullet. Just remember it will be hard to bring him down. He already believes nothing good will happen to him."

He stood up again and moved to the window, where the morning light had already begun to recede. "There's one other thing," he said quietly. "I mean, it's part of what I meant about breaking your heart, Worth."

"What do you mean, sir?" Worth said.

The professor turned slowly to face him. "I mean, what's out there?"
"I don't really follow."
"What secret is out there for him to expose? Because he'll find it."
Worth shrugged and shook his head, as he might have in class when he had no answer. Roger wondered again at his ability to deny, as he always had, the worst possibilities. On many days his ignorance of the blessed was a great virtue, but now, in this deadly game, Roger wished that he could look at Brent beside him and realize what could be at stake. As usual, though, the stalwart mien, even in the face of Ogden's broadest invitation, meant that Roger would have to worry for them all.

"Be sure, Worth," Ogden said, "before you go ahead with this. One thing we have learned about Crain is that he knows us very well."

•   •   •

The asphalt of the beltway around Fairington curved to the end of sight, liquid in the September heat, its constant mirage renewing itself to the Patterson Forest exit and the beckoning Exxon, where Roger, pausing long enough from his postmeeting reverie to notice his gas gauge on empty, stopped to fill up the car.

Lately, when he needed to think, he had taken to driving alone, sometimes long distances toward no particular goal, just to be alone and to stop answering telephone calls from people worried that Worth Patterson would lose. He had not gotten any real work done in a month, he figured. From the ancient coin machine — preserved from the days the station stood at a country crossroads outside Fairington proper — he bought a Pepsi and, leaning against the feeding car, downed it in one drink, wiping the bottle's sweat on his face. He studied the highway behind him that circled the city in its man-made ravine, gesturing north to Washington, south and west to Atlanta, east to the sea, paring back the land, revealing in turn the abandoned field of a farmer, his outbuildings a jumble of weather-dark boards, a rusting combine at rest between them; ahead, the brick and siding sprawl of a manufacturing plant, trucks poised at the loading ramp, a huge American flag hanging in the still air behind the neat link fence. A man on a tractor outside the factory gate mowed and gathered the grass, stacking it like hay on the ground, as though the grass growing and the man mowing reenacted the life of the farm now ended.

At that very spot, probably after drinking a Pepsi from the same machine, Roger and old Herman Siler had discussed buying the farm for a plant site, speculating on the location of the highway to come and the changes in fortune it would determine. How powerful, Roger thought; the whim of a bureaucrat could alter the path two miles east or west. What fear it inspired in normally confident men. For him, however, with Worth in office, Washington always seemed close.

Above the scene Roger spied the long, bespectacled face of Joe Crain, perched in the white margins of a billboard on the far side of the highway. VOTE FOR JOE CRAIN—HE'S ONE OF US! How simple, Roger thought; how corrupt.

"You work in Washington, mister?" said the teenage gas jockey, handing Roger his charge card. Puzzled, Roger started to deny it, until he saw the boy perusing the congressional license plate and he remembered he was driving Brent's car.

"As a matter of fact, I do."

"You want to keep your job?"

"Going to try."

"Well, you better get on Joe Crain's good side—he's gonna clean out that crowd running down our country, yessiree Bob."

The paralysis of the day prevented what might have been an overly snappy rejoinder, and Roger bit his tongue as the smiling fellow gave him back his receipt. He climbed into the car, but before he could escape the lot he saw the latest Crain flyer blow across the pavement. Yesterday he received an anonymous copy of the state-of-the-art anti-Patterson solicitation, not a difficult item to come by, he realized, since five hundred thousand had been mailed nationally to the names on the NCN computer list. Delbert got one in New York, and evidently so did the local Exxon. The flyer featured an overexposed photograph of the senator at a black-tie reception shaking hands with a smiling Ambassador Dobrynin, against an overlay of the usual Soviet assault troops. Beneath the pictorial, a broadside:

By Day He Votes
AGAINST our Canal. AGAINST our Unborn Children.
By Night He Drinks With
THE RUSSIAN AMBASSADOR.

FIGHT PATTERSON

WHILE YOU STILL CAN

He puzzled over the handbill and then remembered the 1950 original. On one matter Crain had been misjudged, he thought. The man did have a sense of humor. Roger eased onto the local road toward home, inserting a cassette to listen to the strange sound of his own voice on tape reciting the memorandum he had again researched and written, at Ogden's request, and which Brent had distributed, along with the first chapter he had done nearly thirty years before, to all Patterson campaign workers so that they could try to understand the fury and danger of what confronted them. At this hour the faithful needed all the clues the old method could provide.

"To: The File/TO, BA

"From: Roger Albright

"Re: Crain

"Even after Narly Ferguson won, Crain didn't get any respect. He didn't like to hear that the campaign had set back race relations for years, maybe decades, that gentlemen kept such talk out of politics. He wouldn't reply to the intellectuals, the newspaper do-good editorialists, the fancy lawyers always trying to do this or that for Negroes, or that Chapel Hill crowd, a lot of them just downright communists and nothing else to call them. Maybe gentlemen had kept race out of politics for fifty years while pretending Negroes didn't exist. That's how your gentlemen are. Your colored man just doesn't exist for the gentleman until the gentleman needs a shoeshine. Maybe your gentlemen did keep Negroes out of politics, but they let them in everything else. And the government, run by gentlemen, too; why, if they hadn't let Negroes in the white man's army there wouldn't have been a riot in Pockston and my father would be alive. And the government? Did the government care about the rights of plain people? Look at what the army did to Pockston, turning it from a nice little town for farmers to trade in and where honest people could make a living into a brothel, with people you didn't know on the street and black and white women and black and white men together, and Yankee money all over the place. And not just in Pockston, but all over the state. The whole state was turning into a brothel with Yankee money and nigger bucks crawling all over everything. No fire, no brimstone, just fact . . .

"After the elections, in fact, it was tough for Crain to find a job. Evidently the big-time boys thought he was tainted goods. With a new wife and baby he moved back to Pockston instead of to Washington with Senator Ferguson. He took his old position back with Youth for Jesus, but that wasn't enough for a family man. Eventually, because he was Harold Crain's son, the radio station put him on as a

sportscaster. In the fall and winter he called the high school's football and basketball schedule and filled in as the number-two man for Caleb College, at eight dollars a game; in the spring and summer he was the voice of the Pockston Bingoes, the town's semipro baseball entry. Seven-fifty a game, plus a dollar and a quarter for gas and supper. On the road one night from Kinston, when the rent was due and the cash stretched too thin to make it, Joe had an idea: he was good at politics — why not speak for himself? Why not stand for the legislature? That paid; not much, but it paid.

"So he ran for the legislature from the front seat of his Dodge, and, because he was Harold Crain's son, he won. The truth was, though, after settling down in Raleigh, Crain didn't much enjoy the legislature. The legislators weren't interested in discussing the right and wrong of a thing, even the good conservative ones. They were interested in getting elected again, mostly. Crain sat hour after hour in the chambers, waiting for his turn in the nearly deserted hall to give speeches no one listened to on the evils of liquor, and sex perverts, and the Red menace. He voted no on every bill when he thought a private interest would profit from public works, which meant he voted no on almost everything. His colleagues became annoyed with him, especially when the reporters deserted the grand pork-barreling pooh-bahs and flocked to Joe as good copy.

"At the end of his second term, Crain decided not to run again. He stayed in Raleigh rather than move back to Pockston, because his wife liked it, and she was pregnant again, and the capital city had more advantages for the family. Youth for Jesus promptly offered him the state directorship, but he was looking for something fresh. Finally, the North Carolina Insurance Consortium, searching for a new lobbyist at the legislature, asked him to take the job, not dreaming that he would. But when Joe Crain recognized the man who was offering him the lobbying position as the same man who had fired him from the sales job eight years ago, he couldn't resist. It was a sign from the Lord. And besides, he needed the money.

"So he traveled across North Carolina, giving speeches about the benefits of being as covered as you could be and parrying the thrusts of misguided people who thought ill of the industry. He kept his hand in politics, of course. His peers liked him more as a lobbyist than they had as a lawmaker, and he prospered, moderately. They marveled at the beneficial effects on a man's personality of learning how the real world worked. Other states' insurance groups, hearing of his ability to make a speech on the evil of comparative fault or the outrage of joint and several liability, offered him honoraria to visit Tucson, or Memphis, or Toledo and address their conventions. He talked less and less about insurance and more and more about

politics: *how the government didn't work and made people not work either; how it deprived honest businessmen of their living, compromised with communists, and made criminals out of little children who wanted to pray in school.*

"He had seen the problems when he was a young man, and he had tried to warn people as best he could. Now homosexuals were everywhere; cities were put to the torch by crazy, welfare-ruined Negroes; the government had lined so many pockets that it had to print worthless money to pay the bills; the gentlemen who ran things didn't have the stomach to lick the communists stirring up the young people on the streets, much less the communists in Vietnam. For years he had turned down offers from long-ago campaign friends to go back into politics. Politics was the problem, he told them. But he was restless. He had to get the message across before everything went up in flames.

"God answered his need for a job as he had before. Crain's old friends from the 1950 campaign had established the National Christian Network and they had so much money they were setting up their own TV station, outside Fairington. They had the buildings up already, big brick campus-like buildings that looked to Joe like truth itself. Inside, the thin metal floors crackled as he walked over the cooling ducts that whirred constantly, pouring chilled air over room after room of computers, and the men in the white coats that tended them, changing the big marked spools of tape whenever this mailing list was called up for solicitation, or this man's dossier for public exposure. Behind the brick buildings stood the studio, set below ground to withstand atomic attack, so that if America itself were a leveled radioactive ruin, NCN would still broadcast. In fact, it would be the only station broadcasting, its already encoded program to reconstruct a mutant annihilated race in the image of God not missing a beat, its message soothing and practical, as the annihilation would be God's plan too, the means to rid His earth of the unclean, the nonbelievers, to let the rapture of the mushroom cloud bring Satan to his knees and the elect to Paradise. "Where is the tower?" Joe asked, looking around the grounds and seeing none. The towers are secret, they told him. The towers are everywhere.

"Joe knew his friends would ask him to be their public affairs director and knew he would accept. Sure enough, the offer came. Every evening at seven o'clock, after the CBS, NBC, or ABC news, the "alphabet news" as Joe Crain called them, the National Christian News went live. 'Now that you've heard their news, listen to the real news.' Homosexuals marching in the streets. Aborted fetuses in mass graves. Christian schools harassed by state authorities. In short, America at war with God, while Christians tried in the final days to hold off an evil government* *run amok, a government that somehow convinced the good people to pay off the wicked. At the end of the half hour, when the screen vibrated with memories of outrage, after each spliced film, each remark had been edited and placed just so, Crain's five-minute editorial arranged the carnage in perspective, the denouement to a violent drama of democracy going slowly, irretrievably mad:*

> *To say no to the government is the proper way for right-thinking men to defend their families. But when men say no the secular media sneer that they are 'against progress,' or 'reactionary.'*
>
> *What are they really telling you when they say this? They are telling you the old lie that sin isn't bad, that toleration of evil is good, and that man is smarter than God.*
>
> *I say no to the leaders of the so-called homosexual rights movement, and the pro-abortion and anti-family movements, and the pot smokers and drug pushers, all of whom are just plain moral degenerates. I say no to the flood of government welfare that is causing the deterioration of the Negro race.*
>
> *I say no to the courts, which have handcuffed the police, disregarded states' rights, and coddled communists all around us.*
>
> *The hoodlums who march in our streets demanding this or that and taking what they please will demand and take until they destroy us all. Such people will never give anything back to this country. What we need is for a million good men to say no. What we need is a revolt against revolution . . ."*

· · ·

By habit Roger drove through the old neighborhood. On the left stood the Siler's brick pile, still disliked by the neighbors for its angles and gewgaws. Roger believed they disliked it less for aesthetic reasons than because it reflected the likeness of the owner rather than being a reproduction of some other time or place. This was a kind of directness amounting to class betrayal. The ersatz period mansions that flanked it on Prospect Drive—the Galways' fake French château, the Newport-style bungalows, the columned Georgians, even the Albright Cape Cod—always seemed, in contrast, a purchase of somebody else's past for the purpose of evading one's own. They wanted to be different from what they were and to be the same as everybody else, Roger thought. They had succeeded brilliantly.

For some time Roger had permitted himself to feel contempt for his neighbors. Their massive self-creation he acknowledged to be similar to his own, with the important difference that they had forgotten what they were before. This normally caused little harm, except when a man like Joe Crain made them afraid. Fear made them lose the ability to resist bad ideas, even ideas presented by Crain, who would take their money and destroy every good thing they had done.

Across the fairway, set back discreetly amid the shade trees of Founders Row, lay the Patterson compound. The senator's leadership once rested on his neighbors' desire to be like him. What Worth can't understand, Roger thought, is that they don't need him anymore, and today Crain can write in Fairington's book as readily as he.

Beyond that, Worth could not seem to grasp that he must change if he would win, and Brent could not make the case. It was close to checkmate. Crain prepared for him an impossible bargain: become something you are not in order to survive. Brutal but elegant, Roger thought.

On bad days Roger believed it was more curse than blessing that he resisted the moving dream of his neighbors. If only, he thought on those days, he could share their new lives with them. They sensed he couldn't and made him pay. He thought after thirty-two years in the town he had maybe three friends: Worth, Billy Roy, and, in his last days, old Galway. And yet he couldn't escape; Fairington was his home. It was his condition to create much of Fairington's wealth and yet remain a spectator to Fairington life. When the black college students marched downtown, he took Brent in the car to witness every night of the week-long demonstration. Lulu was even more convinced he was mad; she would not go downtown without the maid network's intelligence that there was no sit-in that day and it was safe to enjoy lunch in the Garden Room without the gamey smell of equality in the air. At the time Roger was not on the side of the demonstrators; neither was he against them. He didn't think it mattered what he thought. Their moment had arrived. Every night the Albright men parked beside the police barricades and from atop his father's shoulders Brent watched the marchers while Roger hummed "Georgia on My Mind"—that was, Brent said once, his primary memory of the civil rights movement, sitting on the shoulders of a balding man in a starched white shirt who whistled "Georgia on My Mind" while police carried the Carver College student body into history.

Later in the eventful decade, Brent and Roger went to a conference on the heady progress of Fairington industry, held on the pristine estate of one of the research companies lured to the land Roger purchased on the Institute's account beside the local teacher's college, which was now, by Roger's generosity and political intercession, UNC-Fairington. Long ago the farmland turned research park had been dubbed "Albright Acres" in the press, the official label proposed by chamber of commerce leaders having been quickly discarded by everyone but them. Roger's panel was challenged from the audience by a shouting scholar, who disrupted the proceedings in what might have passed for counterculture fashion and presented the gathering with an ominous picture of the true structure of Fairington life. The city, he explained, was organized around a group of six hills, on each of which stood a factory complex. All the factories were surrounded by worker neighborhoods, which were insulated from the rest of the population by a calculated set of freeways, the largest of which neatly cut off the black community in the southeast part of the city. Each of the six hills, industrial fortresses, really, was connected to a major boulevard, all of which emptied into Trade Street, which in turn had its climax at Textile Square and the Galway and Albright headquarters buildings. Clearly, the scholar concluded in grand crescendo, Fairington was a city designed for the pleasure of industrial capital.

The cocksure style of the disputant allowed no deference to the patrons on the panel who made his harangue possible. And confrontation was not the style of the North Carolina Textile League, whose members retained their well-coached executive postures. So Roger astonished his colleagues all the more by rising to engage the fellow in a debate on the present state of scholarship in the social sciences. He moved his argument to climax quickly by striding to the blackboard, sketching the city limits of Fairington, and underlining the notorious six hills. "At the base of each hill," he intoned, "near the citadels of industrial capitalism above, is a softball diamond. All of these softball diamonds are connected by roads that eventually empty into this boulevard here, Commerce Street, which finds its terminus at the Old Tyme Ice Cream Shop. Thus, I submit, sir, that Fairington is designed for the convenience of softball players, who have their seat of power at the Old Tyme Ice Cream Shop, and that this conclusion is just as valid as yours . . ."

He continued down Prospect Drive and slowed to turn on reflex, forgetting that the family home was no longer the family home but a pleasant Cape Cod owned by someone else. He had sold the house a week after the divorce was final, shipping Brent's effects in a UPS truck. He used the money to buy three condominiums, where the furniture from the house was haphazardly distributed. The main condo, or the Big House, he lived in. The second, dubbed the Little House, he gave to Brent, and the third he kept for a while and then sold at 300 percent profit. Intrigued, he bought two more townhouses, which he also sold at his leisure for large returns. He worked on the sales in his spare time, after dinner on odd evenings, installing a telephone in the bathroom so he wouldn't waste any time. One month he made three-quarters of a million dollars on the john.

Chapter Fifteen

1978

THE North Carolina State Teachers' Federation made a habit of endorsing Worth Patterson, and they continued it faithfully in the unsettled election year of 1978. The Fairington Coliseum exhibition hall was filled, and the teachers, who had given the students the day off for the occasion, quickly dispatched the creamed chicken, yellow rice, and green peas efficiently set out for them. Brent remarked that the school lunchroom cooks should have had the day off too, rather than be made to cook for the teachers. But the teachers were not a particularly flush group, and they looked like they enjoyed their creamed chicken, yellow rice, and green peas, and even the gummy peach pie they got for dessert.

If the teachers were not well heeled they were earnest, and being government employees they took their politics seriously. In the summer they volunteered and walked the precincts. Their pedagogical style discouraged rudeness. Anybody would take a campaign full of teachers. And the teachers liked working for Worth Patterson. Any dollar spent on education was a dollar well spent, he often said, even when no teachers were listening.

But this time the teachers weren't hearing about those dollars spent for education. They didn't hear anything about money at all. As a result of a focus group secretly arranged by Brent, and the senator's grudging approval of "repositioning" urged on him by Ogden, who didn't know what a focus group was, they heard a new, tough, repackaged Worth Patterson tell them that they, as teachers, were a "threatened group" and that he pledged the "strict and quick enforcement of the law" when teachers' lives and well-being were jeopardized by "marauding groups of violent youngsters" who wandered the halls of America's schools with knives and guns. "The authority for our schools," he declared, "has been too often usurped by faceless judges and Washington bureaucrats whose ill-advised policies, launched with the best of intentions, have produced a generation of murderous illiterates."

As the senator wound up with an anecdote about a fictitious aunt who kept order in her mountain classroom with a pistol, Roger, on the podium with Ackerman to begin satisfying his promise of public support, searched the tables for Brent. He saw him, behind the television cameras, half-leaning against a pillar. It's sad, he thought, that his success should come from Worth speaking with the greatest sincerity these odd words that he didn't believe.

The television crews had gotten the day's footage and clicked off their spotlights. The print reporters still listened, notebooks ready, but most looked like they had their stories and were coasting out the day. It was playing well, Roger thought, surprised at how Brent's new concoction provoked the predicted response. Pavlov with a smile, the boy called it. Worth had lashed out against truants and vandals with a scoutmaster's passion. He was in fine voice, and his military bearing, firm features, and thick gray hair seemed more popular than ever with the considerable female contingent of the state teachers. Roger felt Ackerman nudge him with a practiced motion so slight the sharpest-eyed auditor would not have blinked. "Bingo," Delbert said, eyes straight ahead. Roger nodded. It was going to be a success.

". . . and then she laid the pistol down on the table and said, 'Boys, you may be bigger than me, but you're not bigger than this pistol, so sit down and do your lessons.'" The fatted crowd guffawed as one, and the waitresses hurried to clear the last coffee cups, sensing that the lunch shift was over. Worth gathered the loose paper of his speech, set to make a final appeal and a speedy departure. The security cop unlocked the fire doors for the main exit. Suddenly, a man in the front jumped from his seat, and Roger froze for a moment, wondering if this was the one who made a threat and meant it. "Senator!" he shouted, reaching for his coat pocket. "Oh my God," Ackerman whispered and lunged toward the lectern, but Roger, planting his feet and summoning his strength, held him back as state troopers pushed to the front and moved to tackle the intruder, standing aside when they saw the man draw a pocket Bible, not a pistol, from his jacket.

"Senator, what I want to know," the man shouted, "what I want to know is why you are so determined to make America weak! Why do you vote against every weapon we could use against the communists? Why do you sit by when little children can't pray in schools and protect themselves from Satan?"

"Now look here, I'm giving the speech," the senator said, shaking his finger at the man. Television cameras turned on the interloper, the suddenly alert crewmen running for position. "Now what you've said aren't true statements," the senator said calmly, turning red from head to toe with the effort, the sweat shining on his forehead. "Those are false statements put out by my opponent and I'm going to set you straight. I've always voted for a strong defense, and I've always been in favor of any child's right to individually pray in schools. I just don't believe, I say I just don't believe that the schoolteachers here want to be in the business of enforcing religion in the classroom."

As the teachers, led by the head table, stood and applauded, the intruder grew enraged.

"Fornicator! Fornicator!" he screamed, sinking to his knees before the lectern, his hands bleeding. "Pray for your soul, damned to the pit! *Iklabba meylabba marronestros connetros plegazel haberzel wazlabba hakesh mombassu skekassu mandros haska vorzit emlabba shaklabba golabba kolabba drolabba labba labbas labbas . . .*"

The troopers pinned the heckler's arms and dragged him away, a belt in his mouth, as the mobile crews followed him and a trail of blood out the door. The teachers, stunned into silence by the outburst that had so violated classroom decorum, stood, and led by their officials at the head table, applauded the senator. "Shit," Delbert said, and then again, and for emphasis, "monkey shit."

The word sounded again and again in Roger's mind. Fornicator, he reflected. Something dirty with a whiff of Latin.

"I think that was tongues," Roger said finally. "And the blood — what the hell was that?"

"Whatever. Asshole was a plant, I'll tell you that. Goddamn plant."

Looking out on the quickly scattering audience, Roger saw that the good speech and the solid, friendly crowd would be replaced on the television screen by a religious nut making strange accusations, an angry, scared candidate trying to answer, and then the crazed scene of blood and glossolalia. The reporters were at the pay phones, already dictating copy. Brent went from phone to phone, working them, trying to laugh it off.

"Did he have a gun?" the senator asked as the traveling party exited, state troopers encircling the side door.

He glanced at Brent for the answer. "No sir. And you handled it fine. You kept your cool."

"Good. I thought so too." The senator wiped his forehead slowly with his pocket handkerchief, his hand trembling as he folded the linen back into place.

"I'm talking with Crain's people tomorrow," Brent said, trying to change the mood. "We might have the break in the debate we're looking for."

"What? I'm sorry. I need to sit down." They sat on dark, low couches in the neon-lit foyer, the senator waving wanly at his well-wishers. One trooper brought him a Dixie cup of water from the fountain and the others nervously watched the departing teachers, hands in their jackets.

•　•　•

From the entrance to Fairington's newest mall, Roger watched the modest but headstrong rush hour traffic progress on the expressway. Patterson High stood in the distance on the right beside the new hospital and the flotilla of doctors' offices that attended it. The NCN complex commanded the crest of a wooded hill gouged otherwise clean by the banking highway, its low-lying Georgian facade and broadcast antenna topped by an ever-blinking red light. "I'd change that color if the Washington bureaucrats would let me," Crain often quipped. Oncoming headlights twinkled as twilight suddenly turned to dusk, and in the new darkness the steel of Roger's car closed around him like a mothy womb. He welcomed with a shiver the anomie that seized him in late afternoon. If only, he thought, if only we all could have lived here without becoming encased in it.

The guard at the entrance to the subterranean parking deck waved him sullenly on, and eventually he came to the underground entrance to Captain Disco, where a valet screeched away with his Lincoln. After he took an elevator to the main floor, the bored-looking maître d', who in his green and gold drum major's uniform must have been the incarnation of the captain himself, directed him to the bar, as happy hour progressed. So this is where the young people go, he thought. Several dozen young women with briefcases and spiked heels, their glasses propped on top of their swept-up hair, stood toe-to-toe with young men in pinstripes and loosened ties. He wondered if there were places like this where old single people went to look one another over. He didn't know any offhand.

All of the drinkers looked familiar to him, as if they might be friends of Pammie and Brent, dressed for a new stage of life, the next page in the photo album. Still, he knew none of them and for a moment he thought he had been stood up. Then he spotted Skip Skidmore waving like a railroad brakeman.

He nodded and walked over to him. "Hello, Skip."

Skip put his beer down on top of the bar and his large face creased with a giant grin. "Why hey, Mr. Albright. How the heck are you? Hope you don't mind this place. I come here for a little pop after work sometimes."

"No, no. This is perfect." He surveyed Brent's boyhood friend, whom he had not seen in years, noting his already broadening stomach and thinning hair, alarmed at how late the hour must be if he was cataloging signs of age in his son's contemporaries. Young Skidmore was always so normal — ordinary would be a cruel word — and when he and Pammie began dating in college, most of the usual crowd had been surprised, by both the fact of it and by Brent's apparent encouragement. Roger had not been surprised, though, even as Lulu, in her seemly cattiness, had gone on about how pleasant but, well, slow young Skip had been, what climbers the parents were, how amused she was that as a matter of honor he had offered to rent Brent's trigonometry homework rather than simply cribbing it. At the root was her delusion that Brent and Pammie's match could be the great culmination to her own desires, perfection squared in the realm of social and sexual appetite. She presumed, he thought, that they would live on Founders Row in the Patterson house, not really wishing to displace Worth and Mandy at once, but taking pleasure in the eventual substitution, any other bothersome details be damned.

"Yeah, things are all right," Skip said, removing his jacket. "Betty and me had a little fellow last year. Skip Junior." He produced a photograph.

Roger put on his glasses to examine the picture. "A fine likeness. I'd say he's a chip off the old block."

Skip flushed. He signaled the bartender, who brought two more beers. "Yeah, we're doing all right. I'm running the Providential agency here in town now, you know, and we just bought the house over there on Renfrow Lane where the Whitleys used to live. I guess you could call it sort of Patterson Forest. The edge anyway. I'm sure glad we got in when we did. Hear the rate's going to be seven percent before long." He shook his head.

"Hard to believe."

"How's, uh, you know, Senator Patterson's campaign? I hear Brent and Pammie are working on that now."

"Oh, he'll do fine in the end. Always a struggle with the NCN. All the money involved."

"Yeah, the holy rollers make me nervous."

Skip's eyes grew wide as he tried not too hard to make room for a very well endowed patron who was bumping her way forward to the bar. "Tight fit," she purred to Skip's Adam's apple as she wriggled through, her breasts caressing his ribs.

"Is this where the young crowd comes to drink?" Roger asked.

"Yeah, this is where you can check out the latest. They all come in with the new outfits—AT&T, IBM. Hard to keep up with 'em from week to week."

Roger watched the young lady to his left calmly pour her Tom Collins down the front of a young man's suit, twisting her glass to pass on the last drop. She stalked out the door, swinging her suit jacket behind.

"Hey, bitch—if you don't want it, what the fuck are you here for?" the spurned lover yelled after her over the din as he wrung out the tie in his beer.

Skip shrugged. "Sorry about the language, Mr. Albright. We get some real irresponsible people in here sometimes."

Irresponsible people, Roger thought—irresponsible. That was what Fitzwater, the high school principal, had called Brent in a quavering tone, probably thinking something worse but only able to summon that most widely derogatory of educators' words to Roger's face, after he had expelled Brent for heading a boycott of classes during the Vietnam Moratorium. "How was he irresponsible?" Roger remembered asking the principal, the man's self-conscious toupee and elaborate manners on edge because of a problem he clearly had no preparation to solve. "He led the walkout at third period and gave a speech telling the students to throw their bodies into some machine—that is when I stopped it." He was misquoting Thoreau, Roger remembered, but it appeared that Brent had the right usage, and that was a hopeful sign.

"How's the football team this year, Skip?" Roger remembered Skip had played for the team, which was sometimes used as a reluctant paramilitary unit by Fitzwater to police the protesting student body.

"Sir?"

"You know, the high school team."

Skip looked around the bar, searching, Roger imagined, for the conference standings in the daily newspapers posted for decoration on the wall. "Things have changed, sir, really changed. They won the league last year, went pretty far in the playoffs, too."

"That is a change. I remember the team being very bad."

"Well—yes sir. But we have the black kids now. They can really play. Team has a new coach, too, a black guy. Has a lot of personality."

"Sounds terrific. I reflect on football from time to time. Playing football teaches discipline, don't you think?"

Skip put his empty mug on the bar and spun it like a top. "Maybe. Mostly it teaches you to get cussed at. Teaches you to take salt tablets when it's hot. Listen, sir, with all due respect, why are we here?"

Roger motioned for the bartender to fill Skip's glass again. "I wanted to talk about Brent. You were his best friend, weren't you? In high school, I mean."

"Sure. Is something wrong?"

"No, Skip. Nothing's wrong. I just want to know some things. What he was like then?"

"What he was like?" Skip's moon-shaped faced furrowed in a dozen practiced wrinkles. "What he was like? Is this some kind of a joke?"

"As a friend. What he was like as a friend?"

"What do you mean? We had good times."

"Until the Spanish Galleon."

"What do you care about it?" Skip said, his voice carrying beyond them, adopting a challenging adolescent tone.

"What happened to that boy, Skip? You were there."

"You know Brent didn't. He couldn't. It was a crazy thing."

"But it all went bad after that, didn't it? And then you started dating Pammie."

Skip turned to leave. "I'm really not into this, Mr. Albright," he said.

Roger held him by the arm. "No, let's talk some more. I'll make it worth your while."

Skip sat down and lit a cigarette. "Trying to quit," he said, spinning it between his fingers.

"My question is—why didn't Pammie marry you?"

Skip shook his head. "I'm not believing this."

"I need to know, Skip. This is important."

"Okay. That's easy. Because she loves Brent."

"Loves?"

"Yeah. She's always loved him, and he's always loved her. They just can't get it right, you know?"

So it was all of a piece, Roger thought. Pammie was trying to explain it, the two of them together, and the violence, that night at Ocean Drive. Brent had tried to make love to her and it didn't come off, and he couldn't understand. It happened right there, in the beach house, after Skip, the best friend and accomplice, had cleared all the other seniors and their girls out, had led them to the Spanish Galleon, where Brent had to confront them after the humiliation. She told him she didn't love him, and he knew it was a lie but he stopped anyway, thinking the failure his.

"Sell me some insurance, Skip," Roger said, removing his checkbook.

"Excuse me?"

"I said sell me some insurance. You must be good at it."

Skip hesitated. "I don't want to sell you any insurance, Mr. Albright."

"Sure you do. I need insurance. I have responsibilities."

Skip laughed. "I'm not believing this."

"What's not to believe? You're an insurance man. I need insurance. Let's hear your pitch."

Skip shrugged and removed a business card from a velvet-encased holder. He placed it in Roger's waiting palm and looked away, gathering himself. "If I were you, Mr. Albright," he began, clearing his throat. "If I were you, I mean with your financial situation and all—I mean not many guys bring to the table what you do—I'd still be thinking about increasing my coverage. I know a lot of the smart guys tell you not to buy whole life any more, because you can get more in money markets. But you get that protection in whole life, too. Now I don't know what you think about term, but if you're like me, you like to own your insurance. That's savings *and* protection, Mr. Albright. Now I'm not going to tell you there aren't any other good companies out there, but I will say flat out that Providential's Dividend-Plus is the best damn product in the industry."

Roger put the card in his pocket. "Thank you, Skip. A very sound presentation." He wrote out a check for five thousand dollars. "Put that in some whole life for me, won't you? I'll trust your discretion on it. I can do that, can't I?"

As he waited for the elevator to take him back to the parking garage, Roger noticed that the dinner tables around the dance floor were already filling up. The drum major did a brisk business, he thought. He wondered if Pammie and Brent occasionally had dinner at Captain Disco, or if they avoided it because running into Skip would be awkward. He winced as the valet screeched around a concrete pillar with the Lincoln, but he gave the kid a dollar anyway, and Skip Skidmore's card for good measure. "If you need any whole life, that guy has the best damn product in the industry," he said, wincing again when the kid slammed the car door as though it were the lid to a garbage can.

•   •   •

The dark lobby of the O. Henry had been covered from floor to marble counters with drop cloths, and workmen were busy removing the chandeliers that lit the way down the long hall to the banquet room, arranging the glass beside the stacks of crystal doorknobs and hammered bronze spittoons. Roger wondered why Judith had wanted to meet there, and he had thought of suggesting another place when she called. But he figured in late middle age she was developing some feeling for historic places about to meet the wrecking ball, and far be it from him to discourage sentiment.

A tall, white-jacketed black man, his head completely bald and his visage firmly set, strode from the shadows toward Roger, looking to neither side and taking no notice of the surrounding disorder. With a start Roger recognized the apparition as Ozzie. The old maître d' made a slight bow, his smooth pate reflecting the dim offering of the workmen's lamps. "Mr. Albright," he said. "Come."

With that he turned on his heels and led Roger back the way he had come, opening the large French doors to the dining room, which appeared bare of tables, chairs, even curtains above the arched windows. They passed through the echoing room, their footsteps a tattoo to the tinkling of crystal glasses and the sounds of laughter and music that had animated the dinner hour in the bustling days. Ozzie gestured slightly, and Roger saw against the far wall the faded paisley damask of an old wing chair. There sat Judith, waiting, her hands clasped before her.

He hadn't seen her more than four or five times in twenty years, he figured, unless you counted the regular appearances she had begun to make on talk shows after she became a journalist of note. He telephoned, though, at odd times. The night in South Carolina he called her from a pay phone outside the police station. She heard him out, babbling about what he had to do, and Brent. "Don't you think," she said finally, "that a lot of this is because Brent's a teenage boy . . . ?"

One day five years later he was riding the Eastern shuttle from New York to Washington when he read Freebaum's obituary. "Donald Freebaum, Noted Sociologist, Dead at 75," the long-prepared notice began, recounting a life of bookish daring that only the *Times* could make properly momentous. There she was at the head of the survivors — Dr. Judith Stern, wife, of the home. He stopped in the Admirals Lounge at National and called. "Oh God, Roger, I'm so glad it's you," she said, her voice smoky with the strain and the sadness. "It was his heart. He said Nixon did it to him . . ."

Roger kept up with her magazine pieces, first as a novelty, and then because he liked them. She had become, in the aftermath of her twenty years with Freebaum, a motherly prod, transforming the conversation of her late salon into the stuff of policy. After Freebaum's death she quoted even more liberally from his books, until it was generally believed that she had authored whole chapters of *Dilemmas of Authority* and *The Most Social Animal*. After a year she went adjunct at Columbia and devoted herself full-time to writing. Soon, propelled by the lifetime of contacts and credibility he bequeathed, ability led her to the excitement of a successful cadre, although nothing quite prepared her, Roger thought, for being so well received by the Money Roundtable. It was a comfort of middle age that one could be a conservative critic of the establishment and live well, after having spent one's youth as a radical critic of the establishment living poorly. If society were as disciplined as Judith would want it, he figured, her own success would be impossible.

Brent was her subject, not him, she insisted in her last phone call, as she explained her errand to Fairington and invited Roger to lunch. Evidently Brent had been her subject for a while, as she had shadowed him in Washington for weeks, to the point, Roger noted, that Brent spoke of her in familiar terms. "Professor Stern," he would say, chuckling. "What a piece of work . . ."

"I always stay in old hotels," she said. "But this is a bit much. They're going to implode it or something."

Her bracelets jangled as she moved toward him in her richly patterned silk dress, which supposedly called attention to itself and not the figure beneath. She tensed slightly as she kissed him on the cheek, and though the signals of her presentation were self-sufficiency and friendly decorum, he felt she reserved something for him beyond that. Or maybe he just hoped she did.

"Well, aren't you going to say anything?"

He laughed. "I've been hearing a lot about you from my son."

"My favorite lunch partner. You should be very proud of him."

Ozzie produced from a suddenly materialized serving tray a full luncheon in covered dishes, the heavy china embossed with the O. Henry logo, an *O* with an *H* overlay, a quill pen splitting the middle. With a practiced motion he flicked a white cloth over the table beside them. He might have made our lunch himself, Roger thought, being too proud to say the kitchen had closed.

"I'm sorry you and Lulu split up," she said as Ozzie left, pushing the serving cart before him down the echoing hall. "I know that was hard."

Her condolences surprised him. Since it had been nearly a year, he rarely heard them anymore. "Damn right it was hard. I never thought she would do it."

"I never thought Donald would die," she said, simply. "It meant so much to me when you called that day. I felt a thousand times better."

"Well, I just had a notion. And thank you. We did the best we could, had some, you know—" He had been drifting toward the assurances of many good years, good times, a healthy child, but caught himself. They both laughed.

"I wanted to tell you that, and to talk to you about my story, so you don't misunderstand. I'm not writing about the campaign. I'm writing about Brent and some other kids just starting out working for old pols in trouble like Worth in trouble. I want to see how these young people are coping."

He chuckled. "Your big chance to get Worth after all these years and you're passing it up. I'd say you were being honorable."

"Honorable? Heavens no. Brent's a better story. Besides, I'm a softie for Institute men."

Honor, or whatever word she would use for it, played a part, although she would never say so, he thought. The bigger part, though, was that she didn't have to go after Worth now. She had been drubbing him for years in absentia, her monthly column skewering the old guardians of Potomac liberalism for their compromises, their impervious tolerance, their jerry-built bureaucracies, arguing that they should be retired because what they proposed wouldn't work and made whatever problem under discussion worse. All of this she wrote in a chatty yet analytical tone, addressed to participants in decades of spaghetti suppers at Cambridge and Ann Arbor and all points between. She didn't need to attack Worth. She could write about Worth's aide and treat Worth as an irrelevance.

"When you figure Brent out, be sure to enlighten me, too."

"Oh, come on. Brent's not so hard to understand. He wants to be happy."

"That's what I mean. What good does it do to want to be happy?"

She sighed. "I think we've had that conversation."

The way she said it brought to Roger's mind the things their distance had not permitted them to discuss over the years. She had no doubt gone through wanting to have children and deciding against it, or trying and not being able to, and they faced each other now with the result. He had hired and fired, celebrated and fumed without apprising her, or really anyone, of how he felt about it.

Still, the lost time had advantages. Some things seemed clearer than they would otherwise. He had thought he understood, for instance, why she disliked Worth, that it was rooted in something like social rivalry — he represented privilege and she could not see beyond that to his work. But now he knew that to be an underestimation — she disliked him deeply not for his manner and status, but because she believed his power to be based on a lie. In this she was one with Crain, whether she acknowledged it or not. For her, Worth Patterson was a lie because he made social progress a form of philanthropy. As for Crain, he always thought social progress itself was a lie, or worse, a swindle.

"It was hard when you left me," she said. "Very hard. I still think about that time."

"I left you? I thought you left me."

She shrugged. "A technicality. You know what I mean. It made me crazy, you with Worth and those self-important fraternity boys. But then something else happened. In the fifties, I think. Television. You all had to buy televisions for your children, and Brent is the result."

He winced, for in making Brent her subject she was not fighting fair, and of course she was making Brent her subject. "Brent is the result of television?" he said, falling back on his oldest strategy, deflating her grand arguments by pouncing on their ever-absurd extremes. She, knowing it, and knowing also that she had touched him with Brent, merely smiled.

"This morning he got his answer," she said. "Crain won't debate."

"You talked to him?"

"Poor thing. He went on about 'consequences' and the 'only opinion poll that counts' and the like. He's very handsome, you know, Roger. Looks like you at that age. I have a start whenever I see him."

Poor thing indeed, Roger thought. He never had a chance. How could he know the depth of Crain's contempt for debate, a useless convention for those who know they are right, dangerous in that the impressionable may be led astray by reason.

In the face of this nightmare, and the consequences of its victory, which Judith knew as well as any, Roger was distraught at her inability to let bygones be bygones and fight Crain with them. He couldn't help but take it personally.

"What do you think is going to happen?" he asked.

"I don't know, really. They think this is their Spanish Civil War." She chuckled, catching herself in the irony.

"I see. So it's national."

She nodded. "NCN wants it to be."

Roger tried not to laugh aloud at the notion of Judith Stern's friends—"neoconservatives" she called them of all things, the whole lot of them, like her, intellectual refugees of the left, thrown in with the evangelical demon rum crowd. How the world turns, Roger thought; one really must work to keep up-to-date.

"One thing I told him I'll tell you, even though it could cost me a source. The man at the Fairington speech was a plant. There may be others."

Roger straightened in his chair, aware that with age he stooped slightly when tired by the press of affairs. He marveled at the many grades of barbarism the Crain camp could muster, the science of psychological assault they had created and codified. Had they polled to determine the optimum presentation, deciding on a hired religious lunatic because of a focus group? Or was it something cruder than that, the cunning of the blackmailer masquerading as technique? Anything seemed possible to people who would mock their own faith for effect.

Try as he might, he couldn't get mad at Judith. He felt, instead, that their present pass was a dismal practical joke. They were, he figured, both players in Crain's outrageous script, at the end of which he transforms from low-life stunt man into a senator.

"How do you stand it? Just watching, I mean. You know what he is. How can you stand it when he denies everything, even what he did to MacGiver?"

She shrugged. "I'm paid to watch. Detachment is healthy. Besides, I've signed things that say everything I believed was a lie."

"It's not the same."

"I've thought about it," she said evenly, stiffening as though challenged by his unwillingness to let her pass off the question. "And it's not my doing. You and Worth and Tal made this little world and you wouldn't let anyone else in. Now no one can help you. Crain is your consequence. I know that's hard and I'm sorry."

Maybe she's right, he thought. Maybe we did bring it on ourselves. He remembered with distaste his only meeting with Crain in all their years of antagonism, a chance encounter at a textile executives' dinner earlier in the year. He thought he should have looked away, but instead he allowed himself to be fascinated by Crain in the flesh. The scourge of liberalism, defender of the faith healer, sage to the legion of television-swept souls stood barely five and a half feet tall in his air-blown hairdo. He had forgotten how short Crain was, and he realized the effectiveness of the most primary illusion Crain perpetrated on the television screen—physical size. He imagined an elaborate series of meticulously scaled sets, constructed in absolute secrecy, resembling the furniture for a child's playhouse, deployed in maximum security, to procure over a period of years the fraud that Joe Crain was a tall man.

Neither spoke, but Roger felt their meeting to be an interview, one in which everything they could say had already been said. Crain made a small bow with a flourish that would have seemed a mockery were it not for the firm sense that he felt this farce to be a genuine show of gentility—the compliment, the *beau geste*, the trappings of a hundred movies choreographed in posture and word before mirrors, rehearsed each evening with his script for the news, a manner he could not make his own but could allude to, as in a mime. I'm not going to give ground, Roger thought. I'm just not going to give ground to the little bastard. Crain stood at his ease, grinning a long time, his expression both eager and blank, not false as a photograph exactly, but as a photograph of a photograph.

Chapter Sixteen

1978

I N his most clinical tone, Professor Ogden told the breakfast strategy group about new research done by a student who had attended Crain campaign training sessions undercover. Their structure was an order of service — Invocation, Call to Worship, Affirmation and Almsgiving, the Word, the Message, the Benediction, all punctuated by familiar hymns with the name of the Master replaced by the name of the candidate: to summon, "Stand up, stand up for Joe Crain, ye soldiers of the cross...."; to dedicate, "What a friend we have in Joe Crain, all our sins and griefs to bear...."; to redeem, "Blessed assurance, Joe Crain is mine, oh what a foretaste of glory divine...." Ogden had suspected the student of a hoax, or perhaps a hallucination, never believing that the secular whips of the fundamentalist legions would take such liberties with the Word, but another observer brought back the same tale. The material would make for a good seminar, Ogden had said, though he did not know in which subject — political science, religion, and anthropology all came to mind; perhaps the best forum, he concluded, would be some of the more adventurous sections of clinical psychology.

The images stayed in Roger's mind throughout the morning. He wondered if anything Worth could do would be enough to stop the tent revival juggernaut. Just that morning the campaign had word of fleets of decommissioned school buses being bought by evangelical churches, ostensibly for Sunday transport, but arriving suspiciously close to Election Day.

The senator stood, reading a press version of the tough new stump speech Brent had drafted. "I guess what you're finally proposing, Brent, is that we tell the truth about Crain," the senator said as he thumped the pages of his copy approvingly.

"For a change," Pammie said.

The senator looked sharply at her over his reading glasses.

"Well, I think it's brilliant, Son," Roger added, trying to be upbeat.

Brent flushed and then laughed as though to dismiss the praise. "Brilliance is not our goal, Dad. We want audience share."

"Audience share," the senator muttered, shaking his head.

"Whatever. It's terrific, Worth," Roger said. "Now you just give 'em hell."

"By golly, that's the spirit. We're just going to do it." The senator thumped his hand on the metal office desk for emphasis. He paced the floor, flipping the pages of his speech and muttering the words, jabbing the air for emphasis. Suddenly he stopped and stared out the wall-length windows of campaign headquarters, squinting in the afternoon sun that danced on the sidewalk ginkgo trees, the green leaves still promising Indian summer.

"There are people who owe me," he said. "And I'm going to start reminding them. There's way too much fear out there, and the first people who have to stop showing it is us."

•   •   •

The rest of the morning the senator spent on the telephone. True to his word, he called in his chips with the men he had built bridges for, or for whom he had placed a protégé in this or that job. He also telephoned the publishers of the friendly newspapers who he felt had been cowed by Crain, reminding them of their duty.

There was no question in Roger's mind that Worth had finally woken up. It was like the old days, when it was fun. Every two years they would crank up the old campaign again, after the first one in '52. Roger developed a reputation as a political operative by managing the little Fairington machine. Ogden kept the office staffed in Washington; he convinced Delbert to organize the operation, and by the end of the second term Worth had the best office in the House, except for the most senior men.

It was still fun even when election became automatic, because Worth drove hard, without even thinking about it, Roger concluded, to free himself from the trajectory. Down home the sophisticates explained his growing liberalism by friendship with the Georgetown set Mandy cultivated. That was fine with Worth. The truth, that he believed the old wrong had to be righted, would be a secret he and Roger shared. When Kennedy offered him the post at Justice — and the prospect of appearing at numerous schoolhouse doors drawl and all to escort the Negro children in — he jumped at it. Ogden was apoplectic — after all, the Senate seat in 1966 beckoned; it was the chance for the Institute to return in glory sixteen years after the recently departed Narly Ferguson had defeated their candidate. Mandy took to her bed. She had tired of the House, too, but she had been sure if Worth left it would have been to an ambassador's post.

Roger applauded, because he knew it was another step on Worth's own path. As things turned out, he won the Senate seat in 1966 anyway, notwithstanding segregationist grumbling, and the Voting Rights Act he helped draft at Justice was going to keep him there. Ogden returned to the upper house in style after all, and Mandy not only got out of bed, she plotted her own social campaign to employ the considerably greater cachet a senator's wife possessed. This time everyone did what Worth told them to do, including Roger, who cheerfully obeyed orders to leave the campaign managing to professionals and do something really important like raise money, a task at which he had few peers.

So the picture of Worth again in command after a faltering start recalled the happy old days. But it also recalled a constant problem. Nearly everything had to be lost before Worth could think of taking action. It was a major fault of Ogden's method: reason, balance, noblesse oblige itself were difficult traits to cultivate, and they didn't coexist easily with killer instinct. The ability to destroy an opponent just for the sake of doing so, to press an advantage to humiliation and beyond, in short, the natural talents of a street predator like Crain, which Roger by necessity had acquired in business, were alien to Worth. He needed a reason for being brutal, an outrage. Fortunately, Crain at last began to oblige him. As usual, NCN held back the nastier stuff for the stretch run. When the Patterson campaign's tougher line began to work and Crain's negatives rose, the first broadside appeared:

NORTH CAROLINA WAKE UP!

BLOC VOTE AIMS TO DEFEAT CRAIN!

WAKE UP NOW, BEFORE IT'S TOO LATE!

Below the nightmare type the authors reproduced a grainy photograph of Senator Patterson shaking hands with the Reverend Pinkerton of Raleigh's Second AME Zion Church, with the legend "WE WILL TURN OUT AN ARMY TO DEFEAT JOE CRAIN," attributed to neither. After the pamphlet drops in rural eastern towns, Crain began to speak on the evils of "bloc voting" and how the "bloc vote" threatened democracy, changing his intonation of the key phrase day by day, from the flat, television-midwestern "bluck vote" to a rich, slow tidewater "blaawk vote," until an ear that had been bombarded by the subtle transitions over a myriad of fifteen-second spots could not tell apart the encoded diphthongs.

It was outrage enough. At Brent's urgings Worth agreed to take up the lance. Roger took some credit for his son's advice. Aware of the tendency of Institute training to dampen the savage virtues, Roger had taken it on himself to arouse killer instinct in the adolescent Brent by playing him at tennis over and over after the boy was better than he was, until hefting the racket and drilling the serve once more past old Daddy was so routine that Brent would try a couple of risky spins and Roger would break him. Furious, Roger scolded him, always in public, so he would remember: "Never, never let me break you. You have the advantage, and by God you always press it." Saturdays he wagered Brent on foul shots at the Patterson High gym, driving there after practice as Brent lingered to shoot alone, enjoying the ease of the unencumbered net. "Reward is a function of risk, Son," he said. "Also nutcutting." He laid a fifty-dollar bill on the foul line, betting Brent, who shot 70 percent from that distance, that he could not shoot six out of ten. Six shots dropped through the net in a row, and Brent pocketed the money. "How about double or nothing?" he asked. "No, Son," Roger said, pleased at the boy's dispatch. "I think you're getting it . . ."

"Now, Hugh, dammit, I'm telling you we're going to win this thing," the senator said, holding the telephone receiver between his shoulder and his ear. "We need your newspaper now, Hugh; You've got to be on board. I know that, Hugh—I know you're grateful. Well now let me ask you this, Hugh, who runs your newspaper—you, or that young editor whose salary you pay?"

Brent tapped the desk top and pointed to his watch. The senator nodded distractedly.

"Hugh, Hugh, listen. I've got an hour and forty-two minutes to get to Chapel Hill to make the speech I was telling you about. You best be thinking about that endorsement. It's your damn duty, man. How the hell could you look yourself in the mirror after caving into the Crain crowd?"

"I've got the car running downstairs, Senator," Brent said. "We're going to cut it pretty close."

In the car, the senator insisted Roger sit beside him. "You remember Hugh, don't you? A little on the gutless side, but I think he's going to come through. Thank God he asked me to do that for Hughie. You know in these little towns you just can't buck the church people, and they're all lock, stock, and barrel for Crain. That is, the ones who give a damn, which are the Baptists. Goodness knows how a churchgoing Presbyterian like me could get on the wrong side of the religion crowd. Maybe I ought to become a Baptist! Not just any old Baptist — but a *foot-washing Baptist*! That's it, Roger. I'll just announce I've seen the Lord and be dunked! We could time it for — what do you think — next week?"

"I don't think Mandy would stand for it."

The senator laughed, and in fact he laughed all the way to Chapel Hill, going over the speech line for line and chuckling. Brent drove the big Lincoln very fast down Interstate 85, which had long replaced the country highway Roger remembered and had become in its maturity less highway than superannuated Main Street, with signage, outlet malls, eateries, and trailer parks stacked up mile after mile. Brent drove eighty, knowing that the congressional license plates would discourage the highway patrol. The last ten miles he drove on the winding blacktop that linked the town and the university to the outside world both seemed to delight in shunning. The road widened to meet the town's limits; in the distance, the domes and towers of the university looked down upon the speeding car. Brent expertly bypassed the town's main street. He drove past Fraternity Row, making a point, Roger thought, of slowing down by the rebuilt Deke house, and cleverly piloted the car to the rear entrance of the Taliaferro Ogden Student Center, where the senator's speech was to begin in three minutes.

As they entered the flat-roofed, cubed structure, Roger could see, without being a professional, that the new edge to the campaign had produced results in the form of a more interested press corps. Where loungers would ordinarily be gathered eating frozen yogurt and watching soap operas, camera crews and mobile units stood, ready to intercept the candidate.

Brent whistled when he saw the media enclave. "That's more reporters than we've had in the last two weeks, total."

"They all came to pick over my carcass," the senator said, his teeth locked in the candidate smile.

"Senator Patterson — Senator Patterson," a dozen voices called out.

Three microphones appeared under his nose. "Today's *News and Observer* poll has you trailing Crain by seven points."

"Now, y'all boys know — and ladies, too, I might add," he said, winking, "you all know that the only poll that counts is the one on Election Day. Besides, that's down from eleven."

Pammie and Brent flanked the senator as he walked into Ogden Hall, with Roger following behind. The room was half-full; some of the students sat reading, or talking among themselves, and the moderator, the chairman of the Political Union, stood at the lectern speaking into a buzzing microphone. The speaker saw them enter and began reading the senator's introduction, with the effect that as the senator climbed onto the platform, he had just been called upon to make his speech. Pammie and Brent left the chair closest to the center camera shot for Roger and sat at the edge of the platform, turning subtly to make head counts of the TV crews.

"I appreciate the invitation of the Carolina Political Union to address you this afternoon," the senator began. "I know that the great man for whom this building is named, Taliaferro Ogden, is passionately interested in the political campaign we are now in for the United States Senate seat I currently have the honor to hold — and intend to keep, I might add — because Taliaferro Ogden is a man who makes everything in life his interest, a great scholar and a great citizen, in the finest sense of that word. Much of the prosperity our state and our nation enjoy today is due to the work of Taliaferro Ogden and other selfless individuals who dedicated themselves to the truth, and who told the truth. Because their voices rang out for truth, great wrongs were righted and the liberties and the prosperity of the people increased."

As the television cameras and reporters bustled into the hall and set up their equipment, more students, attracted by the excitement, wandered toward the remaining seats until every one was filled; the walls, too, were soon lined by the curious.

"I had the honor as a young man to stand beside Taliaferro Ogden in many fights for truth. The Senate campaign of 1950 was one of those fights. In that ugly year and time, when hate-mongering and scandal were the stock in trade of the opposition, I first met my present opponent. Our meeting was not a happy one. I have the sad task of reminding you, students, most of you not even born when McCarthyism's blight was on this land, that it was Joe Crain's voice broadcasting the hate-filled racist lies and Red-baiting slander that brought down Dr. Ernest MacGiver.

"Today we hear again the same hate-filled racist lies, the same Red-baiting slander employed by my opponent, except this time he is not broadcasting over a radio microphone but over his own television station financed by over seven million dollars of other people's money.

"I am older than you and have seen the damage that lies can do. I have seen — "

"Fornicator! Fornicator!" a voice from the back cried out, with the same sickening edge as in Fairington before. "Be cursed before God!" His heart racing with the now-familiar words and their renewed threat, Roger searched through the glare of the floor lights to find the intruder. Since the Fairington incident, Brent had hired private detectives to screen the crowds for disrupters. In fact, three had been rousted at the last stop, and he knew of one today. But apparently the net wasn't entirely effective. Already, the television cameras had found him, a simple-looking blond young man, in the parka and jeans of the student. "Fornicator!" he shouted, his voice growing stronger. "Burn in the pit!"

The senator's jaw tightened and he gripped the lectern in physical resolve to push on.

"The truth is that my opponent is a hypocrite. He pretends to be a man of the Christian faith, and yet his views directly contradict the most basic ideals of Christian — "

"*Daddam daddam nitwasa vimami bocassa namit hikasim owasa dimitis sayodam matodan sitada nowami . . .*" The words came fast, and, though incomprehensible, they had a meaning about them. The speaker, under the television lights, stood as though in a trance near a corner of the hall; like the first one, he was a plain young man. The gifts of prophecy, Professor Ogden had lately lectured them all, including speaking in tongues and the handling of snakes, represented to the faithful a form of vision, a purity evidenced by the practitioner that saw to the heart. "He stood there," Ogden had said, recalling a long-ago Pentecostal meeting, "stroking the head of the rattler like a puppy, its fangs all juiced and puffed out and its body curled up the man's arm with the rattles just going to town. And a woman fell down on the ground and wiggled around and screamed, 'I can take the serpent, give it to me now, Lord, give it to me now, Lord,' and somebody put a copperhead on top of her and she wrapped it around her waist." He tamped down his pipe and relit the black tobacco. "North Georgia, 1935 . . ."

". . . The truth is that my opponent is a pretender. He claims to be speaking for the 'little man,' the 'outsiders,' but in fact a number of his backers are the richest, most influential men in the nation, who would use my opponent to enlarge their already vast privileges—"

". . . *nausikit tatorka katelbam majemus nomeresa sabonu mehadum rofizes dolfos papinu salaminit carpasa bazela nokkula* . . ."

"Fornicator! Fornicator!"

"Spill thy seed in the path of Baal!"

"The Christ, the Living God!"

"Fornicator! Damned before Christ!"

More accusers stood, each shouting and pointing at the podium. Roger counted eight in view, but there could have been more, as the light faded past the first few rows. He looked for the campus cops but couldn't see them either. Brent had tried to make arrangements with the local police, always a touchy proposition, and especially so on campus. The state trooper detachment stood at the front to guard Worth but made no move against the protesters, who arranged themselves strategically at the rear. Worth pressed on, growing hoarse.

". . . . The truth is that my opponent is a bigot. I don't mean by that the obvious, but that he is prejudiced against everything and everybody that he doesn't understand. And that's plenty—"

"*Beelzit balzehak notdemus* . . ."

"*Ikthassa hohassa memurrit* . . ."

"*Koxuker kalzeke niturkos* . . ."

". . . the only holy and apostolic . . ."

"Fornicator! Fornicator!"

"Soiler of the womb of Mary."

"The blood of Shabas, the blood of . . ."

"*Bemshabas bemshabas bemshabas* . . ."

"The seed of Ham! The seed of Ham!"

"*Nimkak norbidit arakolita* . . ."

"*Daddam daddam daddam* . . ."

The protesters' ire fed on each resumption of Worth's speech. Worth warmed to the attack, too, as though by angering the hecklers he had found a surrogate for Crain. A contingent of campus police finally arrived, with Brent at their side, arguing with a civilian in a bow tie Roger figured was the dean of something or other. The show of force on campus by the Crain people was yet another stroke, Roger realized. Brent had prepared with local authorities routinely for disruptions since the first incident, but the university setting presented special problems. Crain had figured correctly that the campus police, even though put on notice by the Patterson advance team, would be loath to take action against the protesters for fear of violating their First Amendment rights to disrupt the senator's speech. So many times Worth Patterson's friend, the university, in its impeccable defense of expression, now seemed helpless not to serve Crain's interests. But then Brent took matters into his own hands. Shoving aside the disbelieving dean, and before the bemused eyes of the constabulary, he and several of the college volunteers tackled the hecklers nearest to them. A small melee ensued and the police, finally confronted with unambiguous violence, broke the fracas up, carrying away the protesters and their attackers.

"You see that?" the senator ad-libbed, gesturing to the battle scene on the floor. "That, my friends, is the viciousness and the ignorance of the Crain mob. He won't debate me like a man. Instead, he sends out these impostors to shout me down. There's no difference between him and the white-sheeted cowards who burned crosses in the front yards of men and women who stood up for justice!"

The students, stunned by the fight on the floor and the fury of the senator's attack, did not at first respond, but rather marveled at the transformed scene before them. The senator continued to ad-lib and the crowd, now aroused, roared with every sentence. The television crews hustled up the aisle to get shots of the senator raising both hands above his head in a boxer's clasp of victory, reveling in the applause, which now had mounted into a standing ovation that overwhelmed the diluted chants of the remaining Crain provocateurs. As the ovation continued, the senator wiped his face with his handkerchief, and, signaling for quiet, returned to his text.

"In conclusion, let me speak to you as a fellow student. I once had the honor of being president of the senior class at this remarkable institution. I did not make the class address as scheduled at commencement, but rather on December 8, 1941, when I resigned from the college to enlist in the

Navy. Back in my day, we did not have much in the way of choices for the future, because we had to go to war. That made things simple for us, though we didn't think we were lucky."

The senator put aside his papers and leaned over the lectern. "Today you students don't have a war to fight, thank God. But the price of freedom has to be paid by every generation, and you will never pay a higher price than standing for the truth. I hope you will support me, still your brother in this place, in the task that lies ahead so that I can return to Washington and continue my work."

•   •   •

Dodging bicyclists and dogs on the worn brick sidewalks, Roger managed, to his satisfaction, not to attract much attention from the students changing classes, enjoying as they were the first noontime of the year when the air was cool enough to leave on the morning sweater. As they had been engaged when he left thirty-six years before, three groundsmen were diligently widening the overburdened sidewalks, one brick at a time, tapping the ground, applying sand, lining the brick up just so, close to the way, Roger supposed, it had been done in ancient Egypt. He climbed the steps of the old library and two girls made way for him, holding open the door. They moved aside, he realized, because they thought he was a professor.

"Men shall know the truth and the truth shall set men free." So declared the portal's inscription, which Roger had read a thousand times. What controversial translation from the Hebrew gave "men" rather than "ye"? The effect was always both familiar and odd, so that he never questioned the words, but thought the biblical profundity sounded as if it were spoken to the Lone Ranger by Tonto. Goodness knows how the new Bible lingo would have it, he mused. Probably something like "When you understand you'll feel better."

You shall know the truth, and the truth shall set you free. Funny, it doesn't seem to work out that way, Roger thought. He remembered coaching the theory with Judith on the very same library steps at spring exam time. He took Hegel, she took Kant, and then they switched notes. "Okay, here goes," she said, one hand shading her eyes for concentration, the other conducting a symphony of the air as she rocked in thought: "Okay, here goes — if you don't know the truth, you're happy, but that's only an illusion and you're not free, because your actions are based on something false. But if you know the truth, then your actions are based on real things. That may make you unhappy, but you only think you're unhappy, right? It's really an illusion and you really are happy . . . ."

He shivered, recalling the trances of the faithful in the student center, the conviction so articulate and yet insensate. The more modern the age, the more primitive the people, Roger thought, seeing again the fascination of the students, the excitement in Brent's eyes as he surveyed the chaos on the floor, creating his own irrationality to combat the awful irrationality that confronted them all. Perhaps I could have done more in the other life, Roger thought, imagining himself in the hall, at the lectern, meeting the irrational head-on as Ogden would have done. Once he never thought it was important. Now he could think of little else that was more important. And it was too late, he thought; he had no lightness of spirit to bring to the task.

The bored attendant in the open stacks waved Roger on, also thinking, he supposed, that he was a professor. Who else would seek passage to the ignored shelves holding undergraduates' theses? They were organized by number and name and his was easy to find: "Patterns of Operation in Piedmont Textile Corporations" by Roger Albright. He sat on the stone floor and turned the thin, onionskin paper. The youthful triumph of the method rolled on before him, punctuated by Ogden's skeptical exclamations — "Really?" and "Your assumption!" — but Roger had rolled on nonetheless, creating industries, cities, wealth from his mind: "One must conclude that the most favorable conditions for capital formation and the cost of labor will develop in the next decade . . ." O truth! O beauty!

Somehow in this place, with a document so broad, yet personal and innocent, written by a younger hand, Roger felt Brent's presence with his own, as he had hoped it would have been in many things. Goddammit, Roger, why are you always so sure? Brent would say. On the last page disappointment, as always, is revealed — the B, clearly written, without comment, and the initials T.O. The legend continued — but then, Roger saw it, with a new postscript. He looked at the markings several times and he rubbed his finger over the vivid ink. Had Brent been here after all? he wondered, trying to understand why the boy would ask such a question:

Isn't it really a kind of destruction?   BPA

5/1/70

May Day, he thought, remembering the day, May 1, 1970; Brent was here reading before May Day, even then running Father to earth. In Roger's mind he saw the students rally again and Brent with them, three thousand marching with the banner of the Vietcong across the green quadrangle to the chancellor's office, and then to the street. The troopers took away the ones who fought, but the chants went on, obscene and clever, calling, "Soo-ey, soo-ey," at the police through the tear gas that cut the heavy spring air.

He remembered waiting at the station, arms crossed, among the officers and the winos and then paying the bail in cash, peeling one by one the hundred-dollar bills from his wallet, as Brent stood beside him, furious. The drove away in the new Mercedes.

"Do you have any idea what this could do to your prospects?" Roger said, feeling as stupid as he was sure he sounded.

"Do you have any idea what your goddamn war is doing to millions of people?"

Roger slammed the brakes and yanked the agile car to the shoulder of the Durham highway, oblivious to the honking drivers who whizzed past. "Don't you ever curse me again," he said evenly, drumming the steering wheel with his fingers.

He turned into Brent's apartment complex and drove past the swimming pool, where a number of bathers had taken advantage of the strike to work on their suntans. He stopped in front of the condo he had bought and leased back to Brent for the tax break. "Just tell me one thing, Son," he said.

"What?"

"Was it over a girl?"

"A girl?" Brent laughed.

"Answer me, dammit. Was it over a girl?"

As Brent struggled in his anger, the girl appeared from the shadows of the condo, her arms folded in front of her. "You sell any shirts lately to the U.S. Army, Mr. A?" Pammie said. "They've been going through some, all those bloodstains."

Roger checked his impulse to ask her what she was doing in Chapel Hill at his son's apartment rather than in class at whatever girls school she went to that year.

"Yes, as a matter of fact. A very good customer. And I'm damn proud of it, too."

"Roger Albright — shirtmaker to the imperialists. I guess these war profits bought you that car."

"Don't mock me, Pammie."

"Who, me?"

"For your information, I've driven lots of cars. I don't need this one, I could drive anything."

Why am I losing control? Roger wondered. Why am I even having this ridiculous conversation?

"I'm glad you said that, Mr. A." Pammie giggled, catching herself, Roger thought, as though possessed of an inspiration she could barely contain. He remembered clearly the murderous look on her face as she picked up one of the smooth river stones from the condo strip garden, not knowing, until years later, why she hated him so. "I'm glad you don't need that old Nazi car." She hurled the rock wildly, barely missing Roger, who thought it was meant for him, as it crashed into the window of the Mercedes-Benz. Then another flew, and another, each denting the gleaming metal with an alarming thump. He started for her, but another round of river rocks drove him back. "Old Nazi car!" Pammie yelled as she planted a big one on the windshield, breaking the glass into a hundred capillaries.

Roger folded his jacket over his arm and crouched, guarding the length of the car like a soccer goalie against the barrage. The curious of the condo village gathered to see the well dressed middle-aged man defend the Mercedes against the girl. "Old Nazi car!" Pammie yelled as she hurled another rock, and another. Rock after rock struck the metal as Roger ducked, not knowing what to do. Finally he stood straight, discarded his jacket, and walked slowly forward. Pammie suspended the barrage. He stood in front of her, hands on his hips, and turned to look at the ruined Mercedes. The gathered crowd stood tensed, whispering, not knowing what violence would occur next. She turned up her chin to meet his stare, which moved in expression from anger to curiosity. For seconds he studied her as though she were a new thing to him entirely. Finally he took the rock out of her hand, weighed it in his palm, and in one motion turned and threw a strike against the sedan, the stone hitting a rear door with such force that it buckled.

"Old Nazi car," he muttered.

•   •   •

The Thumpers' farm lay twenty minutes west of Fairington on Lake Jowett, a sprawling backwash of the Catawba that had been dammed behind the flow of an electrical generating station. The dam had deposed small farmers from their property years before. A number of the newly landless moved to Fairington to work in the factories the dam's power made possible. Exclusive residential properties soon grew up on the banks of the lake, though the unpredictable ebb and flow of the water, which fluctuated due to the requirements of the spillway, provided the lakefront properties from time to time with more frontage than advertised in the form of oozing, foul-smelling lake-bottom muck. The developers (Winston Galway among them) had ameliorated the embarrassment by building a lake within a lake, using concrete and oil drums, sheltering the numerous launches and sailboats of the Lake Jowett Yacht Club so that they would not be left high and dry on their owners' docks when the water fell. The financiers had also installed huge blowers, which erupted from the surface like the mouths of metal science fiction monsters, to oxidize the still waters and do battle with the algae that had begun to clog the lake surface. The blowers proved effective, but not at all pleasing to the eye, and Galway himself thought of placing lighthouse shells on top of them, flying flags of varying colors; now the uninitiated thought the machines were picturesque buoys, and in fact they served as such each year when the All-Carolina Waterskiing Festival took over the waters.

Most of the residents on Lake Jowett built their homes as near to the shore as possible, but Billy Roy bought his frontage and twenty acres as a buffer for the house he constructed high on a hill dominating the vista.

"No two ways about it," Pammie said. "Looks like a tobacco barn. Always has. Pretty tacky, all right."

By default Roger found himself driving Pammie to the Thumpers' party, the last of the season's barbecues held each year so late as to be also a harvest celebration, the open-fire ritual roasting of pigs an offering to the wandering gods for the good fortune and continued bounty of the clan. As usual Pammie had dressed inappropriately for the event, this year in a skin-tight leather outfit with pink, 1950s-style sunglasses stuck in the middle of her false beehive hairdo, along with high stiletto heels that Roger thought a hooker might wear. He supposed it was her comment on the proceedings.

If he had a daughter, he would expect her to appear in some modest country garb.

If he had a daughter. He remembered the party the night of the '66 election, which he and Lulu threw at their house. A glorious evening it was, with Brent and Pammie and their friends mixing with the drunk and happy adults. As a boy he never saw his parents drink and couldn't remember a gathering of more than twenty souls in one place for any social purpose except church, and yet there were the kids, and no one thought a second about it. Eventually he chased the boys from the bar, and they then chased the girls God knows where. He found Brent and Pammie sitting outside the door to the upstairs guest bedroom watching Delbert Ackerman and a campaign secretary wrestling half-clothed on the four-poster. Brent was fifteen and Pammie was thirteen.

Roger parked at the edge of a ditch at the back of a long line of cars, suburban Jeeps, and pickup trucks in front of the Thumper compound. He started to get out and open the door for Pammie, worrying, as she sat gossiping about one Thumper or another, that the large sequins meandering up and down her leather ensemble might rip the upholstery of his Mercedes as she extricated herself. She did have a destructive effect on Mercedeses. At the same time he figured that he had escaped what he thought she wanted to say to him, as their conversation had not reflected the closed doors and tensed exchanges of the Patterson campaign under siege.

But before he could move from his seat, Pammie gripped his thigh and held him. He knew he would hear what she had to say after all.

"It's not right what you're doing," she said, her touch still firm against him, as though he were a wild animal that could be calmed and then trained by it. "You're hurting Daddy."

"What are you talking about?"

"Ever since you started hanging around the campaign—it's just not working, the chemistry's wrong. No, I mean it. It's all wrong. Whenever Brent wants to do something you shoot it down. Don't think nobody notices. Brent does. Daddy does."

"Pammie, now you don't—"

"Just wait a minute, I'm going to say this. I thought it was because you had really different ideas about things. But that's not right. You're jealous of Daddy. Always have been."

Her speech drove him into silence for a moment. He weighed, as he thought he must, her charge, as direct and serious as it was and how much it left unsaid.

"Pammie, you can't understand the relationship I have with your father — it goes back years, and there are things between us that you can't know or appreciate. As for me hurting the campaign, Brent asked me to spend time, and I'll gladly leave whenever he asks. I've told him to tell me to get the hell out whenever he wants."

"He won't do that."

"Why?"

"Because he wants to prove to you he can do it. He wants you to see. Can't you tell?"

"I don't know, really — "

"As for the other stuff, I know."

"Know what?"

"I know the other stuff, about Lulu and Daddy. That's part of it too. You keep stirring that up, using it all the time."

He stared at her, wondering first at his own blindness over the years. That was why Lulu had not been concerned. She had put the whole thing on Pammie. Put it on a little girl. She would forbid Pammie to tell Brent because then the boy wouldn't be able to function, but she would have this woman's pact with the girl who would be her son's lover, to stop things before they got out of control. Of course Pammie despised him. And all along he had ignored her as a moody child.

"Lulu told me," Pammie said. "Before the time at the beach."

"What happened was a long time ago," he said, looking straight ahead to the lights of the Thumper house. "And there's probably nothing to it." He couldn't face her; he was angry again with Lulu for everything.

"I still think I could manage it. We could adopt, you see, and if I ever got pregnant by mistake — you see, I'd tell him I couldn't — I'd get an abortion."

Roger winced.

"But of course you don't want that. You want a real son, not some castoff. Well, not to worry, Mr. A. Brent knows something's wrong. There's always something wrong. But he'll never know what. That's why she told me. She knew I'd never tell him."

How could she, Roger thought. How could she put the responsibility on a little girl? "I'm sorry, Pammie. About how all this turned out."

"I know you are, Mr. A.," she said, patting his leg. "After all, how many fathers get exactly what they want? Your best friend's daughter loves your son. He loves her. What they want to do is live together and have your grandchildren in a house down the street. Your son wants to go into politics with his father-in-law, who happens to be a senator. The Albrights and the Pattersons. What could be more perfect?"

"Nothing's that perfect. I mean even if it was, it wouldn't be. You've got to—"

"Stir things up? That's what you do. We'd have some swell Christmas dinners, don't you think? After about the third drink everybody would get real relaxed. But you'd stir things up just enough to make sure we'd never be happy."

Laughter and quick footsteps sounded on the gravel outside the darkened car as the Thumpers' guests continued to arrive. Roger felt the discomfort of potential discovery. He had to leave the chamber that held them, diffuse her speech in the cool Piedmont night.

"Oh, Mr. A, I'm such a spectacle," she continued. "Everybody says so. A spectacle. Poor Pammie, they say, made a fool of herself at Provisional Class. Got mixed up and sold her body at the Bargain Box. Can't even get Brent to marry her."

"Stop, Pammie."

"No, if it wasn't that, it would be something else. You'd see to it."

He wanted to tell her that she had it all wrong, that it wasn't him, but events, that things happen, that he was trying to control it all. But where would he begin?

"Pammie, we need to go," he said, opening the car door.

She laughed. "You are scared," she said, reaching over him to close the door he had opened. "Even though you know I won't tell, you're scared anyway." Without warning she kissed him, hard, and he gasped when he felt her hands on him, stirring his old glands. He sat, trapped by her weight, her breasts against him, her breath in his ear, her heel raking his leg.

Suddenly she sat up and gathered her purse. "A thrill for you, Mr. A? You got turned on. I felt it. That's what it's like for me when I kiss Brent. Every time it makes me crazy." She pushed the door open and ran up the driveway.

•　　•　　•

The Thumper house was indeed a larger-than-life replica of a tobacco barn, two stories tall, constructed from logs and planking taken from old curing sheds on the land Lake Jowett covered. Below the roof's exposed beams stretched three sheaves of freshly cured bright leaf, which Billy Roy changed each year. In contrast to the rustic living room, with its rocking chairs and refinished rough-hewn oak tables, stood the kitchen, which compromised on no convenience from the Cuisinart to the microwave. Behind it was the game room, with Billy Roy's color TV, pool table, and wet bar, replete with scores of neatly stacked and spotless N.C. State highball glasses.

Funny, Roger thought, when Billy Roy was building the place the person who took the most interest was Walton. It touched the engineer in him, he said. He and Billy Roy had spent weeks building the house together. Every year since Walton had his heart attack and died Billy Roy had given the Walton Prize in Textiles at State.

Outside, the lawn that Billy Roy had won away from the forest played host to several hundred guests whose wardrobes ranged from Roger's business suit to the bib overalls of those who favored the authentic touch. Most, however, wore the standard khaki and plaid ensembles that Pammie mocked with her biker-girl getup. The busiest participants were the two local men Billy Roy had hired to cook the barbecue, the preparation of which was a major logistical affair. The pit, actually a trench, was dug several feet deep to host a hardwood fire, which, having burned for most of the day, produced by nightfall a plentiful bed of charcoal for the final searing. A rotisserie, the spit of which appeared to be the drive shaft of a fairly large automobile, skewered two pigs. Each rotated slowly while Billy Roy supervised a liberal basting. Greased aluminum siding reflected on the subjects while the team examined and punctured and examined again to verify that the meat neared completion. The fat oozed and bubbled; the chefs nodded in expectation of the feast. On the opposite side of the sloping yard stood a heated tent under which was spread the rest of the fixings: huge quantities of sweet coleslaw, Brunswick stew, potato salads, yams, baked beans, creamed yellow corn, white corn on the cob, cornbread, spoon bread, banana bread, banana pudding, buttermilk, and iced tea, sweet. A white-jacketed waiter served cocktails from a table to the rear, and behind him, the MarvelTones, the younger Thumpers' favorite beach band, had succeeded the bluegrass ensemble that had begun the entertainment.

This year more than others the tableau seemed to be a slow-motion movie in which Roger found himself both an actor and a witness. Pammie's attack—the proper characterization of her behavior, he believed, not that she wasn't entitled—had struck too close to the mark, and he felt disoriented in this familiar place.

By the light of the torches he saw Pammie approach the barbecue pit, presumably, Roger thought, to enjoy her handiwork. Coyly she took his arm and kissed him on the cheek, smiling broadly at Billy Roy. She stared at the roasting pigs.

"Aren't they going to cut the heads off?" she asked, frowning. "I don't like them with their heads on."

"Lord no, honey, we're not cutting the heads off," said Billy Roy emphatically. "The brains melt down real good and season the meat, don't they, boys?"

The two authorities nodded.

"I think I need a drink," Pammie said, disengaging herself from Roger. She eyed him and then the rotisserie again. "Uncle Roger, you could at least see to it that the poor dears had their heads cut off."

Billy Roy took off his apron and wiped his hands with it. He looked solicitously after Pammie as her pumps rejoined their uphill struggle on the lawn. "You don't think she's on drugs, do you?" he whispered to Roger.

•　　•　　•

By memory Roger found the path into the woods, plunging farther from the fading human sounds. He traced the familiar path by the crinkling of the snapped pine needles and the warning hoot-hoot-hoot of the night owls. The dock sat only a hundred yards through the trees, but he couldn't see it through the blackness. Suddenly he emerged, bursting from the trees in a half-run to accommodate the incline. The company's powerboat sat by the pier, rocking in the spare light of the quarter moon now revealed. He climbed into the stern, Brent having already sat amidships and claimed the wheel. That's as it should be, Roger thought. Some things have progressed to a natural end—the son at the helm, the father a passenger, finally.

"Go ahead and drive," Roger said.

Brent popped the top to another beer; the liquid fizzed over him, agitated by its portage. "Damn," he said. Brent turned the ignition key and the big outboard whinnied to life. He guided the launch away from the dock and set out between the buoys for the middle of the lake to take the measure of the unpredictable water.

"You remember the first time I let you drive?" Roger said. "You ran her right into the shallows on the other side."

"I was thinking the same thing."

"You know Billy Roy grew up underneath this damn thing."

"Say what?"

"Just what I said. His farm was right down there."

Roger pointed down, beneath the bottom of the boat.

Brent looked into the lapping, murky water. "I thought he was from Wilkesboro."

"That was later. Billy Roy figures from the old map he was born somewhere near the breakwater of the yacht club, thirty-five feet down."

Brent turned starboard and idled the engine, pointing the bow in the direction of the phantom homestead beneath the yacht club's deck. "Jeez — they must have had that place a hundred years. Tough to get it just washed under like that."

"What the hell you talking about?" Roger guffawed. He removed his jacket and opened a beer for himself. "Best thing ever happened. The government gave his father thirty-eight hundred and seventy dollars for that old farm. More money than he'd ever seen. Then he died."

Brent laughed. "Makes it all worthwhile, doesn't it."

"Listen, Son, that was a lot of money in those days."

The moon rose higher over the hills to the east and the lake water reflected the choppy light. Brent turned easily to port to make a great circle, weaving between the blowers, silent in autumn.

"I ever tell you the story about how we almost got run out of business?"

"Bits and pieces."

"Old Winston Galway tried to run us out of business. You know that."

"Something about a patent. The senator fixed it."

"Fixed it? Fixed it? Hell, Worth couldn't fix a lawn mower in those days. What he did was take on all of Galway's lawyers and argue the best damn law case you ever heard. Yes sir, but for Worth old Galway might have put us under. Worth was brilliant. It was just me, Billy Roy, and Charlie Walton by then. And oh yeah, one seamstress — our last employee."

"Neither one of you much talks about it."

"It was a long time ago."

Roger sat down and stared over the stern at the lights on shore showing dimmer as they drew close to the quiet center of the water, so enclosed in darkness that he imagined it a vast, still inland sea.

"Did you know, Son—did Worth ever tell you how he bopped Marilyn Monroe?"

"Never heard that, Dad."

"Goddamn just bopped her, on Jack Kennedy's boat. I went down there with him, down there to Palm Beach. That's how Worth really took off in politics, you know. Because he and Jack Kennedy were asshole buddies from the navy, so Kennedy had it set up for him. He was like that, you know, Kennedy."

"Gosh. Did the senator enjoy it? I mean, were there Mafia guys there or anything? Did JFK watch?"

"Now what the hell are you talking about. A man bops a girl—sure he enjoys it. He bopped her, he bopped her, he bopped her, end of story. Worth bopped Marilyn Monroe. How many men can say that? I mean in the great scheme of things."

"I see your point."

Roger popped a new beer for each of them. "Don't get me wrong now."

"About what?"

"About Worth and me. We looked out for each other. I was behind him all the way, pushing him to run for this or that, backing him up. And Worth—well, when we needed that money, you know it was Worth's thirty thousand that got us past old Galway. Not one thought about it, just sent over thirty thousand dollars."

"That did it? Thirty thousand dollars?"

He laughed, spewing beer across the bow. "Listen, Son, it's not the first million, it's the last dime you don't have that gets you. Oh—I forgot Billy Roy. He chipped in a hundred seventy-eight dollars. Went to his momma. 'Momma,' he said, 'Momma, I need the money now.' She didn't ask him a thing, she just got the money. The old lady kept it in a refrigerator down in the basement because she didn't trust the banks. She just gave it to him. Probably that old government money. 'The Lord provides,' she said."

Roger sat back in the stern, his face pointed to the celestial procession. "The Lord provides."

"So on your theory of the last dime, it wasn't Worth's thirty thousand but Billy Roy's hundred seventy-eight dollars that put you over the top."

"Yep." He pointed into the black water. "His momma's hundred seventy-eight dollars."

Roger leaned over the side of the boat, his face close to the water. One by one he filled the empty beer cans with water and then he stood up and threw them toward the shore, each falling far short with a muffled splash and sinking to the bottom.

"You want this last one?" He rocked on his heels, holding out the final Budweiser.

"Nope. You kill it."

Roger took a long draught and coughed.

Then he stood up and balanced himself against the stern, leaning delicately against it as he peed into the wash of the boat. "You can't get too caught up," he said.

"What are you talking about?"

"Just that. Worth could lose, you know. He's not always going to come out on top."

"Oh shit, Dad. Don't give me that. We're going to beat Crain. It would just be impossible for that shithead to win."

It was wrong, Roger thought, to believe that old men resisted the world; it was truly the young who resisted. Their resistance often produced the heroism that saved a culture in battle, but in less valiant times it led to embitterment. This was a less valiant time. For him to tell Brent that Worth had flaws, had committed wrongs, could lose — all contrary to the Institute mythology lodged in the boy's ever-resistant mind — would seem a self-serving lie. Moreover, the one transgression that would be most illustrative he simply had no words to discuss.

"All I'm trying to do, Son, is to get some reality into this thing. There's more, you see. More for you to do after this."

"You don't get it, do you?" Brent shouted, his voice drowned out by the roar of the motor as he revved the engine up again and banked hard by the final buoy, close to the flood tide. "You just don't get it. This isn't some game that you play out to get to another game. This is the most important thing that will ever happen in our little world. This is about you and me and Worth and the professor. Jesus, Dad, they're coming after us."

"I know, Son. But at the end of the day it's just an election. There will be others."

"You're wrong," he said quietly. "They're coming after us. It's finally caught up. All these years you've been telling the rednecks — you know, sell your farm so the government can build a dam, move to Fairington and work in the mill, better yourself, love black people while you're at it, change your whole fucking life because you weren't dog shit to begin with, and by the way vote for people who let you know in a thousand ways they're better than you are, because they are. Well, now the game's up, because they've finally found somebody who tells them they aren't dog shit, they never were, they don't have to better themselves, they don't have to love black people, they don't have to do anything but just be the redneck assholes they are. And they're coming after us with two-by-fours. If we don't stop them here, it's over, forever."

"Son, it doesn't do any good to exaggerate."

"No — it'll be over. Look at the polls. I study them every day. You and Worth have been running a race. You educate one, like Billy Roy, and he comes over to our side. You educate enough while the rest just stay asleep, and we win. That's what we've done so far. But you see Crain won't let the other ones sleep. He's going to wake them up, bring them from every trailer park in every hick town and tell them it's okay to kick our ass. And they will, boy, they will. And he's got the money to find every one of them. If we don't stop him we're lost. Maybe if we could have kept the game going another ten, twenty years, you know, he wouldn't be a threat. Hell, maybe it would take a hundred, and then maybe that wouldn't be enough."

Roger tossed his dwindling cigar at the crown of the buoy. "Goddammit," he muttered as it missed the mark. He wanted to say something to Brent that would persuade him the world wouldn't end if Crain won, that it wouldn't even be much altered. But as he listened he began to be convinced that it might be.

"Your problem, Dad, is that things just don't matter to you. There's always something else."

"Not true, my boy," he said, growing angry, but then deciding to let it go.

"Whatever," Brent said, waving the comment away. "Whatever. But you know what makes me the maddest?"

"What, Son?"

"That he made me hate them."

"Who?"

"Crain made me hate the rednecks. You see, I can't be like you. I hate them for what they're doing. And I've worked all my life not to. And I hate Crain for making me hate them. Do you have any idea what I'm talking about?"

"Son, people aren't going to be led if they don't want to be."

"I know that."

"Now I want you to promise me something."

"What?"

"You promise me that whatever happens you won't go off half-cocked."

"What are you talking about?"

"Just promise me. You won't go off half-cocked."

"I can't promise you that."

Roger spun Brent around and held him by the shoulders, trying unsuccessfully to catch his averted eyes. "Promise me, Son. Promise me."

"Just drive the damn boat, Roger. You're always driving anyway, man."

They crept along the opposite sides of the launch and exchanged seats. Roger revved the engine to sudden full throttle, and the boat jerked forward, pointing to the far reaches of the lake, away from the houses. "Hoo-ee!" he cried over the spray and the burning engine. "You're going to see something now, Son. You're going to see something now."

The lake and the sky expanded together, as the big boat sped through the necks and inlets and marshes that the water had cut through the hills. The banks on either side sat silent and dark, and the straining motor drowned out the croakers and the flying fish and almost the far roar ahead. Roger remembered long ago taking Brent that far, to that part of the lake to fish, but going no farther, it being enough to say that the rest was forbidden. Roger sped relentlessly on, the speed itself driving the boat. "Hoo-ee," Roger cried again, "hoo-ee!" and then he saw it, and Brent saw it too, the waters rushing over the concrete waterfall ahead. Dead-on lay the edge of the dam itself. Roger fell back as the slipstream caught the boat and threw it into the white water that roared louder and louder. Fear raised the cool pressure at the back of his neck. The current carried them as a pebble until he turned starboard and steered the craft broadside, bellying out of the tide at the edge of oblivion.

Roger idled the boat. He clambered shakily to the top of the hull, and, holding the launch's windshield, motioned Brent to do the same. Grappling for balance, Brent climbed behind, swaying before catching his sea legs. Arrayed below, beyond the dam's wall, lay the spreading valley of the Catawba, falling hundreds of feet by nature and man. In the far distance glowed the lights of the city, sparse at first, and then clustering together to form an aurora on the horizon.

"That's Fairington to the north, isn't it?"

"There it is all right," Roger said. "Whatever happens, Son, we can go back there. Crain can't touch you there. Besides, he won't be able to hold it together. That's the real truth, Son. Nobody can hold it together very long."

Chapter Seventeen

1978

THE usual editorial sources criticized Crain's bloc vote stratagem as being, even for him, too crude an appeal in an age when crude appeals were passé. Indeed, at first the ploy seemed doubly inopportune, since it brought forth for the first time an attack strategy from Worth Patterson, as well as a rise of three points for the senator in the polls during the week after the Chapel Hill speech. Nonetheless, Roger noted that the yelping of the Crain partisans had grown more intense, creating the kind of pure frenzy on which Crain thrived. Perhaps, he thought, that was the real gambit.

Even so, momentum was with the Patterson forces. Reading the last good statewide polls, either side would have said the two campaigns stood even within the statistical margin of error. All evidence pointed to a final ten days of campaigning in dead heat, each side with enough money to bury the other in ads. Brent had every reason to be ebullient about pulling even, and he was, to the point of reminding Roger of his earlier doubts about negative campaigning. Roger replied that the Institute men hadn't done any of that really, and they hadn't. What they had done, and Roger duly credited Brent and Delbert with the result, was to make the public Worth tougher. They had erased his wimp image and increased his numbers by countering the associations of weakness and betrayal fostered by Crain's own negative campaign. Worth's offensive strategy thus worked as the best defense yet employed.

Emboldened, Brent and Delbert pressed their argument for a last-ditch character assault against Crain. Despite his reservations, Roger too enjoyed the film clips of the MacGiver campaign Delbert resurrected, with the stark racial ugliness of Crain's handiwork punched up for thirty-second spots, the crude handbills displayed as evidence. To continue the volley, Delbert supplied footage of Crain's NCN commentaries on stolen library reels obtained from a secret source. Not even Brent knew the mole's name. The spliced venom against the "Red" Chinese, fluoridation, and the Beatles made Crain sound shriller than any debate, and the dated film caught him before his television makeovers, so that he looked as forced as he sounded. Worth, who also enjoyed rubbing Crain's nose in it, insisted only that what they charged had to be true.

They attacked as though casting for game fish, watching the line spool out, waiting for the strike and the run. When the ads had played for the thirty-six hours it took to get back an audience sample, the Crain people responded by calling the spots lies and simultaneously sought to enjoin the use of the old NCN films on the basis of claims ranging from copyright infringement to common law theft. The attack had to be working, Roger thought, or else they wouldn't be so testy.

It was the larger calculus that concerned him. Crain was forever figuring, and he wouldn't have drawn Worth out without some larger purpose than energizing the Neanderthals. Neither would he launch an uncoordinated campaign. Roger thought it was all of a piece, and the fact the Institute men didn't comprehend it unsettled him.

The first clue, a warning really, had come from a friendly newspaperman. "What do you make of the charge?" he asked Brent, several days after the Chapel Hill speech. "Charge?" Brent replied. The reporter laughed. "I guess you could call it that." Brent looked at Roger and shrugged broadly. I hope, Roger thought, it can all remain such fun for him.

Shortly thereafter reporters generally inquired about the senator's bachelor days in Washington, his private habits and preferences. Background stories appeared, almost as a means of covering the bases, as though the curious word — *fornicator* — antique yet potent, had challenged their professionalism. The spectacle panicked Roger, despite himself. He realized that if this was Crain's purpose, and if the rumor hardened, not even a friendly press could save them. Aside from the secret he feared most, Roger was generally amazed that the tamer Patterson secrets — the tainted money, the curious filial estrangements — had gone unreported, as they had for so many years. He realized anew one stubborn legacy of the Institute: the press indeed, as Crain complained, stood solidly for Patterson, and nothing short of a smoking revolver in his hand and a warm dead body beside him would make the papers. More deliberately than usual Roger read the major dailies, searching for the exception, which he didn't find. As a concession to time spent on the matter, *The News and Observer* ran a reprise of the senator's past liaisons, dressing up old Washington society columns from Worth's bachelor days with a whiff of stale champagne. The impression, after all the fuss, was only of a garden-variety playboy, providing mere background to background.

So the press corps did not warm to Crain's hints. The powers that be seemed eager to print and reprint Brent's statement deploring the "dirty tricks" of the Crain campaign, "reminiscent of Nixon's discredited tactics." Editorials deplored the choreographed heckling of Chapel Hill and Fairington and speculated hopefully that it would backfire among the multitudes of the quietly religious who did not share Crain's partisan harnessing of the Word. The news stories emphasized the late momentum of the Patterson campaign, giving it additional life by their attention.

Still, the possibilities of Crain's plan haunted Roger, even as each day brought better news. The worst sign, Roger thought, was that Worth grew even more resigned. A quiet fatalism that the optimistic mistook for serenity hung over him. Roger thought he must have been warned.

"What do you think they have?" Worth said, catching Roger alone with the papers.

"Maybe nothing," Roger said, trying, as he had for too many years, to remember, to be reassuring, even though this time they both shared the risk.

"It's not like him to lie back, the bastard."

"I know."

"You think he'll do something, don't you."

"I just can't say."

Worth stepped back into the doorway of the small break room. "Che sarà sarà," he said jauntily, with a small wave. A curious gesture, Roger thought, Worth's small retreat — as though he had stepped back on the station platform to bid farewell to a departing train.

•   •   •

The Simpson *Argus* was a small-town daily that had been purchased by a supporter of Joe Crain's named Henry Broadus six months before the primary elections. Although filings with the FCC, which would require such disclosure, showed nothing, Roger believed that Broadus, who had no visible means of support for his right-wing writings on superior Caucasian cranium sizes, Federal Reserve usury, and similar stock topics, was financed, in fact if not in name, by NCN. Appearing at every speech in the same blue business suit, with ties too narrow and shirts too wrinkled to indicate that he otherwise made a habit of the wardrobe, Broadus shouted questions not so much for answers as for effect. This investment by NCN, which appeared to amount to the purchase of a raffish press pass, struck Roger as yet another odd-fitting piece to Crain's puzzle.

They timed the story for the day *The News and Observer* poll would declare Patterson ahead. "Patterson's Homosexual Lover Tells All," the *Argus* headline blared, as truck distribution Broadus didn't possess delivered the paper to strategic corners all over Raleigh. In the second paragraph the reader learned that one Phineas Patterson, the senator's mysterious father, and not Worth Patterson, was the subject. Beneath the story the *Argus* printed a gray photo of a thin, mustachioed young man who declared that Phineas often had sex with him for money in a known gay brothel off Dupont Circle in Washington. Though shocking, it was, as homosexual scandal goes, uninspired. Nonetheless, the story worked after a fashion, as a vast, embarrassed silence fell over the political world and Broadus grinned his idiot's grin on every six o'clock newscast from the Great Smokies to Cape Hatteras. NCN had thrown its stooge to the wolves for a sound bite: instead of the day being dominated by the new Patterson momentum, the airwaves were filled by pictures of the Senator denying the story and threatening a libel suit.

If that had been all, the blow could have been minimized and rendered into a mere diversion. But the day following the senator's denial, Crain littered eastern North Carolina with handbills featuring a blurred photograph of a dapper older man identified as Phineas Patterson on a street corner said to be in Paris, France, his arm draped around a smiling young man of color. The legend below read:

HOMOSEXUAL FATHER OF WORTH PATTERSON
IN PARIS, FRANCE, WITH "FRIEND."
DO YOU WANT HOMOSEXUALS TO HAVE THE RIGHT TO *ADOPT BABIES?*
TO *TEACH YOUR CHILDREN?*
RECRUIT TEENAGERS FOR *ACTS OF SODOMY?*
JOE CRAIN SAYS NO.
WHERE DOES WORTH PATTERSON STAND?

Roger had never seen a picture of Phineas Patterson, and his first re-action, as he was certain the first reaction of the Crain handlers had been, was that the resemblance was stunning. They could have been twin broth-ers rather than father and son. The wide lapels and ties suggested a current photograph. How could they have gotten it? he wondered, and with a young black man, or was he Arab? Indeed, a black lover squared the circle, fulfilling every ancient fear. It was a grand coup.

"Aren't you coming?" Worth said, gesturing downstairs to the meeting of the campaign strategists convened to respond to the emergency.

"They don't need me," Roger said. "I'm certain whatever will be done will be the correct thing."

Worth laughed. "Oh come on for old times' sake. At least you're off the hook, aren't you. They got the wrong scandal. The bastards. Now it's just me and poor old Daddy. I tried to warn him."

So he did have an inkling, Roger thought.

"Poor old Phineas. All he wanted was to be left alone, and I did this to him. Well, you'll miss my speech."

"What are you going to tell them?"

"To leave me the hell alone, let me handle it my own way. No more talk about polls or strategies. The bastards ruined a lifetime of work. Maybe a little dignity will salvage some of it."

"It's not your fault, old buddy."

"Sure it is."

"Do you want me to come down with you?"

"No. Tal will understand. And you. The rest will just have to make the best of it."

Roger wanted to do something to fix it, as he had a hundred times be-fore, but Worth had confirmed what he knew already—that having Roger go down there and fix it wouldn't do. Worth would find his own way, and a few would understand the seriousness of the blow—not the homosexu-ality, on which the strategists would focus, but the truth revealed that the Patterson name had been a deceit.

"It was well played, don't you think?" Worth said.

Roger nodded, for he agreed; the strike was adroit in its concealment and execution, well conceived in the honor of the ruthless. Clearly each step had been modulated, measured out by necessity, so as not to commit any political waste, not to attempt the opponent's decapitation unless and

until the polls said you had to. Then Crain could be insulated from any
real choice in the matter—the percentages dictated it, the forces of evil
arrayed against him were too strong for commonplace methods, God's
hand led him to smite Satan's legions. Nothing personal, really, not even
in the prideful signature of the poster itself, constant even in its meter to
the MacGiver campaign. It was not personal at all, just Crain's little vanity,
the artisan's mark on squalor.

The strategists' reaction was to downplay and maneuver. "If this is the
best they can do, let's just walk away," Brent said. "Scare this Broadus
asshole, no comment on the rest, keep on our themes." This was sensible,
Roger thought, except it misconstrued the character of Crain's attack. The
thrust was not tactical, but directed at Worth's will.

"Pure genius," Delbert muttered as he drafted Worth's denial.
"They've womanized him. Six weeks for us down the drain."

Roger studied Worth's press conference to appreciate Delbert's point.
The very act of denying the charge portrayed indecision, and the matter
on which he appeared indecisive trumped the image they had worked to
build. That was why it was pure genius, along with the drop-dead picture
of Phineas. Homosexual fathers are not easy to explain to the average voter,
especially when you have the spitting image staring back from a compromising handbill. The poster claimed a place in Roger's mind, along with
the picture of Willie Simpson that stayed there always. It was funny how
you carried some things with you, Roger thought. Willie Simpson's face,
for example, so proud and tranquil, yet framed as on a wanted poster. Now
Phineas, trapped in the lens, was condemned to reveal the only secret he
thought worth keeping.

Crain, as usual, stood to the side while his poisons worked. He timed
the spectacle as though by stopwatch while the gossips digested the story
of the expatriate Patterson heir, and the public weighed the assertions and
denials. Finally, when it had played out for a day and there was no new
angle to turn, Crain arrayed himself before several American flags and
taped his ad:

Whatever my opponent is, he isn't one of you. You know that whatever he is, he deserted you long ago to run with the liberal crowd
that makes fun of us, and our families, and our God. Everywhere I
try to speak to you, my opponent's friends shout me down. You know

the ones I mean — the lesbians, the ERA crowd, the curious ones who hold hands with each other, even outside churches. Why, they were doing it outside the First Baptist Church in Charlotte just the other day — George Arnold's church, a strong man of God. They take up money for my opponent in those bars where they go to commit sodomy. Well, you know where I stand on that.

Now you send them a message. You tell them Joe Crain doesn't compromise. Joe Crain won't say that somebody has a civil right to be a degenerate. And I don't care how many of them demonstrate against me. We may lose this election. The other fellow may get enough money from the Hollywood celebrities who fornicate with each other like jackrabbits, and from the homosexuals, to beat me, but that's fine. All right then, I'll lose. I will not sell my soul to be a senator.

Now, I'm going to tell you the truth about liberals. When liberals say that to keep up with the times you have to be tolerant of degenerates and open to new experience, when they say you have to change your beliefs to keep up with what they call progress, what they really want you to do is give up who you are and what you believe so that you can be nobody and believe nothing. That's the definition of liberalism, my friends, and since my opponent doesn't know what he is, I'll tell him — he's a liberal. I'm a conservative, and I know where you stand on that.

The quick, clean shot to the heart — and it was quick and clean; because Crain had the honor of the assassin, there would be no lingering butcher's job — had its immediate and definitive effect. The trappings of the campaign remained, signs healthy, trends favorable, Brent's organization peaking, confidence rising with the numbers, a pink, feverish glow of progress deluding even the pros. Each day in the bunkerlike headquarters Brent examined the daily polls, gave punchy interviews, framed the day's news bite, issued orders to troops who worked past quitting time so that they might keep their jobs past election, and in the background Worth cheerfully disengaged. Relieved in retreat, vagueness came upon him as the morning mist, humor taking over from passion, irony from attack. He was totaling up accounts that only Roger and Ogden, and perhaps by now Delbert, could recognize, Brent too young and too intoxicated to imagine the possibility that what he saw and heard was a sham or that a man could give up so much.

The exemplary thing about Worth had always been the life plan, not the life, Roger admitted. Now, looking back at the ease with which he shed it, Roger could not say that even the life plan was ever really Worth's at all. In fact, it had been everyone's but Worth's. Giving up the life plan was Worth's choice, but in offering it up to Crain, an awful thing indeed to contemplate, he offered it up for Roger, for Ogden, for everyone else who had borrowed it, himself oddly immune from the loss, and indeed refreshed by his ability to walk away. Like MacGiver he sat in his hotel room, or in the backseat of the car, fiddling with this or that for hours. Like the young advisers before, Brent did not know what to do. How Crain incapacitated! In telling the enemy's personal truth and making it into a political lie, he took from his opponent the ability to act but gave him the ability to become himself. After the truth had been told within the lie, the victim spoke wonderfully anew, as though freed from the possibility of his own success by a powerful drug.

The candidates met once in the campaign, passing in the corridor at WBT in Charlotte. The station had scheduled back-to-back television interviews hoping for an impromptu hall debate; Brent had arranged to arrive a half hour early for the Patterson taping, on the chance they could waylay Crain on his way out. "Well, isn't this a coincidence," Worth had said as he grabbed Crain's arm and dragged him from his entourage into the white light and humming meters of the press Brent had assembled for the ambush. With his throwaway smile he put his arm around Crain as they both, by instinct, gave the thumbs-up sign, Worth acting the part that Brent had coached, giving the photographers a chance to record for the unknowing the fact that Senator Patterson looked much more the part. Even so, Crain wouldn't engage. "You got me," Worth said audibly in Crain's clutches, and then, sotto voce, "you bastard." Crain's handlers swept him away, angry at the ambush, not noticing the glee in their master's face.

The physical meeting drained Worth more. The next day his wit turned plaintive, and then progressed to the metaphysical. Finally he journeyed to a still farther remove, to the bewilderment of the now-alarmed managers, turning his campaign speeches to parables. Some days he took as his text the New Testament, others *Alice in Wonderland,* and before difficult crowds, *The Wonderful Wizard of Oz.* Observing success in the matter,

Crain switched off the negatives without a further allusion to cardinal sins, and instead told anecdotes about family values.

•   •   •

Roger suggested the Albright Corporate Conference Center grounds at Bright Star for the campaign's election-morning rally in order to secure a location easily policed for Crain's hecklers. Brent drove them quickly on the interstate past Raleigh, and on the two-lane highway east to the old farm, the land stretching flatter and flatter, exposed by harvest's end, the old gray dirt bared in the open furrows.

"You remember what he said?" Worth asked, Roger knowing what he meant—what Dr. MacGiver had said on the same stretch of highway on runoff day twenty-eight years before.

"Something about the beach," Roger said. "About all of us visiting him and Emma at the beach."

"You know, we've bought out there too, on Ocracoke. You could sail from Belhaven, across the sound, maybe drive there and spend the night at the River Forest. But the channel — -"

"Senator," Brent began, interrupting him in the firm tone he had adopted in the last days. "Senator, remember that Governor Black will introduce you. He got pissed off at your last reference to him as Pontius Pilate. Or what he could understand of it. I've written some make-nice talk for you."

"Thank you, Son," Worth said, putting the papers in his pocket.

"Worth, why in the world would we drive to Belhaven and sail to Ocracoke?" Roger asked. "That doesn't make any sense."

"Probably not. They do have that nice oyster casserole at the River Forest."

Brent steered the campaign Lincoln into the long drive that led to the igloolike corporate modules clustered around the old plantation house in the distance.

The assembled crowd was larger than any in the campaign and far larger than they had expected. The weather had stayed warm, and the spectators lounged on blankets, eating picnic lunches, expectant. Perhaps, Roger thought, this was how it was when the great times were upon them—secession, war, depression—and the people listened to the assured men before them. In their faces Roger could see the expectation. The coming to judgment was upon the people, and though they pretended to despise the politicians, they wanted very much to like them. They had determined that the climax had arrived, that Crain and Patterson were colliding, that something important, even if only a man like themselves standing up to speak, was to happen, and that they should be there.

The governor greeted Worth at the edge of the podium, and the senator, by reflex, hid his distaste. "Hello, Hank, old buddy," he beamed.

"Worth—looks like you got a bunch of good Democrats today."

The governor, a self-made brick millionaire from the low Piedmont pine bogs, had never liked Senator Patterson much, having complained on numerous well-liquored evenings about the superior air of the "Fairington crowd." True to form, during the rise of the Crain campaign he did not extend himself beyond the most grudging gestures on the senator's behalf, believing himself vulnerable to "Joe's boys"—those dissident erstwhile Democrats, mainly in the rural east, which was the base of the governor's support, who were loudly organized by the opposition. On election morning, however, when it could do little good or harm, he played the enthused master of ceremonies, preening before the faithful and the curious, discussing the end of the football season two weeks hence, the beginning of basketball practice two weeks before, the weather, and the virtues of a straight ticket, his means of minimally boosting Patterson. When he had created the necessary frenzy he announced triumphantly that he was a "yellow-dog Democrat" who could smell Joe Crain out as the skunk at a garden party anytime. He read a telegram from the president, which Brent had arranged through Hassell, sending his regrets that he could not attend in person this fine and spirited gathering, but that he needed, in fact the country and the free world needed, Worth Patterson in the Senate, that Worth Patterson was one of the most important leaders the nation had, and that he implored the Democrats of North Carolina to turn out and reelect their senator.

"You notice that Hank made his speech without once endorsing me," the senator said to Brent, smiling and applauding as Governor Black held his arms out before the crowd's thunder.

"Yes sir. I noticed that."

"He's half afraid I'm going to win this damn thing and that Crain is going to run against *him* next time."

The governor strode from the microphone and grabbed the senator's hand, shaking it like a water pump. In the same motion he brought him to the edge of the platform, holding up the senator's fist in political communion. Still basking in the whistles and cheers he bear-hugged Worth, catching him unawares and almost crumpling the speech notes the Senator was retrieving from his pocket.

"Thanks for warming them up for me, Hank," Worth said as the florid magnate wiped his forehead with a handkerchief and prepared to sit down.

"Anything for you, Worth old buddy, anything at all. You know that."

The crowd quieted involuntarily, some standing to see the senator, some holding small children on their shoulders. Roger thought they looked a bit like spectators who couldn't decide whether they'd rather see a baptism or a hanging.

"You see," Worth began, "the problem is, Joe Crain doesn't believe we can do anything together to make society better. We should just cut our losses, you see, and get on to the next life. That makes it tough to be in government, because you can't do anything. You just walk around putting people in jail for disagreeing with you."

Roger could feel Brent tense beside him. This was not the speech he had written. There was nothing about strong defense, lower taxes, or the tobacco price supports. It was just Worth, an uncooperative candidate who refused to make his last sound bite.

"I have this other view, that people acting together can make society better. I didn't say perfect, or even more moral, just better in an ordinary way—more jobs, better schools, that kind of thing. I believe in doing what you can with what you know, and I'm modest about how much you can know, especially about what the Good Lord wants.

"I also believe that the future will be good, which Crain doesn't. If you have faith in the future, see, then you have a vision. You might not know what it is all the time, or even most of the time—the vision, that is—I mean you might not see it, but it's out there. And to take hold of it, this future you can't quite see from where you are, you have to take hold of possibilities, even people and ideas that are different from you, and to be changed by that.

"So I disagree with Crain on this, too. He thinks to change means you're weak. That's backward. To change means you're strong. And I will always ask you to be strong. Sometimes it's hard, but I will always ask you.

"I will say one thing about morals. I believe it is morally right to appeal to the best in people, and by that I mean their spirit of cooperation and fair play. I believe that's the American way, and I've always tried to do that, rather than making people afraid. That's not moral. I mean dividing people because of fear. It's always out there, the fear, but that's not the better side of people, so I don't appeal to it.

"Another thing my opponent accuses me of, and this he's right about, is being rich. I am rich, and I didn't make any of the money I have. My grandfather made it and left it to me. If that moves me to be on the side of the poor, then I don't apologize for it. Despite what you might think, poor people don't get much out of the government, and I'm proud to help them get what they do get. That's a test of a strong people, too, helping the poor, although Crain thinks it's a sign of weakness.

"The old Saint Paul, a far better politician than I, preached to the church at Corinth, which was torn up like we are. Saint Paul told them they had to love one another. That they had to put aside their pride, because they didn't know enough to be proud, because we can see ourselves but dimly in this world. Later we may see all things, and the truth will be apparent then, when now it is hidden. We see through a glass darkly, he said, meaning a mirror, of course.

"So, my friends, if you ask me what to do about this or that in Washington, if you ask me what I can do for you, I can say what I have always said, tried to say, that I will look in that mirror and try to make sense of it, and that I will always think of you, and the children, and the country, and the fields so pretty this time of year, and the cities we built, our jobs, the dreams that keep us young, and everything that keeps us going. I'll do that and I'll try to remember us in our best moments, at our best times, and I will try to represent that to the world the best that I can, as long as you give me the power to do it. And if you don't want to give me that chance to serve anymore, then I'll just say thank you and slip away a happy man, because you've already given me more than I could ever deserve."

There rose from the crowd a long moment's murmur and then a roar passed over the podium, feeding back through the microphones. The governor sprinted to the edge of the platform and glanced about quizzically. Then gently he led the senator to the edge of the dais to receive the ovation, holding him firmly by the elbow and then taking one step back, smiling, clapping nervously, waiting, Roger thought, for the crowd below to shout for Barabbas.

•   •   •

They filed quietly from the bandstand and the bleachers into the parking lot and the field beside that was cordoned off with red and blue plastic flags that flapped in the sporadic breeze. They drove their pickup trucks and Chevys and Fords out of the roped-off grassy fields, away from the buildings and toward the highway with its billboard pointing east on U.S. 64 to the self-proclaimed "Largest Tobacco Auction in the World." They drove, Roger imagined, back to the town to stamp the afternoon's invoices or to the farms that began at the highway's edge, where the last tasks of the season's cycle waited in the fallow fields. The cars and trucks departed to the direction of a highway patrolman two by two, and he wondered if Worth had made any sense to them.

He wondered also if Brent would ever forgive them for voting for Crain, or indeed if he would himself. It had been so long since he had thought of voters as people. That was a flaw, he realized, a flaw built into the Institute. He never evaded it, but he had never had to confront it either. The Institute somehow left out of graphs the fact that moving people from point A to point B on a self-actualization chart required their consent. He thought the whole thing started with those Walker Evans photographs in *Life* magazine Ogden had in his office. Once he had those to stare at, he got out of the habit of meeting real people. Brent had done that far better than any other Institute man, Roger thought, and for his trouble he led a far more tortured life.

"Delbert wants to know if you have a copy of Daddy's speech for the Hardee's dedication," Pammie said to Brent, who still moved slowly about the platform, trying to compose himself. "He also wants to know what to say to the reporters about the copies of the speech he was supposed to give this morning."

"Just tell him to say that we screwed up and the senator will give that speech this afternoon in Fairington, or tonight in Raleigh, or he might just make paper airplanes out of it. Whatever. And there won't be any copies of today's speech; they have to work from notes. Oh yeah — come with me to the car and get the Hardee's stuff."

They walked to the Lincoln, which by then stood alone at the edge of the lot. He unclipped a copy of the Hardee's speech from a loose-leaf binder. Two hundred voters would be present at the Hardee's opening in Spring Hope, and Miss Nash County would cut the ribbon, assisted by the senator and a vice-president for marketing with Hardee's Hamburgers International. After that Brent had to return to attend to the details of democracy on election eve. Roger had seen his punch list, which included making sure the hired muscle had enough ammunition to secure the phone banks and double-checking the auxiliary generators in case Crain's people cut the headquarters' power lines. A pretty picture of democracy for youthful idealists.

"Here, take this to Delbert, will you? And let's drive back together, okay? I need to be with you. Chuck can drive the senator."

Roger watched as the two of them walked toward the grounds of the conference center, away from the sodded-over tobacco field that served as the gathering place for crowds such as today's and for concerts of the Tri-County Symphony that Lulu sponsored. Restoring the old manse had been Lulu's idea, as she watched it become more functional than her taste would permit in the hands of its pragmatic farmer owners. The last straw had come when they tore down the breezeway and turned the smokehouse into a toolshed. The carriage house had been converted to a tractor garage long before, probably in Charles's time. The nearby icehouse now stored old tires. When the owners forsook painting for fiberboard siding, Lulu resolved to put an end to it. "We've got to do something," she said simply as she and Roger drove west on 64 one Sunday afternoon, past the Bright Star turnoff toward Fairington.

He knew when she said it she meant restoring Bright Star. Several times he had thought to buy it back, but as easy as it would be to do, something stopped him. His willfulness still told him not to turn back. But in truth, he did want to return a little bit. He had sentimentality enough to enjoy the curious old place. It was not pride that restrained him, he realized, but superstition. Here stood the failures that made him, and the certainty of his end. Even a place in the graveyard, which was always tended by virtue of the deed, stood waiting. The memento mori had made him work harder than most, not, he thought, for an empire; that would be unfitting. What he wanted was the simple life on a grand scale, and he thought he had attained it. Insecurity had motivated him well, but it was time to move on, and she knew it before he did. As in other things, he underestimated her. "You're right," he said, and blessed it.

She soon set to work, with architects and county officials, preservation experts and historians. He had never seen her so determined. It was then he knew, without her saying it, that this was an important thing for her, that she was attempting a restoration not only of the house, but of their life together. He bought her a condominium nearby so that she could oversee the work herself, so anxious she was for it. Each layer of paint uncovered, each original brick recovered, each artifact retrieved from the grounds she handled as a personal article of salvage, a reclamation by her of the idea she had fallen in love with. Never was she in better spirits than when he joined her and she showed him his scoured past. No longer afraid of the house's spell, he wondered if he should fear hers. Was his present state so marred that she had to rip him up by the foundations, re-create him out of existence?

The finished house and outbuildings, serene and ornate in their genuineness, stood as a curio amid the contemporary pods hatched around it for the business purpose of gathering executives in sports clothes to wear name tags and eat catered food. Roger had insisted on the conference center, and Lulu, indifferent to all plans but her own, understood well enough that the place, to be tolerable to Roger, had to have some function. Purchasing the tobacco land and the house, the tidy dirt-and-shell approach, the icehouse, the smokehouse, the carriage house — he could not agree to it without the objects made new for some purpose. Besides, he explained to her, constructing the conference center would permit the whole project to obtain Industrial Revenue Bond financing. So she acquiesced in his counterrestoration, if that was what it took to save the whole, agreeing that the curved white modules and their darkened glass would rise beside the manse, that the Albrights' gift to the county would reserve the grounds for corporate retreats while opening the house to all. Then, with that balance, he could accept the proclamation of the Nash County Historical Museum; the hoopskirted docent greeting tourists on the veranda, the ersatz rooms, the facsimile furniture, the reproduced portraits of people who never lived there. "Representative of the period is the central staircase, with its dramatic sweep that leads the visitor upward," she would say, her voice climbing as the auditors ascended, consulting their guidebooks. He knew it was not enough, but he loved Lulu some for trying.

Why did he always run from it? Failure, he thought, was not the worst thing, by far. By contemporary standards Crain was a success, an up-by-his-bootstraps striver, made good in religion, in television, now in politics. No, failure was not the worst thing; to realize that, he figured, was to become at once less optimistic but more civilized. The sentiment carried with it a superiority he sensed in the old place, a kind of character he had often disdained but that now seemed attractive. Charles Albright, after all, was a failure. But he thought clearly, was gentle with women and children, determined in things that mattered, and dutiful to the end.

That was what Lulu fell in love with, he concluded with a start. She fell in love with the farm boy Roger Albright worked a lifetime to banish. Funny how the very biggest things can get ruined almost without notice.

So too, he figured, did the Institute fall to the law of unintended consequences. The Institute created its own meaning, insisting always that life would, by golly, be improved, and checking like a schoolmistress to make sure none of the unwashed were left alone. In opposing such fussiness Crain flourished. He restored that perfect id the Institute would extinguish. Worth had no way to argue with him, even if Crain would argue. With the Senate at stake, the two of them were reduced to shouting half-truths on television to people who didn't listen. Once, Roger reminded himself, Charles had persuaded men of far less education, in argument far more complex, to sacrifice more for the greater good. Some failure.

Pammie and Brent stood by the iron gate of the graveyard, shivering in the snappish breeze of the advancing afternoon that stripped the few remaining leaves from the ancient pecan trees lining the drive to the house and brought the gray clouds of a gathering storm. They could have stood there at any time, Roger thought, master and mistress, at the end of a journey home, the carriage empty, the horses stalled, a stop at the well for a draught of water, she bothered by the cold, gathering his vest around her shoulders, together the perfectly ambiguous heirs to the protean estate.

Brent opened the gate and led her to the center of the old stones, the mottled obelisk of white marble that marked the general. What could draw him there after all this? Roger wondered.

Brent rocked on his heels, squinting to read the monument's elaborate script:

Here Lies in Beloved Memory
Roger Pettigrew Albright, Maj. Gen. CSA
1828–1898
A Chivalric Warrior for a Noble Cause
A Christian Gentleman as was Said of the Chevalier Bayard
"Sans peur et sans reproche"

Roger knew the inscription by heart. What the hell does it mean? he thought. God save me from foreign languages on my tombstone.

He watched as Brent moved to the next monument, the clean marble square marking Charles. "Brightest and Best are the Sons of the Morning" the legend read, an exhortation rather than a boast. It is a simple plot, Roger thought, well kept and honest. Perhaps the boy would choose us after all, if it came to that.

But it always comes to that, in one way or another, he figured. Being an Albright is a pretty good thing, given the alternatives. It had taken him a lifetime to admit that; he hoped the boy would feel the same way without as much trouble.

Roger felt drops of rain and by habit looked south and east over the stalk-marked fields where the clouds from the sea came. The furrowed land rolling upon itself calmed him as it once had, and he felt the silence of it at the end of the day, the repose that spread even over the highway behind. The quiet, especially in autumn, had once invigorated him, but now it made him melancholy, a harbinger of endings in a place of endings. Two boys, oblivious to the coming storm, played tag as miniatures about the edge of a haystack, flushing a covey of quail that flew straight up and then dispersed against the darkening sky. The wind whipped up and Roger made his way to his rented car. He turned on the road toward Fairington, now busy with the daily traffic of the town. Behind the flashing light of a school bus, he stopped and watched the mechanical sign wave its warning to the drivers who craned their necks out of windows, thumping their fingers against the steering wheels in rhythm to the afternoon disc jockey, all waiting for the big machine to lumber again down the country highway. The children descended one by one, each looking both ways, hesitating and then dashing across the road. The blinking red aileron swung slowly to its original position and the bus clanked into gear.

As Roger prepared to follow the procession, he saw by the roadside one boy left from the school bus odyssey, a small boy in a yellow slicker. He raised his hand to Roger and smiled a gap-toothed grin. Something in the boy's face, Roger thought as he drove past, or maybe it was the yellow slicker — he could still smell Brent's yellow slicker. Or was it his own yellow slicker that he smelled? He met the gaze of the small boy, saw his brow furrow. He was lost. Roger lingered, wanting to help. But the line of cars moved on, the driver behind sounded his horn, the moment passed, and

Roger too headed down the highway. He looked back and saw the boy running through the last drops of rain toward the gravel driveway and the simple dandelion yard, to the frame house set back from the road, to the familiar things, no longer lost. Whose yellow slicker was that? Roger wondered. Anyway, it was a long time ago. The storm passed — there would be no more rain toward Fairington. He placed the visor down against the large low sun that drew all westward, there in the line of pilgrims, now lengthening. Ahead he saw Brent and Pammie's car, and he rode behind them for a hundred miles, until beside the interstate arose the glass towers of Fairington, and they turned as one toward home.

IV

——✖——

GOOD SEATS
FOR THE END OF TIME

1979–81

Chapter Eighteen

1979

WHEN he was a boy Brent had wanted to be an astronaut, to carry the lightness of the future with him above the earth, rotating in harmonic calculus to the voice of Mission Control, his path perfectly predictable, his spirit perfectly free. Roger bought him a mock space suit and a poster with the names and dates and flights of the spacemen, the American ones, that is, and he followed the story of mechanical faith and manly courage through the first adventures of the Mercury men: Alan Shepard, Gus Grissom, and then John Glenn, whom he thought unduly celebrated, for any of the others could have orbited had they been given the chance. He tracked the glories of his heroes the way other boys traded in the fame of baseball players, swapping their faces on cards, searching long hours for the right paraphernalia to capture the right stuff, and demanding it adroitly so that at Christmas and birthdays there would appear the genuine Mission Control flight screen, a to-scale Freedom 7 with removable cockpit and singed heat shield, a helmet like that worn by Gus Grissom that played, when the correct string was pulled from the rear, instructions — complete instructions it was claimed — for blasting away from the Cape Canaveral sands, past the Bermuda tracking station, past the booster rockets that fell into the Atlantic, past the last turquoise light of earth into the great looping circles of time.

Gus Grissom was his hero, a Mickey Mantle of astronauts, with a name that Brent knew alone would have qualified him for the Yankees Murderers' Row had he not dedicated himself to carrying the glory of American know-how past the wild blue yonder. Years later, Gus Grissom's death depressed him for days, and he was powerless to hide it, even amidst the sophisticated manners of high school. Gus Grissom — to have escaped, actually escaped the earth — and then to be incinerated on the launchpad during training! When Grissom died, Brent felt again the call to ride the rockets. Once before, when he was younger, it had passed the phase of boyish fancy and become a pact with fate. He had sneaked into the adult section of the public library to find out how you got to be an astronaut, learning that it took many years as a test pilot in mere airplanes, that being a military man was the favored entry. He studied the requirements for West Point and Annapolis. But what he really wanted was the Air Force Academy, brand-new in the Colorado mountains. "Send Me Men" the legend read above the main gates; Brent saw the photo in the issue of *National Geographic* he searched out over and over from the piles of the yellow magazines that Lulu kept on the slats above the insulation in the attic. He would learn to fly airplanes and then to fly into space.

Brent so immersed himself in the study of space travel that Lulu began to worry about him, and she received suggestions that he be checked out by Dr. Bernstein, known as Dr. Bonkers by the kids at school who had been sent to see him and answer dumb questions about what comes into your mind when he says oatmeal. Dr. Bonkers smiled a lot and didn't say very much, didn't even ask him what came into his mind when he said oatmeal, but asked him what he thought about Roger and Lulu, questions Brent was glad to answer and expand upon, giving him the entire history of the household until Dr. Bonkers looked at his watch and said that his mother was waiting for him outside.

"Does this mean I get to go to military school now?" Brent asked. A lot of the boys who went to see Dr. Bonkers disappeared a short time later, and it was said that they went to military school, to the smart-looking places Brent read about in the advertisements at the back of *National Geographic*, places that promised "individual guidance, five hours of homework nightly, and expert character-building grades 7–12, all set in the beautiful Adirondacks" above the picture of a determined boy in a high beaver hat and a coat with epaulets. The girls who went to see Dr. Bonkers disappeared too, except they went not to military school but "to Virginia," like Lucy Johnson, who had a body in the fifth grade and got caught without any clothes on in the bathtub playing with her little brother's thing.

"Do you want to go to military school, Brent?" Dr. Bonkers asked, closing the door that he had just opened, raising his bushy eyebrows that had more hair it seemed than his balding head, looking down over the half-glasses that fell to the tip of his nose.

"I might want to."

"Why is that?"

"Because, see, it would maybe give me an angle on getting into the Air Force Academy."

"Un-*hunh*," Dr. Bonkers said, opening the door again and ushering him to the waiting room where Lulu sat, her purse in her lap, her hands folding and refolding a Kleenex. She glanced at Dr. Bonkers who nodded his head slowly and closed the door behind him, and then she stood up, smoothed her navy blue dress with the high white collar, and removed the keys to the navy blue Chrysler from her purse.

"If we don't hurry," she said, "we'll be late for the orthodontist."

That night, when he was upstairs in his room constructing his model for the new Saturn rocket, Brent heard Roger and Lulu arguing, yelling at each other. He stopped and listened, for it was rare that so much as a raised voice was heard in the house, much less Lulu's sobbing and Roger's ice-cold staccato office speech.

". . . Somebody had to do something about it. I just took matters into my own hands," Lulu said, her voice quaking.

"I will not have it, do you understand?" Roger insisted, punctuating the command by slamming the door to the den. Brent heard his slow footsteps climb the stairs.

"Son?" Roger said, poking his head though the half-closed door, his face flushed. He tossed his jacket on the bed. "Let's see — is that uh, some kind of rocket you're working on?"

Brent paused, remembering to contain his impatience at Roger's naïveté. "It's the new Saturn booster platform, Dad. Just in at Morley's yesterday."

"Great!" Roger picked up the rocket assembly and examined it under the Tensor lamp Brent had bought for close work.

Brent winced. "Dad. Please — it's still tacky." He took the booster platform gently from Roger's hands and set it back on the corkboard.

Roger sat on the edge of the bed. "Don't you need some more light in here?" he said, switching on the bedside lamp.

Brent nodded without looking up. "Sure, Dad. Thanks."

Roger cleared his throat. "Son, I've been meaning to talk with you about this astronaut thing. You know how I've told you that a good businessman checks out all his variables before he makes a decision."

"Variables?" Brent looked from the model and squinted at Roger.

"Those are the parts to a decision. Like putting the model together."

"Oh."

"You see, Son, I think you may have overlooked something in the astronaut plan."

"I don't think so, Dad." Brent bent back over the model.

"Well then I guess you know, Son, that an astronaut has to have twenty-twenty vision."

Brent's hand shook as he put down the rocket. "Twenty-twenty vision?"

Roger nodded. "Yes, Son. I was in the service and I know how they operate. You've got to pass flight school, and for that you've got to have perfect eyesight. They just won't take you otherwise. A lot of my friends were washed out during the war because they couldn't pass the eye test."

Brent took off his glasses and held them toward the window, where he had set up the telescope to work on his constellations. He squinted at the glasses, which became a blurry haze as he moved them farther away.

"Maybe I can fake it," he said. "You know, memorize the chart. I know a lot of guys at school who do that."

Roger placed his hands on Brent's shoulders. "I don't think so, Son. Mission Control checks you out pretty thoroughly. I don't think many men get by."

So that was it. Brent thought for a second he would break his glasses in a rage, but what good would that do? Something out there, or really something in him, in his eyes, in his body, was going to keep him from being an astronaut, keep him from fulfilling the only mission in life he ever wanted. How stupid all this junk was, he thought, surveying the Mercury program posters, topographical maps of the moon, and cross-section diagrams of the Milky Way on the walls, the rows of meticulously constructed model capsules and boosters, the experimental space station that was his pride sitting on the shelf, and even the satellites, which were tedious to make but which he felt obligated to study, hanging from the ceiling, in the chronological order of their launch.

"You can still enjoy flying, Son. It's not the end of the world. I enjoy flying myself. Why don't you and I get the plane and fly up to Washington on Saturday and have a day to ourselves? We can go to the Smithsonian if you want, and then maybe we can see the Senators play. I think they're home against the Yankees."

"They'll lose," Brent said glumly.

He called the Air Force recruiting office the next day to make sure Roger was right. Roger was right. He considered the idea of being on the technical side of the space program and flirted for a month or so with becoming an ion propulsion engineer. But he kept remembering the sad smile of Deke Slayton on the astronaut card, Deke Slayton who had a heart murmur and would never go into space but would have to make do on the ground, radioing his buddies who circled the world and then asking them when they got back how they liked it.

• • •

"You sure finished that number for Union Carbide in a hurry," Delbert said, grabbing the speech Brent had just finished, a speech that went to great lengths to extol free enterprise to a group of conventioneering chemical company executives who presumably needed no convincing.

"It's an easy sell, Delbert. Have a good trip."

Ackerman waved good-bye while putting on his jacket and stuffing Brent's speech into his briefcase. In a continuation of the motion he tossed a copy of his itinerary on the desk of the secretary he and Brent shared and kicked open the door to the office, which just last week the workmen had finished stenciling with the proud new name: "FUTURE MANAGEMENT ASSOCIATES, Delbert Ackerman, President."

Brent removed from his wallet the business card Delbert had made up for him. "Brent Albright, Associate" it read, and below, Delbert's new motto — "We don't manage your business for the future. We manage the future for your business." Brent placed a dozen of the cards in his jacket pocket. He had to make some calls that afternoon.

"We need the Pan Am Building for credibility," Delbert had told Roger when he asked how a business that wasn't making any money could afford the highest-priced digs in Manhattan. "They think we're just parlor pinks. Nothing impresses these bastards like a good address. Of course, I don't need to tell you that."

The first three months after the election, Brent moonlighted at the Ford Foundation, or the Tank, as Delbert called it, as a specimen in the Oral History Project, recounting to graduate students his experience as a historical victim of right-wing direct mail campaigning. Rising to the role, he held roomfuls of staffers spellbound with stories of the barbecue and chitlin circuit, the grass-roots organizing of the evangelical churches, the tactics of the NCN, and the perverse personality and politics of the new senator from North Carolina they were all learning to hate. Sorrowfully the program directors nodded their heads. Later, they invited him into their offices, and, closing the doors to the open square halls that looked out from the tinted glass and the wooded atrium toward the United Nations and Turtle Bay, they asked him if it was true, what they'd heard, that Mobil Oil was hiring in the public affairs division.

At a seminar held by the New School for Social Research he found himself seated on a panel with Dick Hassell, who greeted him like a comrade from old. Hassell looked a little paunchy and jet-lagged, no doubt from his new job at Lehman Brothers. After the midterm elections, Hassell had quit the White House staff, leaking to the *Times* his disappointment that "the President, alas, sacrifices policy for politics." He had written a very long article for *The Atlantic* recounting the stages of his disillusionment and pointing out who among the White House staff used cocaine. On the basis of the article, Lehman had hired him to "quarterback Washington — sensitive matters," as Hassell explained it, shouting to Brent over the din of P. J. Clarke's. "But that's not where the real action is," he said. "I'm trying to get into the deal flow."

At first Brent had felt guilty asking for the large speaker's honoraria he seemed entitled to command for stories of failure, but Ackerman, who courted him, with Roger's blessing, to join FMA's public relations consulting business, had cured that weakness. "Make the bastards pay, kid. Never work cheap," he counseled. After several weeks of entreaties, Brent had succumbed, exacting from Delbert a promise he could veto client projects if they were ideologically objectionable. Delbert seemed insulted by the idea that FMA's projects could ever be ideologically objectionable. Thinking of new ways to market the business after Brent came on, Delbert arranged evening focus groups with women executives to test a new line of Future Management Associates personal services. "Only the cream for you, kid," Delbert promised. "Hey, loosen up, okay? There's nothing ideological about this. I'm walking my share, too. I even give you the young ones."

Brent had to admit Delbert was right. Providing a walker service did increase their business. Soon the focus group participants began directing projects in their corporate divisions to FMA, and Brent kept busy writing presentations for seminars on corporate assertiveness, or on the proper things to say when interviewed on television by hostile reporters. One technique his clients thanked him for, usually the only one they remembered, was Brent's instruction to use the inquisitor's first name when the questioning got hot. Such as — "You know, Roberta, this business about widget waste killing small babies is all just scare talk."

Not that the marketing technique was risk free. One lady bank vice-president, after taking Brent to dinner at Le Cirque, demanded that he beat her with the whips she kept in her dumbwaiter or else she would accuse him of raping her. After he had unenthusiastically shredded her gown and given her the pleasure of the thongs, she asked if he wouldn't please pour a decanter of red wine vinegar down her back. He complied and fled. The next day, at the lunch to which she had arranged his invitation, she sat beside him in porcelain profile, her fingernail tracing his kneecap, while they heard, in a private dining room of the Century Club, an economist from the Money Roundtable discuss the advantages of returning to the gold standard. As she had assured him, there were plenty of corporate public relations officers to accept his business card. "I told you," Delbert had said, "that once we get on the list there would be no stopping us." He was right about that. Once the word got out that Future Management Associates could write a mean speech, the luncheon invitations rolled in, even without assistance from the focus groups. FMA became an opinion maker, a firm whose ideas helped shape boardroom decisions. In his new station, when attending meetings of the Money Roundtable, Brent took time to wander the halls of the Century Club, pausing to meet the gaze of the young Henry James whose portrait stared from the wall, taken by the clear, strong eyes, the delicate amusement. What, Brent wondered, would Henry James say in a hired speech denouncing Regulation Q? What was Regulation Q?

The secretary had already left for lunch and Brent locked the door behind him as he went out for his afternoon walk. He turned up Park Avenue and found a place on the sidewalk among the multitudes, starting, by habit, to stroll uptown toward Lulu's but deciding against it. A mile north stood her apartment house, where even at that moment Pammie would be studying and Lulu would be trying to get her to eat more than she wanted for lunch. It had been more unsettling than he would have thought for Pammie to announce, after she had accepted Lulu's invitation to live with her in New York, that she was quitting her political activities and preparing for a new venture: a master's degree in business administration.

"B-school," Brent had repeated dumbly when she appeared at the office early one Friday afternoon with the news.

"Yep. But I have to take some remedial courses to retool. Calculus, economics, accounting."

"What do you want? Money—is that it?" He found his checkbook. "How much—ten thousand, fifteen, twenty?"

She laughed. "You always take care of me. No, no money. I don't want anything. It's fun, really. Very weird. You get a calculator with your initials carved on it and one of those briefcases like I've always wanted, you know, with a little pocket flap for everything."

He knew she was seeing Hassell. It was inevitable, he figured. He believed Hassell had put the whole idea of business school into her head. She denied it, improbably, after repeating some elegant phrase he knew Hassell had to have coined about the world being divided into people who are investment bankers and people who aren't. He had to listen to lines like that at least once a week while trying to support Pammie in her new vocation.

Meanwhile, personal life continued much the same. For example, every Thursday Lulu invited him to dinner. On these occasions, although the important things had split asunder, he would feign normalcy and regale his mother and Pammie with stories of pale glory servicing the mischievous clients of Future Management Associates.

"... so he had taken the company plane to Philadelphia and left his car in New York. But he forgot that he'd left his car so he thought some guy had stolen it when he got out of the meeting. He didn't give a goddamn about his car, you know, just another Jag, but it had his wife's special backgammon table in it and he knew he'd catch hell. So he got the Pennsylvania Highway Patrol to issue an all-points bulletin. Then he remembered he'd left it parked at La Guardia. And this guy is CEO of one of the fifty largest industrial corporations in the United States."

Lulu laughed politely. Pammie cleared the table. "That's hysterical," she said. "I'm so proud of you. You know, retooling and all."

After supper that night, when Lulu left to meet Walter Degley for the early show at the Carlyle and Pammie retired to the calculus, Brent took his evening constitutional, marching south in the darkness, wandering as far as Soho, where he sampled the after-hours clubs and their pleasures, then walking north again before dawn, huddled against the buildings with his coat drawn around him so that the bums and the hustlers would think him one of them. Dawn refreshed him, and he hurried to Grand Central Station, where he stood to greet the commuting executives already muttering to themselves the day's order of battle, the first lines of sweat on their foreheads. They passed him on the escalator, their eyes fixed on the struggle, leaving behind in the slips of the concourse the trains that would at the end of the day reverse routes and take them north to Greenwich, or New Canaan, or Darien. He waited there until the gigantic clock hand in the archway above the ticket counters stood straight up at nine, and he heard, far up Fifth Avenue, the bells of St. Patrick's toll the hour.

• • •

"By the waters of Babylon, there I lay down, and wept, when I remembered Zion . . ."

Roger watched Brent move slowly through the line, past the old women whom he imagined there every day, past the self-conscious parishioner seeking a special prayer. In the dark solace of St. Barts he watched them kneel, the penitents, holding their briefcases, the *Journal* or the *Times* underneath an elbow, their expressions relieved of worry in the sanctuary's haven, removed for a moment from the getting and spending outside on Park Avenue.

"The Body of Christ. The Blood of Christ. The Body of Christ. The Blood of Christ. The Body of Christ. The Blood of Christ . . . ."

Maybe it was the repetition that calmed him, Roger thought. Delbert said that he seemed better when he returned, refreshed at least, as though morning communion served as a rehabilitation program for his dimly understood paralysis. Roger didn't think it right to be disturbed by Brent's immersion in a perfectly laudable Christian ceremony, but he was. Certainly, he reasoned, if Crain stands for anything it is that Christianity can be taken too far. This could be part of the man's curse — that Brent would be touched by the hysteria, too. When the priest reached him, Roger saw that Brent seemed confused as to what exactly to do, and he both dipped his wafer into the cup and drank from it, causing in the priest a brief stir, a hitch in the economy of grace.

•   •   •

While in New York during the months he stood vigil for Brent, Roger received an invitation to meet Nose for lunch. He found her table at the restaurant Rendezvous, which she proclaimed to be her favorite in Manhattan for its high prices and atmosphere of rococo intrigue. Roger didn't particularly enjoy the rich food that her newspaper paid for, but he was fascinated enough by his companion, who insisted he call her Angela. It was thoughtful for her to so insist at the outset, he realized; otherwise, what else would he call her?

"Perhaps you would like to know how your friend Senator Crain is distinguishing himself on the Hill."

"Please, Angela," he said. "Senator Crain is not my friend."

She laughed, a deep contralto laugh, her remarkable bosom shaking her body from crossed ankles to flowered hat. She motioned for the waiter to fill the glasses again with the white wine she had had brought up from the cellar, and she leaned over the table, placing her hand over his, arresting him for the moment with the merry and piercing gaze that overwhelmed the objects of scrutiny from behind her aquiline, finely powdered, deep-nostriled trademark.

"Everything Judith said about you is true," she said. "You are quite extraordinary. A throwback. A charming throwback. Anyway, I asked you here because we have mutual purposes."

"Oh?"

"Yes. This is quite between-you-and-me-ish, but the new Senator Crain has a bounty on his head."

"What do you mean?"

"I'm sure I don't have to spell things out for you, Roger. There are players who want him out."

"Spell things out for me, Angela."

She looked casually to either side and smiled at the passing maître d', measuring his steps away from the table before speaking. "There are rumors that the Bureau has him on film, my dear," she whispered, flushing and fanning herself with her napkin. "In the most—and I emphasize that—the most compromising way."

Roger sat amazed, conversationally helpless for several moments. Nose waited patiently, averting her eyes from his indisposed state and skipping her gaze over the heads of the diners at tables beyond, her eyes navigating the room like the pilot of a small plane flying in the treetops.

"You see, it puts me in an awkward position," she continued, still looking beyond him with a distant smile. "These nasty sort of sexual things are not really my cup of tea. I was trained quite differently, as you can well imagine. Garden parties, the duchess of Kent, that sort of thing. But my goodness, gossip isn't at all what it used to be."

"It's preposterous," Roger finally managed to say. "Simply preposterous. Crain has no sex drive at all. None. Not normal, abnormal. Just none."

Nose shrugged in a tinkle of bracelets. "Yet there you are. I offer it to you not as proof of the fact, but of the bounty."

"But you see it's all false. There's nothing to it. Why would you want to involve yourself in something like that?"

She studied him for a moment, her cultivated eyebrows in a furrow. "I think the problem here is that you don't recognize me as a serious person," she said finally. "But I am a very serious person. I police manners, you see, and in Washington, manners are, well, the most important thing. What I mean is that Senator Crain will smash through the surfaces of things and tear about. That can't be allowed. We get these types, and not only here but in London, Moscow — everywhere, really. They enjoy smacking heads, you see, because they're right, and what's a little blood when you're right? So I police the surface of things and do away with them, if I can. Without apology. The surface of things keeps us civilized. That is the most important thing. So you see, Roger, that is why you must help me."

He took a drink of wine. Improbably, she scandalized him. "What can I do?" he asked.

"Tell me something bad about Joe Crain."

He shook his head. "But I can't."

"Why?"

"I don't know anything bad about Crain."

"After what he's done to you?" she said. "You must know something."

He paused to consider once more the strange but correct answer.

"I don't know anything bad about Crain. Evil yes, bad no."

She motioned for the check. "Pity."

•   •   •

Sometime after the election Roger came to understand that Crain's followers voted for him not because he was changed but because he was the same. This made him even more melancholy, because all along he had wanted for Crain to have been changed, for his sullen frankness to have been replaced by network coaching, for money and a prospective Senate seat to have moderated him. But no, he was the same. He was the same as your ugly family dog. He just stood there, guarding the shack, Everymutt in rebellion against progress. Or—and here Roger corrected himself, for it was important to try to understand—not progress, for that was a loaded word, but change. If change would mock God and make you feel unworthy, then to hell with it.

But at least he understood the failure better. Oh, the Institute had performed well, its ministers had gone forward, trained to think and speak in every newspaper, every law office, every laboratory, every duly licensed place of reason. The Institute had built a palace of facts and invited the people in, but alas, too many of them declined.

He didn't know which came closer to breaking Odgen's heart: the several fanatics who truly believed Crain's program, or the many voters who thrilled in its empty protest. He thought it was the latter, for to be told that the method itself was irrelevant, told really that the world wasn't broke, so don't try to fix it anymore—not even with a thanks and well done, mind you—hurt more than Crain's shameful stratagems. You could lose an election, Ogden had said, but don't let them break your heart. He gave Worth the warning, but he meant it for himself.

That Judith had stayed out of the race when the danger to Ogden and the consequences for all were so vast was something he could not dismiss, even after a year. At least the others had acted honorably to resist, out of instinct if nothing else. Instead she indulged in a forty-year-old pique.

He realized he could be blaming the messenger. After all, she'd been right about Worth's weaknesses and the outcome. But Ogden—surely she saw it would kill him. Even that, in the end, didn't matter enough, he figured, and now she had to live with it.

He asked her once what Crain had talked about when she interviewed him. "The rapture," she said. "He talked a lot about the rapture."

"But you're not of the faith."

She shrugged. "I guess I was a project. He told me what to do if I suddenly saw people on the street fly up."

"Fly up?"

"You must know. When they take off into the sky."

"No, I don't know."

"That's when the end of the world happens. When they start to fly up."

He supposed she meant some theory of the elect summoned upward at the end of time. "So they—the elect—will just fly heavenward, briefcases, umbrellas, and all."

She shrugged. "Why not? It's as good a plan as any. He seemed very sure."

"Well, it is kind of melodramatic. Revelations is like that. What the hell did Crain say you were supposed to do?"

"When?"

"When you see the elect . . . fly up."

"Oh yes. That's important. You fall down on the sidewalk, cover your face, and don't let anyone take you away to the holding station."

"The holding station?"

"Right. But if they do, and you go to the holding station, don't let anyone put your hand over a machine that looks like a grocery store checkout thingamajig."

"A what?"

"You know, the thing you put the plastic wrappers on and it reads the numbers."

Thus Crain pitied the poor infidel, providing her with the secret of outsmarting that great counter of the sheep and the goats: don't get caught with your hand on the thingamajig.

Judith called soon after the election for dinner, but he declined with some excuse. She called again, and again he demurred. She hadn't called since. He couldn't face her, even after a year. He knew this was irrational, that what happened wasn't her fault, but it was still important. She could have tried to stop the juggernaut and didn't. It awakened memories of how she had once hurt him, and how Crain hurt them all now, in a far more malignant way; namely, by believing that to be right was the most important thing in life. It was an ancient fallacy that had broken far too many hearts.

Chapter Nineteen

1980

THE funeral procession stretched a full mile down Patterson Way. The only signs of life along the boulevard that led from downtown Fairington to the highway and the Patterson grounds at Lake Jowett were the city police in their black armbands who guarded the intersections and the curious children in front yards who interrupted their games and watched from the edge of the street, perhaps wondering why on this Saturday the rest of the world was so sad. The mourners made Fairington's largest funeral party since the death of Oswald Patterson nearly sixty years before. Ernest MacGiver, attended by a nurse, hobbled into the sanctuary, leaving his wheelchair at the door, his chesterfield buttoned to the chin, his face twisted to a grin by stroke, his eyes fixed on the casket at the head of the aisle, perhaps imagining that it was really himself inside and not Taliaferro Ogden, so confused he was by yet another funeral, the one event that permitted release from his room. "Ogden dead?" MacGiver asked loudly, looking around the church for someone to answer. An usher tried to lead him to the back, where seats remained, but he shook his head, dismissing the man as though he were a junior professor, and proceeded toward a full pew where he stopped and looked around in confusion, raising his cane as though to call for order.

"He thinks it's his pew," Lulu whispered to Roger as another usher joined the first to try to shepherd MacGiver on.

"They don't know him," Roger said.

"Argggg." A short, violent sound issued from Dr. MacGiver as first one usher, then the other tried to take his elbow. The congregation sat, quieted by the impasse. Finally, Worth moved deliberately across the rows to where MacGiver stood.

"Dr. MacGiver. It's Worth Patterson," he said, motioning for the ushers to leave.

"Patterson?"

"Yes sir. Worth Patterson."

"Tal dead?"

"Yes sir. Tal is dead."

The old man shook his head and tried to speak, but then he looked at the casket and at the pew beside him and only shook his head again.

"Would you, sir, do my family the honor of sitting with us?"

The senator offered his arm, and MacGiver took it, hobbling down the aisle, his face straight ahead.

"So much death," Lulu said, fanning herself as she sat beside Roger, who drove her, with Brent in the backseat, toward Ogden's corner in the Patterson graveyard. Even that, Roger thought. Oswald would even provide Ogden's cemetery plot. Brent cleared his throat, and Roger for a moment thought he would speak, perhaps even remove the dark glasses he had worn through the service, but no, he had just cleared his throat, that was all, and Roger knew there would not be a word, not even to remark on the absurdity that in Fairington divorce didn't give a family an excuse not to attend funerals together. Ahead, Roger saw the first caravan of headlights pass from Fairington into the gray Piedmont hills. The convoy stopped for the crossing of a hound, the first car careful to see that the animal was fully on the other side of the highway before proceeding. The dog watched several of the line pass and then loped across the stubbled fields.

"Can you imagine that trash Joe Crain showing up here today? For— this?" Lulu said, unable as ever, Roger remembered, to call death by name. Crain had sat unremarked in the vestibule, nodding at salient points in the brief eulogy. He left quickly afterward, stopping for a moment before the open casket in order, Roger figured, to make sure Ogden was really dead.

Lulu turned to the backseat and took Brent's hand in hers, massaging it as though to assure herself that he was there with them. "It is our family's comfort that we have always stood by the right kind of people," she said. "It is in the worst times that you count on the right kind of people."

The caravan passed through the old cherub-laden iron gate onto the Patterson "farm," as they called it, really a gentleman's stable by a lake.

Roger chuckled as he saw the roadside filled with pickup trucks and old Chevrolets and Fords, dusty from the long drive from the Georgia mountains where Taliaferro Ogden came from. The slope of the Patterson grounds stood two deep with his kin — men, women, and children who had waited there all morning, through the city church service, to claim him, never mind that he had left them decades before and would be buried beside a rich man. As the cars from the city formed in parked rows the singing began, echoing over the far shores of the lake. "Blest Be the Tie That Binds" they sang in deep throaty unison, all in their Sunday clothes, the wives in dark dresses and thick hose, the husbands in their stiff blue suits, the scrubbed children held firmly. The sound of it, so deep and pure, so unexpected, stilled the newcomers, and Roger could do nothing but stand by the open car door until the last verse stopped. He looked for Worth, who, like him, stood still in the sound.

There, in the gathering, as he and Worth prepared to lift the heavy casket, he felt again the understanding they shared of Ogden, and of the days when he had showed them the future. The memory of those first weeks stirred within him, before he had known the method, before Worth had known the plan, when they had been two spirits lifted from a dark time for different reasons into possibility. What a remarkable bargain governed Tal Ogden's life, Roger thought, surveying again the finality of the Patterson graveyard, the corner of the ground reserved for the able minister, Greek to the Romans. What a remarkable bargain, what remarkable fruits, now brought to a sad and uncertain end.

It seemed so plain, but yet so unknowable, Ogden's desires for them all. Plain because the method's aim was plain: knowledge for power, power for good. Yet, had they stumbled over that last part? He was satisfied, given human mistakes, that they had led well, but had they used power for good?

Several times Roger had wanted to ask Ogden the question, but he never knew quite how. Now they would never hear his judgment. Not that he would share it with them if he still lived. Year by year Ogden had receded from view, subtracting himself until the method stood alone, without intrusion from the human, perpetual and pretty, unblemished by ego, but vulnerable for that reason, too. Subtracting himself required unnatural discipline, Roger believed, because Ogden was not like that, not the Ogden of those first days, when the passions and the ideas crackled together and made young men and women change their lives. It was an act of will for

Ogden to become a system, just as it was an act of will for him to cleanse the Patterson millions. To finish the second legacy, really the first charge of his life, Ogden spent his last months making of Oswald's remaining unclipped coupons a foundation, dispensing the money as fast as he could to the startled impoverished, a self-imposed penance for the calculation of motive and return he had earlier attached to philanthropy. Whatever the virtue of subtraction, the cost had been high, Roger saw. In the end, Ogden became incapable of performing even simple charity in the first person, his good works manifest finally in a legal fiction. On the hillside, though, Roger didn't dwell on the last days, but made himself remember the first, when they all were young and had much to say to one another.

Together Roger and Worth walked through the gate to the small marked plot at the corner of the graveyard. When they reached the casket, the bagpipes began, keening in a near-human wail, rising and rising. The grave had been dug in a businesslike fashion, in sight of Oswald's monolith, but discreetly away from the family arrayed before him. The pallbearers formed and balanced the weight on their shoulders, steadying themselves for the last distance, Worth and Roger at the head.

•   •   •

"I never understood my father," Worth said as he and Roger walked the sands near the breakwater at Ocracoke, a late-afternoon haze rising from the storm at sea to obscure the Pattersons' new house at the point.

"What do you mean?"

"I mean just that. He lived in Grandfather's house, my house, even after he was married to Mother. Spent his time building that golf course. He loved the golf course. He knew every blade of grass. He installed the first bent-grass greens in North Carolina, you know."

Roger sifted through the hash of data he carried on the famous and the obscure, in specific the important subject of the Patterson family, but he could not locate that fact about bent-grass greens. "I didn't know that."

"Yes. Even before Pinehurst. Most contented man I ever knew."

A Lab retriever sped past them on the beach, a tennis ball in his mouth, running to the whistled command of his master, who walked casually past through the surf's edge. He nodded and smiled absently at the senator and his guest.

"I think you should go into teaching," Worth said suddenly.

"Whatever for?" Roger said, puzzled by Worth's interest in his retirement.

Worth shrugged, "Oh, mainly to get you out of the house. You're rich as Croesus and you spend your time in a condo eating TV dinners."

Roger enjoyed the suggestion of new possibility, an offshoot of Worth's remarkably upbeat manner. We're really just like kids, free again, he had said earlier in the day—except, Roger thought, but did not add, they had never really been kids. Or free.

"I know you're planning to sell the company," Worth continued. "There's no use in denying it."

"How do you know that?"

"It's the reason you fought me on the fair trade bill. It hit me about a month later."

Roger wondered if he had been transparent about the fair trade matter and the company. He didn't think so, and no one else, not in the press, nor in the campaign, not even Brent himself, who would have been the other likely source, had commented. Worth, he figured, simply knew him very well.

"This teaching thing. What made you say that?"

"Oh, I don't know. Judith mentioned it—at lunch, I guess, discussing how to get the Institute back in shape. You know, she's been awfully good since the election."

Worth's suppleness still amazed him. The ability to combine with Judith in some scheme for the Institute—Judith Stern, his good friend! He's better able to adapt to his own failure than I am, Roger thought.

"I think Judith's worried about you," he said. "And I am too."

"Lot on my mind, that's all. The business—you were right about that."

"Nice piece of legal work. Who are you going to use?"

"Some New York bunch. They're all the same. I'd give it to you if you were practicing."

"Thanks, but that would be sticky. Look, the business is on your mind, I know, but you could do that in your sleep. There has to be something else."

"Oh, you know what it is."

"Yes. Young Lochinvar of the pines." Worth stopped and shaded his eyes against the afternoon sunlight, waving his walking stick at a shrimp boat coming home against the speckled water, its labored motor sounding finally over the lapping tide. Roger noticed that on Ocracoke Worth went nowhere without his walking stick, a great gnarled rod of driftwood that he wielded with a priestly flourish, to enforce his will on the waters, he said. The stick arose from the Gulf Stream, or drifted from Bermuda itself, Worth said when asked of its origins. Bermuda was only three hundred miles due east, he reminded people regularly, brandishing his staff, which defied apparent physical properties by being immense and feather light at the same time. The stick had proven its powers, Worth recounted, in the building of the beach house, which appeared to Roger, from all angles, as a phantom glass dwelling rising from the perpetual fog. It was, in that way, magical, and Worth saw to its construction fully hoping for it to be. A house, he had said, sighting the gables from the surf by his staff, was the right thing for a man to build when he tired of war.

"Brent came last month," Worth said.

"So you mentioned."

"He wanted to stay here. I told him he couldn't."

"Why?"

Worth stopped at the edge of the surf and waved his staff at a flock of gulls settling on the water. They obeyed his cryptic command, circling upward from sea to sky and then alighting again.

"Because he needs to sort things out for himself. He thinks I can help him, but I can't."

Roger shook his head. "You probably could. I can't anymore. Never could, really."

"Nope. Nobody can help him. That's what I told him. Nobody. He's on his own. There's no fate, or destiny, worth much; he doesn't owe anybody, least of all some dead people, anything in the world. Let the dead bury the dead, I told him. Funny thing coming from me, eh? But I told him. If he wanted to come here and stay, it was to worship some dead thing—what I was, and what he wanted me to be. And I told him I wasn't that dead thing and I never was, and he'd better go make his peace with the living, like I was trying to do."

Roger took off his soaked shoes and looked to the sea for a sign; maybe Worth was right, having lived the wrong side of the question for so many years. Better make your peace with the living while you have a chance.

"Do you think you made headway?"

Worth thrust his stick vigorously into the sand. "Oh, I don't know. The boy just has to choose, and with his eyes open. I told him if he needed advice he might try his father, whose advice I'd been taking for forty years."

"Ha," Roger said. "He won't even talk to me."

"I know."

The senator stopped again and turned to face the ocean. The waves overtook his crusty deck shoes, the wind snapped at the billowed edges of his shirt. He drew a finger to his forehead as though bringing forth a thought.

"I told him whatever you've done, you've done for him. To keep him from a mistaken life. He said he didn't understand. Congratulations, I told him. You've become a man. You don't understand your father, either."

The whine of a motor sounded down the beach. At the same instant a dirt bike appeared, dipping between the dunes, cutting through the loose mounds. Worth put his hand to his brow to shade his eyes. "Will you look at that," he said, chuckling. "From horses to motorcycles in a year."

Abigail's blond curls bounced up and down to her squeals as she clung to the bike's driver, who had a matching set of male blond curls. They raced by, teasing the water, the bike's wheels tossing up shards of wet sand that the sea quickly reclaimed. "Hel — lo Dad — ee," Abigail called, tossing back her head and waving as best she could as her companion kicked the bike into the dunes.

"The boy's father owns a fishing boat in Ocracoke, and the boy himself is barely civilized," Worth said, shaking his head. "He speaks real High-tider. Abigail teaches him grammar. God knows what he teaches her."

"I can imagine what Mandy thinks."

"She wants to send her off to school in Virginia, of course. But I put my foot down at that. I'll be damned if I'm going to have a second daughter taken away from me."

He paused and looked back at the fading figure of the motorcycle, winding back to the village. "And besides, I think Isaac is a fine boy. Reminds me of how we started out, when old Sir Walter Raleigh landed up the beach. Makes you remember what a damn near thing the whole business was. No, I like Isaac just fine. I've had enough of these overcivilized types."

Roger knew that Sir Walter Raleigh had never set foot in North Carolina, but he had spent half a lifetime disciplining himself not to step on Worth's punch lines for the sake of accuracy. It had been far more entertaining, and socially useful, to observe and encourage as Worth ad-libbed his way into history.

Worth motioned ahead with his walking stick, and they turned to walk the mile back to the house. The tide had begun to run, the surf gaining its strength, pounding its authority into the docile shore. Ahead lay the cottage peeking through the haze and over the dunes, themselves anchored by sea oats and hard, tufted grass, the front of the house offering a full-windowed panorama of the ocean, the sun decks littered with squat wooden deck furniture. "I'm sorry to miss Mandy," Roger said, knowing full well she had vacated at the first mention of his visit. They had come not to like each other very much over the years, and one or the other felt like a third wheel whenever they were with Worth.

"Don't worry about making her go. It would have been something else if not you. She's going to divorce me."

"Good God—has she said anything?"

"No, she doesn't know it yet. She can't handle the way things are now."

"You mean about leaving Washington."

"Well that, partly. But other things too. Phineas, for example. I called him the day that poster came out. I think I told you. Didn't tell anybody else. Just kept it to myself. But I thought he had a right to know what the son of a bitch had done. I got him right away, just rang him up. Funny, he'd sent me that number fifteen years ago and I never once used it."

"So what did he say?"

"It was as though we had talked last week, you know, very familiar. He had been following the campaign in the *International Herald Tribune*, he said. Oh, but about the poster—he just laughed. He said the boy was an Algerian who had a flower shop down the street. He remembered the picture, too. The couple said they were tourists; young couple he said, from Charlotte. Talked about home a little bit. He took them to the shop because they wanted some cut flowers. The boy's name was Franz, he said. Perfectly nice boy with all sorts of girlfriends. He apologized for causing me trouble. I told him I would forgive him that if he forgave me everything else."

On the sun deck sat Isaac and Abigail, back from their ride and dripping happily from a swim they had apparently just taken with their clothes on. Their banter stopped as Roger and Worth rinsed their feet in the outdoor shower and climbed the steps.

"Isaac, let me introduce you to Mr. Roger Albright, an old friend of mine," Worth said, ignoring the fact that his daughter and her caller sat dripping wet.

"Hoi, oi'm Oike," the young man said, standing, and trying unsuccessfully to dry his hand on his shirt before offering it. "Roight pleased."

"Pleased to meet you too, Ike," Roger said, noticing the extraordinary diphthongs experts believed to be Elizabethan but that he always assumed the result of genetics run amok. "Hey, Abigail. You should get your dad here to shell out for a real swimsuit."

Abigail blushed and giggled, but then she stood. Draping herself sari-like in a towel, she asked, just as Mandy would, "Maybe you'd like something cool to drink, Mr. Albright. It's not too early for a cocktail, is it?"

He glanced at Worth, who winked. "No thanks, Abigail. I've really got to get going. I have to make the ferry at six."

Roger packed in the guest room with the view over the small cove to the harbor, where the fishing boats chugged brazenly to their berths, skimming between the sailboats and the cabin cruisers. In a world of acquaintances, Worth was his closest friend. The years of joined and divorced purposes scarcely mattered beside the fact that they survived and remembered. Even the things that divided them brought the same end.

"So I told Brent," Worth said as he watched Roger pack, "that if he turns his back on you he will end up hating himself."

"If I just hadn't given him to Ogden. God, I shouldn't have done that. I thought it was the best thing."

"Listen, Roger. Just stop it. You had to give him to Ogden. The boy was breaking bad."

Roger was surprised at how good it felt to hear that, even if he wasn't sure it was true. "Well, you know the problem. And on top of everything — when we went through at least we had the good days coming. We had good days. Now he gets the bad."

Worth laughed. "The good days? You old romantic. We fought like hell. Don't worry — he'll cope. He's a tough kid. Remember, he worked for me."

Roger took his suitcase in his hand. "I just don't think he'll come back, Worth. That's the bottom line. I'm afraid the well has been poisoned. I'm afraid it was poisoned from the start."

A tug sounded over the settled bay, gulls chasing it and the ferry to berth.

"Nonsense. You're his father, I told him. Always have been, always will be. He'll come back when he's ready."

Roger shook his head. "Thanks. But I don't think so."

"Oh, stop it. Of course he'll come back. You're easy. Now my grandfather, he was a real son of a bitch. Drove all of his children out except my father. That, you see, is what I admire about Phineas. That he stayed. How he put up with it I'll never know."

"Worth, the world has been raised on Oswald Patterson stories. Oswald Patterson—"

"Was a monster, a braggart, a thief, a great man. Take your pick."

•   •   •

Two weeks later, Worth called from Paris.

"You're where?" Roger asked.

"In Phineas's apartment. He's made dinner—we're having a great time. I brought pictures."

"Jesus—when did you decide to go?"

"Tuesday, I think. I just got on the plane and left. Was going to surprise him, but I called ahead. It's the thoughtful thing to do."

They both laughed until the operator came on.

•   •   •

"That's really what I wanted to tell you," Judith said as she warmed her hands on the coffee she had brought for the both of them. "He's fine, he wants you not to worry."

When Roger finally agreed to meet her he thought it would be pleasant to sit outdoors. Too late, he remembered that the March air in New York held little of the same promise of spring as in Carolina. She had been quite insistent. She had news about Brent.

"How can I not worry? He won't return calls, he stays out all night in these clubs—"

Judith laughed. "He's young. You remember how that was."

He blushed despite the cold, because he did remember, all the more vividly with her beside him. They sat in Central Park by a concrete pond, ice still at the edges; in temperate months it held miniature boats skippered by city sailors, some piloted by remote control, others under sail. The boarded-up clubhouse behind them stored the vessels for the winter.

Around the pond stood bronze statues of *Alice in Wonderland* characters—
the Mad Hatter, the March Hare, Alice herself, with retinue. Roger could
think of few spots on earth so civilized, so well executed for the pleasures
of modern city man who was bound otherwise, except for the escapes of
imagination and taste, by the geography of the metropolis.

"Do you see him often?" he asked.

"About once a week. He calls when he wants to talk. We have a good
time. We talk about you, mostly."

"Really?"

"He's puzzled. He wants to start at the beginning."

"What's the point?" Roger said brightly, hoping to mask his uneasiness.
From Judith's look, he was unsuccessful.

Judith took his arm and drew closer to him on the bench. "He's never
been on his own, you realize. You, or Tal, always planned. The campaign
was awful for him. Just awful."

Roger shook his head. "He won't even talk to me."

"You're very strong medicine. He has to stay away from you, but he
can't admit it. Doesn't that make sense?"

"No."

"I would ask you to use your imagination, but I know that's no use.
Listen. What has happened to him is very serious. When you went into—
this thirty years' war—many things had already happened to you. You had
your own life. He hasn't."

"I guess I can see that."

"Good. Progress. I wouldn't have said anything; one of the elements of
our, our friendship is that we keep confidences. But I knew how things are
between you, and I look for any sign. Last week he said, 'When you see
Roger, tell him I am all right,' and he caught himself, as though to recon-
sider, but he left it there. So—here I am."

He wondered what secrets she would tell Brent, and he started to ask,
but she stilled him. "I think one thing he's wary of, in talking to you right
now, is that he's afraid you'll ask him to join your business."

"Well, Jesus, all he has to do is say no."

She sighed. "It's not that simple. He has to be ready to say that."

The absurdity of Brent fearing a campaign to have him work for a company that would soon no longer exist arrested him for a moment. "Believe
it or not, I had no plans to bring him in," he said.

"Really? I thought you would."

"No."

She sat back and shaded her eyes from the afternoon sun with her hand as she looked south to the crest of buildings at midtown's edge. "I've always wanted to ask you something," she said, squinting.

"What's that?"

She pointed to the horizon. "Which one of those is yours?"

"That's what you always wanted to ask me?"

"I just wondered. It always seemed such an odd thing. That is, to know someone who owns a building like that in the first place, and then not to know which one it is."

He counted under his breath. "The fourth one down. Beside the black one."

"Hmm," she said. "It's big."

"Pretty good for a country boy."

She laughed. "A country boy. The funny thing is I remember when you were one. You were sweet to me, Roger. I want to thank you for that. At the time I was too young to appreciate it."

Her saying that lifted him unexpectedly, the words sounding as a true memory from their past life. He had been sweet to her. Suddenly he felt jealous of his son's secrets. He looked again to the midtown horizon and pointed to the Albright Building.

"Take a good look. I'm selling it. That and the whole company too."

She looked at the building, and then back at him. "What in the world for?" she asked.

"I don't know exactly."

"Roger—it's your work."

"I know. Maybe that's why."

He remembered the ramifications of what he told her. "Now listen, Judith. What I just said is inside information. If you trade in the company's stock before I sell, it's a crime."

She tried to keep from laughing, but couldn't. "I don't know how."

"How what?"

"I don't know how to buy stocks."

"Well then. I guess we don't have a problem." He relaxed, taken aback by his own skittishness. "Anyway, I'm glad I told you. Now you see why I have to talk to Brent."

"I guess so."

"I don't want him to read it in the papers."

"Do you want me to say something?"

He thought for a moment. "No. I need to do that."

She stood and buttoned her coat to her chin. "Just remember, country boy, don't try to solve this like a problem."

"What do you mean?"

She sighed. "I can't explain it if you don't know. Donald didn't get it either, God rest his soul. Why can't I know any men who believe life is anarchy?"

"Wait, you don't need to walk—we can share a cab."

"No thanks," she said, kissing him on the cheek. "I remember the last time that happened. I'll take the crosstown bus."

He watched her walk away in her well-worn flat shoes, her handbag gathered firmly to her side, her gait relaxed yet wary, a woman of the city sure of her direction. He thought he had been wrong about her in an important way for many years—he had been wrong to believe she lived alone. Now he believed himself more guilty of that than she. No, she seemed quite at home in the human mess, happy even. As she disappeared into the park's shadows, sadness overtook him, and he felt again that his life had been a mistake. How different things would have been with her, he thought. She called what he did his work; he always liked that.

•   •   •

The Flyers Club stood hidden amid the pinnaclelike buildings that shrouded the winding, narrow streets near the stock exchange. "Mr. Albright for Mr. Albright," Roger said to the doorman, whose placid expression shielded a wink as he led the way from the nondescript entrance up the frazzled carpet that so irritated Roger, even though he used the club only when he had business on the Street. He had asked Brent to meet him there, or rather left word with his machine on the slim chance he would sense somehow the moment of the day and accept this invitation, having refused the rest. He picked his way through the covey of leather chairs arranged in the high-ceilinged room, propellers hanging as trophies above the old boys reading papers. A group of younger men sat drinking in the corner, near the fire that burned every day of the year in the large hunting hearth. One by one, some casually, others boldly, they turned to look; silence fell among them as one of their number, dressed in yellowish suspenders—Roger thought they were mauve, though he was generally lost beyond the primary colors—rose to greet him. Hassell—could that be Hassell? Roger thought. Good Christ. Hassell, a member of the Flyers Club?

"Roger! Roger, my man! This is so great. Unbelievable. Really, this is so great. We just got back from the printers. It's a done deal." He draped his arm around Roger's shoulders and whispered hoarsely. "We've been in the men's room counting the cash."

Roger thought Hassell was drunk, or perhaps just giddy from his all-night labors.

"Thank you, Mr. Hassell. And the rest of you, for your efforts. Have any of you seen my son, Brent?"

Hassell laughed, too loudly, Roger thought. It was overly familiar, the laugh, not nearly as deferential as his station would demand. He hoped it was the strain, and the lack of sleep, and not that his investment banker was an idiot.

"No sir. Not Brent. I haven't seen him here."

He declined their entreaties and sat alone by the fire, taking the glass of scotch the waiter delivered. He stared at the faces that peered down dully from the curled photographs on the wall above, the smiles of aviators beckoning their fellows upward, recalling the origins of the club for gentlemen adventurers of the air, a function the current membership had long forgotten.

In the men's room counting the cash, he repeated to himself. The Street makes vulgarians out of Rhodes scholars as easily as a butcher makes hamburger. Pretty soon every crook in America would be here buying and selling with somebody else's money and smart boys like Hassell would get rich helping them. They even had Joe's boys now to confuse the public while the smart boys did their work. It would be picked clean, he could see that. At least he didn't have to know the crooks he sold to; that was the greatest service Hassell had done, and the only one a good clerk couldn't also have performed. Still, there was a seductiveness about the way the smart boys played the game. All they had to do was empty their in-box into their out-box, forget the names of the company being interred and the crook burying it, and a couple of million would fall their way. It was easier certainly than inventing something, as I did, Roger thought.

For all of Brent's troubles, Roger was glad he hadn't ended up one of the smart boys. It would have been easy for him to do it, Roger figured. A new job, a new wardrobe, a new way of looking at the world. Maybe he could even get a brief taste of fame, appearing on a talk show or dashing off an article to demonstrate his prescience. And it would have been fun. The Hassell circle appeared to be having a lot of fun, swashbuckling about as they did from deal to deal, club to club. At least he and Brent distrusted the same things. That could be a start.

All right, Son, he thought, gathering himself, imagining Brent in the chair facing him, the elusive interview. All right, Son, I'm ready.

"Who am I?"

"I don't know."

"Where did I come from?"

"I don't know."

"Why did I do these things?"

"I don't know."

"What should I do now?"

"I don't know."

A rush of air accompanied the entrance of five or six gentlemen of a certain age, ruddy faced from the afternoon merriment, all marching openhanded to greet Roger.

"Can't keep Roger Albright down, that's for sure!"

"Roger, old man, congratulations! When are you going to give us poor suckers a piece of the action!"

"Roger—good show. Never can fool old Roger Albright!"

Roger stood. "Gentlemen, thank you," he said. "Let me present my son, Brent."

"The young kingmaker!" said one of the ruddy-faced, clapping Brent on the shoulder. "A chip off the old block!"

The gentlemen retreated together to the bar.

"So you see, that's really why I asked you here," Roger said.

"Why?"

"Because I sold the company this morning, for two hundred and fifty million."

"Why?"

"Because I thought it was the best thing."

"Why?"

"To turn us into money. That's all we are now, we're just pure money, as pure

as anything could be. You don't have to worry about anything else, about being anything or doing anything. We come from nowhere, we are who we want to be, we don't have to do anything for any reason. We're just pure money."

The old boys looked up testily and stared before returning to their papers. Perhaps you have to be past retirement age before you are at liberty to talk to yourself, Roger thought. Anyway, that's how it would go. Something like that. Even if the boy came, it wouldn't go well.

Outside, on Wall Street, the wind blew the day's stray paper up the narrow divide against the traders who walked elbow to elbow past the Exchange, not knowing that with all their diligence and luck this day they could not have made as much money as Roger Albright had without trying. A siren below scattered the masses, for a moment its alarm commanding the road. The ambulance fought through the crowd and passed from view, the light receding, the army of Mammon joining again as the struggle continued. Meanwhile Roger sat, waiting for Brent.

Chapter Twenty

1980–81

ROGER believed it had been since the war. He hadn't eaten Christmas dinner without family since the war.

"Have some dark meat," Mandy ordered.

He dared not refuse, and he helped himself from the platter she fairly hurled at him. At least, Roger thought, as he nodded and murmured thanks, he was not the primary object of her fury, that being the ancient and dapper little man who reigned at the end seat of honor, another interloper, but one who had owned the Patterson manse long before she ever set foot in it. When Worth returned from Paris he had brought Phineas back with him.

"Aren't the children eating together?" Phineas asked, giving a reassuring squeeze to Abigail, who sat in worshipful attention at his left, a posture she had not altered, Roger surmised, since his arrival.

"Right. They're with Lulu today." Roger wondered at the way the old man simply picked up with Pammie and Brent when he had never known them; yet he did somehow, imagining them from the several letters a year that Worth had written, from the snapshots he'd sent.

"Holidays are the hardest times to be away," Phineas said. "You never get used to it."

"We're all here now, Dad." Worth passed Phineas's plate to the head. "And Roger's just as good as family. Mandy's table gets as big as it needs to at Christmas."

She glowered.

"Granddaddy, where is that secret panel? You know, in the library?" Abigail had brought an old house plan Phineas had framed for her to the table. He had intrigued the girl with tales of passageways and private compartments, and she hadn't believed him until one day he pressed the nose of a green marble gargoyle over the library hearth and revealed a hidden closet. Apparently he had ordered the construction of a half dozen similar false panels throughout the house, most of which had fallen out of use and memory. Recovering the old blueprint from the gargoyle's sanctuary, Phineas led Abigail on explorations that set the girl to pronounce that she wanted to be an architect. Phineas then regarded her as fair game, and they spent much of the day and night together going over his current portfolio, which included, Worth had told him, an entirely new Fairington, rendered boulevard by boulevard, appearing to Worth's unschooled eye a bit like a Buck Rogers movie set.

"We can talk about that later," Phineas said. "I'm sure your mother wants you to eat like a lady and socialize properly."

Abigail wasn't the only one Phineas instructed. For example, he believed that Worth and Roger took too much exercise for their age and declaimed to them on the topic, saying that since he hadn't been around when they were young and had required advice on other matters, he would make up for it by teaching them how to be old. Exercise became counterproductive, he continued, when one realized that the rules of fitness reversed themselves at a certain time in life. After that, good health was best maintained by husbanding one's energies, staying in bed as much as possible, never walking when one could ride, and, whenever one was in company, sitting in a prominent place so that conversation partners gathered around, limiting exertion.

Thus the old gentleman held forth on the useful arts. What had started as a week-long visit turned to one month, and then two.

". . . and I was saying to Dad—about the Institute, I mean—that we really could make a go of it. You know it's never really had our ideas in it, always was Ogden, always—we can't kid ourselves on that score . . ."

Roger managed to tune Worth out when he got particularly rhapsodic about plans for the new Institute, as he did periodically when he became anxious about doing something useful with his time. Unfortunately, Roger thought, the presence of Phineas made Worth ambitious again. Roger admitted this to be a great advantage of vigorous parents: as long as they are active they make you feel young, even as they tell you how to be old. Therefore, Roger concluded, I have to be the one, without the elixir of youth to handicap my senses, to hold to the truth: that the Institute is not a present vehicle for ideas, but a pleasant memory of a world that no longer exists; that to bring it back would not create a movement, but a museum.

". . . Judith's plans for the conference space are exciting. Of course we need to build away from the main hubbub . . ."

Worth's apparent alliance with Judith puzzled Roger. In his view they had no right to conspire, especially on a subject of which he disapproved. The two of them had huddled, however, for the past six months. Somehow, for Judith, Worth's defeat had wiped the slate clean; the entitled was no longer entitled, and forty years could be reclaimed without shame. She also felt guilty, he figured, and she ought to. As for Worth, the amazing amnesiac, he forgot she had ever disliked him.

Another aspect of Worth's youth movement that Roger distrusted was the new spirit of Christmas. Much to the delight of the table, Worth presented him with an elaborately wrapped gift—a silk shirt, scandalously comfortable, monogrammed on both pocket and cuff, in a cream color not duplicable at the wash-and-wear looms of Albright Industries. He could never wear such a thing, and Worth knew it. Badgered for a display, Roger draped the shirt over his shoulders as a cape.

"Thanks," Roger said. "I think."

Worth and Phineas made fun, while Mandy, her disgust towering over them, cleared the still-laden serving plates. Roger was alive to the irony of the gift but was puzzled by how little the gesture affected him. Could it be that I have lost the capacity for sensation? he wondered. Lately he had thought a good part of himself had gone numb, as though he had misplaced the experience that permitted him to enjoy such things as clever gifts. He dimly remembered enjoying them, and the memory increased his growing sadness. Try as he might, he couldn't remember the specifics that had consumed his days when he had chased the chimera of a worldly mark. Was it inevitable that to live a purposeful life required that sensation be stripped away until planning for the next moment finally obliterated the present and one was left confused at the sentiment of others?

He thought it must be too late to recover pleasure in simple, elegant tasks. He had observed the evidences of such a temperament—the well-made garden, for example, with superior tomatoes. Or expertly played croquet. Not once had he felt unburdened from the dull complexity of accomplishment; now he feared that his habits were so intractable he was incapable of it. Partly, he admitted, he resented the old example, again leading the way.

Worth looked at his watch and leaped from his chair, as though summoned by some errand. He busied himself with helping Mandy clear, taking a large casserole in his hands almost to the kitchen, but then setting it aside on the buffet. He started to make some remark, thought the better of it, and removed the dish through a swinging door toward the sound of clattering plates. Then the telephone rang, and before the second cadence could begin, he leaped through the door again and picked up the receiver in the hall.

"It's for you," Worth said to Roger, grinning meaningfully to the rest of the table and gesturing to the waiting telephone.

Roger wondered what sort of joke gift this was. One of those girls on the telephone who said nasty seasonal things for a fee?

He picked up the receiver. "Merry Christmas, Dad," Brent said.

Roger closed the door to the dining room and sat down on the stairs. "Merry Christmas, Son."

"I don't know what the scene is down there, but this is pretty excruciating."

"Really?"

"Yeah. Pammie's freaked out about school, as usual, and Mother invited Walter Degley, who showed up with peppermint schnapps."

"How are you, Son?"

"Oh, okay. Don't worry about me or anything. I'm really all right."

"Well, it's been a long time."

"I know. I'm sorry."

"No need for that. No need at all."

The crackle of distant voices sounded over the line, other families, Roger surmised, assuring each other that everything was fine and nothing was anyone's fault, that a blameless set of missteps had brought relations to a state of disarray.

"I had lunch with Judith last week. She's real up about the Institute stuff."

"I'm glad she's excited. I have my doubts."

"I figured."

"How's your mother?"

"Oh, she's fine. Just a little bit of the blues."

"Well, you should watch that. Be especially attentive to her. I know having you and Pammie there is a help."

"I will. Listen, Dad. I know things haven't been great, but they're better now, they really are."

"I know, Son. I know whatever you've done there's been a good reason."

"Well, I can't say if there's a good reason, but there's a reason, anyway."

"I know."

"I may have some news."

"News?"

"Yeah, in the spring. I may have some news in the spring. I'm thinking about coming down for the Institute opening. You'll be there?"

Roger laughed. "Of course I'll be there. How could I miss it?"

"Good. Great. Well, I've got to go. I love you, Dad."

"I love you too, Son."

Roger hung up the receiver, trying to remember if he had ever told Brent that he loved him, that is in maturity. He couldn't remember that he ever had, or had heard the same from Brent. It seemed more natural than he would have thought.

He returned to the table and sat down. All waited expectantly.

"Well?" Worth said.

"That was Brent."

"And?"

"Oh. He said he's coming to the Institute opening."

"Terrific. Terrific news. Isn't that terrific? Just terrific."

"Yes, Son," Phineas said. "Did he mention Pamela at all?"

Roger paused to think. "No, not really."

Worth ladled out some of Mandy's special Christmas trifle for him, and he ate two helpings, washed down with the champagne that Worth brought forth. Roger thought that he might really be enjoying all the odd things about the day after all — the strange family table, the peculiar gift, the long-awaited call from the prodigal. Perhaps he had made the first step toward correcting his temperament.

"It's much too warm for Christmas," Mandy said. "I can't seem to get into the mood."

"May I be excused, Mother?" Abigail asked, eyeing the telephone, no doubt, for some personal holiday reconnoitering, Roger thought.

"Yes, you may. I really don't know what to do with myself in this weather. I mean, I'd like to have a fire, but then we'd just roast."

"Did Brent say anything about seeing Judith?" Worth asked.

"And with Pammie away studying," Mandy continued. "Goodness, that's not like her at all—"

"Golf," Phineas said.

"I beg your pardon?" Mandy rejoined, as all eyes turned to his end of the table.

"Golf. It's a perfect afternoon. We should all go out for golf."

Mandy lit a postprandial cigarette and edged her lipstick with a folded napkin. "Phineas," she said menacingly, "no one here is going to leave to play golf."

Phineas made a small Gallic gesture.

"Terrific idea. Dad, that's a terrific idea. Roger, you have your clubs, don't you? Well—just play out of my bag."

They trooped across the yard to the club, leaving Mandy to sit amid the ruins of the meal. The pro shop was closed, but they found two carts with keys by the back door. Phineas insisted that he ride in the odd cart with Philippe, the dog he had brought with him from Paris, which Mandy had consigned to the outdoors. You boys go on and ride together, he had said. You have things to talk about.

"Mandy can go if she wants," Worth said as they motored off the first tee on the deserted course. "But Abigail stays. Dad can bring his friend to stay, too. He doesn't mention it, but it bothers him, you know, the separation. They've been together for twenty-eight years."

Not a car moved on Founders Row or anywhere the senses reached. The solitude of the afternoon, marked only by conversation and their golf shots, made Roger think for that time that the three of them were alone in the world. The strange afternoon heat thawed the hard ground, still caught in the memory of last week's frost, and a mist rose up at their feet, settling in its mass before them and then reaching into the air until it, too, dissipated. They played the fairway shots from memory.

"We'll make a life," Worth continued. "I know the objections. I don't know how to raise Abigail. I wouldn't spend time with her, blah, blah, blah. But dammit, that's my first commitment—before anything else. The girl deserves to have something passed on."

Phineas sped up beside them. "Roger, either you're bunkered or in the cherries," he said, pointing ahead in the gloaming to the fairway hazard and stand of cherry trees. "I've sent Philippe along to scout."

They followed Philippe's trail on foot. Phineas picked up his long-running apologia for Oswald Patterson. "Father was a wonderful man," he said. "Very funny, and brilliant. Self-taught, basically."

"Well, there was the railroad matter," Roger said. "Too bad about that. I suppose without that no telling how far he would have gone."

Phineas whistled to Philippe. "He was right, don't you think? There were people trying to stop the railroad, just for spite. They resented him. Jealousy, terrible jealousy. You see, Father created, and he let me create. People are jealous of that. It was all jealousy."

Roger couldn't help but reflect on how mistaken he must have been about Oswald Patterson, or how deluded Phineas must be now, to so reimagine a man of settled reputation, a man who had bribed legislators, bullied the Interstate Commerce Commission, bought a town lock, stock, and barrel, and made all but one of his children hate him, or so the legend went.

"It's not the common picture, I know. The truth is, my sisters made the myth up to get back at him, because of money. They were all stupid and envious and I have outlived them."

They came upon Philippe, standing over Roger's ball. He was a low-lying, perky, American-style beagle hound. "I'm curious," Roger said. "How did you name him?"

"The namesake was a very bad man. So I named a dog after him. But you see, now I have grown fond of the dog."

Roger's lie was playable, and he resisted, as always, the temptation to improve it. He prided himself — no matter how bad his game might be, no matter how punitive the result — in playing within the rules of golf. Many better players did not. Fortunately, his position among the trees left him a satisfactory angle to the green, which lay below and to the right through the mist. As he stood over the ball, however, he was overtaken by a sense of déjà vu and found himself strangely unable to continue. He remembered himself envisioning the present moment at that very spot fifteen or sixteen years ago. He had been searching for Brent and had come upon him there, his golf bag balanced easily on his back, an iron in his hand as he approached his ball in the cherries on a clear summer evening, at dusk. He had set out to summon the boy for supper, thinking about a half-dozen other things, overburdened by his chore as dinner's herald, and there he was at that spot. Roger did not want to call him and instead stood still, watching, seeing for the first time the figure of the man in the boy, knowing he was a boy still, but seeing the future in that stance and motion at the day's last light, and then, curiously, seeing himself and a strange old man there too.

"I remember when we were laying out this hole," Phineas said easily, disengaging from the spectator's stance to light his pipe. "You see how the land slopes naturally to the left and then to the right, beyond this cherry grove? It was like that, this rolling, changeable landscape, all through these acres, before anything else was here. Both simple and various, really; a perfect classical landscape in the middle of an old dairy farm. Needless to say, the prospect is hard to protect when you're building. That's why I really wanted the golf course. We would have made more money, of course, if we had sold everything for lots, but you could preserve something, at least of the character of it, maybe even improve it a bit. I never told Father that part, but I believe he thought it was an aesthetic value, as he would have said, which drove me to the opinion, and he permitted it. But the point is I told the workmen plainly to preserve this stand of cherry trees and they cut them down anyway. So we stopped everything, I mean the entire project, to hunt down more cherry trees. Had the devil of a time. Finding more cherry trees, I mean."

Worth drove up, having found his ball in the rough. "You've got yours?" he said to Roger.

"Yeah — can't decide between the five and the six."

Worth looked at him quizzically. "But you always hit a five."

Roger removed the five iron and, as usual, hit short and to the right. "You sure didn't want a six," Worth said, as he had several hundred times before when witnessing Roger hit from that distance. They rode ahead, making tracks in the moisture on the wintered fairway.

"He wants to die here," Worth said as they watched Phineas approach his fairway shot and strike it cleanly, short and straight, in the clever manner of the successful octogenarian. "We drove out to the farm yesterday, and he began picking out his plot. Sort of upsetting really, but he was matter-of-fact about it. He told me he always knew I would come and get him. Just come and get him. He wasn't going to come back until I did that. How do you figure it? I asked him what the strangest thing about being back was. You know what he said? We were in the parking lot, by the clubhouse, and he said that he thought the strangest thing was how big the cars were. Everything that could happen in fifty years, and he thought the strangest thing was how big the cars were."

They played the front nine, drinking from the flask Phineas had brought. Then, at the turn, something made Philippe run home, and they went back too.

• • •

At Worth's urging the state sold a parcel of land adjacent to university property to a newly formed foundation whose purpose was to build a permanent home for the Institute. Ogden had never wanted a building, because he thought the idea of his life would ossify in brick. That was truly superstition at a high level, Roger thought. It made little difference now, for Ogden was dead and the Institute nearly so.

Roger took a seat in the rows of folding chairs workmen had unloaded for the groundbreaking. He watched as they brought forth bunting for the dais and large flags to frame the new green banner that would hang behind the lectern in large relief. Brent had promised to meet him there, and he came early to prepare himself, thinking, uneasily, that he might not recognize his own son.

Judith too had called the day before, to confirm that he was coming. There was a hint of official business in her voice, and he surmised that she had made him part of the program, although he had declined formal offers. He had no idea what the order of things would be. Judith had said the spirit would be festive, and from the looks of the decoration it seemed she meant it, though he was hard-pressed to recall anything they should be celebrating.

Indeed, bad news had greeted them on all fronts since the most recent elections, which saw Worth's defeat ratified in large and small races from coast to coast. Perhaps he faced the grim picture more than others, as he had occasion to frequent the world that Joe's boys and the smart boys now ruled. Walter Degley had invited him only last week to speak on a panel at the Money Roundtable, and out of curiosity at Walter's gall he had accepted. Walter was on the program committee, it was explained, and besides, there were younger men who wanted to meet the legendary Roger

Albright. In any event, being duly, if perfunctorily, flattered, he accepted and found himself the featured specimen in a discussion entitled "High Yield Debt and the New Spirit of Enterprise." How the new spirit of enterprise differed from the old lust for money he would be hard put to say, but then again his role was not to comment on theoretical matters. The Money Roundtable had plenty of people for that. His job was to explain how one actually made a pile.

When he looked over the room at the Century Club, he didn't recognize any of the faces peering back at him. In fact, when he went on these ventures he seemed to know fewer and fewer of them. Perhaps he hadn't gotten to New York as often as he might, but he couldn't help but notice just how foppish the crowd seemed to be, all of them turned out like Hassell in colored shirts with white collars and oddly printed French ties that glittered in the light, many wearing braces decorated with animals that peered out at angles through their open chalk-stripe jackets. And the hair oil. The only place he saw so much hair oil being worn by young men was in the George Raft movies he watched from time to time when he couldn't sleep. Not too long ago, the only sort who dressed like that were Englishmen, or members of the Council on Foreign Relations. Now, simple bankers did, and the intellectuals who serviced them. He felt like a bumpkin in his baggy Brooks Brothers suit.

The toastmaster, an excitable fellow, introduced him with the passion one would reserve for the discoverer of a great vaccine, rather than a guy who had done well in the rag trade. He made what he had done — that is, build and sell a business — sound noble in a way that was both flattering and disturbing. At a time when he knew his own failure, all he heard from these people was that he was a great luminary, a success they would emulate, and that there was some higher value attached to his ability to enrich himself continually. It was as though they were inventing their own virtue; that they commanded not only the finance of the nation, but its myth-making, too, and rather than try to make the country better, they were going to make of their lives a glorious tale.

". . . the establishment turned down all attempts by Albright Acquisition Corp. to obtain financing in the so-called quality debt markets, but Roger Albright, who wanted to make this deal happen, had the insight — no, the genius — to convince the financiers of the buyout group that his assets, undervalued because of the hidden worth of his real estate, could support high-yield bonds. The skeptics call them junk, as you know, but they really represent the democratization of the market for corporate control, and Roger Albright, a proven innovator in manufacturing, found himself on the cutting edge of finance.

"Now, after six months, Roger Albright has been cashed out, half of the redundant manufacturing capacity has been cut, the work force has been reduced by four thousand, the intellectual property has been licensed or sold outright, and the entirety of the high-yield debt is being serviced by the remaining plants at full production with reduced nonunion labor costs. The real estate did turn out to be the crown jewels, and after a national road show, plans have been announced — and fully funded, I might add — to rehab and franchise the historic cotton mills as full-interior shopping malls. A nationwide anchor tenant will be announced shortly, with possibilities for the financing of similar ventures in industrial spaces across the country. In eighteen months, analysts believe that Albright Acquisition Corp. — transformed into a real estate development company — will turn to the equity markets for its first public offering. Ladies and gentlemen, the Albright Industries deal is a home run, and we have with us today one of the first heroes of the restructuring of America . . ."

The truth was, Roger hated being an avatar of the new age. The dismemberment of Albright Industries he believed to be a shameful waste. He had sold a business, not a collection of trinkets to be auctioned off. The euphemisms for cutting jobs could only come from science fiction, and the glorification of it sickened him. He wondered, as he rose from his seat on the dais, if there was anyone in the room who was not mad. The experience was so deflating he could barely speak, and since he had no desire to make remarks, he called for questions and sat down.

•   •   •

"Dad? Dad?" Brent's voice startled Roger from his reverie.

"Well, hello there," Roger said heartily, having rehearsed his tone, and thus been able to adopt it even though taken by surprise. He stood and shook Brent's outstretched hand, surveying his son in jaunty costume — ski sweater, leather jacket, sunglasses, a bit in need of a haircut, but nonetheless looking at home in the warming day on the raw land.

"You were pretty lost in thought."

"Oh well — I'll tell you about it. You're looking fit."

"I'm okay. You're looking well yourself."

Roger laughed. "More of an achievement for me than for you."

He had thought of six or seven topics he wanted to bring up, from Judith's new mission, to the Hassell comedy, to Nose's vendetta, but he kept his peace, believing that this meeting was more Brent's than his.

"I'm really sorry I've been out of touch," Brent said.

"I said that was all right, Son. We all have those times when we have to be off to ourselves."

"Right. For two years. No, it was inexcusable—but unavoidable. After we lost, I just couldn't face you, or the senator either, for that matter. I was so ashamed. You see, I'd let him down and proved what I was always afraid of—that I wasn't as good as you. You would have won that election. You would have figured out a way to do it. It would have been impossible, but you would've done it anyway."

"No, Son—"

"Yes, you would've. You can't tell me you wouldn't have. I thought if I could win this election I could finally have done something. I could finally feel like your son."

"What do you mean by that?"

"I mean that—I never could put it this way until we lost and it all came down—I was holding out that election as one last proof. But I've never felt like your son, you know? I was always some *thing*, doing this or that for some purpose, and you were always this strange man, watching me. I was always supposed to be doing my part in some grand plan—but I never could figure out what it was. I just figured it must be winning this election, that had to be it. And then when I won, I would have done it, whatever it was, and I'd be free."

A great sense of sadness overcame Roger. He marveled at his ability to communicate to Brent exactly the opposite of what he wished: that he knew the perils of the great plan, and instead of warning Brent away from it, had watched as he submerged himself, until the boy believed (and how could he otherwise?) that it was what he wanted.

"You know, I told you not to go off half-cocked," Roger said.

"I remember. Did a lot of good, didn't it."

"What you said about having to do something, or prove something—that's not what I ever believed, Son. I always wanted you to be free of that."

Brent nodded ruefully. "You know who made me see that? The senator.

It's funny. I wanted to live with him for a while. He wouldn't have it. Practically ordered me out of the house—in Ocracoke, I mean. Said I had to work out whatever it was with you. It was eerie."

"How do you mean?"

"My relationship with him—and this gets back to the problem—was very strange, I think, for a work relationship. I had to sort that out, too. I mean, he was my boss, but he knew me so well, knew every reaction I would have, what I was thinking, sometimes. He—well, between the two of us, it was just too much. And then I failed him, too. I had to get away."

"I see."

"I'm trying to get on with it. A new life, I mean. But it'll take a little while." Grinning broadly, Brent reached into the inside of his jacket and removed one fat, embossed letter, and then a second, and then, magician-like, a third, a fourth, a fifth. "Go ahead," he said, handing them to Roger.

Puzzled by the ornate script announcing some of the land's greatest universities, Roger opened the first and read through a paragraph of congratulatory prose declaring that Brent had been accepted in the entering class of the School of Policy Applications. So more or less read each of the others—the Economic Culture Studies Program, the Consortium for Social Planning, and more recognizably, the Department of Political Science. He handled the letters, one by one, as documents of weight and import. "We are pleased to invite . . ." "Because of your Institute record and obvious promise . . ." "The faculty is delighted . . ." The wealth of good news and future reward made Roger light-headed. The letters were as medals of an illustrious legion. If only, he thought, one could be accepted in such a way regularly.

"That was my news," Brent said. "But I didn't want to let on until I was sure."

"Wonderful. This is wonderful."

"Thanks." He laughed. "You're really surprised, aren't you?"

"Well, yes."

This admission, and the truth of it, so obviously gave Brent pleasure that Roger wished he could have been more surprised at other moments between them. The fact was, however, that he hadn't been surprised much at what Brent had done, that is, officially done, because after Ogden took him, Brent had pretty much always done what was expected.

"Judith was helpful. I mean, it's a bit of a cliché, I know. The academy and all that. But I just couldn't work with Delbert anymore. He's gone completely native, drove me nuts. Then I had these issues with Pammie when we stopped seeing each other and that all got resolved. School seemed like it'd be fun."

"I am very proud of you, Son. Always have been. If you're sure, then I'm sure this is the right thing."

They sat as workmen commanded the aisles to place the last touches on the dais and test the sound system. It felt good to be surprised, Roger thought. There was lightness about it, not knowing what to expect, and, as chance would have it, coming upon a happy result.

"I'm sorry I couldn't tell Professor Ogden," Brent said. "I would have liked to tell him. Do you think he would have approved — I mean, really? He never thought I was smart enough."

"I never knew what the old man really thought. Who cares? He never approved of me."

Brent looked incredulous. "Never approved of you? You? You were part of the charmed circle. Part of the legend."

Roger shook his head. "No, Son. He thought I threw away my talent. Sold out. No sir, he never approved of me. But it's all right. It really is. If you want to be a scholar, who gives a damn what Ogden thought? You can't be bound to somebody else's idea for your life."

Trumpets sounded behind them, and they turned with the gathering crowd to see a procession of red, white, and blue banners floating in the slow breeze. Next came a half-dozen high school girls with glittery tights and the boots and epaulets of drum majors, each clutching a baton. The band in uniform that followed them took seats on the dais and on command played "Stars and Stripes Forever," conducted without a score by a be-whiskered leader. Behind them on a stage decked with bunting, flags of principalities and organizations unfurled. A boy and a girl in colonial dress planted in the ground before the dais a staff bearing a flag of bleached white with a green spreading oak. They stood aside as Judith and Worth walked together onto the stage, holding between them a red banner that they draped over the lectern. "The Institute" its gold letters proclaimed.

So Worth and I were a bit too much together for the boy, Roger thought; well, that had a devilish justice to it. He thought Brent's plans still a bit earnest; he might have expected the boy to announce passage on a slow boat to China rather than graduate school. Still, this was good, a proper strength. He studied the youths around them, well dressed, confident, innocent of the days ahead, and he imagined Brent wondering just how he would fit in — learned older man, angry politico, the student ever young. The boy had always been between one world and another, Roger thought. Since he now knew the true fact that Professor Ogden hadn't approved of Roger Albright, and he'd lived enough to understand it, maybe he'll see he has more company than he thought.

Worth and Judith took seats at either side of the dais, and for a moment the company was still. Then a breeze stirred the flags, and from the center of the mise en scène a black youth in a dark suit walked forward and began to read:

> And the time being come that they must depart, they were accompanied with most of their brethren out of the city, unto a town sundry miles off called Delftshaven, where the ship lay ready to receive them. So they left that goodly and pleasant city which had been their resting place near twelve years; but they knew they were pilgrims, and looked not so much on those things, but lift their eyes to the heavens, their dearest country . . .

It was not the words that arrested Roger, though the passage, which he believed to be part of the story of the Pilgrim voyage, was interesting enough. It was the rich and lilting voice of the young man himself. He knew the preacherly cadence, had heard it ten thousand times before, on well-tended streets, in complacent restaurants, and country gas stations in the dead heat of summer; on streetcars and trains until those passed away; in the nursery and the locker room, and on his own shop floor, and lately in his offices — Yessir, Mr. Albright, the voices said, in agreement without connection, or, This way, Mr. Albright, through half-opened doors.

> . . . the tide, which stays for no man, calling them away that were thus loathe to depart, their reverend pastor falling down on his knees (and they all with him) with watery cheeks commended them with most fervent prayers to the Lord and His blessing. And then with mutual embraces and many tears they took their leaves of one another, which proved to be the last leave to many of them . . .

The vigorous old English phrases and the sight and sound of the young man reading them unsettled him, but in a good way, as though he witnessed something worn and dull made new. He sensed that the recital of the strong, the essential American-ness of it, resonated among the others too and lifted the gathering to a strange anticipation. He wondered if the strength and correctness of the incongruity also excited the young man, so resolute in his simple garb, speaking the simple words. Or, despite himself and good intentions, did he feel put upon to speak the words of these white men on behalf of other white men?

> ... After long beating at sea they fell with that land which is called Cape Cod; the which being made and certainly known to be it, they were not a little joyful. Being thus arrived in a good harbor, and brought safe to land, they fell upon their knees and blessed the God of Heaven who had brought them over the vast and furious ocean, and delivered them from all the perils and miseries thereof, again to set their feet on the firm and stable earth, their proper element ...

The firm and stable earth, Roger repeated to himself; their proper element. He thought of another black man, who had been young when he was, who also had addressed the white man's world with much hope. The picture of Willie Simpson on the crude wanted poster of a political broadside came before him again, as it did from time to time, thanks to Crain. What had happened to Willie Simpson? Willie Simpson had been full of promise too. He rose through the cruel and static world white men made for him, to the doors of West Point. Despite it all, he drove himself to the appointment, only to have Crain take it away and make his own face a thing for thousands to hate. Did Willie Simpson make good? Could he make himself not be bitter? Maybe he went to college anyway, fought the ugliness and succeeded in a job, endured the smirks of the loan officers and bought a house, battled for his children against the street, and resisted all impulses, even as they came every day, to run to another place, because his place was here, his proper element. Maybe he got a son; maybe he raised him hard and well, taught him about Joe Crain — not to hate him, because that was weak, but to understand and defeat him. And then one day Crain would meet the man he dreamed about, and he would know the face when he saw it, Willie Simpson, again, except this time Willie Simpson not young and afraid, but Willie Simpson a grown man and unafraid. Then Crain would know it was over, and if he had any sense left about him, he would praise his God as a merciful God for the instrument being Willie

Simpson, who would tell the truth about him and let him go in peace, rather than somebody else, somebody who would have brought the fire he deserved.

Roger wondered if Brent recognized the possibility; he felt sure he did. From such lately despised quarters absolution could arise, absolution from the regrettable fact that was the real thing haunting Brent, Roger feared: that he and his like would never defeat Crain either, that the sins of the fathers would be forever visited on them.

Still, it was progress that the survivors, though never able to attain final victory, could learn to listen with the heart and that way to be delivered of the vast and furious ocean that so baffled and challenged, and took so many lives.

Finished with his reading, the young man stepped back and joined the other players. Judith walked to the lectern and met there a young girl carrying a silver bowl. "This is our first celebration," she said. "I welcome you all. Now we have the giving of proclamations and medals."

She opened a scroll and read. "Roger Albright was born on a farm in Nash County . . ." He sat motionless as she recited his story, lingering over the association with Ogden and tenure with Worth. It was definitely his life as told by her, and he liked the sound, even as she ignored the commercial wars that had taken the measure of his energy, knitting together his life behind the scenes of politics and ideas as though it were his one true calling. The odd and exciting thing was that as she said it, he began to be persuaded.

". . . always supportive with his time and counsel to the great causes of the day, he provided to the business world a conscience and to the people the fruits of a brilliant imagination and a large heart . . ."

That was the way he would have had it, anyway. Maybe the key to this thing is getting on the record. She kissed him on the cheek while presenting him with the bowl and the sash that she fitted on him at the dais, knowing that he would not don it himself. "Life Achievement Award 1981" it read. He wondered if he had to march in the processional; to guard against that he waved and walked determinedly from the dais before she could conduct him to a chair.

"We now turn to first principles," Worth said, moving from the stage to the ground below. A young boy carried the Institute standard behind him, and together they walked to a cordoned-off space of earth. With the tip of a polished spade Worth motioned to the spot, and the boy thrust the staff into the red earth below. "On this spot we will build the new Institute," Worth said, "which will be a place of strength and renewal." He pushed the spade into the ground. "Now we all must turn the earth." He walked to the front row, and, helping Phineas from his chair, conducted him to the spot. Phineas, with a goodly thrust, delivered the first red clay. He picked up a clod and showed it above his head. "May we, God willing, produce from this element, earth, the first fruits of knowledge, and then, by our steadfastness, make of our knowledge power for good."

"Oh shit," Brent muttered.

"What?"

"Never mind," he said, nodding as Judith stepped forward to take the spade.

She dug briskly. "I ask that we may learn from the people." She grounded the spade at Worth's feet.

He motioned that all should rise, and as the band played "Columbia, the Gem of the Ocean" ushers conducted the audience, row by row, to the appointed ground, where all took their turns with the red clay. Roger thought of saving a clump as a memento, with his silver bowl, but thought the better of it.

"Whose idea was this?" Roger asked Worth, gesturing to his bowl as the line filed past.

"Oh, I don't know it was anybody's in particular," he said. "You get to keep it for a year."

"Okay. I remember how these things work."

"Just don't want any confusion. We're on a budget, you know."

•   •   •

Roger caught up with Brent, who waited for him to receive congratulations from several well-wishers.

"Pretty strange event," Roger said, removing his sash and placing it in the silver bowl.

"I loved it. Terrific energy."

"Terrific energy? I don't know exactly what that means."

"It's okay, I don't either. We're all learning."

Roger handed the letters back to Brent. "I haven't even asked you where you'll enroll."

"Don't know yet. The West Coast maybe. Judith thinks Berkeley. Someplace I haven't been yet."

"I'll help you any way I can."

"I know. Thanks."

Brent led them out of the way of oncoming workmen who carried off the already dismantled dais and bandstand.

"I'll get back home, Dad," Brent said. "I don't know how just yet. It's just not going to be the way we planned. I can live with that, if you can."

Roger nodded. "I can live with it. Hell, I welcome it." He thought about telling the boy how often he thought of the scholarly life he had left behind, but he figured that detached approval was the better course.

"As I said, I've been thinking a lot about losing the election. Not all about failing, but in a positive way, too. The way I figure it, the Institute had to have done something awfully good to call out a thing as bad as Crain. And what happened to us will happen to Crain, too; he probably knows it. One day he'll just see the guy, somewhere, in a sound bite, and he'll know his time is up. It doesn't matter that it won't be me. Really."

Judith appeared, carrying the Institute banner. "I guess I'm the keeper of this thing," she said. "Another one of Phineas's ideas. I feel like I'm reliving the Bull Moose campaign."

She stopped and studied the two of them, Roger with his arm around Brent's shoulder, Brent taller by the margin of the hair he retained and Roger lacked.

"Am I interrupting something?" she asked.

"No — no," Brent said. "I have to get going. I'm meeting some people over in Durham."

"Where are you staying the night, Son, or are you going back?"

"I'm staying in Durham. But listen — why don't I drive to Fairington tomorrow and we can have dinner and I'll bunk over in one of the condos."

"Well, just stay with me, if you can."

"I'd like that." Brent checked his watch. "Listen — gotta take off. Judith, it was great. Terrific energy."

They waved as Brent jogged away, his shirttail below his leather jacket. In a prank on time, Roger believed, Brent actually had gotten younger since the last days of the campaign, had shed the constraints of his previous life and through some alien but life-giving process had maneuvered himself again to the edge of manhood. He didn't know what strange boy had metamorphosed, but he seemed agreeable enough, and Roger looked forward to getting to know him.

"That looked to have gone very well," Judith said.

"Yes," Roger said buoyantly, "I think it did. You've been watching over him, haven't you?"

She looked up at him girlishly, pleased, he thought, at her success.

"I just listened to him. Gave a little advice. It was a pleasure. He helped me, too."

"Oh? How so?"

"That would be telling."

"I'm very grateful."

She shivered in the March breeze and he helped gather her sweater around her shoulders. "Walk with me?" he asked.

She nodded. "Wait." She took the sash out of the silver bowl and re-folded it. They walked toward the town, passing the hurrying students, their heads down with the burden of their book bags, some already sporting the slight clothes of spring.

"Those were nice things you said about me up there," he said.

She took his arm. "You deserve nice things. And awards. Awards are inspiriting."

They had walked nearly the length of the grounds, almost to the front of the old campus. Suddenly, Roger became aware that they were at the place where they had sat together forty years before to watch a pa-rade and things had begun between them. He stopped amid the trees, grown larger now around the spot where they had lingered, drawing the moments from memory. He could have been twenty again as it all came back to him, and he knew in a deeper way than mere recollection what it was to be with her that day, and the intervening years fell away alto-gether, easing as the burdens of the recent past gave way to the distillation of the far past. He floated light as the air in the sensate memory, until it was the present that appeared strange and improbable, and his true self appeared as that figure before him on the ground, watching the parade, his life beginning.

"Do you know where we are?" he asked.

"Exactly. This is the spot, under that oak, where we sat and watched the Fourth of July parade and then went to my apartment. 1941."

"And?"

"And what?"

"Don't you feel it? I can feel every moment, everything about it. I could be there again. I am there, right now. It's the truest thing that ever happened to me."

She sighed. "I'm not sentimental, you know that. But I am hungry. Why don't we get something to eat."

They crossed the street and went into a restaurant in which several large television sets played tapes of old basketball games. It was only midday, but students jammed the place, drinking and eating sandwiches bearing the names of sports heroes he vaguely recalled. He couldn't help but think that maybe these youngsters could be making better use of their time. They took a seat by the window.

"You and Worth get on famously these days," he said.

"I like him now. Since he's not a senator anymore he's a nice man. Some people just take longer to grow up."

"I know the both of you want me to run the Institute."

To his satisfaction she squirmed in her seat ever so slightly. "I think that's natural."

"No, you think it's therapeutic. Poor old Roger—needs to do something. Get his mind off things. Well, I'm going to be just fine, thank you."

"So you don't want to run it."

"No, I don't." He thought when he heard the words how sure he was of it. "No—I think you should run it."

"Me run it? The Institute? I didn't even think you let girls in."

He shrugged. "This is the new Institute."

He produced a pen and wrote names on his napkin. "I'll serve on the board," he said, turning the paper so she could see his handiwork. "You'll need me on there because this is a very strong board. You probably haven't even thought about your board, since, knowing you, all you've been doing is putting together the staff."

"I thought that should come first."

"Wrong. First you need a strong board, then a capital campaign to get them committed. Getting the building up will create presence. Nothing like bricks and mortar to get the money flowing. Look here." He underlined the names of the ten industrialists and bankers he had scrawled out. "This should be your board. And me—that's eleven."

"Roger—why would these men, and they are all men, by the way, join this board? We're not going to do things they'll like."

"They'll come on because I ask them. They'll give money for the same reason. Worth doesn't really understand fund-raising even though he says he does. Rather than bother with it he and Phineas would pay for the whole thing themselves. That would be a mistake."

She took the napkin from him, and the pen. "We can plan the Institute later. Why don't we order? I'm starving."

Outside, students massed on the sidewalk as afternoon classes let out. They looked so different and yet so much the same, the constancy of age and temper somehow overriding the fashions of the day. He found himself among them, saw the street again as it was when he walked it regularly, felt the rhythm of the long afternoon settling back in his consciousness. Yet here in this most familiar of places—and probably because it was the most familiar of places—he noticed the time and realized he was a stranger.

"This is not the way I thought my life would turn out," he said.

"You mean having lunch, or in some larger sense?"

"Everything. I had no idea I wouldn't have a business, or a wife, or that my son wouldn't talk to me. Mainly I thought everything would be the same, or somehow more so. But instead of everything being the same it's all very odd. Now I wake up in the morning confused. I really do. I have no idea what's going to happen."

"That's good."

"What's good about being confused?"

"It means you're not dead. You see, Roger, I'll tell you a secret. Everybody's confused. It's healthy to be confused. High time you started."

Roger exulted as he realized yet another character weakness to be virtue in disguise. Confusion was good and proper, healthy in fact. All types of possibilities opened.

"So how do I start?" he asked.

She looked around the filling room with satisfaction. "You've already done it—this is a great start. You got us good seats in a popular restaurant."

Good seats in a popular restaurant. Maybe it was a sign, he thought. Maybe worlds ended and began in just that way.

"Are you free this afternoon?" he asked.

"I thought I'd spend it with you."

He liked the idea, and the way she said it. Why not enjoy the afternoon with an old friend in a place that held so much of the past and the future, a familiar and strange place such as this. We can finish lunch, he thought, and take a walk, and talk about everything we know, and then it will be time to think about supper.

AUTHOR'S NOTE

This is a work of fiction. Other writers, however, have in-
fluenced me in the interpretation and rendering of historical
events. Of particular influence among scholars has been the
work of C. Vann Woodward, Howard Odum, and Warren
Ashby. Memoirists and journalists to whom I am indebted
are George S. Patton, Junius Scales, Elizabeth Drew, and
Hal Crowther.

I acknowledge the influence of these writers, but absolve
them from the arrangement of fact and circumstance in these
pages, which is mine alone.